i'll stand by you

SHARON SALA

sourcebooks
casablanca

Published by Sourcebooks Casablanca, an imprint of Sourcebooks, Inc.
P.O. Box 4410, Naperville, Illinois 60567-4410
(630) 961-3900
Fax: (630) 961-2168
www.sourcebooks.com

Printed and bound in the United States of America.
RRD 10 9 8 7 6 5 4 3 2

Chapter 1

ADORABLE GRANT ROLLED OVER IN BED AND SHUT OFF the alarm as a familiar cramp rolled across her belly. The monthly miseries had arrived, and by the smell coming from the baby bed where her son, Luther Joe, was sleeping, the baby food jar of prunes she'd fed him last night may have been a mistake. Between her cramps and Luther's runs, it was not the optimum way to start a workday, but she had already learned the hard way what it was like to live on leftovers.

She made a mad dash down the hall to the bathroom and came out a few minutes later carrying a tube of ointment for Luther's diaper rash. There was nothing glamorous about being a seventeen-year-old unwed mother, but after giving birth, she had vowed never to complain about getting her period again.

She hastened her steps as she headed back to her bedroom. Luther was awake and beginning to whine, and she didn't want to wake Granddaddy until the very last minute.

"Hey, little man," she said softly as she hurried toward the crib.

Luther was big for his age and already pulling himself up and standing inside the baby bed. His little, fat hands were curled around the spindles, and he was chewing on the bed rail, probably trying to cut teeth, but it had yet to happen. As soon as he saw her, he smiled that toothless baby smile she loved while saliva dripped down onto his chin and points below. He clutched the bed rail and squealed as she approached.

Dori chuckled. "Shh, now! You're gonna wake Granddaddy."

The mere mention of his favorite male sent Luther's gaze straight toward the door.

Dori sniffed, then rolled her eyes.

"Ooowee, Luther Joe! You sure do stink. Here, lay down a minute and let Mama get you all cleaned up again."

She unsnapped the crotch of his pajamas and began to clean him up while making faces at him, then laughing as he tried to mimic the expressions she was making. It was a game they'd been playing for almost a week now, and she was convinced that he was going to be a genius. As soon as she finished, she picked him up out of the crib, settled him on her hip, and headed for the kitchen.

It was still dark outside, but Dori's job as a dishwasher at Granny's Country Kitchen began at six a.m., when they started serving breakfast. She settled him into his high chair, handed him a teething biscuit, and started making coffee and warming milk to put in his cereal as she glanced out the kitchen window. The sky was still dark, but she could see darker, heavy-looking clouds. May was always a rainy month and this May was no exception. Maybe if she hurried, she'd get to work before it began.

Within minutes, she had bacon frying and beaten eggs in a bowl ready to scramble. She was putting bread in the toaster when Luther let out a big squeal. She turned to see her grandfather entering the room. He was slightly stooped from so many years as a roofer but still in fine form for seventy-six.

"Mornin', Granddaddy."

"Morning, honey," Meeker Webb said and wiggled his fingers at Luther, who squealed again and whacked his teething biscuit on the tray of the high chair.

Meeker eyed his granddaughter closely as he kissed the top of her head and swiped a piece of crispy bacon. From the day she'd been born, he'd always thought she was the prettiest thing in Blessings, Georgia, and still did, although her blue eyes weren't as sparkly as they used to be, and she didn't pay much attention to how she looked anymore.

He'd given up trying to get her to tell him who Luther's father was. He had already figured out that she wasn't telling because of what she feared he'd do to him. She wasn't a run-around girl, and she hadn't had a boyfriend when she turned up pregnant. Meeker might be old, but he wasn't stupid. Somebody had his way with Dori and left her to suffer the consequences alone.

"Looks like rain," he said as he poured himself a cup of coffee.

Dori nodded as she strained off the bacon grease, then poured the eggs into the hot skillet and began to stir.

"I know, Granddaddy. I'm going to leave just as soon as I feed Luther."

"I'll feed ole buster here, and you sit yourself down and eat breakfast for a change. You're wasting away. I can eat after you're gone."

She hesitated. He already did so much for her, but his offer was tempting. She sure didn't want to work all day in wet clothes.

"But your breakfast will get cold," she said.

He tweaked her ear.

"I know how to heat it up, now, don't I?"

She grinned and handed him Luther's bowl of cereal. She dished herself up a serving of eggs and bacon, grabbed a piece of toast as it popped up, and ate standing up.

Meeker frowned. "Honey, the least you could do is sit down."

"No time," she muttered, talking around the mouthful of food she was chewing.

Within minutes, she was in her bedroom, throwing on clothes without care if they matched or not and brushing out tangles in her long, dark brown hair. She used to take pride in her appearance. Before her parents were killed, everyone used to talk about how much she looked like her mother, with her baby-doll features and little turned-up nose, but she couldn't see how it mattered much anymore. Her pride, along with everything else, had taken a great fall when she turned up pregnant, and like Humpty Dumpty, she didn't know how to put herself back together again. She grabbed an umbrella and then stopped off in the kitchen before she left.

"I'm going now," she said and kissed her little boy good-bye. "Luther Joe, you be good for Granddaddy."

Luther grinned and blew bubbles with a mouthful of oatmeal, which made Meeker grin.

Dori rolled her eyes. "Don't laugh at him, or he'll just do it again."

"Why not?" Meeker said. "You used to do the same thing, and I laughed at you."

Dori hugged her grandfather's neck.

"I hope you know how much I love and appreciate you."

Meeker squinted and gruffly cleared his throat.

"I love you too, girl. Now hustle or you're gonna get wet. Luther and I will be just fine."

Dori blew him a kiss, then put on her raincoat and, after she stepped out onto the porch, opened her umbrella.

The sun had yet to come up, but the streetlights lit the way out of her neighborhood toward downtown Blessings. She took a deep breath of the cool morning air as she came down the porch steps. It even smelled like rain. Without hesitation, she lengthened her stride and shifted into work mode.

She'd never made it to a high school prom, and her days of going to football games and school trips were over. She'd tried homeschooling, then decided it was a waste of time and took the GED. Now she was almost through with online college courses on building websites. She could have felt sorry for herself, but all she had to do to get past it was think about her baby. She wouldn't trade him for all the parties and dances in the world. She paused briefly to check for traffic as she reached the corner, and when the first drops of rain began to fall, she started to run.

***

When twenty-year-old Johnny Pine's alarm went off, he rolled his long-legged self out of bed with a groan. Five a.m. came far too soon, but he needed the extra hour to do a load of laundry and make breakfast for his little brothers before he sent them off to school. When he was little, his mama never made him breakfast, let alone got out of bed. But he remembered what it felt like to go to school hungry and was determined that wasn't happening to his brothers.

Marshall was ten and in fifth grade, and Brooks, a.k.a. Beep, was seven and in second grade. Although they were young enough to still need a mother, that wasn't happening. Their mother had overdosed on meth two years ago and was buried in the Blessings Cemetery. Their daddy was doing time in prison with no hope of ever getting out. Johnny was all they had left, and he wasn't going to be the next one to fail them.

He headed for the bathroom on bare feet, wincing at the feel of grit on the floor. He'd meant to sweep up last night after dishes and the boys' homework, but he'd forgotten. Maybe he'd have time if he hurried through his shower.

A short while later, he was in the kitchen, stirring oatmeal and sipping his second cup of coffee. The washer was on the spin cycle—so far, so good. He eyed the oatmeal, then turned off the fire and set the pan on a back burner as he went down the hall to wake up the boys.

The Ninja Turtle night-light in their room used to be his. It was cracked, and one of the turtles was missing an arm, but it still worked, shedding a pale green glow on their faces. They both had black hair like Johnny's, and when they got older, he suspected they'd look a lot like him, as well. He did what he could to keep them in line but feared he was a poor substitute for a parent. If he hadn't already been eighteen when their mama died, the state would have taken them away from him. Now he kept everything on the up-and-up for fear they still might.

He turned on the light in the room and then leaned over the bed they shared and shook each one gently.

"Hey, Marshall. Hey, Beep. It's time to wake up. Oatmeal is done. Get up now and don't dawdle. You can't be late for school."

The boys were mute as they rolled out of bed and padded across the hall to the bathroom to pee. He got out their clean clothes and then set their shoes side by side on the floor before he left the room. He could already hear giggling inside and knocked on the bathroom door as he passed.

"Quit piddlin' around and get dressed!" he yelled.

Silence followed his footsteps as he went back to the kitchen. The washer was through spinning, so he dumped the load of wet clothes into the dryer and turned it on. The clothes would be wrinkled when he got home this evening, but at least they'd be clean and dry. They might be living life at the bottom of the barrel, but they didn't have to live it dirty.

He glanced at the clock. Already a quarter to six and he still hadn't fixed their lunches. They qualified for the free lunch program at school, but he wasn't putting that kind of stigma on the boys if he could help it. He got out a can of Spam and began making sandwiches. Marshall liked mayonnaise, Beep wanted butter, and he liked mustard. He made one for each of the boys and two for himself, added a banana apiece in their lunch boxes and a honey bun in his, and then left them on the corner of the table as the boys entered the kitchen. They were dressed, but their hair was a wreck. He'd work on that later.

"Sit," he said. "I'll dish up the oatmeal."

"Can I have raisins in mine?" Marshall asked.

"I don't want no raisins," Beep muttered defensively.

"You don't want *any* raisins," Johnny said, absently

correcting the grammar as he dished up the hot cereal and dumped a handful of raisins on top of Marshall's serving.

Beep frowned. "That's what I said."

Johnny grinned and kept dipping. Conversation ended as they began to eat. Oatmeal was not his favorite breakfast food, but it was hot, cheap, and filling, and that was that. Maybe when he won the lottery, they'd eat bacon and eggs.

He swallowed his oatmeal in eight bites, turned around, washed and rinsed his bowl, and put it in the drainer.

"Put your bowls in the hot water when you're through," he said and then pointed at Beep. "And don't be putting any oatmeal in the dishwater again. Eat it. Don't waste it."

Beep nodded without looking up and shoveled another bite into his mouth.

"If he don't want it, I'll eat it," Marshall said.

"If he doesn't want it," Johnny said, correcting his grammar too.

Marshall shrugged.

Johnny frowned. "Don't shrug that off," he said shortly. "When you don't speak properly, people think you're dumb, and we've got enough to live down without people thinking we're stupid, understand?"

Marshall blinked. "I'm sorry, Johnny."

Beep looked nervous. If Marshall was in trouble, that probably meant he would be in trouble too.

Johnny eyed the anxious expressions on their faces and sighed.

"Look, guys, you're not in trouble, okay? I just want you to be the best you can be, and that means no lazy talk, okay?"

"Is *ain't* a lazy word, Johnny?" Beep asked.

Johnny nodded.

Beep beamed. "Then I ain't gonna say that no more."

Johnny grinned and left the kitchen shaking his head. It was time to cut his losses and end the grammar lesson, or they'd all be late.

He scratched his chin as he paused in the hall. He had time to shave or sweep, and he opted for sweeping. He didn't want to walk on that gritty floor again tonight, and since he drove a bulldozer for Clawson Construction, no one there cared if he had whiskers.

By the time he was through, the boys were too. He sent them to brush their teeth and then went to look for rain gear. Marshall was outgrowing his hooded jacket. If Johnny had time this coming weekend, he'd stop by the Salvation Army resale shop and see what they had in stock.

"Guys, hurry up!" he yelled as he tossed the jackets by their backpacks and strode across the hall and into the bathroom. He eyed their hair and grabbed a comb, yanking it through their hair just enough to give it a semblance of propriety.

"Dang, Johnny! You messed up my 'hawk," Marshall said as he re-combed his hair with his fingers until he had his Mohawk hairstyle back the way he liked it.

Johnny rolled his eyes and grabbed his youngest brother.

"Stand still, Beep. I just need to get this..." Johnny stopped and frowned, then looked closer at the knot in his little brother's hair. "What the hell is that in your hair?"

"You cussed," Beep muttered.

Johnny parted the knot with the tip of the comb.

"Is that gum? Did you go to bed with gum in your mouth again?"

Beep shrugged.

"Crap on a stick, boy, you aren't gonna have a lick of hair left if you keep this up," Johnny said and pulled a pair of scissors out of the drawer in the vanity.

Marshall eyed the latest surgery absently, then pointed at the other bald spots near his little brother's right ear.

"At least it's on the same side," he offered.

Johnny rolled his eyes. The kid's head was beginning to look like he had ringworm, which would definitely set him up as a target if any of the kids noticed it.

"Don't let anybody pick on you," he said.

Marshall put his hand on Beep's shoulder. "If they do, I'll whup 'em," he offered.

"Every man has to fight his own fights," Johnny said as he tossed the hair ball into the trash. "No more gum for you at night, bud," he said gently and gave Beep a quick hug.

Marshall frowned, listening as the rain began to hammer on the roof above them.

"Oh man, it's raining. We won't get to go outside at recess," he grumbled.

"There's always recess another day. Go get your stuff," Johnny said. "I've still got to drop you off at Miss Jane's so she can take you to school later. And don't make her have to wait for you when school's over. Get your butts out to the van."

"Okay, Johnny, we promise," Marshall said.

He was old enough to realize how fragile the framework of their little family really was—Beep not so much. If Miss Jane got mad at them and quit being their babysitter, then that would mess up Johnny's job, and

Johnny couldn't lose his job, or they'd be homeless, and he didn't want to be homeless. Daddy was in prison and wasn't ever coming out, and Mama was dead and buried. He lived in fear of what they'd lose next.

Within a few minutes, Johnny had loaded them into his old SUV and was driving across town to Miss Jane's Before and After. She called herself a part-time day care, but since she refused to wipe baby butts, her only service was taking kids to school and picking them up afterward. She furnished an after-school snack and expected them to sit quietly and do homework until they were picked up before suppertime. Miss Jane also did not tolerate roughhousing, which meant the Pine brothers were on notice at least once a week.

Johnny accelerated slightly as he approached the incline where the old railroad tracks used to be. Even though the train no longer ran through Blessings, it was still the demarcation point for the wrong side of town. While Johnny had grown up there, he had himself a plan. He was going to take his family into a better way of life or die trying.

Ruby Dye frowned when she heard the rain peppering against her windows. Rain was never a good sign for a beauty shop. The Curl Up and Dye had a reputation to maintain, and humidity played hell with a hairdo, especially Vera's and Vesta's creations. The Conklin twins were inordinately fond of hair spray and used it liberally, although it had a tendency to turn hair into a helmet on high-humidity days.

She glanced at the clock. It was almost seven a.m. If she left now, she'd have time to do a load of towels at the shop and mop the floor before Willa Dean Miller showed up for her weekly shampoo and style.

Willa Dean ran the local travel agency. Last year, she'd booked a trip to Italy for Patty June Clymer after Patty divorced her preacher husband for fornicating with a local whore. The divorce had caused quite a stir in Blessings, and Willa Dean's business increased dramatically after Patty June came back talking about good-looking Italian men.

But Ruby wasn't in the market for travel beyond going to the salon, so she put on her raincoat, gave her own hair a last check, and flipped a curl back in place.

Ruby liked to change her hair color on a regular basis as a walking advertisement for what she sold, which was beauty in a bottle. She'd been blond and curly for the past two months and liked the look. It brought out the green in her eyes. She grabbed her purse and umbrella as she left the house, grateful for her covered porch and carport.

She had a Garth Brooks CD playing in her car and the windshield wipers seemed to swipe rhythmically to the music as she drove toward Main. On impulse, she swung by a drive-through at a local bakery and picked up a dozen doughnuts. The twins were cranky on rainy days, and a little sweetening up might be in order.

Today was also Mabel Jean Doolittle's birthday. Her manicurist was a real sweet girl, and while Ruby hadn't bought her a gift, Mabel Jean would be just as happy with a jelly doughnut and a week of free booth rent.

On the other side of town, semi-newlyweds Mike and LilyAnn Dalton were still sleeping. Mike had a spa/gym down on Main Street that was temporarily closed for renovations, and LilyAnn had taken off work today for her monthly doctor checkup. She was four months pregnant and still struggling with morning sickness. Added to that, her emotions were on a perpetual-motion merry-go-round. Between the daily drama of throwing up and bawling for no reason, this was getting on her last nerve. However, Mike was over the moon that there was a baby on the way, and when she felt better, she'd be on the same page. She'd wasted far too much of her life already.

Unlike most of the other businesses in Blessings, Granny's Country Kitchen never suffered a loss of business on nasty days. In fact, bad weather had a tendency to draw more people to warm, cozy places, and there was nothing more comforting in the South than hot biscuits, sausage gravy, and a great cup of coffee.

The waitresses were turning in an unusual amount of orders, and Walt Warden, the morning cook at Granny's, was turning them right back out just as quickly. The customers continued to come in, but then lingered because of the rain. Before long, the place was packed, and there were a half-dozen people waiting for to-go orders as well.

Dori never looked up from her job. She scraped leftovers, rinsed, and loaded dishes into the commercial-style dishwasher without hesitation. It took ten minutes for them to run through the superhot cycles, another five of rinse and heat dry, and then a couple of minutes of cooldown before she took them out again and stacked them back into service for the cook and servers. It was a nonstop process that kept her in constant motion. By the time the breakfast rush was over, it was after ten a.m. and she was ready for a potty break.

She glanced up as the back door swung inward and the owner, Lovey Cooper, came in, shedding a raincoat and umbrella as she went. Lovey smiled at Dori and waved at Walt, who was scraping down the grill.

"Busy morning?" she asked.

"Yes, ma'am," Dori said as she took off her rubber gloves and waterproof apron before heading to the bathroom.

After she finished, she washed her hands without looking in the mirror, a subconscious act reflecting the disgust she had with her life.

She was concerned about Luther's little bottom. It was pretty raw from that diarrhea, and she felt guilty all over again for giving him the whole jar of prunes. Without a woman to ask for advice, raising her baby was a case of "live and learn." Unfortunately, Luther was the one suffering the consequences.

She dried her hands quickly and went back into the kitchen. The last dishwasher load was just about done, and she was gearing up mentally to be ready for the lunch crowd. Her daily shift was from six a.m. to two p.m., at which time the second-shift dishwasher, Larry Bemis, would come in and work until close. She glanced up at the clock again. Eight more minutes on her break—just enough time to call home—so she slipped into the back hallway for privacy. When her granddaddy answered before the second ring, Dori knew Luther was down for a nap and Granddaddy was making sure nothing woke him before it was over.

"Hello, Dori. Everything okay, honey? Did you make it to work before the rain?"

She smiled. "Hi, Granddaddy. Everything's fine. It rained on me some, but I didn't get too wet. Everything okay there?"

Meeker Webb chuckled. "You are a worrywart just like your grandma was. Everything is fine, including me and buster. There's food in the kitchen, and the roof don't leak, so we're high and dry. Can't ask for anything more."

She laughed. "Okay. I hear you. I love you. See you this afternoon."

"Deal," he said.

She dropped the phone back in her pocket and returned to the kitchen, put the apron and rubber gloves back on, and began emptying the busboy's latest tub of dirty dishes. One thing was for sure: scraping out other people's leavings was a deterrent for overeating. She was as thin as she'd ever been in her life.

———

The rain at Johnny's job site made removing stumps easy, and Floy Beaudine had six of them he wanted out. But Floy had also warned Johnny not to tear up his pasture with the bulldozer if the ground got too wet.

Johnny had three stumps out before the ground got soft, and now the dozer tracks were making ruts in the pasture. It was time to stop. He was in the act of loading up the dozer when his cell phone rang. He jumped up into the truck cab, out of the rain, to take the call, and then, when he saw it was the school, his heart skipped a beat. They never called unless there was a problem.

"Hello?"

"Johnny Pine?"

The woman's voice was clipped, the disdain in her voice a faint, long-distance slap on the cheek.

"Yes, ma'am."

"This is Principal Winston. Your brother Brooks was fighting at school. He's in the office, and you need to come get him."

Johnny thought of those bald spots on the back of Beep's head and muffled a groan. He'd feared as much.

"Is he all right?" he asked.

"He has a black eye, and his nose is bleeding. It seems a bit crooked. It might be broken. We thought you would want to get him checked out."

Johnny gasped. Little kids didn't usually do much damage to each other, but a broken nose was a lot more than a scuffle.

"Broken? What the hell happened to him? Who did that?"

"The children were sent to recess in the gym because of the rain, and some of them were—"

The skin crawled on the back of Johnny's neck.

"Some? As in more than one jumped on Beep?"

She hesitated. "Well, we're still investigating the—"

"I am on my way, and you better have the responsible parties in the office when I get there."

"Now see here, Johnny! You—"

"It's Mr. Pine to you, ma'am, and we'll continue this discussion face-to-face."

He hung up and got out of the truck. Minutes later, he had the dozer loaded and was driving back to town, talking to his boss as he went.

"Mr. Clawson, this is Johnny. I got three of the stumps out of Mr. Beaudine's pasture before I had to stop because the ground got too soft. I was just loading up when I got a call from school. Beep's been hurt, so I need to run him by the ER, okay?"

Clawson liked Johnny Pine and had known him for years. Johnny was the best worker Clawson had, and he never asked for favors. It was not a problem to grant this one.

"Sure, it's okay, Johnny. We can't do any more dozer work today because of this rain, so go on home when you're done. I sure hope your brother is okay."

"Yes, sir. Thank you very much."

He hung up the phone and kept on driving. By the time he got the truck parked and headed to school in his SUV, he was so mad, he was shaking.

Chapter 2

MAVIS WEST, THE SCHOOL SECRETARY, LOOKED UP from inside the big, glassed enclosure of the principal's office and saw Johnny Pine coming in the front door. He was easily over six feet tall, with wide shoulders and long legs, and his face was downright handsome. *Strange how the bad boys always turned out good-looking*, she mused. And then she saw the frown on his face and the length of his stride and glanced at the little boy on the cot near her desk. She liked the Pine boys. They had good manners and they were smart. It wasn't their fault they came from bad blood. Then the office door opened, and Johnny Pine was coming inside.

Johnny's anger was on simmer as he walked into the office. Then he saw Beep's swollen face and bloody hands, the ice pack against his cheek, and his backpack lying beneath the cot, and he stifled the urge to put his fist through a wall.

"I want to speak to Mrs. Winston."

Mavis sat up a little straighter. "She's in conference with—"

"Who did this?" he asked.

"It's not my place to—"

At that point Beep woke up, saw his big brother, and started to cry all over again.

"I fighted my own battle, Johnny, but there was too

many. They said I had cooties in my hair, and I told them I didn't, and they shoved me down on the gym floor and started kicking me and calling me names."

Rage washed over him in waves as he scooped Beep up in his arms.

"They kicked you?"

"Yes."

"In the face too?"

Beep nodded, his eyes welling all over again.

"How many?"

"Four."

"All of them from your class?"

"No, they were fourth graders."

Johnny looked back at the secretary and spoke, his voice so soft she had to lean forward to hear properly. "Miss Mavis, either you open the door to Mrs. Winston's office for me, or I'll kick it open."

Mavis jumped up to block the way.

"I told you she's in conference. She's dealing with this. It's not your place to—"

"Well, yes, it by God is my place. This little boy was attacked by a gang of older boys in the school gym, which is school property, and no one has seen to his welfare beyond a fucking ice pack. Did he tell you all he'd been kicked?"

Mavis hesitated, but truth came out. "One of the teachers on duty in the gym witnessed it."

"Why didn't you call an ambulance? Did anyone call the police?"

Mavis gasped. "We didn't see a need to call an ambulance, and the police have no place here. This is a school problem and will be dealt with here."

Johnny looked down at Beep and wanted to cry. His face was swollen, and his nose *was* crooked on his face.

"If he was kicked all over by a gang of boys, that's assault, which is illegal, and he could have internal bleeding. Either I talk to her now, or you'll all be talking to a lawyer. Do I make myself clear?"

All of a sudden the principal's door opened and Arlene Winston slipped out, quickly closing it behind her.

"Please lower your voice. I'm dealing with this in the proper manner," she said.

Johnny tightened his hold on his little brother.

"I'm sorry, Mrs. Winston, but you do not tell me how to react to this outrage, and you're not dealing with shit. Four older boys attacked a little boy, and if there are broken bones in his body or internal bleeding that you have ignored, there's going to be hell to pay. I'm taking my brother to the emergency room. I *will* have the names of the responsible parties, because their parents are paying for the medical bills incurred from this incident. Their little bastards better suffer some serious suspension time too, or shit is going to hit the fan all over town."

Mavis watched her boss's skin color go from a highly incensed pink flush to pasty white so fast she had to look twice to make sure she was seeing properly.

Principal Winston flinched. "I understand the ringworm issue started everything and—"

Beep hid his face against his brother's chest as Johnny interrupted.

"Ringworm? Did I hear you actually say that? He doesn't have ringworm. He got gum stuck in his hair, and when I cut it out, hair came with it. That then raises the question, are you implying that if Beep had ringworm, then the boys had the right to kick the shit out of him?"

Arlene Winston paled. "You are putting words in my mouth. There's no need to make such a—"

"There is every need," Johnny said softly. "Just because you don't like this little boy's last name doesn't mean he deserves less than any other kid here. I am not making empty threats, and you know me well enough to know I mean every damn word I say."

He started toward the door, then paused and turned around.

"Considering the way this has gone down, I believe I'll just get Marshall out of school now too. I feel the need to keep my family close today, since it seems I can't trust the public school system to do it for me. If Beep is able to come back tomorrow, then they'll both be back. If he's not, they won't. And if anyone looks cross-eyed at either one of them over this, I will make you *and* them sorry."

Mavis glanced at the principal, who nodded reluctantly. Mavis used the school intercom to summon Marshall Pine to the office to be checked out of school.

Sitting up in Johnny's arms made Beep's nose bleed again. Mavis handed him a handful of tissues and then patted his leg. Johnny considered the gesture as coming a little too late and focused on Marshall coming up the hall. He knew when Marshall stumbled that it was a reaction to Beep's face.

"What happened?" Marshall asked as he entered the office.

"Please pick up your brother's backpack under the cot and we'll talk in the car," Johnny said.

Marshall scooped it up, pausing long enough to give the women in the office a look of disbelief, and then followed his brothers out of the office and into the rain.

Mavis looked at the principal.

"What do you want me to do?" she asked.

"Get the school lawyer on the phone and start calling parents," Mrs. Winston said. "Don't tell them what happened. Just tell them I need them down here now."

"Yes, ma'am," Mavis said and scurried back around to her chair as Arlene Winston went back into her office to face the four boys in question.

Johnny drove to the clinic with Beep in his lap. He knew it wasn't legal to drive like that, but he couldn't bring himself to let him go. The windshield wipers swiped rapidly through the downpour as the rain continued to fall.

Marshall was quiet all the way to the clinic, but his fingers were curled into fists and Johnny knew he was contemplating revenge. It was an unfortunate aspect of how the Pine men rolled, but this time it had to be different because they couldn't give anyone an excuse to let this slide.

"Hey, Marshall."

"What?"

"I am telling you to let me deal with this. This is more than just two kids fighting, okay?"

Marshall eyed his little brother. "Who beat you up, Beep?"

Johnny shook his head. "No. I said we're not going there. Four older boys did it, and right now that's all I know."

"They said I had ringworms. They said I had cooties," Beep mumbled.

Johnny patted Beep's arm. "We're going to get you x-rayed, buddy, and if everything is okay, when we get home, we'll have a family discussion, okay?"

Marshall patted his little brother's leg as Johnny drove into the ER parking lot, then parked as close to the front as he could get. He took off his jacket and put it over Beep's head and face to protect him from the rain before he carried him inside.

Thelma Crown, the ER receptionist, quickly recognized the family.

"We need to see a doctor," Johnny said. "My little brother was attacked at school."

Thelma hid her shock, but the others in the waiting room did not. That would be all over Blessings before sundown. She slid a clipboard across the counter.

"Fill this out for me and take a seat. As soon as—"

But Johnny didn't budge as he pulled the jacket off of Beep's little head, revealing the extent of his injuries.

"No, ma'am. We need to see a doctor now. He was kicked repeatedly about the head and body by four older boys, and I need to make sure he's not bleeding internally."

This time, Thelma didn't bother to hide her shock.

"I'm sorry. You can put him in that wheelchair while I call the nurse's station."

"No thank you. I'll carry him," Johnny said.

Thelma made the call, and moments later, a nurse and a doctor came out pushing a gurney.

When Johnny laid him down, Beep cried out.

"Johnny, don't leave me!"

"Don't worry, buddy," Johnny said softly. "You're not going anywhere without us." He held tight to his hand as they rolled him back.

—∿—

Halfway through the noontime dinner service, the busboy at the Country Kitchen began throwing up. Lovey immediately sent him home, but it left the waitresses in a bind. They didn't have time to clear tables *and* wait on their customers, so Lovey made a few adjustments in the staff.

"Hey, Dori, I need you to grab a tub and cart and help the girls bus some tables."

"What about the dishes?" she asked as she began taking off the gloves and apron.

"Just hustle and we'll make it work," Lovey said.

Dori took down her ponytail, smoothed down all the loose ends, and put it back up again. Then she straightened the blue-and-white-striped shirt she was wearing, checked her jeans to make sure they weren't wet, and pushed a tub and cart out into the dining area straight toward an empty table full of dirty dishes.

Customers were still seated at the tables on either side. A trio of men at one of the tables smiled at her and went on about their business. But the four women at the other table were parents of kids she knew from school, and the looks they gave her weren't kind. She kept her head down as she cleared the table, then wiped it down and set it back up. As she moved past, one of them called out.

"Dori Grant! You've changed so much I almost didn't recognize you. How are you doing?"

"I'm just fine, Mrs. Parrish, thank you for asking."

But Lorena wasn't through.

"And how is that baby of yours? I guess he's getting bigger. What is he now, four months?"

"No, ma'am, he's six months old."

Mrs. Parrish smiled at Dori, but it was not a friendly smile.

"Now what was it you named him? I know I've heard it."

Dori started moving away. "His name is Luther Joe Grant, after my daddy."

Parrish's smile thinned. "Well, that's sweet, but I would have thought you'd name him after *his* own daddy and not yours."

Dori stopped, then looked the woman squarely in the eyes.

"Why would you think something like that, Mrs. Parrish? It's pretty much tradition in the South to name babies after parents and grandparents."

Lorena Parrish sniffed.

"Well, I guess that's so, especially if the identity of the parent is in question," she drawled.

Dori gasped. She tried to hide it, but her eyes quickly blurred with tears, and to make it worse, Lorena Parrish was still talking.

"However, *your* people aren't from the South, now, are they? I mean, everyone knows you're a direct blood descendant of Ulysses S. Grant, the man in charge of ravaging this country during the War of Northern Aggression."

Across the room, Lovey Cooper had been eyeing Dori ever since Lorena Parrish called her down, and she could tell by the look on Dori's face that she was being insulted. Lovey never had liked Lorena much anyway and decided it was time to call a halt to what looked like an inquisition. She strode across the floor and slipped a hand across Dori's back, patting her gently to make sure Dori understood she was not in trouble.

"Ladies, I'm going to have to interrupt this fascinating history lesson and insist that you let Dori get back to work. We're a little shorthanded right now. Honey, if you'll just get those last two tables for me, that will be enough."

"Yes, ma'am, I sure will," Dori said, thankful for the reprieve.

She could hear Lovey's sharp, high-pitched voice shift into an oversweet tone as she addressed the table of women.

"Lorena, you're looking fit as a fiddle. I guess that new marriage is agreeing with you. I have to say I wouldn't have had the guts to take on a fifth husband like you did. They're so dang hard to train and all."

Lorena Parrish was laughing with everyone else, but she was pissed and Dori knew it. Her face was a ruddy shade of red.

Johnny was sitting beside Beep's bed in the ER and Marshall was sitting silently in a chair against the wall, overwhelmed by what had happened to his little brother and intimidated by the sight of all the scary equipment.

Beep's nose had already been set and both eyes were turning black. His nostrils were plugged with little wads of cotton to stop the bleeding. The clear plastic guard they'd put over his nose spanned the upper portion of his face like a mask. He was drifting in and out of sleep, exhausted from the events of the day.

Marshall glanced at Johnny. "When can we go home?"

"We don't go anywhere until the doctor tells us it is okay," Johnny said.

A single tear ran down Marshall's face.

"Is he gonna die?"

"No, of course not," Johnny said, but he was beginning to worry. Beep was getting quieter, and all he could think about were dire consequences, like blood clots and concussions.

He glanced up at the clock. They'd been in the ER over three hours, and he was ready for some answers.

No sooner had the thought crossed his mind than the doctor came in carrying X-rays.

Dr. Quick had delivered Brooks Pine, and he was pretty angry about what had happened to the little guy. But criticism was left for others. His job was to fix him. He pulled a couple of X-rays out of an envelope, turned on the viewer light, and slid them up onto the screen as Johnny and Marshall moved up beside him.

"So, here's the verdict, guys. Mr. Brooks here has some healing to do. Besides the broken nose, he also has two cracked ribs, a large contusion on his spine, and one on his thigh. Look here," he said, pointing to the X-ray. "These fine lines on the fourth and fifth ribs are hairline fractures. Other than the broken nose and a couple of loose teeth that should reseat themselves, I don't see any other injuries to his head or neck."

Johnny felt sick. He wanted to cry, but he had to be the strong one.

"What do we do? How do you fix this?" he asked. "Are you sure that's all? He's getting sleepy. Are you sure he doesn't have a concussion?"

"Adrenaline crash," Dr. Quick said gently. "No concussion, no intracranial bleeding."

"So he wears the nose guard to protect the nose, but what about the ribs?" Johnny asked.

Dr. Quick patted Beep's leg.

"Just no roughhousing or lifting for a few weeks and they'll heal. He's young and kids' bones are very pliable."

Just to prove he wasn't as sleepy as they thought, Beep piped up with a question of his own.

"Do I still have to take a bath?" Beep asked.

It was the perfect comment to lighten the moment. Dr. Quick laughed.

"As long as you let your brother wash your face so you don't mess up the good job I did on your nose, you'll be good to go. A warm bath might even make some of the aches you're going to have feel better," Dr. Quick said.

"Shoot," Beep said.

"You have to take a bath," Marshall said. "I wouldn't want to sleep with you if you got stinky."

Beep winced as the movement of facial muscles caused him pain.

"I sleep with you even when you fart," Beep muttered.

Marshall looked embarrassed.

Dr. Quick caught Johnny's eye. "Could we speak privately for a moment?" he asked.

Johnny followed the doctor out into the hall. His heart was pounding, and he felt sick to his stomach. "What's wrong? Is something else wrong that you're not telling me?"

"No, no, I'm sorry. I didn't intend to frighten you. I wanted to tell you that I have reported this to the police and they are on their way to talk to Brooks."

Johnny was relieved that decision had been taken out of his hands. He focused on what Dr. Quick was saying.

"I'm speaking out of line, but you're pretty young to have the responsibilities you have, and I don't want to see you railroaded. I think you need to see a lawyer to protect your rights. At least make sure the responsible parties pay for the medical bills and hope the threat of a lawsuit makes the school take the appropriate action."

Johnny's shoulders slumped. "I can't afford a lawyer, Doc. I threw the word around a lot when I picked him up from school, but that's not going to happen."

"You know Peanut Butterman, right? He has the law office above the old bank."

"Yes, sir," Johnny said. Everyone knew Mr. Butterman. He was one of Blessings's true characters.

"Give him a call and tell him I referred you. Every so often, he takes a case pro bono when he thinks someone is about to get railroaded. I think this would be one of those cases."

Johnny was surprised and embarrassed. "I don't want charity."

Dr. Quick put a hand on Johnny's shoulder. "This isn't about your pride, son. It's about Brooks's and Marshall's welfare through the rest of their school days. In other words, tie a knot in their tails now, before shit gets out of hand."

Johnny got it. His pride didn't matter as much as their safety. "Yes, sir. I hear you. And thanks."

"You're welcome. I'm very sorry this happened, but the police should be here soon. They will want to interview Brooks and let him say his piece. They'll go to school and get those statements as well. You let Peanut work his magic, and you stay out of trouble in the process. Peanut will get the names of the parents, and the medical bills will go to them through him."

Johnny went back inside the room as the doctor left.

Marshall was still holding Beep's hand. "Are the cops gonna sweat Beep?" he asked.

Johnny rolled his eyes. Someone had big ears, and he didn't know where Marshall got his vocabulary. That sounded like something out of an old gangster movie from the 1940s. "No, Beep is not in trouble, and the police are only going to want to hear his side of the story."

Marshall frowned. "You can't trust 'em."

Johnny stared at his brother in disbelief. "Marshall! Where is all this coming from? Since when have you become an expert on bad police procedure?"

"I watch TV. I know how it goes down," Marshall said.

"I think your TV choices could be better, and we'll be talking about that as well in our family meeting. In the meantime, you will be quiet, and you will be respectful when the police get here. Do you understand me?"

Marshall ducked his head. "Yes, sir."

Beep reached for Johnny's hand. "Don't leave me alone with the cops," he said.

"What the hell?" Johnny muttered. "Have you been watching those shows with Marshall?"

"Yes."

"Where?"

"At Miss Jane's after we get through with homework. She watches old cops-and-robbers movies."

"Good Lord," Johnny muttered. He was going to have to have a talk with the sitter too. Could this day get any worse?

There was a knock on the door, and then a uniformed officer from the Blessings Police Department walked in carrying a tripod and a camera case.

Johnny breathed a sigh of relief. He knew and respected Lon Pittman. He would be fair. "Hey, Lon," Johnny said.

"Hello, Johnny. Dr. Quick has reported an assault on Brooks Pine, who I am assuming is your little brother, Beep. Can't say as I ever knew his real name before today. I am going to video his statement, okay?"

Johnny nodded. "Dr. Quick told us he called you. Beep will answer your questions. Won't you, buddy?"

Beep blinked and tightened his hold on Johnny's hand.

Lon was shocked at the condition of the little guy's face and hated that his presence was adding to his discomfort. He quickly set up the camera and once it was in place, he moved just out of camera range. "It's gonna be okay, Beep. You remember me from Career Day at school, right? I came in and talked to your class about obeying traffic laws and how you look both ways before you cross streets. I just want you to tell me what happened."

Chapter 3

BY THE TIME BEEP FINISHED RECOUNTING THE STORY, Lon was shocked at the viciousness of the attack and trying not to show it. He had everything on video, including Beep's broken nose and swollen face, the missing patches of hair on the back of his head, as well as the large contusions on his back, thigh, and belly, which was turning a darker shade of purple where his ribs had been fractured.

Lon turned off the camera. He would get the other boys' statements as well, but there was no way on earth to explain away what they'd done. Four older, bigger boys had ganged up on one younger and smaller boy and kicked him until they broke him.

Lon paused at the foot of Beep's bed and patted his foot.

"I'm sorry this happened," Lon said.

Beep blinked. "It won't happen again, Officer Pittman."

"Oh yeah?" Lon said.

Beep nodded. "I'm not gonna sleep with gum in my mouth no more, so they won't be mad."

"Anymore," Johnny said, "and none of this was your fault, Beep. Your hair is not their business. They are the ones who did something bad, okay?"

Lon was sick to his stomach. Poor kid, still thinking it happened because he didn't "look right." He slipped his copy of the doctor's report into a folder as he began gathering up his things.

"I think that covers what I need. Y'all take care," Lon said. He left quickly, anxious to get to school before it let out, leaving Johnny and the boys in the ER.

Johnny glanced at Beep, then slid his hand across Marshall's shoulder.

"Marshall, you stay here with your brother until I get back. I'm going to find a nurse and get us checked out. I'll be right outside, so don't worry, okay?"

Marshall nodded. "I can handle it. I'm not a kid anymore."

Johnny frowned. "Yes, you are, and I intend for you to stay that way until you're old enough to say that and claim it. Understand?"

"Yes, sir," Marshall said softly.

Johnny laid a hand on Marshall's head to soften his words and then walked out of the room. His stomach was in knots. The boys who'd hurt Beep belonged to three upstanding families. He was convinced the boys would not be punished and Beep would not get justice for the assault.

Inside the room, Marshall leaned across the bed and whispered in Beep's ear, "Who hit you first?"

Beep's eyes welled. "Lewis Buckley."

Marshall's eyes narrowed. "He won't do it again."

Beep was worried. He'd never been in this much trouble before and was afraid to go back to school.

"Everyone is going to hate me," he whispered.

Marshall frowned. "Why? You didn't do anything wrong. Besides, I'll take care of you, and if they don't like me, they can kiss my ass."

"You said a bad word," Beep said.

Marshall shrugged.

"I won't tell," Beep added and then closed his eyes, too miserable to talk anymore.

———ᴧᴧᴧ———

When Mavis saw Lon Pittman enter the school building with an expression on his face similar to the one Johnny Pine had been wearing, her heart skipped a beat. He *had* called the cops. She glanced over her shoulder. She could still hear raised voices inside the principal's office. This mess was about to get worse.

Then the office door opened and Lon Pittman walked inside carrying a tripod and a camera case.

"Afternoon, Mavis, I need to speak to Mrs. Winston."

Mavis shifted nervously in her chair as she straightened her jacket.

"I'm sorry but she's busy right now. If you don't mind—"

He tapped his badge. "She can get unbusy. This is police business."

Mavis nodded. "I'll just let her know you're—"

"Are those kids in her office?"

"What kids?" she asked, knowing full well the ones he meant.

"Don't play dumb with me, Mavis. I am not a happy man."

"I wasn't playing," Mavis muttered and then rolled her eyes as she realized she'd just acknowledged she was dumb. "I mean… Oh, never mind! Just a minute and I'll see if—"

"I asked you a question. Who's in the office with her?"

Mavis shivered. She liked her job just fine, but she'd never signed up to defy authority. The police trumped Mrs. Winston whether she liked it or not.

"The kids and their parents," she answered and watched a muscle jerk at the corner of his left eye.

"Perfect. Now if you'll just open the door for me," he said.

Mavis hurried to the door, knocked once, and then turned the knob so that the door would swing open. As soon as Officer Pittman was inside, she shut it behind him.

Lon walked in with his chin up and his shoulders back and set down his things.

Arlene Winston was stunned to see the police and realized this was spinning out of her control, but this was not the time to panic.

"I'm sorry, Officer Pittman, but you—"

Lon held up his hand as he coolly eyed the four boys and their parents.

"No apology necessary. I see all the parties in question are here. I came to take statements about the assault."

Carl Buckley's face flushed with anger. He turned on the principal even as his wife was trying to calm him down.

"Assault, my ass! Who the hell called the cops?" he demanded.

Lon heard the challenge in the banker's voice but didn't rise to it.

"I received a report from a doctor in the ER. Surely you know that when any child is brought into a medical facility with suspicious injuries, those injuries have to be reported to the police," Lon said.

"Injuries? Exactly what kind of injuries are we talking about?" Buckley asked.

"The child in question has a broken nose, broken ribs, loose teeth, and large contusions on his back, belly, and leg."

Sally Rankin stared at her twins in disbelief and then covered her face.

Coach Sharp's wife looked at her son as if he were a stranger and then began to cry.

Carl Buckley's wife slumped forward in her chair and would have hit the floor if Buckley hadn't caught her.

Coach Sharp cursed beneath his breath, but it was from panic, not anger.

But it was the banker, Carl Buckley, who had a reputation to protect, and he was ready to bully whomever it took to make all this go away.

"How dare you come in here and treat us like criminals?" Carl shouted.

Lon saw the rage on the banker's face and the smirk the Buckley boy was wearing, and began pushing what he knew would be emotional buttons. He glanced at the principal.

"I was not aware that the parents were part of the assault," he said.

Sally Rankin gasped. "We weren't, but if we had been there, I can promise none of this would have happened."

"Then Mr. Buckley misspoke. Dealing with criminals is part of my job, and when they are underage, dealing with their families does occur," Lon said, pointing at the video camera with the remote. "This will be taped for security purposes. So, Mrs. Winston, if you don't mind, I need to commandeer your office and ask you to step out—"

"But I—"

"Did you participate in or witness the attack?" he asked.

"No, but—"

He opened the door to her office and then stepped aside, waiting for her to leave, which she did, but with indignation. He closed the door behind her and turned to face the room.

"Parents are allowed to be present since the perpetrators are minors, but since they were not witnesses, they have no voice in what is said. Do I make myself clear?"

Coach Sharp nodded.

"Yes, sir," Sally Rankin said.

"Do we need to call a lawyer?" Buckley asked.

"I'm just taking statements, not charging them with anything, Mr. Buckley."

Buckley's nostrils flared. Just as he opened his mouth to complain even more, his wife elbowed him in the ribs and shook her head.

Lon pointed at the boys who were sitting by their parents.

"Boys, stand up and bring your folding chairs over here in front of me and take a seat, please."

The boys were beginning to look anxious. It was becoming apparent that they might actually be in big trouble. They stood, glanced at their parents for backup, and when none was given, dragged their chairs to the middle of the room and sat down.

Coach Sharp stifled a groan. Lon had efficiently moved all four boys so that they would be sitting with their backs to their parents. There was no telling what might come out of their mouths.

Lon turned on the camera, identified himself, stated the time and date, and then gave instructions to the boys.

"This is a video camera which I will be using to take down your statements. Now, all I need you to do is answer every question I ask truthfully. For the record, please state your name, age, and grade in school, beginning with you."

He pointed at the boy to his left. Not only was he the largest one, but he was also the only one who didn't look scared.

"Lewis Buckley. Ten years old. Fourth grade."

Lon pointed at the boy beside Lewis, who quickly responded.

"Kevin Sharp. Nine years old. Fourth grade."

"Billy Ray Rankin. Nine years old. Fourth grade."

"Bobby Jay Rankin. Nine years old. Fourth grade."

"Thank you," Lon said. "Now who wants to tell me how the altercation with Brooks Pine began?"

No one moved. No one spoke. All but Lewis were pasty white and shaking. Lewis was still smirking. Lon thought of the Pine kid's battered body and needed to wipe the smirk off his face.

He pointed at Lewis and Kevin.

"I'm going to need you to remove your shoes, and, you, please remove your shirt. I will be booking them in as evidence."

Lewis reeled like he'd just been slapped.

"But these are my new shoes," he argued.

Kevin plastered his hands on the front of his shirt.

"I can't go nekkid in school."

Lon shrugged. "There's blood on Lewis's shoes and on your shirt. That makes them evidence in the assault. Our crime lab will take samples of the blood, and if it matches Brooks Pine's blood, then it helps prove your part in the assault. Please take them off."

Lewis swiveled around in his seat, his eyes widening in panic.

"Daddy?"

"Please face me," Lon said. "Your parents are not in trouble. You are."

Lewis was upset but tried to hide it as he took off his shoes.

"You can keep the shoes. Daddy will buy me some more," he announced loudly. "I don't want anything with that skuzzy kid's blood on it. He's nothing but white trash."

The Buckleys were tight-lipped and red in the face.

Lon kept his focus on Lewis, who seemed to be the ringleader of the four.

"Who is white trash?" Lon asked.

"Beep Pine," Lewis said. "Everybody knows it. Daddy says their family is white trash."

"How did the boy's blood get on your shoe?" he asked.

Lewis shrugged. "His nose popped when I kicked him. I guess it happened then."

Carl Buckley went numb. Hearing the casual manner in which his son had just spoken did not bode well for the outcome of this meeting. His wife put a hand over her mouth to stifle a moan. She was both horrified and ashamed.

"Are you the only one who kicked him?" Lon asked.

"No," Lewis said. "Kevin and the twins kicked him too."

"You kicked the most!" Kevin argued.

"We only kicked his legs and belly," the twins said.

The parents couldn't look at each other and wouldn't look at Lon.

Lon just kept pushing. "Exactly why did you kick him? Why would any of you boys want to hurt him?" Lon asked.

"He had ringworm!" Lewis yelled.

"He had cooties!" Kevin Sharp added.

The twins ducked their heads. They were already aware that they'd crossed a huge boundary. Their mother had already called both of them bullies earlier. They were screwed.

"I didn't want to do it," Billy Ray said.

Kevin elbowed him in the ribs.

"Ow! That hurt!" Billy Ray cried.

Kevin glared. "Don't lie. You were laughing when you kicked him."

Lon held up a hand and elevated the tone of his voice.

"Boys! Keep your hands to yourself. And by the way, did Brooks Pine tell you he was hurting? Did he ask you boys to stop?"

Lewis shook his head. "No, he didn't—"

Bobby Jay interrupted. "Don't tell another lie, Lewis. We're already fucked!"

Sally Rankin inhaled so loudly both boys actually ducked their heads, expecting her to grab them up by their shirt collars and wash their mouths out with soap.

Ruby Dye was cutting Rachel Goodhope's hair when Vera Conklin came in the back door of the Curl Up and Dye. She'd gone out to get lunch for herself and the girls, but she had come back with more than their food. She set the sack down on the table in back and hung her wet raincoat on a hook as she headed toward the salon.

She raised an eyebrow at her sister, Vesta, which was part of their twin-speak for "Boy, do I have something to tell," smiled at Ruby's customer in the styling chair, and pointed at Mabel Jean, who'd just finished doing Rachel's nails.

"Mabel Jean, your salad is in the sack on top. Vesta, your club sandwich is probably on the bottom. Ruby, your burger is in there somewhere, and if it's squished, it's not my fault. They pack up to-go orders at Granny's Country Kitchen like they're running out of sacks. Hi, Rachel. My goodness, that new haircut is going to make you look ten years younger."

Rachel beamed.

Then the ladies watched Vera take a step back and put her hands in the air, somewhat like Preacher Lawless down at the Freewill Baptist Church right before he called upon the good Lord for forgiveness of their sins.

"Ladies, I'm about to bust with my news. I just heard about the most horrible thing."

Ruby stifled a smile. Vera was all about the drama.

"What happened?" Ruby asked.

"The youngest Pine boy got beat up by a gang of older boys at school this morning. They said his nose is broken and he's bruised and bloody all over. They also said when Johnny Pine came to get pick him up, he read them the riot act and then took the little guy to the ER."

They looked at each other in mutual horror.

"Good Lord! What is this world coming to, anyway?" Ruby muttered.

"Who would do something so awful to a little kid?" Rachel asked.

"If gossip is correct, it was Coach Sharp's son, Carl Buckley's son, and Sally Rankin's twins."

Ruby shook her head. "Considering two teachers and

a banker are the parents, doesn't sound like the little Pine boy is going to see much justice."

"I don't know about that," Vera said. "After Dr. Quick treated the Pine boy, he called the police. Something about a legal responsibility to report assaults on children, I think."

Vesta glanced at the clock. She had almost twenty minutes before her next appointment.

"I'm calling Junie down at the police station to see if they arrested those kids."

Ruby frowned. "No, don't! Whatever's happening, we'll find out soon enough. Better to leave gossip alone when kids are involved."

"She's right," Vera said. "Besides, Lisa George teaches fifth grade math, and I'm doing her hair after school. She'll talk. She can't keep a secret for beans."

Rachel Goodhope frowned. "How old is the Pine boy?"

"They said he was in second grade," Vera said. "There are just the three Pine boys left, you know. The older brother, Johnny, is raising his two little brothers, and this probably hit him real hard, him being the only one responsible for them anymore."

"Why is that?" Rachel asked.

Ruby patted Rachel's shoulder. "Because their daddy is in prison and their mother overdosed two years ago and died. Johnny came close to losing the boys to Social Services then, and if they want to, they could make this an issue and take the boys away from Johnny by claiming he's not a responsible parent."

"But he's not to blame," Rachel said.

Ruby shrugged. "Since when has that mattered?"

"Well, I think that's terrible," Rachel said.

Ruby nodded. "So do I," she said, then gave Rachel's hair a last squirt of hair spray and spun the chair around. "All done. What do you think?"

"Good," Rachel said, eyeing her new cut. "I like it a lot. Thank you, Ruby."

"You're welcome, sugar. Let's go up front and get you down for next week, okay?"

Rachel gathered up her things, making sure to get her umbrella. She didn't want to mess up her new hairdo before she sported it around a little. She thought about the school incident again as she was driving through town, which reinforced the decision she'd made years ago not to have children. Rachel Goodhope would always be a work in progress.

Dori had managed to eat most of a grilled cheese sandwich between emptying and loading the dishwasher and was taking a breather to ease her aching back when one of the waitresses came in to get a refill on corn bread muffins for one of her tables.

"You won't believe what I just heard. A gang of older boys beat up the youngest Pine boy at school this morning. His brother took him to the ER and the doctor called the cops to report the assault. Shit is hitting the fan, big-time."

Walter the cook looked up as he refilled the bread basket.

"Who were the kids who beat him up?" he asked.

"Coach Sharp's boy, banker Buckley's kid, and Sally Rankin's twins."

Dori was horrified.

"Why would they do something so awful?"

"They didn't say, but you know how mean kids can be. His last name is Pine, which automatically makes him a target."

A wave of heat washed through Dori so fast, she felt faint. She had been so busy trying to survive her personal mistakes that she had never thought about Luther's life that far into the future, but now she was realizing what he had in store. He was a bastard child, and there was nothing that would ever change that fact. By virtue of birth alone, he would become a target. Sick to her stomach, she tossed what was left of her food in the garbage. She remembered Johnny Pine as a quiet, good-looking guy who always seemed too serious. Now she knew why. Her heart hurt for Johnny's little brother, for her little guy, and for all children who become victims of someone else's ignorance and rage.

Now that she'd delivered her gossip, the waitress grabbed the bread basket.

"Thanks, Walt. I gotta get back out on the floor, but I'm making a prediction now that nothing happens to those boys. When power and money is involved, it never does."

Dori thought of Johnny Pine's lot in life as she began scraping plates. He'd been a couple of years ahead of her in school, but she didn't remember him ever having a girlfriend or being involved in many school activities. With parents like his, he must have felt like he had a lot to live down.

And then her shoulders slumped. Her parents had been decent people, just like her granddaddy. They had good names and good reputations. She was the one who'd messed all that up. The only thing she could do was never make that mistake again.

Her steps were dragging by the time her shift was over, and it was still drizzling when she left the restaurant. She could call her granddaddy and have him come pick her up, but it was more trouble than it was worth for the time it took to get Luther bundled up and buckled into his car seat. Besides, it wasn't far, and walking back and forth to work was the only time she had left that was her own.

She sidestepped puddles as she walked, trying to stay beneath the overhangs of various businesses as she headed home. The wind was just strong enough to make holding on to the umbrella difficult, and so she kept it clutched tightly in her hands and pulled close to her head. Someone honked as they drove past, and she started to wave until she realized they weren't honking at her and kept walking.

A gust of cold wind blew rain against her pant legs. They would be soaked by the time she got home, but getting wet was not a problem, just a situation easily remedied. She thought of the little Pine boy again and wondered if Johnny was as afraid of his responsibilities as she was of hers. Luther meant the world to her, but he'd already started life with one strike against him. She had to find a way to make sure that her mistakes did not hold him back. She put her head down and kept moving at a fast clip, and by the time she got home and walked in the back door, she was both cold and wet.

The house was quiet except for the television she could hear playing in the living room. She left her raincoat, umbrella, and wet shoes in the mudroom, and as she went to change clothes, she saw Granddaddy and Luther asleep in the recliner. When she saw the show they'd been watching, she smiled. Watching people hunt alligators was one of Meeker Webb's favorite pastimes, and it must have agreed with Luther. He was sprawled out in his grandfather's lap, relaxed as a cat sleeping in sunshine.

She hurried to her room to change into something dry and then began gathering up a load of clothes. There were always clothes needing to be washed. As she worked, she added items to the growing grocery list and then decided to run the dust mop on the hardwood floors. It was a quiet job, and one that needed doing. By the time she had finished, both of her guys were waking up.

When Luther saw her, he let out a squeal that woke Meeker. After that, there was no containing Luther. He wanted his mama, which meant whatever else she needed to do, she would be doing it with Luther riding shotgun on her hip.

Chapter 4

JOHNNY TOOK THE BOYS HOME, PUT BEEP TO BED, AND left Marshall sitting beside him watching TV. He went to the kitchen to make some coffee, and while he was waiting, he called Miss Jane at the Before and After to tell her they were with him.

"Are they sick?" she asked. Jane considered it her duty to guard against germs as well as bad behavior, and didn't want them anywhere near the other kids until they were well.

"No, ma'am. Beep was hurt at school today."

"Oh, well, I'm sorry to hear that. Did he get hurt on the playground? I've been telling people for years that those old monkey bars aren't safe."

Johnny didn't hesitate to explain. He wasn't going to sugarcoat one bit of what happened.

"No, a gang of older boys beat him up. He's hurt pretty bad."

Miss Jane didn't like racket, but when they were behaving, she did like the Pine boys.

"Well, that's just awful. I'm so sorry to hear that. Was it that gang from the depot?"

Johnny took a deep breath, willing himself not to react to the slur about the boys from his side of town who hung out at the abandoned depot, playing music with their band.

"No, ma'am. They were from your side of town. It

was Coach Sharp's boy, Banker Buckley's son, and Mrs. Rankin's twins."

He heard a gasp and then nothing. Just when he thought she was going to hang up, she asked him one more question, her voice shaking.

"How bad is he hurt?"

"They broke his nose and ribs. He has multiple contusions, a swollen mouth, loose teeth, and his eyes are black. I will let you know when to expect them at the Before and After again."

"Oh, Johnny, I am so sorry."

"Yes, ma'am, so am I," Johnny said and disconnected.

Now that he'd taken care of the immediate, he needed to think about long term. He poured himself a cup of coffee and sat down at the kitchen table with the phone book. It was time to call that lawyer.

———

P. Nutt Butterman, Esq., known around town as Peanut, heard about the school incident from his secretary, who heard about it from her sister-in-law, who heard it from her husband who was a bus driver for the Blessings Public School system. Soon afterward, Peanut got a heads-up call from Paul Quick about doing pro bono work for Johnny Pine. He had a fondness for underdogs and admired Johnny Pine for keeping his family out of the Social Services system. He quickly agreed to help and was debating as to whether he should approach Pine on his own or wait for him to come in when his secretary knocked and then stepped into his office.

"There is a young man named Johnny Pine on the phone. He wants to know if you would see him today.

I didn't know what to tell him because technically you don't have an appointment open, but your next appointment is already late. She lives about five miles out of town, and the way it's raining, she may have decided not to drive in."

"Put him on the phone," Peanut said. "I'll talk to him now, and we'll go from there."

She nodded and closed the door on her way out.

Peanut sat down, waiting for her to put the call through, and when he heard Johnny's voice, he leaned forward with his elbows on the desk, ready to go to war. He did love fighting for the underdogs.

"Hello, this is Butterman."

"Mr. Butterman, my name is Johnny Pine, and I think I need a lawyer. Dr. Quick gave me your name to—"

"Quick already called me," Peanut said. "Sorry to hear about your brother, and I just want to let you know this one's on me. By the way, what's your brother's name again? Quick told me, but I didn't write it down."

Johnny hesitated, a little overwhelmed that this had happened so easily. "His name is Brooks, but everybody calls him Beep."

Peanut chuckled. "I can appreciate a good nickname. I tried to hold a grudge against my parents for what they named me, but the oddity of my name has made it memorable. When someone in the area is in need of a lawyer, my name is the first one they think of."

Johnny relaxed. The man was definitely friendly and seemed very down-to-earth.

"I appreciate this more than you know."

Peanut grabbed a pen and a notepad. "My pleasure. Now, the first thing we'll need to do is make sure the parents are aware they will be responsible for the medical bills incurred from this, so I'll get their personal info. I know Dr. Quick called the police. Has your brother given his statement yet?"

"Yes, sir. Officer Pittman came to the ER and videoed it. He said he was going to school to get statements from the kids when he left."

"Perfect. I'll get a copy of that or a transcript. Now, do you want to ask for damages?"

Johnny was a little shocked. "No, no, I don't want to sue anyone. I just want to make sure they pay for the medical bills and that there are proper consequences for those boys. I don't want anybody paid off, so to speak, to make this go away."

"Then that's what we'll aim for," Peanut said. "Let me talk to the police and see what charges, if any, are going to be filed. Give me your contact number, and I'll be in touch."

Johnny gave him his phone number and then a few moments later, hung up. He didn't know how this was going to turn out, but it felt good to have legal aid on their side.

When he glanced at the clock, he realized lunchtime had long since come and gone, and headed to the boys' bedroom.

"Hey, Marshall, did you bring your lunch home?" he asked.

"Yes, it's in my backpack."

Beep's eyes welled with tears. "My mouf hurts. Don't want nothin' to eat."

Johnny frowned. The pain meds they'd given Beep in ER were beginning to wear off. "I'm sorry, buddy. I'll go get your new prescriptions filled and pick up some soup. How about chicken noodle? It's your favorite, and you won't have to chew."

Beep nodded.

"Can I eat here in our room with Beep while you're gone?" Marshall asked.

Johnny had a rule about eating food at the table, but today was a day for breaking rules.

"Yeah, sure. And you can have a root beer with it, if you want. There are a couple in the refrigerator."

"Can I have one too?" Beep asked.

"How about you and Marshall just share one, and if you want more, you guys can open the other one."

"Okay," Beep said, but the tears overflowed and started to roll.

Johnny sat down on the side of the bed and patted Beep's knee. He wanted to cry with him.

"I'm so sorry, buddy. Hang in there. I won't be gone long." Then he pointed at Marshall. "You're in charge. Use your common sense, please."

Marshall nodded.

Wasting no time, Johnny was back out in the rain. His clothes were still uncomfortably wet, but there was no need changing until he was home to stay. He was sick to his stomach about what had happened and knowing Beep was in pain made him angry. He wanted revenge. He wanted those boys to pay. But how would justice ever be served when the perpetrators were still kids too?

It wasn't going to be up to him to seek revenge though. He had the law and a lawyer on his side. Surely they would make things right. All he needed to do was what he'd been doing: take care of business. He started the car, and after a quick glance at the aging house they called home, he put the car in gear and drove away.

First stop was at the pharmacy to drop off the prescriptions. He intended to get what groceries they needed while they were being filled.

LilyAnn Dalton was shelving bottles of shampoo when she saw him come in and quickly stopped what she was doing to talk.

"Johnny! We've been hearing horrible stories about Beep being hurt at school. Is that true?"

"Yes, ma'am, I'm afraid it is."

LilyAnn's hand subconsciously went to her belly and the baby she was carrying.

"Is Beep okay? I can't believe that happened."

"He's home, but he has a ways to go before he's able to go back to school."

Mr. Phillips, the pharmacist, walked up as they were talking.

"Johnny? Is your boy okay?"

"He will be," Johnny said and handed him two prescriptions. "I need to get these filled, please."

"I'll get right on it," he said and hurried off.

LilyAnn lowered her voice.

"Was it really Coach Sharp's boy? And Buckley's? And the Rankin twins?"

He nodded.

Her eyes widened, stunned that "good boys" would do something so awful.

"Someone said they kicked him. Is that true? Is he hurt bad?"

Johnny sighed. He hated repeating this over and over, but better the truth from him than gossip on the streets.

"Yes, it's true. The truth is they hurt him bad. His nose and a couple of ribs are broken. His mouth is swollen. They loosened some of his teeth, blacked his eyes, and he has deep contusions on his back and leg."

The horror of what he was saying shocked her to tears.

"Oh my Lord! Why, Johnny, why?"

A muscle jerked at the side of Johnny's eye.

"Because his last name is Pine. Because I cut gum out of his hair, and they decided he had ringworm. Because they're mean, entitled little bastards who believe they are better because of who they are and where they live. I'll be back in a little while to get the medicine."

He walked out with his head up, grateful for the rain that hid his tears.

By that night, Blessings was in an uproar. There was a contingent of residents who were horrified that four decent boys from good families had been taken to the police station and booked like common criminals all because of a little fight with one of those Pines.

And then there were the others who were horrified that one small boy was brutally beaten by a gang of boys, all older and bigger than him, regardless of his name. There hadn't been an acrimonious division like this among the residents since the day Georgia seceded from the Union and went to war against the United States of America.

⸻

Unaware of the growing turmoil in town, Dori was washing dishes and listening to her little boy's babbling as he whacked a teething biscuit into crumbs against the tray of his high chair.

Meeker was in the living room, watching television. Every now and then he would rub his chest and burp. Something he'd eaten didn't agree with him. He yawned and stretched and burped again.

"Damn chili," he muttered and got up, heading for the kitchen to get some antacid tablets.

Dori smiled when she saw him walk in.

"Hi, Granddaddy. Do you want something cold to drink?"

"No, honey, I'm fine. That chili I ate is barking at me. I just need some antacid."

She frowned. "The chili was fine. It was all those pickled jalapeño slices you put on it that's making your belly hurt."

He grinned. "You sound just like your Grandma Caroline," he said as he dug through the cabinet for the medicine, then popped a couple of chewable tablets in his mouth.

Luther pointed at the bottle and squealed.

Meeker laughed. "This isn't candy, boy! You stick to your cookie…or what's left of it."

Dori eyed the crumbs, both on the tray and the floor, then rolled her eyes at the wads of crumbs between Luther's fat little fingers.

"You are a mess, Luther Joe. I think it's time you get a bath and get in bed."

Meeker eyed his granddaughter, judging the slight slump in her shoulders and the lack of color in her face. She looked tired.

"Five a.m. comes early, doesn't it, girl?"

She shrugged. "It's early all right, but I also get home early too, which is fine by me."

He admired her attitude and her fortitude. Despite her fragile appearance, she was a tough little thing. He'd always felt a little guilty about Dori's situation, thinking if there'd been a woman in her life, things might have turned out different. Then he looked at Luther. But if things had been different, then they wouldn't have the little guy, and that would have been a tragedy indeed.

"I believe I'll have that cold drink after all," he said, getting a cold Coca-Cola from the refrigerator and taking it with him as Dori got a clean wet washcloth and began cleaning up Luther and his mess.

Rain was still hammering against the roof and blowing against the windows as she carried her baby down the hall. He was patting her cheeks with his fat baby hands, and when he poked a finger in her mouth, she pretended to bite it.

Luther squealed.

Dori laughed.

Their nightly ritual continued.

The rainstorm had moved on and the house was quiet by the time Dori crawled in bed. Meeker was snoring in his bedroom down the hall, and she could hear Luther in his crib on the other side of the room, sucking his thumb. She sighed, glad the day was over, but the moment she relaxed, she thought of what had happened to Johnny Pine's little brother and then of Johnny, imagining how afraid she would have been if it had been Luther who'd been hurt today. In an odd way, they were both in the same boat: teenagers raising kids. The only difference was that she had her grandfather. Johnny didn't have anyone. She wondered who he talked to when he got scared, and then she rolled over and closed her eyes.

Johnny got a text from his boss sometime during the night, telling him to take the day off, since it was too wet to run a dozer, to take care of Beep, and to just ignore what people are saying.

Johnny's stomach rolled, wondering what kind of uproar the incident had started. From what his boss said, it sounded like people were mad at them, which figured, even though Beep was the victim.

He shoved a hand through his hair and got up to go check on the boys. They were still asleep, so he started coffee and then went to take a shower and get dressed. If shit was going to hit the fan, he didn't intend to face it butt naked.

He showered quickly, then wrapped a towel around his waist and squirted some shaving cream in his hand. He couldn't remember ever seeing his daddy clean shaven or dressed up, and his need to be a polar opposite was ingrained. All three of the boys had their daddy's black hair, which marked them yet again as "one of those Pines," but they didn't have to mirror his ways.

As soon as he'd finished shaving, he got dressed and went to the kitchen for coffee. His brain didn't kick into full gear until that first swallow of the dark brew slid down his throat.

He was debating what to make for breakfast that Beep could swallow comfortably and decided on oatmeal, which was their old standby, so he measured out the right amounts of oats and water, added a pinch of salt, turned on the heat, and as soon as it got hot, he began to stir.

He heard a door open and knew one or both of the boys were awake. A few moments later, Marshall appeared in the doorway.

"Beep's nose is bleeding," he announced.

"On the way," Johnny said, turning off the fire and putting a lid on the oatmeal. It could finish cooking by itself or he'd put it back on the heat later.

He could hear Beep crying even before he reached the room, and his heart sank. For the first time since their mother's death, he felt her absence in a way he would never have imagined. Beep needed cuddling, and Johnny had never been a cuddler for either of the boys. He teased them. He corrected them. He fed them and loved them, and they knew he loved them, but now there was a need for more—and he felt horribly inadequate for the job.

He stopped in the bathroom on the way and grabbed a wet washcloth and a hand towel and then crossed the hall into their room.

Beep was sitting up in bed sobbing. His hair was standing on end and his eyes were so swollen he could barely see. A thin trickle of blood was seeping out of one nostril and his pillow was spotted with more of the same.

At that moment, Johnny hated those boys with every ounce of his being. He slid onto the mattress beside Beep and held out his arms. Beep crawled into his lap and went limp against Johnny's chest as he continued to cry.

Johnny suspected he was not only in pain but also overwhelmed by the memory of yesterday's horror and afraid of a repeat once he was back in school. He held him close as he wiped tears and blood off his little brother's face, talking softly.

"This isn't bad. It's just a little blood," Johnny said and then glanced up at Marshall, who was looking anxious, and gave him a wink to reassure him too. "He hurts and he is sore all over, Marshall, but he's not worse, okay?"

Marshall nodded, then burst into tears.

"Oh hey! Guys, come on now. You're breaking my heart," Johnny said, his voice shaking. "Come here, Marshall. I need a hug."

Marshall fell into Johnny's outstretched arm, his shoulders shaking with muffled sobs.

Johnny laid his cheek against Marshall's head and stifled the urge to join them.

"My nose is bleeding," Beep cried.

Johnny pulled himself together, gave Marshall a quick hug and a kiss on the top of his head, and then gave him something to do.

"Bring me another wet washcloth, will you?"

Marshall bolted from the room, wiping snot on the back of his arm as he went while Johnny tended to Beep.

"Now, let me see that little nose."

Beep tilted his head.

Johnny gave it the once-over and noticed that the gauze that had been in his nostril was missing, probably lost during sleep.

"I see what happened, Beep. That bandage Dr. Quick put up your nose fell out. We'll get some fresh gauze and fix you right up, okay? Are you hurting too?"

Beep nodded.

"More medicine coming up," Johnny said as Marshall came back with a wet cloth. "That's perfect. You go get dressed while I help get Beep settled. I made oatmeal. If you're too hungry to wait, help yourself."

"Can I have raisins?" Marshall asked.

Johnny grinned. "May I have raisins, not can I, and, yes, you may. You're gonna turn into a raisin one of these days."

Happy for the freedom of making his own cereal, Marshall threw on some clothes and bolted for the kitchen before Johnny changed his mind.

Beep shifted against Johnny's chest and looked up.

"Are you gonna settle me now?" he asked.

Johnny grinned.

"Yeah, buddy. I'm gonna settle you now. After we get you dressed, do you think you might try and eat a little oatmeal?"

Beep frowned. "I don't want no raisins."

"You don't want any raisins," Johnny said.

Beep sighed. "I already said that."

"I know, buddy. Now let's get his bloody shirt off and get you a clean one, and then we'll get your medicine."

Johnny grimaced as he eased his arms out of each sleeve and then stretched the neck opening before pulling it over Beep's head. The bruises were larger and darker, making him look even more fragile. He couldn't believe that this had happened and had no idea how it was going to play out.

―――

Ruby Dye turned the Closed sign to Open as she unlocked the front door of the Curl Up and Dye.

Today was likely to be unusually hectic. Vesta was sick at home, and Ruby and Vera were picking up her appointments. No one was getting a lunch break, but they were confident they could do it.

Ruby and Vera had already divided up the clients over the phone last night, so she began checking supplies to be sure she had the right products on hand. One of the ladies she was picking up for Vesta was Jane Farris, who ran the Before and After day care. Ruby liked Jane, although she thought she was a little uptight. It was Ruby's opinion that if you're going to run a business involving children, you should at least enjoy being around them. Jane talked about them like they were dirty puppies who peed on floors and chewed on furniture, which she was certain was not the case.

A short time later, Ruby's first appointment showed up, and then Vera and Mabel Jean walked in together and the day began. What she hadn't planned on was an hour-by-hour playback of everyone's opinion on the assault of Brooks Pine. By the time Jane Farris arrived, Ruby was stunned by what she'd been hearing, and Vera's cheeks were an angry red.

Mabel Jean was working her nail file like a chain saw and gritting her teeth to keep from arguing with the clients who were so disrespectful to a family down on their luck.

They were shocked by the number of people who thought the whole thing should just go away.

Mabel Jean left to run an errand, and Ruby was sweeping up hair from her last appointment when Jane Farris arrived. By the time she'd hung up her jacket, Ruby was ready for her.

"Morning, Jane!"

Jane waved.

"Good morning, Ruby. I sure appreciate you

working me in to your schedule. The older I get, the more I appreciate the luxury of someone doing my hair for me."

Ruby beamed. "And that's just music to my ears. Come on back and we'll get started."

Jane noticed Luwanda Peeples deep in conversation with Vera but didn't interrupt to say hello. Luwanda's husband was on the city council, and the way she carried on, you'd have thought he was one step down from being president of the United States.

As soon as Jane was seated, Ruby snapped a cape around her neck and escorted her to the shampoo station. Jane was unusually silent, and Ruby purposefully didn't initiate a conversation, sensing her need for peace. After she'd finished the shampoo and conditioning, they moved back to her station to blow-dry her hair. Ruby combed through Jane's hair with her fingers, getting a feel for the texture and thickness.

"Vesta uses a curling iron rather than rollers on your hair, right?"

Jane was eyeing herself in the mirror, trying to remember what she had looked like when she was young, but she'd forgotten. All she saw now was a middle-aged woman with a round face, a wide nose, and double chins. She was lost in thought when she suddenly realized Ruby was asking her a question.

"I'm sorry, what did you say?"

"Vesta uses a curling iron, right?"

"Yes. I don't have the patience for rollers and sitting under a dryer anymore." Then she smiled. "I take that back. I shouldn't say *anymore*, because I never did like to sit still. Some things never change, I guess."

The moment that came out of Jane's mouth, Luwanda Peeples took her private conversation with Vera to the room.

"I'll say that's right, Jane. Some things never change, like another member of that no-good Pine family in trouble with the law! I've been telling Vera here what a crime it is that four decent little boys were taken to jail for nothing more than a little scuffle. Everyone knows the Pines are just white trash. The mother is dead from drugs and the father is in prison, and yet that Pine boy got off scot-free after the fight and those dear boys are the ones in trouble. They all go to my church, and I think it's a crime what happened."

Ruby had just brushed a hank of Jane's wet hair around the bristles of a vent brush and had the dryer only inches from her scalp when Jane spun her chair around so fast Ruby lost her grip. The brush slipped from her hand, tangling in Jane's hair as it dangled down the back of her neck.

Jane could have cared less. She was so angry with Luwanda, she was shaking.

"I can't say you don't have a right to voice your opinion, but if you're going to gossip, Luwanda Peeples, then you need to get your facts straight."

Luwanda's eyes widened in shock and then narrowed in anger. The emanating hiss she emitted was reminiscent of a pissed-off snake.

"That's not gossip! I heard it straight from Buckley's gardener who also does my yard."

"Well, I know for a fact that everything that came out of your mouth is a big fat lie, and I got it from Johnny Pine himself!" Jane shouted.

Ruby wondered if she needed to stop this before it got any worse, but she was privately pleased to hear someone speaking up for the Pines, and so she said nothing. However, an unwise decision is usually recognized only in hindsight, and such was the case.

"I don't lie!" Luwanda shrieked and leaned forward in the chair.

The hair spray Vera just spritzed went down the back of Luwanda's neck, but she didn't seem to mind.

"So tell me how it's okay for four older boys to gang up on one little boy who is much younger and smaller?" Jane snapped.

Luwanda sputtered. "Well, he must have been doing something to—"

"Oh yes, he did something all right! He got gum stuck in his hair. His brother cut it out and sent him to school, where four bullies decided not only to taunt him for it, they kicked him all over the room."

Luwanda gasped. "That's not how—"

"That little Pine boy is one of *my* boys. He's seven years old and in the second grade. He's barely past a baby and now, because of those little thugs, he has a broken nose, broken ribs, loose teeth, black eyes, and deep muscle contusions. Your little choir boys brutalized him and I, for one, am furious about it!"

Luwanda's lips flapped but no words came out.

Vera was shocked. She knew he'd been hurt but had no idea to what extent.

"Are you serious? They did all that?" she asked.

"Yes, they did. I spoke to Johnny myself. They had to take him to the emergency room, and he can't go to school for Lord knows how long. And Johnny didn't call the police; the doctor did. Assault is against the law and the victim was a child. It was his duty."

Luwanda tore off her cape, flung a twenty-dollar bill on Vera's counter and grabbed her purse as she took a step toward Jane.

Jane stood, the vent brush still dangling down the back of her neck and her fingers curled into fists.

Right in the middle of the Curl Up and Dye, the two middle-aged women sized each other up like two broody setting hens with only one nest between them.

"I never took you for a lover of white trash," Luwanda snapped.

Jane's eyes narrowed. "White trash isn't a location, Luwanda Peeples. It is how someone acts, and in my book, you just put yourself right in the Dumpster."

Luwanda gasped. "I won't forget this!"

Jane shook her head. "I should hope not. Maybe next time you'll get your facts straight instead of spreading lies."

Luwanda charged for the front door at a lope while the rest of the women watched her go. The door squeaked as she yanked it open, and then she slammed it shut behind her.

Ruby thought to herself that she needed to oil those hinges. The silence afterward was almost uncomfortable until Mabel Jean came in the back door. She took one look at the women and grinned.

"What did I miss?"

Ruby looked at Vera, and then they both looked at Jane and burst into laughter.

Mabel Jean's grin widened.

"Come on. Really. What happened?"

Jane plopped back down in Ruby's chair.

"I'm not going to apologize," she muttered.

Ruby carefully unwound the vent brush from Jane's hair and turned on the dryer.

"And you should not. Do you part your hair on the right or on the left?"

Chapter 5

YESTERDAY IT WAS RAIN THAT HAD KEPT GRANNY'S Country Kitchen busy, and today it was the elementary school scandal. Everyone had taken sides, and they weren't shy about voicing it. Granny's was the best forum in town.

Lovey held an early morning employee meeting in the kitchen, cautioning her employees not to get involved in the growing disagreement, but it was all they could do to take and serve orders without commenting, because everyone had an opinion.

The waitresses kept Dori and Walter filled in on what was being said as they hustled in and out with orders. But the uglier the comments became, the angrier Dori became. A little boy had been seriously injured, and half the town seemed to have forgotten that. She was banging pots and clanking cutlery with obvious vehemence, voicing her opinion of the whole mess in a somewhat subversive manner.

Walter slapped another couple of hamburger patties on the grill and then put some buns off to the side to toast. He didn't know what to make of Dori's behavior. Normally she was so quiet, he almost forgot she was there, but not today. He looked at her again and decided she wore anger well.

Dori caught him looking at her and frowned.

"What?"

"I was about to ask you the same thing," Walter drawled and then went back to cooking.

She turned her back on him and began emptying the freshly washed dishes from the conveyor.

When two o'clock rolled around, it was none too soon for Dori. She got her things and started home, then remembered she needed diapers for Luther Joe and turned left at the corner toward the supermarket.

The farther away from Granny's she walked, the better she felt. After yesterday's rain, everything smelled fresh and clean. Too bad the rain couldn't wash away the ugliness in Blessings.

She was thinking about what to make for supper as she crossed the street and walked into the supermarket parking lot.

Someone honked a horn and shouted her name. She looked up and saw Pansy Jones, her neighbor from across the street, smiling and waving. She smiled and waved back as she entered the store.

Intent on wasting no time, she grabbed a shopping cart and headed straight toward the baby aisle. She turned a corner by the deli aisle and walked straight up on two girls from her old class who were there with their mothers.

The minute the girls saw Dori, they gave her a body scan that would have made Homeland Security proud, smirked, then looked at each other and giggled. Their mothers just stared.

Dori gritted her teeth and kept moving, hoping they would ignore her, but such was not the case.

A curvy redhead named Jenn actually stepped in front of her cart to stop her.

"Well, hi, Dori!"

The last thing Dori wanted was for them to think she was running away.

"Hi, Jenn. Hi, Leigh. It's good to see you."

"Yeah, uh…you too," Jenn said. "So how's it going?"

Dori smiled. "Oh, good, and you?"

Leigh giggled and fluffed her blond curls.

"We've been shopping for prom dresses. It's only a couple of weeks away."

"Are you still dating Freddie?" Dori asked.

The girls rolled their eyes at each other and then giggled again.

"Ugh, no. You are so behind times, girl. But that's to be expected, considering…"

Normally the hateful tone would have sent Dori ducking her head in shame, but something had clicked in her today. Maybe she should have gotten angry a long time ago. She laughed, which made everyone stare.

"Speaking of being behind…are you still failing chemistry? I mean, I used to tutor you, remember? But since I'm not in school anymore, I just wondered if someone else was helping you pass."

Leigh's eyes widened. Her lips parted, but she was too shocked to answer. Her mother decided to take offense for her daughter and grabbed Dori by the arm.

"See here, Dori Grant. You have no right to criticize my girl. After all, she's still in high school and you're… you're not. You're nothing but a dishwasher."

Dori smiled even wider as she pushed the woman's hand from her arm.

"Mrs. Glover! So nice to see you again. I know I've jumped the gun a bit on growing up, but it's not as bad as you might think. Actually, *I* have already graduated high school. I passed the GED and am taking college classes online."

Mrs. Glover blinked. She glanced at her daughter and then back at Dori Grant, trying to figure out how all that could happen in light of her fall from grace.

Dori just kept talking. "I'm leaning toward website design. It's something I can do from home and make decent money at the same time. As for washing dishes, aren't women always the ones washing dishes? The only difference between me and you is that I'm getting paid for it. I'd love to chat, but I need to finish shopping and get home. I don't mind my job, but I sure miss my baby boy."

Mrs. Glover's cheeks turned pink, but there was little she could say. She *did* wash the dishes at home and got little thanks for the effort, and for that matter, got little thanks for anything. She watched Dori Grant for a few seconds and then turned and glared at her daughter.

"It's time we got home. I have a thousand and one things to do yet today."

"But, Mama, I thought we were going to get some of that yummy banana pudding from the deli to take home."

"You're always wanting to spend my money. If you were working for your money, you'd have a different idea about how to spend it, I can assure you. If you want banana pudding, we'll make it at home."

Leigh was not pleased, but she knew that look on her mother's face and didn't argue. She glanced at Jenn and rolled her eyes, then followed her mother out of the store while Dori was standing in line to pay for diapers at the checkout.

Dori waved at them as they passed by her, but they ignored her presence. She couldn't remember when she'd felt this good.

Unlike Dori, Blessings's youngest criminals weren't feeling all that great. Because of their transgressions and subsequent arrests, their futures were still in free fall.

The twins had been dropped from the track team.

Lewis Buckley was no longer part of the basketball team.

Coach Sharp had personally kicked his own son off the football team that he coached.

And Peanut Butterman's presence on behalf of Brooks Pine was keeping the parents anxious. They hadn't voiced a single complaint about paying the medical bills and knew they would continue to be responsible for any and all medical treatments until Brooks Pine's doctor had released him.

They were certain Johnny Pine was going to sue them for damages and suffering, because if the shoe had been on the other foot, they would have done it to him. Because of the ages of the perpetrators, the district attorney had agreed to a closed hearing. The ruling disappointed the warring factions in Blessings. Fresh fodder would have done wonders for the fires of their indignation.

Two days later, Dori came home from work to find Luther Joe fussy and her granddaddy worn out. She apologized profusely that the baby had been a bother, took him out of Meeker's arms, and told Meeker to go to bed. Meeker didn't argue.

By nightfall, it became apparent that Luther Joe was sick. Dori suspected an earache because he kept pulling at his ear as he cried. Shortly after midnight, Meeker was back up with her, and they took turns trying to comfort the baby throughout the rest of the night, but to no avail.

Along toward daylight Dori finally got Luther to settle. He was dozing in her arms but whimpering in his sleep.

"I'll take him to the pediatrician in the morning," Dori said and then looked at the clock and sighed. "Lord. It's already morning."

"I can take him so you don't have to miss work," Meeker said.

Dori frowned. "I don't know, Granddaddy. I think I should—"

"Honey, we're in this together. I don't clock in anywhere but here with my two favorite people. You go to work, and I'll get him to the doctor. By the time you get off work, we'll at least have one dose of medicine in him and you can take over from there."

Dori still felt guilty. "This is my responsibility," she said.

"And we're still family," Meeker countered.

Luther Joe whimpered again and then let out a wail. Dori put him up on her shoulder and began patting his back and rocking him in her arms.

"My poor little man," Dori murmured and then caught her grandfather's look and gave in. "Okay, you take him to the doctor, and I'll take over when I come home. Tomorrow is my day off and that will give me two whole days to get him feeling better."

"That's the ticket," Meeker said. "I'm going to make

coffee; then I'll take over and you get ready and go to work. I'll call after we get back from the doctor, okay?"

"Yes, okay," she said as the baby continued to fuss. She kissed him on the cheek and then started down the hall toward their bedroom. "Let's go get a dry diaper, okay?"

Less than an hour later, Dori was out the door and on her way to Granny's Country Kitchen. She'd missed sleep before, and it would happen again. All she had to do was make it through her day.

She didn't know until she got to the restaurant that today was the day of the closed hearing at the courthouse.

Dori could only imagine what Johnny Pine was dealing with and said a quiet prayer as she started washing a new load of dishes. Her thoughts slid back to her own little boy, and she wished she were the one with him at the doctor's office. It was times like this when she was reminded adult life could really suck lemons.

It was almost noon by the time Meeker called her.

"Hey, honey. It's me. Luther has an ear infection."

Dori groaned. "Oh, that's what I was afraid of," she said. "So what did they do?"

"The doctor gave him a shot to head it off and some medicine for him to take orally. He's asleep right now, and we're fine."

Dori frowned. "A shot! He's never had a shot before. Did he cry?"

Meeker chuckled. "Hell yes, he cried. He let them know how pissed he was, while he was at it."

Dori felt sick. His first shot and she hadn't been there for him. "Poor little guy. You don't have to sound so proud of it."

Meeker chuckled. "It's a guy thing, honey. He's good. We're both good. See you later."

"Yeah, see you later," she said and ended the call.

Walter had been listening to her call without apology. "Is your boy sick?" he asked.

Dori nodded. "Ear infection."

"That's tough," Walter said.

Dori nodded. "He got his first shot today. He cried and I wasn't there," she said and then burst into tears.

Walter looked a little anxious and went back to his grill. Crying women made him nervous.

By the time 2:00 p.m. rolled around and Dori's day was ending, Johnny was on his way to the courthouse with the boys. It would be the unveiling of Brooks Pine's injuries.

Once the citizens of Blessings figured out they would not be present during the hearing, they regrouped and began gathering out on the courthouse steps as well as lining the halls inside, their curiosity shining for all to see.

Johnny was as prepared for what lay ahead as he could be. He had dressed the boys in clean jeans and new red T-shirts, and made sure they'd combed their hair before leaving the house. But there was a knot in his stomach as he drove uptown. Confronting the boys who'd caused Beep so much pain was going to be hard for all of them. Beep was scared to see them again, and Marshall was in big-brother protective mode. Johnny needed to know justice would be served.

By the time they arrived, the parking spaces were filled up on both sides of the street, and the growing crowd in front of the courthouse was daunting.

Marshall leaned forward.

"Why are all these people here?"

"Minding everyone's business but their own," Johnny muttered and circled the courthouse to look for an empty parking space.

As he stopped at a stop sign, he noticed a young woman waiting to cross and then recognized Dori Grant. He watched her glance toward their car as she started to cross, and he could tell by the look on her face that she'd recognized him too. To his surprise, she smiled shyly and waved. Before he could wave back, she was gone. A little startled that he'd momentarily lost focus, he turned the corner and finally found an empty space.

Marshall got out on his own as Johnny helped Beep out of the car. He could tell by the way his little brother was stooped over that he must be in pain.

"Hey, Beep, are you hurting?" he asked.

Beep shifted the plastic mask on his face to a more comfortable position and then ran a hand across his tummy.

"A little."

"Do you want some help? I'll carry you in if it's too far for you to walk."

Beep looked at Marshall and then ducked his head.

"They'll think I'm a baby," he muttered.

Johnny frowned. "To hell with them. We don't care what they think."

Beep eyed the set of his brother's jaw. "You said a bad word."

Johnny sighed. "Hold my hand, okay?"

Beep nodded.

"You can hold mine too," Marshall whispered.

Beep latched on to both of his brothers and up the sidewalk they went.

The sun was warm on their faces as they walked past bushes of blooming azaleas rife with honey bees and butterflies. Intent on what they had yet to face, they also missed seeing the hummingbirds darting in and out of flowers. A squirrel was sitting beneath the old oak on the courthouse commons, scolding all who walked past, while another was on the back of a bench beneath it. It was an idyllic scene in the midst of chaos.

Johnny shortened his stride for Beep, who was moving like a little old man stiff with arthritis. Marshall stayed in step right beside him with his chin up and a frown on his face, a miniature version of his big brother.

The crowd at the front of the courthouse was noisy and bordering on disturbing the peace. With nothing but a sidewalk separating the people wanting justice for Beep from the others wanting it all to go away, it wouldn't have taken much for trouble to begin.

But then someone noticed the Pine family coming up the sidewalk and word began to spread. Voices lowered and then trailed off into total silence as the full extent of Brooks Pine's injuries became apparent. Shock spread silently through the crowd. It was no longer about the haves and have-nots. It was about a very small boy who appeared to have been beaten within an inch of his life.

A woman from the back of the crowd called out, "God bless you, child."

A man took out his handkerchief and quickly wiped his eyes and blew his nose.

Embarrassed by the stares, Beep stumbled and then

cried out in pain from the jolt. If Johnny and Marshall had not been holding on to him, he would have fallen.

Ignoring the countless onlookers, Johnny stopped and knelt. "Are you okay, buddy?"

Beep was holding his belly.

"It hurt me here," he said, rubbing his side where the ribs were broken.

"Put your arms around my neck and hold on," Johnny said and slid his arms beneath his little brother's backside as he stood.

Beep hid his face in the curve of Johnny's neck. He'd had enough notoriety for one day.

Marshall was anxious. He didn't know what to think about all the people staring at them and was grateful when they finally got inside.

They had to stop at the door and go through a metal detector, which slowed down their progress even more, but there was a bright spot on their horizon. They were no longer on their own. Butterman was waiting for them on the other side of the detector. Johnny caught his gaze and Butterman winked. It reminded Johnny to relax. They weren't the ones in trouble.

They passed through the halls without looking once at the people lining the walls, and when they reached the judge's office, Butterman led the way inside.

When Johnny realized the boys and their parents were already there, he paused in the doorway, giving all of them a look none would challenge.

One by one, they looked away.

"Take a seat here," Butterman said, indicating chairs on the other side of the room and then glancing at his watch. "We still have a couple of minutes."

Johnny sat down, and as he did, Marshall took the chair beside him. As soon as Johnny sat, he eased Beep into his lap, seating him with his back against Johnny's chest. He felt Beep flinch and knew he'd seen the boys, and at the same time, the parents were getting their first look at Beep, as well.

"Dear God," Mrs. Sharp said and then clapped a hand over her mouth as Coach Sharp stared in disbelief.

Carl Buckley's lips went slack, and then he glanced down at his son, as if seeing him for the first time as a person capable of doing something that horrific.

Mrs. Rankin moaned and then covered her face.

They had all agreed on one lawyer to represent them, because the boys had been equally charged, and now he sat staring at the boy across the room and knew the best they could hope for was leniency from the judge.

P. Nutt Butterman was in his element. He'd seen the panic on Brooks Pine's face as he'd faced his attackers. He was sorry as hell the kid had been hurt in such a vile manner, but he was more than satisfied to see how scared the others were now.

"I want to go home," Beep whispered.

Johnny patted his leg. "I know, buddy. So do I, but we have to be here for a while, okay?"

Beep's voice was soft, but it carried. Every mother in that room heard the fear in his voice and was horrified that a child of theirs was the cause.

A secretary opened the door to the judge's chambers and then stood aside.

"Judge Brothers is ready for you," she said.

When they stood, Beep hung back with Marshall and whispered in his ear, "Don't let them hurt me, okay?"

Marshall's voice took on the tone of a holy vow. "I promise, Beep."

But for Johnny, rage swept through him so fast it made him shake. He made no attempt to temper his voice. "No one's gonna touch you, buddy. I promise."

Butterman was shocked. He'd been so focused on the actual physical injuries Brooks Pine suffered that he hadn't realized the depths of the emotional impact, as well. He put a hand on Beep's shoulder.

"And I'm going to help your brother keep that promise."

Beep looked up. In his eyes, these men were giants in stature, way bigger than the boys who hurt him. It was a reassuring sight.

They were the last to enter and took the remaining empty seats as Judge Brothers came in and sat down behind his desk.

Johnny eyed the man closely. He saw manicured fingernails and the collar of a silk shirt beneath the robes and his heart sank. The man's appearance spoke money. Would their lack of social standing be the undoing of any justice for Beep?

Only time would tell.

Chapter 6

JUDGE BROTHERS HAD READ ALL THE FILES, SEEN THE video interviews, and knew to the last stitch what injuries Brooks Pine had suffered. He also knew the parents of the perpetrators were considered upstanding citizens of Blessings, but in his eyes, their progeny did not get a free pass because of their parents' reputations.

He could see the four boys had been coached to be on their best behavior. They were sitting upright, hands in their laps and appropriately penitent expressions on their face.

And then there was Brooks Pine. Smallest kid in the room by far and looked like he'd been run over. And he was scared. Judge Brothers had seen plenty of scared kids in his courtroom during his career, and it was clear this boy was the victim, not the perpetrator.

"Good afternoon," Brothers said as he began. "Just to be clear, this is not an opportunity for lawyers to plead their cases because guilt has already been recognized and admitted. As I adjudicate sentencing, I don't want to hear a parent speak out in argument or a lawyer interrupt what I have to say. Do we understand each other?"

While everyone else nodded, Beep shrunk back against Johnny, trying to make himself as small as possible, and then closed his eyes. The judge's voice was loud and sounded angry. He wanted to go home.

Judge Brothers saw that the boy was frightened, but

his job wasn't about making friends. It was about meting out justice.

"I want to call attention to something very obvious to me before I go on. I want Lewis Buckley, Kevin Sharp, and Bobby Jay and Billy Ray Rankin to please rise and come stand at the front of my desk."

The boys glanced at their parents and then did as they'd been told.

"Now will Brooks Pine please join them?"

Brooks sighed so loud it almost sounded like a groan, but he stood up without hesitation and walked two steps forward. There was less than a foot of space between him and Lewis Buckley, and the obvious difference in their sizes was immediate.

"Now, boys, will you please turn around and face the room."

All five boys turned.

"Parents, I want you to take a good look. If there were any lingering notions you were harboring regarding this child's participation in the beating your sons gave him, I hope you have the good sense to let them go. Brooks, you may sit back down."

Beep pressed a hand against his belly as he walked back.

The four boys were still facing the room.

"All of four of you turn and face the bench."

The boys hesitated, looking around the room for a bench. Their lawyer had to whisper for them to turn and face the judge before they complied.

"I've read your statements," Judge Brothers said. "But I want to hear it for myself." He looked straight at Lewis. "Lewis Buckley, what prompted you to attack Brooks Pine?"

Lewis stuck his hands in his pockets and started to slouch.

"Stand up straight. Take your hands out of your pockets and answer me!" the judge snapped.

Lewis blanched. That demanding tone of voice sounded too much like his father's voice to ignore. He quickly obeyed.

"Beep had ringworms. He's white trash, and we didn't want him near us."

Brothers frowned. "According to the evidence, that statement is false. Brooks Pine had no such disease. In fact, he was a perfectly healthy child until you attacked him."

"Well, we thought he had ringworm," Lewis said.

"And so for that you attacked him?"

"I just pushed him away," Lewis said.

"Did you kick him while he was down?" Brothers asked.

Lewis shrugged and looked away.

"I won't tell you again. When I ask you a question, I want an answer, not a shrug. Did you kick him while he was down?" Brothers snapped.

"I guess," Lewis muttered.

Judge Brothers looked at the next boy. "State your name."

"Kevin Sharp, sir."

"What part did you take in this attack?"

"I guess I kicked him some too."

"Did he do anything to you?"

Kevin shook his head.

"I can't hear you either. Speak up," Brothers said.

Kevin shuddered. "No, he didn't do anything to any of us."

"And yet you deemed it necessary to hurt him. You did know you were hurting him, didn't you?"

"I guess I didn't think about it," Kevin muttered.

"Was Brooks Pine bleeding?"

"Yes, sir," Kevin said.

"Was he crying?"

Kevin's chin dropped against his chest. "Yes."

Judge Brothers looked past Kevin to the twins. "State your names."

"Billy Ray Rankin."

"Bobby Jay Rankin."

"You are twins, right?"

"Yes, sir," they echoed.

"Was Brooks Pine asking anyone to stop hurting him?"

"I guess," Billy Ray said.

"Yes," Bobby Jay said.

"Why didn't any of you stop?" Brothers asked.

The boys all looked at Lewis and then at the judge.

"Lewis is the leader. Lewis didn't stop, so we didn't stop," Kevin said.

Carl Buckley's stomach roiled. At the moment, he didn't much like his son.

The judge eyed Lewis again. "So you're the leader?"

Lewis nodded and then remembered the judge wanted answers. "I guess."

"What do you think makes a leader?" Judge Brothers asked.

Lewis smirked. "My daddy says leaders get what they want out of life."

The judge's frown deepened. "Is that so? So what did you think you were going to get for harming another person as you did Brooks Pine?"

Lewis didn't hesitate. "Show him his place. White trash always needs to be shown their place."

Carl Buckley felt ill. He'd said those very words without a notion of how they would be used.

Judge Brothers glanced at the banker, then lifted a hand. "I've heard enough. This meeting was to rule on the crimes of assault and battery for which you four boys were arrested. If I did what should be done, you would all four be sent to the state reformatory for youthful offenders. However…"

The hair stood up on the back of Johnny's neck when he heard the judge beginning to hedge.

Here it comes. He's going to let them off.

The judge continued. "I think you boys need a 'come to Jesus' moment of your own. You scared that little boy within an inch of his life, and then you nearly ended it with your callous and vicious behavior. The first part of your sentencing is that you will be sent to the state prison this Saturday on a bus with other juvenile offenders such as yourselves who've been ordered to go through the Scared Straight program. You're going to get an up-front and personal look at what it's like to live behind bars with killers and criminals of all kinds."

Johnny exhaled with relief as the four boys burst into tears.

Mrs. Buckley moaned and covered her face while her husband shifted nervously in his seat. It wasn't going to look good for the bank president's son to be in such a program, but he knew better than to say so.

Sally Rankin wouldn't even look at her twins. She knew they were bawling because she'd seen their shoulders shaking, but her heart was fixed on the little boy in Johnny Pine's arms.

Coach Sharp was pale and shaken. His wife was staring at a spot on the wall above the judge's desk. She'd mentally clocked out of this meeting the moment she'd seen Brooks Pine.

Judge Brothers continued. "After you return to Blessings, you will report every Saturday for the next twelve months to Officer Pittman at the police station, at which time he will give you community service duties to perform. You may not participate in any family activities on that day. You will work at whatever Officer Pittman sets you to do and nothing else, and you will not be late. You will not be excused for any reason or for any holiday that happens to fall on a Saturday. Consider yourselves on parole. If you mess up in any way, if you so much as look cross-eyed at Brooks Pine again, or for that matter any other kid in Blessings, I will make it my personal quest to see all four of you incarcerated until you have reached the age of sixteen years. Do I make myself clear?"

The boys were nodding and sobbing.

"I'm sorry. I didn't hear an answer," Judge Brothers snapped.

"Yes, sir," they said in perfect unison.

"Take your seats," he said.

They shuffled back to their seats, their steps dragging, their chins on their chest in abject despair.

Judge Brothers looked straight at Brooks.

"There are quite a few people who were interviewed regarding your behavior, young man, and not a one of them had a single bad thing to say about you. They did say you were very smart, in fact, accelerated in learning for your age. They said you were kind. They said you were friendly. A couple of teachers said you talked too much, but don't feel bad. That's what they used to say about me when I was your age."

Beep was listening intently. He'd already figured out the guys were in big trouble, which made him really nervous. He hadn't understood the bit about what would happen to them if they did something bad again and was certain they would take it out on him.

Judge Brothers wrapped up the hearing with one last word to Johnny Pine.

"Mr. Pine, I understand you have taken on quite a task in raising your younger brothers, and I want to tell you that it seems you are doing a fine job instilling your young men with some common sense and courtesy. I hope you are satisfied with my sentencing. I'd hate to see you enact a bit of your own revenge for what has happened, because even while I would certainly under-stand your reason, I wouldn't want you standing before me and in trouble with the law. Your brothers need you."

Johnny looked the judge squarely in the eye.

"I am satisfied, Your Honor, and truthfully, there isn't anything I could do that would make up for what they did. By their actions, they have forever changed the child he was, and I won't forget it and neither will he." Then he looked at the parents. "Having money doesn't make you good people and where you live doesn't make you right. Don't paint us with our father's sins."

Peanut Butterman resisted the urge to gloat. He liked being on the winning side in a courtroom, but this time it was more than about who won. It didn't always happen, but this time justice was served.

When they left the judge's office, the halls had somehow been cleared of curiosity seekers. Johnny stopped, then thrust out his hand.

"Mr. Butterman, we can't thank you enough. I know your presence in this mess was crucial to this outcome, and we are grateful."

Peanut clasped Johnny's hand and shook it vigorously.

"It was my pleasure," he said. "And just so you know, I admire your guts. If you ever need a lawyer, I'm your man."

"I thank you for the offer, but I hope that day never comes."

Peanut laughed. "All my clients say the very same thing." And then he glanced up the hallway. "Where did you park?" he asked.

"At the backside of the courthouse," Johnny said.

"Follow me. I'll show you another way out."

Johnny followed Butterman through the back halls of the courthouse, carrying Beep in his arms, with Marshall matching him step for step. Butterman bid them goodbye at a side door.

When they started toward the car, the sun was still shining. The two squirrels had disappeared up into the branches of the massive oak, and the bees and hummingbirds were still dive-bombing the blooming azalea bushes.

Johnny heard Beep sigh.

"You all right, buddy?"

He nodded.

Marshall wasn't convinced. "Don't be scared, Beep. I won't let anybody hurt you again."

Johnny frowned. "There won't be a need for fighting

again, okay? You don't go to school and get in trouble on your brother's behalf, understand?"

Marshall frowned.

Johnny frowned back. "I mean it, Marshall. The judge lowered the boom on those boys. They're scared stiff and won't be doing anything wrong. If they do, he'll put them in a prison for kids. And no one else is going to try being a bully because they will know what happened to Lewis and his gang. It's over, okay?"

Marshall thought about it, glanced up at his little brother, and then looked at Johnny. "I won't start nothin'," he promised.

"Anything. You won't start anything," Johnny muttered. "Who wants ice cream?"

Both boys smiled and answered in perfect unison, "Me."

Johnny grinned. "Me too."

—∿∿—

Word soon spread about the boys sentencing, which ended the ongoing pity party in Blessings. People who'd taken the side of the well-to-do slipped back into their daily lives as if nothing had happened. The only people still dealing with it were the parents, who had to pack their boys up the following Saturday and send them off with a busload of youth offenders to the state prison. They didn't know which was worse, their fear for what might happen to them before they got home, or how they were going to live down the humiliation their sons had wrought.

The following Monday, Johnny took the boys back to school and stopped in the principal's office before he let them go.

Mavis West, the school secretary, saw them coming, panicked, and rang for the principal.

Mrs. Winston answered absently. "Yes?"

"The Pines are back. You need to come out."

The principal dropped the phone and bolted out of the office just as the Pines came in the door.

"Good to see you back," she said and glanced down at Beep. "Well, Brooks, you seem to be healing quite well." Then she looked up at Johnny with what she hoped was a concerned expression. "Are there any medical issues we need to know about? Does he have medicine he'll need to take through the day? We keep the medicine in the office, so you'll need to—"

Johnny interrupted. "What *you* need to do is make sure my brothers are not targeted because of your lax attention to bullying on school grounds. Beep needs to skip recess until his ribs heal, and he's fine with that. Marshall wants to sit by Beep during their lunchtime until he's convinced no one else is gonna hurt his little brother. I assume that will be acceptable. Miss Jane will resume bringing them to school and picking them up after it's over. I expect them to come home in the same condition they were in when they arrived. Do we agree?"

Arlene Winston was taken aback by what she viewed as aggression but could not bring herself to argue the point, considering the fact the school had just escaped a lawsuit of massive proportions.

"Yes, of course we agree," she said and lifted her chin. "We have all the children's best interests at heart."

Johnny's eyes narrowed. "That's good to know," he said shortly, then went down on one knee to talk to the boys. "You're both gonna be fine, okay? Miss Jane knows to pick you up this evening. Beep, Marshall will sit with you at lunch, so don't be scared."

Beep's eyes filled with tears. He was scared and not afraid to admit it. "Everyone's gonna hate me," he whispered.

"No, they won't, and I promise I won't let that happen," Mrs. Winston said forcefully.

Beep wouldn't look at her. She'd let it happen before. He didn't put much faith in her vow.

"It'll be okay, Beep. You got me," Marshall said. "Come on. I'll walk you to your room."

Beep threw his arms around Johnny's neck and hugged him, then followed Marshall out of the office.

The moment they were gone, Johnny turned on the women.

"What happened to my brother has changed who he might have been. I am trusting you to nurture what's left. Don't disappoint me."

Then he walked out of the office without waiting for an answer.

Mrs. Winston went into her office without looking at Mavis. There was nothing left to say.

―――∿∿―――

Luther Joe's ear infection was gone by Monday, and Dori went back to work with an easy conscience. Her workday was normal, as was the evening spent with her granddaddy and her son. They went to bed without an inkling of what fate had in store.

―――∿∿―――

Dori was dreaming that an ambulance was driving past their house with the sirens blasting, and then she came to enough to realize that Luther was screaming and their smoke alarm was going off. She flew out of bed, grabbed her purse and the diaper bag, and threw the straps over her shoulder. She rolled Luther up in a blanket and yanked him up in her arms as she ran out into the hall yelling for her grandfather.

Smoke was getting thicker and she could feel the heat above her head. She had to get the baby into fresh air, but she wouldn't leave Meeker behind. She was still screaming when Meeker came staggering out of his bedroom, carrying his cell phone in one hand with the charger cord dangling from the other.

"Fire, Granddaddy! Run!"

"I'm right behind you!" he yelled, calling 911 as he went.

They cleared the house within seconds, Dori in a T-shirt and sweats that she'd been sleeping in, and Meeker Webb in jeans and an unbuttoned shirt, both of them barefoot.

Luther was still crying and could not be consoled.

Seconds later, they could hear the fire sirens and then police sirens. They looked at the house, which was now engulfed in flames, and then at each other. Dori's heart was hammering so hard she could barely think.

"Oh, Granddaddy! What are we gonna do?"

Meeker pulled his little family close as the smoke and flames shot high into the air.

"We still have each other, honey. We'll figure it out like we always do, okay?"

She leaned against his strength as Luther continued to wail. The closer the sirens became, the louder he cried, and no amount of consoling made it better.

Within moments, rescue vehicles began lining the streets and driveway while their yard was filled with firemen stringing hose from the nearest fire hydrant to the house.

Someone grabbed them and pulled them farther away from the fire as neighbors began to spill out of their homes. Water spewed into the air, blowing the fire-heated mist back to where they were standing.

A paramedic put a blanket over Dori's shoulders and then gave one to Meeker as they assessed them for burns and smoke inhalation. They stood at the far end of the driveway as the smoke above the burning house turned into a whirling cloud of sparks and fire. They stood, watching in disbelief as the roof of the house finally fell into the inferno.

In the midst of all the noise, Dori thought she heard her grandfather's voice.

She turned.

"What did you say, Granddaddy?" she asked, then realized he was clutching his chest, his face wreathed in pain. Breath caught at the back of her throat as she grabbed his arm in sudden panic. "Granddaddy, what's wrong?"

Their gazes met.

"I'm so sorry, girl," Meeker mumbled and then crumpled at her feet.

She didn't know that she was screaming. All she could hear was her world coming to an end.

Johnny was asleep when he heard the sirens. He jumped out of bed and ran to the window to see flames shooting high above the treetops. A house on the other side of the railroad tracks was on fire, and he said a quick prayer for the people involved.

Seconds later, both Marshall and Beep came running into the room.

"What's happening?" Marshall asked.

Beep grabbed Johnny's bare leg. "I can't see," he said.

Johnny picked him up, still careful not to squeeze his healing ribs, and settled him on his hip.

"What's on fire?" Beep asked.

"I don't know," Johnny said.

"What if that's Miss Jane's house?" Marshall cried. "It's in that direction. What if Miss Jane needs help? We should go help her."

Johnny frowned. "No, we don't go chasing fire trucks, boys. The firefighters and police will take care of whoever is in need."

Marshall's eyes welled with tears. "She helped us at the Before and After when one of the kids started to say something mean to Beep. She told him bullies didn't belong in her house and if he didn't hush, she'd kick him out and his mama could find someone else to get him to school."

Johnny frowned. "I didn't know that."

Marshall shrugged. "It's over, like you said."

Beep began to cry. "I don't want Miss Jane to burn up."

"Boys, boys, this is getting out of hand. We don't even know for sure what's on fire. We don't even know if it is a house, while you and your imagination have Miss Jane in danger."

"Then we should go see to make sure," Marshall said.

Johnny sighed. There was no way they'd settle back down to sleep now until they knew for sure it wasn't Miss Jane.

"Go get your house shoes and a jacket apiece. We'll find out what's going on, and then when you see it's not Miss Jane, you will come right back here and go to bed, okay?"

"Yes, we promise," Marshall said.

"Yes," Beep added.

Johnny put Beep down. "Go. I'll meet you guys in the living room."

They scurried out of the room as he grabbed pair of jeans and slipped them on over his underwear. He got a long-sleeved T-shirt and pulled it over his head as he hunted a pair of socks.

He heard footsteps in the hall and knew the boys were already heading to the living room. He glanced back out the window and shuddered. Flames spiraled toward the stars like red-hot dragons' tongues licking at the sky.

They drove in silence, taking back streets to keep from running into rescue vehicles or traffic, but when Johnny finally drove up on the scene, the skin crawled on the back of his neck.

"Yay, it's not Miss Jane's house," Marshall said.

"Yay!" Beep echoed.

Johnny knew who lived there. It was Meeker Webb's house, where Dori Grant lived. He thought about the smile on her face the day he'd seen her last, and how she'd waved as she'd crossed the street in front of him. Now this! He knew all too well how fast life could change, and he hoped they were okay.

He started to back up and drive away when he saw paramedics wheel a blanket-covered body toward the ambulance. His heart sank. Now he was as bad as the boys; he had to know if she was all right. Moments later, he saw her come around the corner of the ambulance carrying the baby, which meant the body on the gurney was likely Mr. Webb.

Even before he rolled down the window, he could hear the baby screaming. When he saw Dori stagger, his first instinct was to help. But what could he do? All her neighbors were there. They would surely go to her.

He waited, watching the ambulance drive away, watching the firemen continue to blast water on the still-burning building, watching Officer Pittman stop to talk and touch her shoulder in obvious empathy.

Finally, a woman walked up to Dori, spoke briefly, looked at the baby, and then turned around and almost ran across the street and into her house. Other onlookers began doing the same, quickly giving their condolences and then walking away, while others left without a backward glance.

The baby was still screaming, and Dori looked like she was going to faint.

He couldn't believe it. They'd all walked away and left her, just like they'd done the day of his mother's funeral. The few people who'd come to pay their respects had done so without a word to him and the boys. He remembered how scared he'd felt and how alone. Even though he still had his little brothers, the weight of the world had fallen hard upon his shoulders.

"What the hell?" he muttered.

"What's wrong, Johnny?"

He glanced at Marshall. Were the boys old enough to understand? He was about to find out. "No one is helping her."

Marshall shrugged. "We can."

Beep got up on his knees to look closer. "She has a baby! I think it's crying. I bet it's scared."

Johnny sighed. He should not have doubted them. "You guys sit tight. I'm gonna go talk to her, okay?"

They nodded.

He gave them another look. "And don't get out of the car. Do you hear me?"

"We hear you," Marshall said. "I'm in charge. I'll take care of Beep."

Johnny smiled and scrubbed his knuckles lightly across Marshall's head, eliciting the groan he knew would come, then he got out of the car and started across the street.

———

Dori was numb. The pain in her chest was surely as deadly as the one that took her granddaddy, but obviously God wasn't through playing with her life. Her parents had been dead so long she'd almost forgotten what they looked like, and now Granddaddy. What else could God take away from her?

And the moment she thought it, she looked at the little boy screaming in her arms and tightened her hold. There was no doubt in her mind that he knew Granddaddy was gone too. That's why he was crying. She staggered, then leaned against a police car pulled up at an angle at the end of their driveway and buried her face in Luther's neck.

"Don't cry, baby boy. Please don't cry. Mama's here. Mama's here."

She felt a hand on her shoulder and looked up. It was Pansy Jones, her neighbor from across the street. Pansy was eyeing the screaming baby anxiously and talking too fast.

"Dori, honey, I am so sorry. I wanted you to know that me and Bart will be praying for you."

Then she bolted across the street so fast Dori didn't even have time to respond.

It seemed that Pansy's approach had given the others the cue. After that, some came with a message similar to the one Pansy gave her, while others just got in their cars and drove away.

She couldn't believe what was happening. What was she supposed to do? Where did she go? She needed help and turned to look for Officer Pittman just in time to see him jump in his cruiser and drive away with lights flashing and the siren sounding with its own version of a scream. Obviously she wasn't the only one with troubles tonight.

Luther was still sobbing, his little hands fisted in the tangles of her hair when she felt another hand on her shoulder. She turned around and then her heart skipped a beat.

Johnny Pine.

She hadn't seen him this close in probably three years, certainly not since he'd graduated. She couldn't imagine what he wanted or even how he came to be here.

"Do you have a place to go?" he asked.

Fresh tears welled and rolled down her cheeks. He was the first to ask, and Luther was still screaming.

Johnny cupped the back of the baby's head and rubbed his fingers up and down the back of Luther's neck, then pointed at his car across the street and the two little heads peering over the dash.

"I know we live on the wrong side of town, but my brothers and I would be honored to offer you shelter until you figure out what you need to do."

Dori's heart skipped a beat. They barely knew each other, but it was the only offer she'd had, and she had to think of Luther first. She looked down at the baby and started to sob.

"I don't know what's wrong. He won't stop crying. He might cry all night."

"Give him to me," Johnny said softly, then scooped the baby out of her arms.

It took Luther a few seconds to realize he was no longer in his mama's arms, and he actually paused in mid-scream to stare at the stranger who was holding him.

"You're gonna be okay, little man," Johnny said.

The baby's gaze was fixed on Johnny's face. He was used to being carried by a man and seemed to like the sound of Johnny's deep voice.

Dori stared at her baby and took it as a sign. She picked up the diaper bag and their blankets.

"You are letting yourself in for an awful lot," she said.

Before he thought, Johnny wiped the tears from her cheeks.

"We've lived through worse," he said softly. "Come on, Dori. We don't live in a fancy house, but it's clean and I can promise you'll be safe."

She stared for a few moments longer, and when Luther Joe suddenly dropped his head on Johnny Pine's shoulder and closed his eyes, exhausted and too worn out to utter another sob, she took it as another sign.

"Granddaddy's dead," she whispered. "I don't have anyone but Luther."

Johnny sighed. "I know the feeling. Grab my arm, girl. It's chilly and it's late."

Dori's last line of resistance was gone. He'd promised safety and shelter, and Luther Joe was asleep. Grief would come later. She glanced over her shoulder one last time at the fiery remnants of home and then slipped a hand beneath his elbow and followed him to the car.

———

Pansy Jones had felt guilty for not offering shelter and was still watching from her living room window. Bart, her husband, had been adamant, warning her before she'd even left their property that he wasn't having some squalling baby in their house, and after twenty-seven years of marriage, she knew better than to argue. She never won an argument.

When she saw the Pine boy cross the street, curiosity raised its ugly head. And when she saw them talking, then watched Johnny Pine soothe the crying baby like it was his own, she immediately wondered if it was. No one knew the father's identity. Maybe it was him!

Watching Dori go with him to their car and drive away conveniently absolved her of guilt. Johnny must be the mysterious father. It was a ridiculous stab in the dark, but believing he'd heard about the fire and came to their rescue made everything better for her.

Chapter 7

JOHNNY HANDED THE SLEEPING BABY OFF TO DORI AND then shut the car door. She jumped at the sound, but Luther seemed oblivious. The quiet inside the car after all the sirens made the air feel heavy. She could still smell smoke and looked across the street at the firemen still spraying water on the blaze. She wondered where they'd taken Granddaddy. It occurred to her that there were no clothes left to bury him in, and then she bit her lip to keep from bursting into a fresh set of tears.

His phone and the charger cord were in the pocket of her sweatpants. Officer Pittman had given them to her after they'd taken him away. She'd have to call Lovey at the restaurant and tell her she wasn't coming to work and then shivered.

She was aware of the two boys in the backseat but too numb to think what to say. They were quiet—so quiet. She could hear their breathing within the silence and then the slight rustle of clothing against the leather seats.

Luther snubbed softly in his sleep then thrust his thumb into his mouth and began to suck.

"Sorry your house burned up," Beep said.

"Yeah, really sorry," Marshall added.

Dori nodded and then leaned back against the seat and closed her eyes as Johnny opened the door and got in.

"Are you boys buckled up?" he asked as he started the engine.

"Yes," they echoed.

Johnny glanced at Dori. Her eyes were closed, but there were tears running down her face. He put the car in gear and drove away, wondering what in hell he had gotten himself into. He wouldn't change what he'd done, but this was a whole new set of problems he didn't really need. Still, all they could do was take it one day at a time, and right now, Dori Grant needed a friend.

"Where's she gonna sleep?" Beep asked.

"In Mama's room," Johnny said.

"No one goes in Mama's room," Marshall said.

"They will now. We have an extra bed and they need one, don't they?"

Marshall leaned against the door for a better look at the woman in the seat beside Johnny. Her hair looked wet and he wondered if she was cold.

Beep was quiet, too quiet, and Johnny knew why. Beep was the baby, the one who'd been unaware of most of their mother's flaws. He was probably bothered by someone sleeping in her bed, but it couldn't matter.

Dori heard them talking but had tuned out what was being said. She kept seeing Granddaddy's face twisted in pain and then watching him crumple to the ground.

Had that really happened? Please God let this be a bad dream.

A few minutes later, they began to slow down.

"We're here," Johnny said as he turned into their drive and pulled up to the house.

Dori opened her eyes.

The streetlights were few and far between, but cast just enough light for her to see the simple frame house and the slices of lights showing through the blinds.

There was a single light burning on the wide, covered porch, and she thought she could see a porch swing.

"Stay seated a minute and I'll help you out. Don't want you to stumble in the dark," Johnny said.

Dori waited, watching as he ushered the boys into the house. His steps were sure as he walked through the dimly lit yard, and it hit her that most of his life he'd been taking steps in the dark. Suddenly she realized how easy her life had been before this. Even with a baby she hadn't planned on, she'd still had a good home and her Granddaddy. Johnny had no one but himself to keep his little family intact.

She looked down at the sleeping baby in her arms, grateful that he'd finally fallen asleep. She didn't think she could handle another round of screams.

Then she watched Johnny come out of the house and lope across the yard toward the car. He opened the door and leaned in, shouldered her diaper bag and purse, and then steadied her as she slid out of the seat.

"You hold the baby. I'll hold on to you," Johnny said.

"Thank you," she said.

He paused in the shadows to look at her.

"This is a terrible thing that's happened, but I speak from experience when I tell you that you will survive it because you have to, and you will be all the stronger for it. Now, come inside. You must be exhausted."

His words were ringing in her ears as she let him lead her inside. The house was warm and smelled like chili—Granddaddy's favorite meal. And then breath caught in the back of her throat. She'd never cook for her grandfather again.

She staggered and Johnny caught her.

"This way," he said and led her down the hall to the extra room. "You heard us talking in the car. The extra room was my mother's room. She's dead. It's clean."

Dori shuddered, wondering if she'd ever be that matter-of-fact about life.

Johnny turned on the light and paused. He hadn't been in here in weeks.

"It looks a little dusty. I'm sorry. I'll clean it tomorrow, but the sheets are clean and—"

She interrupted. "Don't apologize for your kindness."

He allowed himself a quick glance and saw a muscle twitching at the side of her eye. He wanted to wrap his arms around her and promise she'd never hurt like this again, but that wasn't true. No one knew what life had in store. Instead, he led her to the rocking chair near the window.

"Sit here while I turn back the bed."

She didn't argue, taking comfort from the warm little body in her arms. She still had Luther, and he needed her. She would find a way to make it. She had to.

Johnny came back to the chair and knelt in front of her, speaking softly so as not to wake the baby. "I shoved the bed against the wall. If you sleep on the outside to keep him from rolling off the bed, you should both be fine."

She'd never been this close to him before and kept staring at his face. She'd always thought him good-looking but what she saw now was the kindness in his eyes.

"Dori?"

She blinked. "I'm sorry. Yes, that will be fine. Luther can sleep next to the wall." Then she looked down at her clothes. "I'm dirty and wet."

"Let me have the baby," he said softly, lifting Luther out of her arms and laying him down. "The bathroom is across the hall. There are clean towels and washcloths in the cabinet. You shower, and I'll put some clean clothes just outside the door and make sure the boys are in bed."

He stood and then laid a hand on the crown of her head.

"My room is the first one on your right. The boys' room is directly across from mine. If you need me, all you have to do is knock, okay?"

She grabbed his hand, her voice shaking. "You are a good man, Johnny Pine."

He felt the calluses on her hands and remembered what she did for a living. Like him, she had stepped into adulthood long before she should have.

"Go get clean and warm while your baby is still asleep."

When she glanced at the bed, he guessed at what was worrying her.

"As soon as I get your clothes, I'll come back and stay with him, okay?"

"Yes and thank you."

He watched her leave and then hurried into the boys' room to make sure they were in bed. Luckily, they'd gone right back to sleep as promised, so he went to look for something Dori could wear. After digging through his clothes, he found a long-sleeved T-shirt that had shrunk in the wash and a pair of gym shorts with a drawstring tie. They'd be long on her, but they were clean and dry and that's what mattered. He laid them outside the bathroom door and then went back into his mother's room and pulled the rocker up by the bed.

The baby hadn't moved.

He saw her cell phone and the charger cord and plugged it in for the night, then turned the overhead light off, turned the lamp on near the bed, and sat down to wait.

Dori stripped where she stood, stepped into the tub, then turned on the water, standing beneath the stream of water coming out of the shower jets without care if it was hot or cold. Except for the sound of running water, the silence engulfed her. Before she knew it, she was sobbing and she couldn't seem to stop.

Johnny heard her crying and closed his eyes against her despair. He knew. He remembered. He glanced at the baby sleeping soundly, his arms flung over his head in limp abandon. He was a cute little guy with a head of brown curls and a slight double chin. A well-fed baby. He could remember the times when he and the boys hadn't had enough to eat and was thankful those times were past.

He leaned back in the rocker and pushed off with his toe. The chair creaked a little on the downswing, but nothing loud and the baby didn't seem to notice. He couldn't remember the last time he'd sat in this chair. He was listening to the water running across the hall when he fell asleep.

Dori cried until the water ran cold before she got out, numb and shaking. She dried without thinking and then remembered she had no clothes. However, when she peeked out in the hall, she saw the clothes and grabbed them quickly as she shut the door. Her hands were shaking so hard she couldn't get the T-shirt over her head, which made her cry a little more. Then she caught a glimpse of her face in the steamed-over mirror and stared, unable to recognize herself for the tear-swollen eyes and puffy lips. She turned away and finished dressing.

The shorts went past her knees but they stayed up, and the T-shirt was long, but warm and clean as she towel-dried her hair. She paused long enough to clean up behind herself and hang up the wet towels. She picked up her dirty clothes and turned the lights out behind her as she left.

The overhead light was off in the bedroom, but the lamplight cast a soft yellow glow on the sleeping baby in the bed and the man sleeping in the chair.

Dori stopped, struck by the complete abandon of Luther's position and the innocence on Johnny Pine's face. He looked much younger in repose, and she remembered he couldn't be more than nineteen, maybe twenty.

She dropped the dirty clothes by the door then took a deep breath as she approached the rocker and gently shook his shoulder.

Johnny woke instantly, momentarily startled by the sight of a girl in their house, and then remembered why she was there.

"You can go to bed now, and thank you," Dori whispered.

He got up and moved the rocker back by the window.

"Remember, if you need anything, wake me."

"I will."

She looked like a kid in his oversized clothes and the grief on her face hurt his heart.

"I'm so sorry," he added.

Her chin quivered, but she didn't cry.

"So am I."

Johnny went to bed but couldn't sleep. He kept thinking about the situation she was in and how scared she must be.

She couldn't go back to work until she'd sorted out where life had dumped her. He had no idea what her situation was regarding money but was guessing her grandfather had most likely made some kind of provision for her. It would just take time to find out where she stood. In the meantime, his job would be to find out what kind of diapers and baby food she needed. The rest would take care of itself.

⸺◦⸺

Dori heard a squeal and then felt little hands pulling at her nose and woke with a jerk. Why was Luther in bed with her? The moment she opened her eyes and saw where she was, she remembered the fire and watching Granddaddy die.

Except for the ache in her chest, she felt hollow. Luther rolled over onto his belly and began rocking back and forth on his hands and knees, drool dripping as he chortled with glee.

Dori sat up. "You think you're something, don't you, little man? And I guess you are. I know you're wet, which I can fix, but I'm guessing you're also hungry, and I'm not sure what I'm going to do about all that."

She glanced toward the window as she turned on the lamp. It must be getting on toward morning. It was then she remembered she needed to call Lovey Cooper. She wouldn't be going to work, and they needed to know.

She looked around for her grandpa's phone and saw that Johnny had put it on the charger for her. She knew Lovey would be up getting ready to go down to the restaurant, so she called her at home.

Her boss answered on the second ring.

"Hello?"

"Lovey, this is Dori. I'm sorry for calling so early, but I wanted you to know I can't come to work anymore."

Lovey gasped. "Honey, what's wrong?"

She started to cry.

"Our house burned down last night and Granddaddy had a heart attack and died while they were fighting the fire."

Lovey Cooper moaned. "Oh, honey. Oh, Dori. I am so sorry. What can I do? What do you need? Where are you? Is the baby okay?"

"Luther is fine. I'm still in shock, but I guess I found out what people really think of me last night."

"What do you mean?" Lovey asked.

"There were plenty of gawkers who came to watch the house burn. They saw Granddaddy die and heard Luther screaming. I didn't think he'd ever stop. Some said they'd pray for us, and then they were gone. Luther and I were standing at the end of the driveway by ourselves when Johnny Pine and his little brothers came to see what was burning. They offered us a place to sleep. He and the boys have been very kind to Luther and me, but with no place to stay and no one to watch Luther, there's no way I can work for you anymore. I'm sorry. I just wanted you to know early on so you can get some-one in for the day."

"Bless you for worrying about us when you've got the weight of the world on your shoulders. Anytime you want your job back, you can have it. In the meantime, tell me what sizes of clothes and shoes you and Luther wear. We'll get you some things gathered up in noth-ing flat."

Dori wiped tears and snot, then exhaled on a long shaky sigh.

"I'm not too proud to take the help. I appreciate that. Dress size is a six. I wear a size six jeans and a size six or a small top. My shoe size is a seven. Luther wears a twelve-month-size clothes and socks for a one-year-old baby. I need diapers, new baby bottles, and any kind of baby stuff someone wants to part with."

"Got it," Lovey said. "Now, you have to promise to call me if you need something, anything. Will you?"

"I promise," Dori said. "And thank you so much."

"You are welcome, honey, and God bless. You'll get through this because you have to, understand?"

"Yes," Dori said and disconnected.

She looked back at Luther, who was chewing on his fist. He was hungry. She had to get busy before he started to cry. She looked around for the diaper bag and dug through it until she found baby wipes and a diaper and quickly got him changed. There was a baby bottle with water in it inside the bag, which was a bless-ing because she'd need that bottle for milk and hoped Johnny Pine had some to spare.

She picked Luther up and settled him on her hip as she went to look for the kitchen. To her surprise, there was a light on under the door to Johnny's room and one under the boys' room, as well. She didn't know their routine, but he obviously started early to get the boys to school and him to his job. Her estimation of his diligence to do right rose even higher.

She paused and knocked on his door, then stepped back.

――――∿∿――――

Johnny woke before daylight and shut off the alarm, then sat up on the edge of the bed in the dark, thinking about the day ahead. He grabbed his cell phone and sent his boss a text, telling him he would be a few minutes late getting to the job site, but that he'd cover it by working through his lunch hour, and then he grabbed a pair of jeans and headed to the bathroom.

After a quick shower and shave, he headed to the kitchen to make coffee then went to wake up the boys.

Sometime during the night, Beep must have had a nightmare, because he was sound asleep in Marshall's arms. The poignancy of the moment was not lost on him as he reluctantly woke them up.

"Hey, guys…time to get up," he said gently as he turned the light on by their bed.

Marshall sighed as he opened his eyes and then shook Beep. "Get up, Beep."

Beep groaned.

Marshall pushed him aside and headed for the bathroom while Johnny sat down on the side of the bed to talk to Beep. The bruises were fading, but he still had to be careful of his ribs and even still wore the protective mask for his nose to school.

"Hey, buddy, come sit in my lap," Johnny said and pulled him out of the bed for a quick hug.

Beep was rubbing sleep out of his eyes as he leaned against his big brother's chest.

"I had a bad dream," he said.

Johnny pulled him a little closer. "Tell me."

"I dreamed our house was on fire."

Johnny sighed. He couldn't regret taking them to the fire last night because of Dori, but he wasn't surprised this had happened.

"Do you remember about the house that did burn last night?" Johnny asked.

Beep nodded. "The woman and the baby are in Mama's room."

"Yes. Wasn't it lucky we had a place for them to stay?"

Beep looked up at Johnny and frowned. "Is she gonna stay here?"

"Not forever, Beep. Just until she figures out what to do next. You saw her crying, right?"

"Yeah. Her house burned up."

Johnny nodded. "Yes, but she was crying because her grandfather died last night too."

Beep's eyes widened. "Like Mama died?"

"Yes, dead like Mama."

"I'm sad for her," Beep said.

"So am I, buddy. So we need to be patient and nice to her, okay?"

"Yes."

Johnny scooted him off his lap. "Thank you," he said. "Now get in the bathroom and get washed, but remind

Marshall to be quiet. We don't want to wake up the baby. I'll make breakfast in a few minutes."

Beep nodded and went to join his brother in the bathroom while Johnny made their bed and then laid out clean clothes for them to put on. Then Johnny headed back to the kitchen to make oatmeal and make sure there was milk for the baby.

As soon as he had the oatmeal cooked, he put a lid on it to keep it warm and had just returned to his room to finish getting ready. He had a T-shirt in his hand when he heard a knock on his door, and he pulled it over his head on the way to answer the door.

It was Dori.

"I'm sorry to bother you, but I was wondering if you had some milk for Luther's bottle."

Johnny smiled as he reached out and rubbed his hand over Luther's soft curls.

"Yes, ma'am, we sure do," he said. "We also have oatmeal, if he can eat it."

Dori breathed a quick sigh of relief. She'd been worrying about food for Luther, and this would work until she could get to a store.

"Yes, it will be perfect. Thank you so much."

"You're welcome. Give me a second to put on my boots, and then I'll walk you to the kitchen and show you where everything is at."

Then he looked down at her feet and saw that she was barefoot.

"We need to get something on your feet," he said and dug a pair of socks out of a drawer. "Here, these will be too big, but they'll feel better than walking barefoot on these old floors."

Dori held the socks and waited while he put on his boots, then he took the baby so she could put them on.

"They feel good. I keep saying thank you, but the truth is there are no words for how much this means to us," she said.

Johnny handed her the baby and then resisted the urge to brush a stray lock of hair from Dori's forehead.

"So, you've thanked me, and I've said you're welcome and I am happy we could help. Now let's go see about the milk and oatmeal."

Dori followed him into the kitchen in her sock feet while Luther kept trying to chew on her hair. Everything went in his mouth these days, but she drew the line at hair.

"The milk is whole milk. Is that a problem?" Johnny asked.

"No, that's what the pediatrician has him on."

"Does it need to be heated?"

"As long as it's not ice cold, it's okay," she said.

Johnny filled the bottle and put it in the microwave without putting on the top.

"About fifteen seconds will take the chill off," Dori said.

When Johnny set the timer, Luther squealed. Johnny looked back at the baby and laughed.

"He knows what that means, doesn't he?"

Dori's eyes welled with tears. "Granddaddy always did that. He's used to being taken care of by a man."

Johnny sighed. He hadn't meant to remind her of what she'd lost.

The microwave dinged.

Johnny took out the bottle and handed it to Dori.

"Check it and make sure it's okay."

She tested it with her finger and nodded.

"It's perfect," she said, screwing on the lid and cradling Luther before poking the bottle in his mouth.

He grasped it with both hands, the look on his face so intent it made her smile.

Johnny saw the love on her face and his heart skipped a beat. Despite her sleep-tousled hair and borrowed clothes, she looked beautiful.

Before he could let that thought take wing, he heard footsteps in the hall and knew the boys were on the way.

"Brace yourself," he said. "Here comes the hungry horde."

Chapter 8

WHEN THE BOYS SAW DORI SITTING AT THE TABLE WITH the baby, they stopped in the doorway and glanced at Johnny, as if waiting for permission to enter.

"Oatmeal is ready," he said. "Sit down."

They bolted toward the table, pushing and shoving to get to their chairs, which was their usual morning routine.

"Can I have raisins?" Marshall asked.

"May I, and yes," Johnny said, tossing a handful of raisins into Marshall's bowl and ladling some oatmeal over them, just like he did every morning.

"I don't want no raisins," Beep announced, just as he did every morning.

"You don't want any raisins, and I already know that," Johnny said, then glanced at Dori and grinned. "Do you have any particular requests for your oatmeal?"

"Sugar and milk?"

Johnny grinned. "I can handle that," he said as he gave the boys their oatmeal.

Witnessing a bit of their regular morning routine was delightful. Not only had he been the knight in shining armor she needed last night, but he also seemed to be a good father figure too. Then she realized he was dipping the same amount of oatmeal into each bowl, one spoonful at a time, and she didn't want to think she would be taking food they needed to eat.

"Do you have enough?" Dori asked. "You guys are going to school and to work, and I don't mind skipping."

Johnny paused, struck by her gentle spirit.

"We have enough oatmeal," he said and dipped the rest of the oatmeal into two bowls, one for her and one for him.

"So, here's the routine," Johnny said. "I drop the boys off at Before and After. Miss Jane takes them to school and then picks them up afterward and keeps them until I get off work. We'll all be home just after five. However, after I drop them off this morning, I'm going by the supermarket to pick up some stuff for squirt. Make me a list of what he needs and—"

"I have some money in my purse. I'm not sure how much, but I'll give it to you, and there's more in the bank."

"Dori. It's okay. We'll work all this out. But right now we're dealing with immediate needs, and that little guy in your arms doesn't care who pays for what. He just wants a dry diaper and food in his belly, right?"

Dori sighed.

"Yes, you're right. If you have paper and a pen, I'll write down just the necessities."

Johnny brought the pad and pen from beside the telephone and slid it across the table.

Beep watched her writing and then glanced up at Johnny.

"Can we add cookies to the list?" he asked.

Johnny knew if he bought all of the other stuff for the baby, there wouldn't be any money left for cookies but didn't want to say so in front of Dori.

"We'll see," he said.

Beep caught the look and hushed. He knew what that

meant—no money. He glanced at the baby and went back to eating.

Dori might have seen the exchange but for the fact that Luther had finished his bottle and had become very interested in the spoon going into his mother's mouth. She'd given him baby oatmeal, but he'd never had the real thing. When he grabbed her spoon on the way to her mouth, the boys giggled.

Dori smiled. "He's a pig," she said.

The boys giggled again, watching as she pried the spoon out of Luther's fingers.

"Bite?" Dori asked as she put the spoon at Luther's mouth.

He opened wide. She gave him the oatmeal and grinned when his eyes widened in surprise. His lips literally smacked when she pulled out the spoon.

"Well, that was a success," Dori said. "I'm guessing it was the sugar."

"I like sugar too," Beep said, watching curiously as Dori spooned another bite into the baby's mouth.

Johnny got up to fill his coffee cup to hide a smile. Beep was seriously interested in their new guests, which was good. He hadn't had much to smile about since the recess incident.

"Hurry up and finish, guys. We need to hustle."

The boys cleaned up the last of the oatmeal and carried them to the sink, washed and rinsed the bowls, and put them in the drainer, then ran to get their backpacks.

Dori was impressed again by their willingness to help.

"Do you want coffee?" Johnny asked.

"Maybe half a cup," Dori said as she gave Luther another bite.

"Got the list finished?" Johnny asked as he set the coffee out of Luther's reach.

She pushed it toward him.

"Oh wait. I need to go get the money. I'll be right back."

She flew out of the kitchen with the baby on her hip so fast he didn't have time to stop her. She came back within moments with her purse, emptied out what cash she had, and pushed it across the table.

"Now, what can I do for you? I'll be here all day. Please let me help," she said.

He started to say nothing as he pocketed the money, and then realized he would be denying her a way to give back.

"The floors always need cleaning. There's a broom and mop out in the utility room."

"What else? I'm good at all kinds of things, I swear— laundry, washing windows, changing beds, whatever you need."

"Can you cook?"

She nodded.

Johnny hesitated to add to her day, but she'd asked.

"We eat really basic food because I don't cook a lot of different things, but there's some hamburger meat thawed out and you can look through the pantry for what else is here and do what you want with it."

"I can make a meat loaf," she offered.

"That would be great," Johnny said and then glanced at the time. He needed to hurry, but he hated to leave her alone.

"You have your phone, so—"

"Officer Pittman gave me Granddaddy's cell phone. He carried it out of the house before he—"

When she stopped and looked away, he kept talking, giving her time to regain her composure.

"Give me your number and I'll write my number down, and if you have a problem or need help, you call me, okay?"

She added the phone number to the grocery list and then watched him copy down his number for her. As he did, she noticed the healing cuts and skinned knuckles on his hands. She didn't even know where he worked.

"What do you do…for a living, I mean?"

"I drive a dozer for Clawson Construction."

"That's a good job. How did you learn to do that?" she asked.

"My dad used to work for Mr. Clawson before he got sent to prison. I hung out with him a lot back then, and Mr. Clawson taught me the rest. He's been a lifesaver for me and the boys. Look, I hate to walk out on you, but I'll be back soon with the stuff on your list. Hang in there, okay?"

Dori blinked, willing herself not to cry.

"Thanks to you, we'll be fine. You made sure of that."

"See you soon," he said and hurried out of the kitchen, yelling at the boys to hurry up as he went.

She took another bite of oatmeal and then gave the rest to Luther. As soon as they were gone, she went back to her bedroom and made the bed, then found a big blanket in the closet and took it to the living room to make a pallet for Luther to lie on. She gave him a teething ring from the diaper bag, covered him up with his little blanket so he wouldn't get cold, and turned on the television to distract him, giving her time to call the police station. Someone there would surely tell her where they'd taken her grandfather's body. Her hands were trembling as she sat down nearby and made the call. The phone rang three times before someone answered.

"Blessings PD, Ames speaking. How may I direct your call?"

"Uh, this is Dori Grant. I'm trying to find out where they took my granddaddy, Meeker Webb, last night."

"Miss Grant, this is Avery Ames. I want to offer my condolences. I am sorry about your grandfather."

Dori was trying to control her emotions, although her shaky voice gave her away.

"Thank you, Mr. Ames. The reason I'm calling is…I don't know where he is."

"Let me check the ambulance logs. Yes, here they are…um, they took him to the hospital, and then Harper's Funeral Home picked him up."

"Harper's. Is that the one on the hill above the Catholic church?" Dori asked.

"Yes, that's the one," Ames said. "Is there anything else I can do for you?"

"No, and thank you for your help."

She hung up, got the phone book, found the number to Harper's Funeral Home, and made the call. She knew Mrs. Harper. She came into the restaurant at least twice a week with her daughter for lunch. Dori had washed the dishes Mrs. Harper had eaten from many times. Now Mrs. Harper was going to do something for her.

"Harper's Funeral Home."

"Mrs. Harper, this is Dori Grant."

Evelyn Harper's voice immediately softened.

"Dori, sweetheart. I can't tell you how sorry I am for all you've lost. How can I help you? What do you need to know?"

Dori started crying. She didn't want to, but there was no way to say all this because the words were choking. "I have to bury Granddaddy, and everything we owned burned up. What do I do? Do I need to come there and pick out a casket? I need someone to help me."

Dori didn't know Evelyn was fighting back tears. All she heard was the kindness in her voice. "Honey, let me tell you what I know, and then we'll go from there. Meeker had already picked out a casket and paid for his funeral. His headstone and burial plot are already in place because it's where your grandmother is buried. If you want flowers, you'll have to contact the florist, but you know they'll do anything you want. As for his clothing, will you trust me to do that for you? I grew up with the man. I've seen him in church enough times in my life to know what he liked to wear."

"In the circumstances, that is good news," Dori said and then wiped her eyes and nose and cleared her throat. "We don't have any other family, so there's no need to delay the service. Can we do this say, day after tomorrow? That will give me time to get some clothes for Luther and me."

"Absolutely. The whole day is open. Would you prefer morning services or afternoon?"

"I don't know," Dori said. "Which is better?"

"Day after tomorrow is Saturday. I'd say afternoon, maybe 2:00 p.m. I'll call the preacher and have him get in touch with you for details. Oh, just so you know, Meeker wrote his own eulogy. I have it on file."

Dori frowned. "I never knew any of this. I can't believe he planned so far ahead."

There was a moment of silence and then Evelyn sighed. "You didn't know about his heart?"

Dori gasped. "What about his heart? He never said a word about anything being wrong."

"All I know is what he told me when he was making all the plans. He said he had a bad ticker. Those were his words. I guess you'd have to ask his doctor for details."

Dori was crying again, and this time she made no attempt to calm down. "He should have told me. I would have stayed home and taken care of him and Luther, but he insisted I go to work. He said I needed the experience. He said he wanted to babysit. He shouldn't have hidden this from me!"

Evelyn Harper sighed. "Dori, honey, Meeker was so proud of you. He said you were going to be something special one day. I'm guessing that he wanted you to have a job on your own, hoping you'd learn to have faith in yourself and your ability to make do. Do you understand?"

Dori heard her, but it wasn't making things any easier to accept.

"I hear you, Mrs. Harper, and thank you for all you've done. You can give the preacher the date and time and furnish him with a copy of the eulogy. I'll call him later. I need to hang up now. I think I'm gonna be sick."

She disconnected as she ran and barely made it to the bathroom before throwing up. By the time the spasms had passed, she was shaking. She splashed cold water on her face and then dried her hands and face without looking in the mirror, unable to face the added guilt.

———~~~———

By midmorning, word had spread all over Blessings about the fire and Meeker Webb's death. The next question after that shocker was what happened to Dori and her baby, but no one had an answer. Her disappearance only added to the drama.

When P. Nutt Butterman heard about Meeker's passing, his first thought was to contact Dori Grant. Meeker had been one of his clients, and she needed to know what provisions her grandfather had made for her. But when he called the police station to inquire as to where she'd been taken, no one knew.

"What do you mean, you don't know?" Butterman asked. "Surely to God you didn't just leave her behind on her own?"

The officer on the desk was instantly defensive.

"I wasn't on duty last night. I couldn't speak to what was done. Pittman was there. Do you want to talk to him?"

"Please," Peanut said.

Moments later, Lon Pittman picked up the phone.

"This is Pittman. How can I help you?"

"Lon, this is Peanut. I'm trying to find out where Dori Grant and her baby were taken last night."

Lon frowned. "I don't know. I was talking to her after the ambulance left with her grandfather's body, and then I got called away for an emergency. Her neighbors on both sides of the street were all there in the yard. I guess I assumed one of them would take her and the baby home, at least for the night. You might check with Bart and Pansy Jones. They live across the street."

"Thanks for the info," Peanut said. "I'll do that."

He disconnected, looked up the phone number, and then made the call and waited for someone to pick up.

"Jones residence."

"Mrs. Jones, this is Peanut Butterman. How are you this morning?"

"Why, I guess I'm fine," she said, surprised by the call.

"I'm calling because you were Meeker Webb's closest neighbor and I'm trying to locate his granddaughter and baby. I was wondering, if by chance, they are at your house?"

"No, they're not here," she snapped.

Pansy's guilt made her answer defensive, and Peanut heard it.

"Did you happen to see where she went?"

"Yes, actually, I did. She and that baby left with Johnny Pine."

That baby. That description alone told him how she really felt.

"Really?" Peanut drawled.

So, without her grandfather's protection, Dori and *that baby* had become a community burden no one wanted to bear. He sighed. Small-minded people got on his nerves, and to his disgust, the woman wasn't through talking.

"If you ask me, it was all rather strange," Pansy said. "I mean, she never would name that baby's father and then out of the blue here comes Johnny Pine to the rescue and takes her away. I'm thinking the daddy finally showed his true colors and came to claim his child."

The skin crawled on the back of Peanut's neck. "I find your comments leaning more toward gossip and supposition rather than fact, and until I knew the truth, I would keep them to myself. In the meantime, thank you for your assistance."

He hung up in Pansy's ear.

Pansy was furious that Butterman had talked to her like she'd done something bad. He didn't have to live with Bart Jones. She'd just done what she'd been told. It wasn't her fault that Pine boy had come to claim his own.

Butterman was just as irked with her as she was with him. As far as he was concerned, she'd said more than enough. He was muttering to himself about the sharp tongues of self-righteous women as he flipped through the file he had on Meeker Webb.

There was a phone number for Dori Grant along with Meeker's contact information. He called the number listed for Dori and got nothing. He decided to take a chance and called Meeker's number next. She answered on the second ring.

"Hello?"

Peanut heard a quaver in the female voice and guessed he'd found his missing heir.

"Hello. This is Peanut Butterman. I'm trying to locate Dori Grant."

Dori recognized the lawyer's name.

"Hello, Mr. Butterman. This is Dori."

"Miss Grant, my condolences on the loss of your grandfather."

Dori stomach roiled. And so it began.

"Thank you, sir."

"Yes, and now to the reason I'm calling. I drew up your grandfather's will, and as you are his sole heir, there are some things you need to know."

"Okay."

"I was told you are staying at the Pine residence. Is that correct?"

"Yes."

"We need to talk in person. Would it be convenient if I came by this morning?"

"Yes, sir, I guess so. Johnny is at work and the boys are at school."

He glanced at the time and then at his daily planner. He had court this afternoon. This needed to be dealt with before.

"Would it be possible if I stopped by about ten o'clock?"

"Yes. Do you know where he lives?"

"I do, and I'll see you then," he said and hung up.

Dori heard the click and disconnected. This was going to be a long day; she just knew it.

Johnny had come and gone over two hours earlier to drop off the things he'd bought, so her immediate needs had been met. Luther was taking his morning nap, and the floors she'd just mopped were almost dry. She'd washed her T-shirt and sweats. They should be dry soon. She'd still be in her sock feet, but at least she'd be wearing her own clothes when he came.

Like all the others in Blessings, Ruby Dye had been awakened in the night by the sirens, and when she got up to look out, the flames she saw over the rooftops to the south had given her chills. But she didn't learn what had happened until the next morning when Vera Conklin called to spread the news.

"Ruby, it's me, Vera. Did you hear about the fire last night?"

Ruby topped off her coffee and carried it to the table as she continued her conversation.

"I heard the sirens and saw the flames, but didn't know what was burning."

"Oh, Sister, it's just awful. It was Meeker Webb's house. It's gone. Burned to the ground," Vera said.

Ruby was horrified. "Oh Lord! Did they get out of the house?"

"All three of them got out, but then Meeker had a heart attack in their yard while they were fighting the fire and died."

Ruby gasped. "Oh no! What's going to happen to Dori and her baby?"

"I don't know. I asked where they were, but Vesta didn't know."

"How did Vesta find out?" Ruby asked.

"One of her clients called to change an appointment and told her about it."

"Lord, Lord, that poor girl. She must be scared half to death, not to mention devastated by her grandfather's passing. I'll need to find out where she's staying. I'm guessing her and her baby are in serious need of some clothing. I'll see what I can find out and get right on that. Thanks for calling. I'll see you at the shop later."

"Okay," Vera said and hung up.

Ruby took another sip of her coffee and then went to get a pad and pen. Ruby liked to make lists. They kept life orderly, and she liked order. She made two headings. One was for Dori Grant. The other was for "baby boy." Now she needed to find out where Dori was staying and give her a call to find out their clothing sizes. Her first appointment this morning was Pansy Jones. Pansy lived across the street from the house that burned. Maybe Dori was at her house. She'd find out soon enough.

—⁓—

Pansy was in a rare state by the time she got to the Curl Up and Dye. Everywhere she went, people were asking her about Dori Grant and her baby. Just because she lived across the street did not make them her responsibility. It was her opinion that if people had been keeping tabs on her like they should have, she wouldn't be raising a little bastard.

The fact that Butterman had basically told her not to say anymore about Dori Grant's whereabouts made her angry. Men were always telling her what to do. The next time someone asked, she was spilling the beans, and Peanut Butterman could just have himself a big old fit and then get over it.

She parked in front of the salon and, when she got out of the car, accidentally shut the tail of her dress in the door and then ripped about three inches of the waist seam before she realized it and opened the door again to free the fabric.

"Oh, well, for heaven's sake!" Pansy sputtered, then tucked the torn bit back under the belt and hoped for the best as she stomped into the shop.

"Good morning, Pansy! All ready for your hair color?" Ruby asked.

"Yes, my roots are starting to show something awful," Pansy said and followed Ruby back to her station.

"We'll get you fixed up in no time," Ruby said and

proceeded to fasten a towel and then a cape around Pansy's neck.

She sectioned off Pansy's hair and began talking as she was applying the color.

"I really like this color on you. It favors your skin tone, don't you think?"

Pansy smiled. Finally, someone wanted to talk about something besides that fire.

"Yes, I like it just fine," Pansy said. "Bart even mentioned it, and he never notices anything."

Ruby laughed. "Isn't that just like a man?"

Pansy rolled her eyes. "You have no idea. Just when I think the man is oblivious to everything, he goes and says something nice like that."

Ruby thought it strange that Pansy hadn't mentioned the fire, especially since it was right across the street from her house. She decided to feel her out.

"So I guess you had some excitement last night. Sure is too bad about Mr. Webb's passing. I always found him to be a very likable fellow."

"Yes, it was a shame," Pansy said shortly.

Ruby waited for her to elaborate, but she did not, nor did she mention Dori and her baby. She kept methodically applying color and humming lightly to herself until she saw Pansy relax, then she tossed another question into the silence.

"So, we're going to start a donation box for clothing and such for Dori and her baby, but we need to know sizes."

"That's nice," Pansy said.

Ruby frowned. "Do you know where I might find her? I want to give her a call."

Pansy clenched her jaw again. Butterman's warning was running through her head, but she'd had enough.

"Actually, I do. That boy Johnny Pine showed up, and she and the baby left with him. I thought it strange myself, but maybe the missing father finally came to claim his own."

Ruby's eyes narrowed. "Well, personally I don't believe a word of that. That young man never turned his back on his little brothers when his mama died, and I can't see him denying a child that would be his, either. So, what did Dori say to you when she left?"

"Oh, that boy came after everybody left. I'd already told her I would pray for her and gone home. I was in my house watching out the window when—"

Pansy stopped and looked at Ruby. She'd just given herself away, and from the look on Ruby's face, she knew it.

Ruby paused, the bottle of color in one hand and a rattail comb in the other.

"You mean everyone went off and left that girl and her baby alone?"

Pansy's face turned a dark, angry red.

"I don't know about everyone. I said my piece and went home like Bart told me to do."

Ruby blinked and then undid another section of hair and began applying more color without looking at Pansy.

The fact that she wasn't talking made Pansy uneasy, and instead of staying quiet, she just dug the hole she was in a little deeper.

"That baby was screaming and screaming. We could barely say a thing to Dori for the noise."

Ruby kept applying color as fast as she could, then finally finished and slipped the plastic bouffant cap on Pansy's head and set the timer.

The silence made Pansy even more uneasy.

"I told Dori we'd pray for her," Pansy said. "I'm starting a prayer chain with our church ladies just as soon as I get home."

Ruby paused, eyeing Pansy curiously, as if she'd never seen her before.

"That's real Christian of you, I'm sure," she said and then gathered up the wet and stained towels and carried them to the back.

Chapter 9

PANSY SAW HERSELF IN THE MIRROR AND FROWNED. She didn't much like what she was seeing and turned her chair toward the front of the salon so she could watch the street instead.

Ruby killed several minutes muttering and slamming drawers and doors in the workroom, and she was still there when the Conklin twins came in the back door.

"Ruby, you won't believe what we just heard!" Vera said.

Ruby pointed toward the front of the salon and then put a finger to her lips to indicate quiet.

The girls' eyes widened, and then they scooted into the small workroom with Ruby and closed the door behind them.

"What's going on?" Vesta asked.

Ruby rolled her eyes. "Oh, I'm just getting a dose of the Christian charity the town of Blessings is so good at handing out. If you belong to the right social circles, they can't do enough. But if you're unfortunate enough to have committed a sin in their good Christian eyes, they conveniently forget God didn't set them up as judge and jury."

Vesta nodded. "Well, anyway, back to our news. You won't believe where Dori Grant and her baby are staying."

"With Johnny Pine," Ruby muttered. "And from

what I can gather, it's because he's the only one with a kind enough heart to take her in. According to Miss Holier-than-thou sitting in my chair with Chocolate Sin stewing on her roots, Dori Grant is a fallen woman with a crying baby that nobody wanted to be saddled with."

"You already knew," Vera muttered and glared at Vesta. "I told you we should have come to the shop earlier. Ruby knows everything before anyone else in Blessings."

Ruby frowned. "Well, I could do without ever having heard this. I am disgusted to the core. I don't suppose either one of you knows where Johnny Pine lives?"

The sisters shrugged. "On the other side of the tracks is all I know."

Ruby rolled her eyes. "I'll find out before the day is done. In the meantime, I better not hear one bad thing said about that girl and her baby or, for that matter, about Johnny Pine." She glanced at the clock. "Pansy's time will be up in a few. I need to get my game face on before I go back out there."

Vera patted her arm.

"I'll go man the front. I don't have anyone until almost noon."

Vesta sighed. "I have a haircut due in a few minutes."

They left the workroom as Ruby began digging through the cabinets. She searched and searched until she found the large plastic jar she'd been looking for.

"Finally," she muttered as she shook a dead wasp out of the bottom and pulled a marker out of the junk drawer.

She wrote *For Dori and her baby* on a piece of paper and taped it to the jar, then took a five-dollar bill out of her purse and dropped it into the jar, like salting a gold mine and waiting for takers. She carried it through the salon with all the ceremony she could muster and set it on the front counter beside the cash register, then flounced back to Pansy just as the timer for her hair color went off.

"That's what I call timing," she said and ushered Pansy back to the shampoo station.

Ruby was still congenial and talkative, but Pansy felt the woman's disapproval of what she'd left undone.

After her shampoo and style, Pansy followed Ruby up to the front to pay. She saw the donation jar and frowned, then reluctantly dug out an extra dollar and dropped it in the jar.

"You are so sweet. Thank you for helping Dori and her baby," Ruby said and smiled big and wide as Pansy made a hasty exit. "Two-faced bitch," Ruby added and returned to her station to clean up before her next appointment arrived.

——◆◇◆——

Johnny was on the job site, pushing dirt to build a pad for Buzz Higdon's new barn. The dozer engine was throwing back heat on his face and legs, but the sun was hotter on his back and neck. If that wasn't misery enough, the hog pen a hundred yards to his right smelled to high heaven.

The hogs were lying in the shade because their mud wallow was drying up, and the flies were so thick around them that they swarmed in little black clouds. He paused long enough to lift the dozer blade and then shifted into reverse, backed up, and turned around to work the pad from another direction. He would not let himself think about the girl and baby back in his house. It would be too easy to become invested in her life.

A lone white heron flew across his line of vision and landed in the shallows of the pond off to the east, but Johnny had no time to admire the scenery. He glanced at his watch. It was almost one. He would be done with this job before long and would, happily, get away from the stench.

Dori cried some more after she'd finished her conversation with Evelyn Harper at the funeral home. She kept imagining her granddaddy's body all laid out on some table with strangers doing only God knows what with it, and no one caring about who he was or how special he had been. She cried until she gave herself a headache, then washed her face and dried her tears and went to check on Luther. He was still sleeping.

She thought about Lovey Cooper spending the day gathering up clothes for them and was grateful for such a good friend. Then she wondered what Johnny was doing and if he regretted his offer to give her shelter. The last thing she wanted was to be a burden to someone again, but right now it seemed she had no choice.

If she'd been home, she would have had cookies baking or a cake in the oven. But this was not her house, and she didn't dare use up foodstuff they might be saving. The floors were swept and mopped. The bathroom had been scrubbed, and she'd dusted the house from top to bottom. It smelled like lemon and pine in every room.

When she'd taken down the curtains in the boys' room to wash, she'd found a stick-figure pencil drawing behind one curtain with the word Mama written beneath it. It was heartbreaking to see the simple drawing, obviously done in secret so that Mama, who was no longer with them, would not be forgotten. She'd noticed the only family pictures were of Johnny and the boys. It was as if this family had begun only after he had become the man of the house. She wanted to hurry up and get the clean curtains rehung, so that their secret would still be safe.

She was pacing the floor and watching the clock when she saw a car turn off the street and come up the drive. *It must be the lawyer*. She wiped her hands on the sides of her sweatpants as she watched the tall, lanky man getting out of his pretty white Lincoln. He looked a little bit like a younger version of Clint Eastwood, and Dori wondered what had possessed his parents to name him Peanut.

The lawyer knocked twice. She took a deep breath and then let him in.

"Miss Grant, I'm Peanut Butterman. Thank you for seeing me on such short notice."

"I thank you for coming," Dori said and stepped aside. "Please take a seat."

Peanut's long legs made the trip from the door to the sofa in three steps, and then he stood, waiting for Dori to sit first. She sat at one end of the sofa. He sat at the other.

"How are you doing?" he asked.

She shrugged, her hands clasped tightly in her lap.

"About like you'd expect. I keep praying this is just a bad dream, but I can't seem to wake up."

He frowned. She looked so young. He couldn't wrap his head around the fact that she was a mother.

"I can only imagine," he said softly. "I can't mend your sadness, but maybe after we talk, you'll feel better about your future. Mr. Webb made sure you would not be destitute."

"Really?" Dori said.

"You didn't know?"

"No, sir. I assumed one day he'd leave the house to Luther and me, but it's gone and I've been trying to figure out how and where we'll start over."

Butterman opened his briefcase and pulled out a handful of papers.

"I will, of course, file all the necessary papers to have Meeker's will go through probate, but considering these drastic circumstances and that you are the only heir, I wanted you to know where you stood, okay?"

She nodded.

"You were correct in that your grandfather left you the house, and the four city lots on which it stood. Yes, it's been destroyed, but it was fully insured. The insurance value on the house was two hundred thousand dollars, so once all of his estate has settled, that money will be yours to rebuild on the site or buy another house if you choose."

Dori was stunned. "That's a lot of money!"

Peanut shrugged. "It costs a lot to build a house; even the most simple of houses can cost dearly. Now, with regards to his car, which also burned up, it, too, was fully insured, and since he had you listed as co-owner on the title, you will be getting money to replace this almost immediately. He had fifty-five thousand dollars in his checking account. There is a safety-deposit box we have yet to open, and since his key probably burned up in the fire, we'll have to get the bank to have it opened by a locksmith, but that's all in the future."

Dori was in shock. She heard what he was saying but could hardly take it in. Granddaddy and her grandmother had always lived a simple life. They'd always had enough but nothing over the top. Now she knew why. They'd been saving it, obviously for her.

"There is also a five-hundred-thousand-dollar life insurance policy that he took out over twenty years ago. You are the sole beneficiary."

Dori gasped, certain she'd misunderstood.

"What did you say?"

Peanut looked up. "About the life insurance? Five hundred thousand?"

She leaned toward him, whispering, "As in…half a million dollars?"

He nodded.

Dori slapped both hands over her mouth to keep from screaming as her eyes welled with tears.

Peanut smiled. He didn't often get to deliver good news in a bad situation, but this time was different and he liked it.

"I would like to suggest that, at this point, you tell no one. You are not yet of legal age, and Meeker had named me executor, so I would be in charge of your inheritance for you, until such time as you turn eighteen. By the way, when is your birthday?"

Tears were running down her cheeks.

"I turn eighteen this coming Sunday."

Peanut's smile widened. "As Meeker's lawyer, I can assure you an executor for your inheritance will not be necessary. You will be legal before probate is finished."

Dori was shaking. "I've been so scared. I thought we were going to be homeless. I would give anything to have my granddaddy back, but I am forever grateful for this."

"How old were you when your parents passed?" Peanut asked.

"Nine. They died in a car wreck a few days before Christmas. The car spun on icy roads and went over a cliff. I barely remember what they looked like. Grandy and Granddaddy were everything to me, and when we lost her, Granddaddy stepped into the gap as best he could for me and we kept our family together."

Peanut nodded.

"And now you have your own little family."

As if on cue, Luther woke up in the back bedroom and let out a howl. "Speaking of family, will you excuse me? I need to change him before I come back."

Peanut smiled. "Do what you need to do. I'm not going anywhere."

Luther's howl was getting louder. Dori broke into a run as she left. She ran into their bedroom just as Luther was making an attempt to crawl over the pillows she'd put around him so he wouldn't roll off the bed.

"Hey, little man. Where do you think you're going?" she asked as she picked him up, cradling him close as she picked up a fresh diaper and the box of wipes and laid him at the foot of the bed, on the blanket she'd folded to use as a changing pad.

He squawked when she laid him back down, and then when he realized she was taking off his diaper, he began to kick and smile his wide-open, toothless smile. She thought it was funny how much babies liked to be naked, but she knew better than to let him be that way long. Inevitably, someone always got peed on, usually her.

"We have company," she said as she removed the wet diaper and wiped his bare bottom, then slid a new diaper beneath his backside and quickly fastened it. "There now, let's go say hi to the nice man in the living room. He brought us some really good news, and I will say we were due for some."

Luther rode her hip like a pro, his hand fisted in her hair to steady his balance.

"Thank you for waiting," she said shyly and then introduced the lawyer and her son. "Mr. Butterman, this is my son, Luther Joe. Luther, this is Mr. Butterman. Please be a good boy for Mama for a few minutes more."

Peanut smiled. "He's a fine-looking young man; big for his age, is he not?"

"Yes, sir, that's what folks say."

"That means you're taking very good care of him," Peanut said. "Have a seat for a few minutes more and then I'll leave you to get on with your day."

She plopped Luther in her lap as she sat back down, positioning him so that he had full view of the man at the other end of the sofa.

"There are a couple more things you need to know," Peanut said. "You have access to Meeker's checking account, do you not?"

"Yes, but I've never used it. Granddaddy had me sign a card for the bank, but he either gave me cash or I spent my income from work on things we needed."

"Good. That way, even though we'll be going through probate, you can still access his money for necessities."

"I have almost a thousand dollars in my checking account, but I'm stuck here until Lovey Cooper brings us some clothes and shoes."

Peanut frowned. He hadn't considered that aspect and promptly took out his wallet and peeled off a handful of twenties and a couple of hundred-dollar bills.

"Here. I think that's about three hundred and fifty dollars." When she started to object, he held up a hand. "Don't worry. I'll add that amount onto my bill when we finalize everything, okay?"

Dori's hand shook as she took the money he'd laid in her hand.

"You are a good man, Mr. Butterman. You have gone out of your way for us today, and I know it. Even though my heart is heavy, you have given me peace of mind."

He nodded. "Have you spoken to the funeral home yet?"

"Yes, sir. We're having the funeral this Saturday at 2:00 p.m. at the Baptist church. I still have to contact Preacher Lawless about details, but that much is firm."

"I'll make note of it," Peanut said and handed her his card. "Call anytime you have a question or need advice. That's what I'm for. Don't get up. I'll let myself out."

He was at the door when Dori called out. "Thank you again."

He smiled. "You are very welcome. And just so you know, I have high regard for Mr. Pine. He has a good head on his shoulders."

Dori didn't say so, but she had high regard for Johnny too.

Luther was still riding her hip when she made a call to the church. After settling with Preacher Lawless about songs for the funeral, she would be done.

Back at Granny's Country Kitchen, the news of Dori Grant's tragedy was the conversation of the day. Lovey had a donation jar at the cash register similar to the one Ruby had set up and had a sign up on the door about her clothing drive for Dori and the baby, so that her customers would see it as they entered. The drop-off point for the clothing was at the Episcopal Church that she attended. The pastor had been happy to participate.

Ruby Dye heard about the clothing drive and funneled all of the information to her clients, should they be inclined to donate clothes instead of money.

Then she thought about what else she could do to let Dori Grant know that not everyone in Blessings was a bigot and thought about sending flowers. Even though there were so many things that girl and her baby needed, sending flowers was proper. She checked the phone book for a number and then made the call.

"Franklin Floral, this is Myra."

"Myra, it's me, Ruby."

"Hello, Ruby. What can I do for you?"

"I want to send flowers to Dori Grant."

Myra Franklin swiveled her chair around to the computer and pulled up a new screen.

"That was a terrible thing, wasn't it?" Myra said.

"Yes. I feel just awful for her. I keep thinking how alone she must feel," Ruby said.

Myra lowered her voice and leaned into the receiver.

"Well, I don't know about being alone. I heard she and her baby are staying with that Pine family."

"Yes, that's what I heard too. I guess it's a good thing

he and his little brothers came along, or she'd still be standing in her yard with her baby, because that's where all of her good Christian neighbors left her after they'd had their fill of sightseeing."

"What?"

"You heard me," Ruby said. "I got it straight from the horse's mouth, so to speak. No one offered her and that little baby shelter. They offered to pray for her, but they didn't see fit to take her in."

Myra sputtered. "Even so, what would make some boy offer to take in a girl and baby unless he had a horse in the race, so to speak?"

"I guess for the same reason he fought to keep his little brothers from going into the Georgia welfare system. Maybe he's just a good person. Now, if you still want my business, I suggest we change the conversation."

Myra sputtered again and then took a quick breath. "About those flowers—what did you have in mind?"

"Do you have any azaleas blooming?"

"Yes, I have dark red and whites in bloom, and one lavender color, I believe."

"The red. I'd like to send the prettiest red one you have."

"That will be fifty-five dollars," Myra said. "Do you want use a credit card? Or I can bill you."

"Just send me a bill," Ruby said. "I don't know the address though."

"Oh, I know where they live," Myra said. "I worked the flowers for their mother's funeral a couple of years back. It's the second house on Admiral on the west side of the street. It has a wide porch that runs the length of the house and a porch swing. I always did like porch swings."

"I want it delivered today," Ruby said.

"I'll get George right on it," Myra said. "Thank you for your business."

"You're welcome," Ruby said and hung up, then glanced at the clock.

It was almost noon. She'd made a little over a hundred dollars this morning and just spent half of it—probably the best money she'd ever spent. She turned around and looked at the salon. All the customers were gone and none were due for at least an hour. She headed for the workroom, where the twins and Mabel Jean were eating lunch.

"Hey, girls, I'm going to run an errand. I'll be back in a few, okay?"

"Sure thing," Mabel Jean said. "I'm almost finished. I'll take the front."

"Thank you," Ruby said. She took off her smock, grabbed her purse, and headed out the back door to her car.

Dori had just finished feeding Luther a baby food jar of applesauce and was heating a bottle of milk. The baby was cranky, and Dori was guessing he was missing Granddaddy as much as she was. More than once she'd caught him staring around the house and watching the doorways. They were obviously in a strange place, and Meeker Webb was certainly missing. He had been Luther's primary caregiver every day. It was no wonder he was confused and fussy. She felt the same way.

The microwave dinged, and Dori took out the bottle and screwed on the top with Luther on her hip trying to help.

She finally got it on and put the bottle in his mouth as she cradled him against her breasts. His little eyes widened as he clamped down on the nipple and began sucking the milk down in noisy gulps.

Dori smiled as she headed to the living room with him in her arms.

"For goodness' sake, Luther Joe, slow down. You aren't anywhere near starvation."

The baby paused in the act of swallowing to grunt and fart. A trickle of milk ran from the corner of his mouth and then he clamped down on the nipple and began sucking again as if nothing had happened.

It made Dori laugh. She was still chuckling as she sat down in the recliner and pushed off to make it rock. In the middle of a smile, she started to cry. Granddaddy would have loved these funny little moments, but there was no one left for her to tell. So she cried a little more and then blew her nose, which startled Luther enough that he let go of the nipple and stared, milk running from the corner of his mouth and down his neck.

Dori laughed. "Did I scare you? I'm sorry, baby boy."

Luther saw her smile and decided it was okay and latched back on to the nipple. He had the bottle finished in no time, and she had him on her shoulder, trying to get him to burp, when she heard another car pulling up the drive. She got up to look and recognized Ruby Dye from the hair salon. She couldn't imagine what on earth she would be doing here at Johnny's. It didn't occur to her that Ruby would come because of her. She was still patting Luther's back and waiting for that burp when Ruby knocked.

When Dori opened the door, Ruby started talking.

"Hello, Dori. You remember me, don't you? Ruby Dye? I own the Curl Up and Dye."

"Yes, ma'am, I remember you. Would you like to come in?"

Ruby sailed over the threshold with two sacks in each hand.

"Yes, thank you, but I won't stay. I'm so glad I finally found you...and there's that sweet little guy in your arms. I used to see you push your son by the shop in his stroller until you went to work full-time. I came to tell you how sorry I am about what happened to your grandfather and your home."

"That's very kind of you, ma'am," Dori said.

"Call me Ruby or Sister, if you like, everyone does," she said.

Dori nodded and kept patting Luther's back, waiting for that burp.

Ruby held up the sacks. "I brought food. If you'll lead the way to the kitchen, I'll put it on the table, and you can put it up later, when you don't have your hands full."

"Food?"

Ruby patted Dori's arm.

"Yes, honey. It's what we do when family loses a loved one—food for feeding the relatives who inevitably come."

"We didn't have any relatives, at least none I knew of. There was just Granddaddy and me left...and Luther, of course."

"Well, then, you can feed yourself and Johnny's family instead of cooking for yourselves, okay? Now show me the way."

Dori led her into the kitchen.

Ruby sniffed as she began taking food out of the sacks.

"This place smells wonderful! Is that air freshener I smell?"

"No, it's just pine and lemon scents from house cleaning."

"Amazing. If you ever want a little extra money, I could sure use you at the shop a couple of times a week. I hate to mop," Ruby said and began emptying the second sack.

Dori stared at the food coming out of the sacks.

"This is so kind of you," she said. "I was going to make meat loaf for supper, but I guess I'll put the hamburger meat in the freezer."

Ruby beamed. "I'm happy to help."

Dori pictured the looks on the boys' faces when they saw the desserts. Beep had asked for cookies, and she'd noticed that Johnny hadn't brought any when he came back with stuff for the baby. Now she could add more money to the pot and put a feast on the table tonight.

"When I stopped by to pick up the pies from Granny's Restaurant, Lovey donated the fried chicken and all the mashed potatoes and gravy. I wanted you to know this isn't all from me. There are lots of people who are pulling for you, honey. You're not alone."

Dori tried to smile, but the tears were too close to the surface. Instead, she buried her face against her baby and started to cry.

Ruby shook her head and opened her arms, pulling Dori and the baby into a motherly hug.

"Bless your heart, bless your heart," Ruby said softly. "The world has definitely handed you some heartache.

But I'm here to tell you that you will get through this and be all the stronger for it after. Understand?"

Dori raised her head, and at that moment, Luther let out a burp of massive proportions.

"Oh Lord," Dori muttered.

Ruby laughed.

Luther Joe followed up the burp by promptly filling a diaper with several impressive grunts.

"Oh dear Lord," Dori said. "I've got to go change him. I'll be right back."

Ruby's laughter followed her down the hall and into the bedroom.

Dori eased Luther down onto the changing blanket and then grabbed the baby wipes and a fresh diaper. Luther was almost asleep as Dori began cleaning him up.

"Yeah, look at you," Dori said softly. "Ate yourself into a coma, burped liked a piggy in front of company, and then loaded up this diaper without taking a second breath. Very impressive, my little man."

Luther smacked his lips and made little sucking sounds as Dori fastened the clean diaper and then put him down for a nap. She covered him with a light blanket and corralled him by piling all the pillows around him again, then gathered up the messy diaper and wipes into an empty plastic sack and took it with her when she left.

Ruby was still in the kitchen when Dori came through.

"Give me a second," Dori said and went through the kitchen and out onto the back porch to toss the diaper into the garbage can.

Ruby was folding up the paper bags when Dori returned.

"I don't know about you, but I always save these," Ruby said and laid them on the cabinet.

Dori washed and dried her hands before going back to look at everything Ruby brought.

"You have no idea how appreciated this will be. It will last us at least a week," Dori said.

Ruby patted Dori's cheek. "I'm happy to help. Have you set a time and date for the services?"

Dori nodded. "Two o'clock. Saturday at the Baptist Church."

"My girls and I have already decided to close up shop long enough to attend the services, so we'll see you there," Ruby said. "Now, I want you to promise me something. If you need help, will you please call me?"

Dori hesitated. "We'll be fine," she said.

Ruby shook her head. "No, I'm serious. If you need something, call me. There are four of us at the shop. We'll make time to deliver it to you, okay?"

"I don't know what to say," Dori said.

Ruby smiled. "Just say yes."

Chapter 10

DORI STOOD AT THE WINDOW A MOMENT, WATCHING Ruby backing down the drive, then went back to the kitchen and began going through the food she'd brought.

The fried chicken, along with the mashed potatoes and gravy, would be supper tonight, and when she found a container of coleslaw, she added that to the menu. There was a big order of ribs from the barbecue place, and she recognized a large to-go order of baked beans from Granny's. Not only had Ruby brought two bags of dinner rolls, but there were also three different kinds of pies and two large bottles of Pepsi. It was an amazing gift, and Dori was grateful to have food to contribute to the family rather than taking it out of their mouths.

She began putting away what needed to be refrigerated and setting the other food on the counter until supper was over. In the midst of all that, the buzzer sounded on the dryer. The boys' curtains were dry. She needed to get those back up before they got home.

It then became a juggling act, getting them on the rods and then up on the hooks without having them slide back off the other end, but she persevered until it was done. She stood back to look at the room, making sure she hadn't disturbed anything they might think would matter, and then hurried back to the kitchen.

It was past noon, almost one o'clock, and she hadn't eaten a thing but a few bites of oatmeal this morning.

Before, the thought of food had turned her stomach, but after the news Peanut Butterman had given her and the kindness of others, the knot in her belly was easing. Because of Meeker Webb's foresight, she and Luther were going to be okay.

She poked through the cartons and dishes one more time, then chose a piece of chicken and some slaw and ate it standing up. A few minutes later, she was cleaning up when her cell phone rang. She dried her hands and answered.

"Hello?"

"It's me," Johnny said. "I thought I'd check in and make sure you're okay."

She smiled, surprised and grateful that he'd called to check on them.

"Yes, we're okay, but you would not believe what's been happening this morning. Granddaddy's lawyer was here and Ruby Dye from the beauty shop came by with a lot of food."

Johnny heard a lilt in her voice that hadn't been there before. Whatever was going on had lifted her spirits.

"That's great. So meat loaf is on the back burner?"

"We have fried chicken, mashed potatoes and gravy, and coleslaw, and some barbecued ribs and baked beans, rolls, three pies, and two liters of Pepsi. I put the meat in the freezer. Hope that was okay."

Johnny laughed. "Of course it's okay. I was just kidding you."

Dori sighed, and he heard it. He knew she was struggling. He remembered the day his world fell in.

"Are you sure you don't need anything before we get home?"

"I'm positive, but thank you, Johnny."

"For what?"

"For asking. For caring. I don't know. Just thank you."

"You're welcome. Call if you need help."

"I will," she said and disconnected.

Johnny knew she was no longer on the line but still held the phone to his ear. It took a moment to disconnect his emotions as he finally dropped the phone in his pocket. He had the dozer on the flatbed ready to haul back into town and was more than ready to leave the pigs and Higdon's pigsty behind.

An hour later, a van from Franklin's Floral drove up to the Pine residence. George Franklin got out and carried a large potted plant to the door, then knocked. He eyed the young girl who came to the door.

"Dori Grant?"

"Yes."

"Sorry for your loss," he said and handed her a large blooming azalea.

"Thank you," Dori said and shut the door as George headed back to the delivery van.

The azalea was stunning, the blossoms a deep crimson red. She put it down on a side table by the front door and then sat down to read the sympathy card.

From Ruby and the girls at the Curl Up and Dye.

All that food and then she'd sent flowers too. Last night, the world she'd known had gone up in flames. Then Johnny Pine opened a door to shelter her and Luther, and the kindness continued to grow.

A short while later, the baby woke up cranky. Dori

felt his forehead, making sure he wasn't getting sick as she changed him, then wrapped him in his blanket and sat down in the rocker and rocked him back to sleep.

—⁓—

When Lovey showed up just before four o'clock with two boxes of clothing, Dori was relieved to see her. This was a woman she knew and admired, and she'd come through for them in a very big way.

"I can't stay, but I knew you would need these," Lovey said as she set the boxes down and then gave Dori a big hug. "Honey, I am so sorry about everything. Do you have any immediate needs? Is there something I can do?"

"No, ma'am. Thanks to Johnny and his brothers, and people like you and Ruby Dye, we're good for now."

"Johnny Pine sure showed those good Christians on your block for who they really are," Lovey said.

Dori shrugged. It still hurt her feelings that the people she'd known all her life had shunned her the moment Meeker was no longer a presence in her life.

Lovey gave Dori a quick hug. "I need to get back. Tonight is all-you-can-eat fried catfish, and you know the place will be packed." And then she saw Luther lying on a pallet in front of the television and smiled. "I've said it before, and I have to say it again. That little guy is the cutest thing ever, and he is growing like a weed. You are doing a grand job, my friend."

"Thank you," Dori said. "I'm really sorry to let you down on such short notice."

"No, no, you didn't let me down. Life just drop-kicked you again, for which I am so sorry. Meeker was a wonderful man, and he will be missed. Oh…I have a list of the people who donated clothing. I'll make sure to put a thank-you in the paper and add your name."

"Thank you again," Dori said. "People are being so kind."

"There are lots of good people in Blessings, honey. Take care of yourself, and if you need anything, you have my number."

Moments later, she was gone.

Dori took the box of clothing into her bedroom and began taking the items out one by one, thrilled by what they'd been given. All of the clothing was clean and in good condition, and in some cases, the pieces still bore price tags. There was a new pair of tennis shoes in her size and a pair of sandals. Someone had included new underwear, a makeup bag with new lipstick, moisturizer, toiletry articles, and a hairbrush and comb.

For Luther, there were baby bottles, lots of diapers, baby toys, a trio of new blankets, and much-needed clothing. She began opening the packages of new garments and took them to the laundry to wash.

Luther began fussing, and she quickly heated up a bottle and stopped long enough to feed him, then laid him down on the bed to play as she continued going through the box, hanging up some of the clothes and putting the rest through the laundry.

Luther was fussing again. When she looked up from what she was doing, she was surprised by how late it was. It was almost time for Johnny and the boys to come home.

The thought made her anxious. She hoped he wouldn't resent what was happening, but she hadn't expected people to acknowledge her in this way. The stuff that kept arriving might make him think she was taking over his space, and hurting his feelings was the last thing she wanted.

—∾∾—

By the time the workday ended, Johnny was ready to go home. He was on his way to Before and After to get the boys, but his thoughts were on Dori. He didn't know what to expect when they got there and was a little concerned with what he and the boys would be facing. She'd sounded almost upbeat when he'd talked to her earlier, but that was hours ago. She could be in tears again, and he wouldn't blame her, but he didn't want the boys scared or upset either.

He pulled up at the day care and got out. The Come In sign was still hanging on the door, so he walked in without knocking and called out, "It's me, Miss Jane."

"We're in here!" she called out.

He walked through the house and into the kitchen, then saw his brothers and grinned. The work island was covered with flour and jars of colored sprinkles. Freshly baked cookies were cooling on a rack. Beep had flour on his nose guard as well as on both hands, and the front of Marshall's shirt had a light dusting of flour, as well.

"Looks like you guys have been busy."

Jane Farris brushed flour from her hands and frowned.

"The boys told me about your houseguests this morning. I want to commend you for your generosity. Is it true Dori Grant's neighbors walked off and left her standing at that fire?"

Johnny eyed the boys. He didn't realize they'd picked up that much of what had happened to her.

"Well, is it?" Jane asked.

"Pretty much," Johnny said.

Jane rolled her eyes. "I could hardly believe it. I go to church with those people."

There was nothing Johnny could say.

"It's a good thing you happened by," Jane said.

Johnny eyed his brothers again and then smiled.

"They didn't tell you?"

"Tell me what?" she asked.

"We were out because they were worried about you. They saw the fire and knew your house was in that area. They wouldn't go back to sleep until they knew you were safe. We were out driving toward your house when we came upon the actual fire. In a way, it's because of you that we were even there."

Jane Farris's eyes widened.

"Is this true? You were coming to see about me?"

Marshall nodded.

"We didn't want you to burn up," Beep said.

Jane grabbed a tissue and wiped her eyes and then cleaned the flour off of Beep's nose brace.

"Thank you, Beep. Thank you, Marshall. It has been a long time since anyone worried about me. Now, let's get a bag so you can take some of these cookies home for your supper."

"That's nice of you, Miss Jane, but don't send too many. Dori said people brought some food to the house today already," Johnny said.

"That's fine. These cookies are kid cookies, anyway. Not really fit for company."

"They're fit for me," Beep said.

Johnny grinned. "Boys, go get your backpacks while Miss Jane is bagging up your cookies. We need to get home."

The boys ran out of the kitchen as Jane added a few more cookies and then gave him the bag.

"Your little guy is almost healed, isn't he?"

"We still have to be careful of his nose and ribs," Johnny said.

"He won't forget that," she whispered. "He won't ever forget. I hate that so much for him."

Johnny frowned. "Yes, ma'am, so do I."

"You are a good man, Johnny Pine. I just wanted you to know that."

Johnny was surprised by her words and the emotion with which they'd been delivered.

"That's kind of you to say, ma'am."

"Give Dori Grant my sympathies. I liked Meeker Webb. He was a good man."

"I will. Thank you for the cookies."

"We're ready," the boys yelled and headed out of the house.

"See you tomorrow," he said.

Jane waved them off, then took the Come In sign off the front door and locked it. She was done for the day.

Johnny put the cookies in the seat beside him and then turned around to check the boys.

"Are you guys buckled up?"

"Yes!" they chimed.

"Is the lady still at our house?" Marshall asked.

"Yes, are you okay with that?" Johnny asked.

Marshall nodded.

"How long is she gonna stay?" Beep asked as Johnny started the car and drove away.

"Until she figures out what she's going to do," Johnny said. "Are you okay with it too?"

"Yep. I'm okay," Beep said and then smiled, and just for a moment, Johnny saw their mother in his face.

"You guys are the best," he said and headed for home.

The boys were talking and laughing and poking each other as Johnny drove through town.

He saw Peanut Butterman coming out of the court-house with a briefcase in his hand, and Myra Franklin from Franklin Floral was carrying a large potted fern to the van.

Officer Pittman appeared to be ticketing a teenage driver he'd pulled over on a side street.

LilyAnn Dalton was walking down the street toward the bank. Everyone seemed to be on their way to some-place else.

He thought of Dori waiting for them and took a left turn at the end of Main Street and headed home.

The farther he drove, the less activity he saw. There were no businesses in this direction and the houses were older. Some yards were in need of mowing and land-scaping was nonexistent. By the time he crossed the old railroad crossing and headed downhill toward Admiral Street, he not only saw but also felt the separation of the classes in Blessings.

He glanced in the rearview mirror. The boys were still giggling and poking at each other, oblivious of their lot in life at the moment. He braked for the turn onto Admiral, and as he looked down the street toward his house, he saw Dori and the baby in the porch swing. Just for a minute, he let himself fantasize that they were one big happy family and that they belonged to each other.

"Hey, look! The girl is in the swing!" Beep said.

"Her name is Dori," Johnny said.

"Hey, look! Dori is in the swing," Beep repeated.

Johnny laughed. He was still smiling when he pulled up to the house and parked.

—◦◦◦—

Dori was wearing new clothing: the white tennis shoes, a pair of jeans, and a blue-and-white-striped Henley. She had dressed Luther in clean pajamas with a pair of new socks on his little feet, and if she hadn't been so sad about losing her grandfather, things would have felt closer to normal again.

Sitting outside had been an impulse, but once she'd settled into the swing and pushed off, the motion was relaxing. Luther was quiet, lulled by the rocking and the sights around him. The chains holding up the swing squeaked just enough to mark a rhythm.

She couldn't believe that this time yesterday, she'd been at home making supper with Granddaddy and Luther. It was hard to accept how fast that world had ended. She wanted to go to the funeral home, but they hadn't called to tell her the body was ready for viewing, and so she rocked a little more as the ache built within her chest.

Luther squirmed and kicked, trying to get his fist into his mouth and a grip on the blanket and accomplished neither, which set off a squawk of disapproval for his situation.

Dori rubbed the top of his soft curls and tucked the blanket around him.

"What's the matter, Luther Joe? Are you missing Granddaddy as much as I am?"

When he wouldn't be satisfied, she laid his head against her shoulder, tucked the blanket around his ears and started patting his back in rhythm to the creaking swing. This was his fussy time. Maybe when Johnny and the boys got home, his mood would shift.

Luther had finally settled again when she happened to glance up and saw Johnny's car. Her pulse kicked as she took a quick breath, a little anxious to face them again. They pulled up into the driveway and parked. When Johnny got out carrying a sack, he was laughing, and something tugged at her heart. Just for a moment, she saw him as a good-looking guy. He was even what girls would call sexy, but he seemed oblivious of the fact. The boys were laughing and poking at each other when they got out, and then they caught her watching and stopped.

She waved, and it was the trigger that egged them on.

"Hi," Marshall said as he walked up on the porch. "Is the baby asleep?"

Dori smiled. "No, he's just a little fussy before his bedtime."

"Can I look at him?" Beep asked.

"Absolutely," Dori said and turned Luther around and sat him back down in her lap.

Beep slipped up onto the swing beside her and then patted the baby's leg. "He's really soft," he whispered.

Dori nodded, eyeing the fading bruises and the earnest expression on his face beneath the nose guard and wondered how anyone could hurt someone this sweet and innocent.

"Yes, he is, isn't he? That's why we have to take such good care of babies, because they can't take care of themselves."

Johnny was standing at the foot of the steps and trying not to stare, but watching Dori interacting so easily with his brothers touched him. Then he caught her looking at him. A little embarrassed, he held up the sack of cookies.

"Compliments of the boys and Miss Jane. They wanted to send you something special, and Miss Jane sends her sympathies." ·

Dori looked at the boys. "Did you help make those?"

"We decorated them and then Miss Jane cooked them," Marshall said.

"That's wonderful. I can't wait to try one," she said. "So let's go in, okay? I think Luther has been outside long enough."

Johnny leaped up the steps and opened the door for her.

She gave him a quick glance and a smile.

"Thank you."

"No problem," he said and shut the door behind them, then immediately noticed the cleaning that she'd done while they were gone.

"The house looks and smells great," he said.

She flushed and then was irked at herself for reacting like that to the compliment. "Thank you," she said and saw him eye the delivery from the flower shop. "From the ladies at the hair salon...because of Granddaddy."

He caught sight of the boys, who were edging toward the kitchen, obviously following the enticing scents.

"Boys, do you have homework?"

"I smell fried chicken," Marshall said.

"Do you have homework?" Johnny repeated.

"A little, but I'm really hungry," Marshall added.

Johnny glanced at Dori.

"It's ready if you want to eat," she said. "Oh, I almost forgot," she said and pulled a hundred-dollar bill out of her pocket. "Mr. Butterman said I would have immediate access to Granddaddy's checking account because my name was also on it, and he advanced me a loan against my final bill. Here's a little more to help with what we'll use."

"It wasn't that much," Johnny said.

"It will be," she said and pushed it into his hand.

"Thank you," he said. "Money is always tight before payday."

"He also said I was on the title of Granddaddy's car as co-owner, which I didn't know. The insurance company will send me money to replace the car. When I get it, I'll start looking for a place for me and Luther and be out of your hair."

He should have been relieved to hear there was a deadline to his charity, but for some reason, it didn't sound as appealing as he would have expected. Instead, he glanced at the boys and pointed.

"We'll eat now. Both of you go wash up, but no dawdling after supper, and no TV until your homework is finished."

"Yay!" they cried and ran toward the bathroom, pushing and shoving as they went.

Johnny rolled his eyes. "That's what you have to look forward to with this one," he said and tapped Luther's little head lightly with the tip of his finger. "I'll wash up in the kitchen."

Dori followed him in, wishing for a high chair. She had the money to get one. All she needed was a vehicle to make it happen.

"Wow!" Johnny said, eyeing the food on the table and all over the cabinet.

"The coleslaw is in the refrigerator. We can microwave the mashed potatoes and gravy to heat it up."

"I can do all that," Johnny said. "I think you've done more than your share today."

"Then I'll feed Luther."

Dori sat down at the table and fastened a bib around Luther's neck and began to feed him applesauce.

Johnny looked over his shoulder and again caught a look of such love on her face it took him aback. His memories of their mother did not include anything like that. He wondered if Dori had felt that kind of love for Luther's father, and then he looked away. It was none of his business.

Chapter 11

THE BOYS SAT DOWN AT THE TABLE, STUNNED BY THE amount of food. Marshall pointed at the large container of fried chicken.

"Is this someone's birthday?"

Dori glanced at Johnny, willing him to answer. He was scooping mashed potatoes on both boys' plates and making little wells in the mounds to hold the gravy and, as she'd hoped, answered for her.

"No, it's not a celebration, Marshall. Some people were kind enough to bring food here on Dori's behalf because her grandfather died."

Beep's eyes widened as he looked longingly at the food, afraid it might not be good to eat.

"Does that mean this is sad food?"

Dori smiled through tears.

"No, honey, this isn't sad food. I think we should call it 'helping out' food. They brought it so I wouldn't have to cook in case I was tired. Understand?"

"I can help you eat it," he offered, then pointed at the platter of chicken. "Can I have a one of those leg things?"

"May I have," Johnny said and put a drumstick on Beep's plate. "What about you, Marshall? Which piece do you want?"

"A big one," Marshall said.

Dori poked another bite of applesauce in Luther's

mouth as Johnny put a larger piece of chicken on Marshall's plate.

"What about you, Dori?" Johnny asked.

"Uh, either a back or wing, please."

Johnny frowned. "There's not much meat on either of those."

She shrugged. "I know, but I like the bony pieces best."

He arched an eyebrow and put a couple of chicken wings on her plate.

"As long as it's a choice and not a sacrifice, they're all yours."

She laughed and was startled that she'd gotten past the sadness long enough to do it.

Luther looked up at her and grinned, applesauce running from both corners of his mouth.

She laughed again at the sight and shook her head.

"You're supposed to swallow that, Luther Joe."

Unfazed by the baby's mess, the boys laughed too.

Johnny's emotions were in overdrive. This was too much like a family gathering, which was a luxury he'd never allowed himself to consider—even if the girl was pretty...even if she had a baby who belonged to someone else.

Johnny finished filling everyone's plates. The boys ate like they were starving. He tried not to feel guilty that he could not provide food like this on a regular basis. He wasn't much of a cook and buying takeout food was not on their budget, but it *was* damn tasty, even if it was sad food.

Finally, they were down to dessert. Dori chose a cookie over pie and then bragged on the boys about how pretty it was and how good it tasted. The boys were beaming, and by the time she asked for a second one, she'd pretty much won their hearts and Johnny's deep respect. She'd seen how important it was to acknowledge their contributions to her situation and responded in the best way possible: by choosing cookies over pie.

"You're a good man, Charlie Brown," he said softly as he handed her the second cookie.

His praise washed through her and filled her up.

"You should try one," she said shyly.

He winked. "You eat mine. I'm going for a third piece of chicken."

The boys worked at finishing off their pie. Dori was trying to eat her cookie and keep Luther's hands out of her mouth while Johnny finished off his third, and last, piece of chicken.

Just as they were getting ready to begin the cleanup, Dori's phone rang.

"Excuse me," she said and got up to go answer it.

"Give Luther to me," Johnny said as he took the baby out of her arms.

"Thank you," she said and ran into the living room to find the phone, then answered quickly. "Hello?"

"Dori, this is Evelyn Harper. I wanted to let you know that your grandfather is ready for viewing, but I won't open his room to the public until you've okayed everything."

Dori's stomach lurched. Just like that, reality reared its ugly head.

"Uh, I'm not sure when I can get there. I'll have to ask—"

All of a sudden, Johnny was right behind her.

"What do you need?" he asked.

"Excuse me just a sec, Mrs. Harper."

"Take your time," Evelyn said.

Johnny repeated himself. "What's happening?"

"It's the funeral home. They have Granddaddy's body ready but won't allow people in until I okay everything."

"Do you have a driver's license?" he asked.

"Yes," she said.

He shrugged. "Good enough for me," he said and dug his car keys out of his pocket. "Take my car and go do what you have to do. We can watch out for Luther until you get back."

It was only because she couldn't get out of this task that she relented.

"Mrs. Harper? Are you still there?"

"Yes, I'm here."

"I'll be there in a few minutes," Dori said.

"All right, honey. I'll be here."

Dori pocketed her phone and looked at the keys in his hand and then at her baby.

"I can take him with me," she said.

He frowned. "No, you can't. You don't have a car seat."

"Or a baby bed or a high chair or a baby stroller or anything else," she muttered and then sighed. "I already feel so beholden to you and now to ask you to babysit and furnish me a vehicle seems like overkill."

"You didn't ask; I offered, which is a different set of circumstances, and the sooner you leave, the sooner you get back. But hang on a minute."

He left at a lope and came back just as quickly.

"This is a key to the house. You might be needing it in the days to come, and the car keys, of course." He dropped them in her palm then curled his fingers around her hand. "It's just help, Dori. At one time or another, we all need it."

She nodded, and just for a moment after he let go, it almost felt like she'd lost her anchor.

"I won't be long," she said and then rubbed her finger along Luther's arm. "Hey, little man, you be a good boy for Mama, okay?"

Johnny smiled. "He'll be fine. Strangely enough, I seem to be good with boys."

She put the house key in her pants pocket and made a quick exit before she changed her mind.

Starting the car made her nervous, and then she had to move the seat forward to better reach the brake, evidence of Johnny's long legs. But as soon as she backed out of the drive, she forgot about who she'd left behind and focused entirely on the journey ahead. The distance to the funeral home wasn't far, but it was facing what she had to do once there that made her sick to her stomach.

She got to the funeral home without incident, but the moment she parked and got out, her legs began to shake.

"I can do this," she mumbled and kept moving forward.

Evelyn Harper must have been watching for her, because she opened the door to greet her.

"Good evening, Dori," Evelyn said and gave her a brief hug. "How are you doing?"

Dori shrugged as tears welled.

"Are you ready?" Evelyn asked.

Dori nodded.

"Come this way," Evelyn said, taking her by the arm and leading her into a viewing room.

Dori crossed the threshold, saw the open casket, and stumbled. "Oh Lord," she whispered.

Evelyn stopped. "Would you like to be alone?"

"Yes."

Dori moved toward the casket as Evelyn walked out and closed the door. She looked at the suit, at the tie, at his hands crossed just above his waist, at the way they'd combed his hair—at everything there was to see until there was nothing left but his face.

He looked like he was sleeping.

Tears rolled as she reached for his hand, but then she flinched. Not only was it stiff, but it was cold—a reminder that he was done with this body.

"Oh, Granddaddy, I am so sad. We are lost without you."

She sat down in a chair beside the casket and ran her fingers along the satin-like finish on the cherrywood, like Grandy's dining table and chairs. But then she remembered that they were gone too.

She cried until her eyes were swollen and her head was throbbing in rhythm with her heartbeat before she made herself get up. This time when she looked, she looked straight at his face, as if willing him to open his eyes and acknowledge her presence.

"I know about all the money you left for us. You saved me when Mother and Daddy died. You saved me again when Grandy died, and you didn't throw me away when I got pregnant with Luther. Now you've saved us again by making sure we aren't homeless and penniless. You were the best grandfather ever. I won't let Luther forget you. I promise."

She took a deep breath, wiped her hands across her cheeks, and walked out of the viewing room and into the office across the lobby, where Evelyn was sitting. Her eyes burned when she blinked and her mouth was dry, but she was almost done.

"He looks fine…just fine, Mrs. Harper. I can't thank you enough for all you did."

Evelyn Harper politely ignored Dori's appearance as she opened a desk drawer and pulled out an envelope.

"It was our honor. I need to give you this. It was in the pocket of Meeker's blue jeans."

Dori took the envelope and quickly opened it. A long, flat key fell out in her hand.

"It looks like a key to a safety-deposit box," Evelyn said. "I thought you might need it."

Dori was stunned that he'd thought to take it with him when they'd left the house. She'd have to let Peanut Butterman know.

"Thank you very much," Dori said.

Evelyn nodded. "So, do we have your approval to open the viewing room to the public?"

"Yes," Dori said, then slipped the key into her pocket and walked out.

The drive back to Johnny's house was anticlimactic. She'd seen Granddaddy's body and faced the fear without losing her mind. By the time she pulled up into the drive and killed the engine, she was numb.

Oblivious to the fact that the porch light was out, she got out of the car with her feet dragging and then sensed movement in the dark and looked up.

Johnny walked out of the shadows.

She paused.

"He's in bed asleep," he said, answering her question about the baby before she could ask.

She shuddered.

He opened his arms.

She walked into his embrace and closed her eyes.

"You did it, girl," he said softly and cupped the back of her head with one hand and slid the other one across her back.

He didn't want to feel a connection with her, but he did; whether it was empathy or something more didn't matter. For as long as she needed him, he was here.

Dori shivered again.

"That was hard," she whispered.

"I know," Johnny said.

Then she remembered he'd buried his mother. Yet another road he'd already traveled before her. She sighed. It felt good—too good—standing there like that. She pushed away from his embrace and then handed him his car keys.

Johnny saw tears on her cheeks, but her voice was steady.

"Thank you again for saving me," she said. "I'd better get inside."

He pocketed the keys and led the way, then locked the door behind them as she headed down the hall to her baby. The sound of her footsteps faded as she entered her room, but the memory of how she felt in his arms was anything but gone. He looked in on the boys, who were in the kitchen doing homework, and then headed for the shower. Tomorrow would come all too soon.

Dori checked on the baby. He was dry and sound asleep with the little barrier of pillows around him. She sat down in the rocking chair, then got back up again and put the key on the dresser, and then found Butterman's card and sent him a text.

I have the safety-deposit key. Call me
tomorrow.

She hit Send and then laid out a new nightgown for
later and left the bedroom. She could hear the shower
running as she walked down the hall and thought it
was the boys until she walked into the kitchen and
saw them at the table with their schoolwork. She eyed
the bottles of Pepsi from Ruby Dye and then glanced
at the boys.

"How's it going?" she asked.

"Good," Marshall said and kept working on his math.

Beep didn't have homework, but he liked to read and
had his nose in a book.

"Are you guys allowed to have pop before bedtime?"

"No," Beep said. "I would pee the bed."

She gave up the idea of a Pepsi.

Marshall looked up.

"You can have one. Johnny does. We don't mind. I
don't like to sleep in pee and Beep only has one pair of
pajamas. Me and him agreed we don't want pop at night
until he's a big boy."

Dori smiled. The boys were adorable.

She got a glass, filled it with ice, and then poured in
the Pepsi. She took her first sip while it was still fizzing
because she liked the tickle of it on her nose. The kick
of caffeine was welcome as the cold drink slid down
her throat.

"Cookies don't make me pee the bed," Beep said.

Dori stifled a grin and looked at Marshall, who
shrugged.

She got the sack of cookies. "To make homework

better," she said, giving them one apiece and then sitting down in one of the chairs with her drink.

Johnny walked in as Beep was swallowing his first bite.

"Hey, can I join this party?" he asked.

Marshall grinned. "I'm almost done, Johnny. Just one more problem."

"Good for you," Johnny said, making himself a glass of Pepsi too and sitting down across the table from Dori.

She pushed the bag of cookies toward him.

He took two, then leaned back in the chair and took a bite. "These are *good*," he said, somewhat surprised.

Dori nodded and took another drink.

"I might need a swallow of water," Beep said as he polished off the last of his cookie.

"You can have a drink of my Pepsi," Johnny said.

Marshall looked up and frowned. "I don't like to sleep in pee."

Beep looked longingly at the glass. "I'll only have one little sip."

Marshall sighed and went back to his problem.

Beep took one small sip and then wiped his mouth with the back of his hand. "That's good stuff. Some hair of the dog," he announced.

Dori's eyes widened.

Johnny frowned. "Let me guess. You've been watching old gangster movies at Miss Jane's again."

Beep nodded. "Belly up to the bar, boys. The drinks are on me," he added.

Dori burst out laughing.

Johnny shrugged. "I know. Who knew Miss Jane had such a fondness for gangster movies? She doesn't seem the type."

"I'm through!" Marshall announced.

"Good job," Johnny said. "Both of you get your baths and into bed. I'll come tuck you in shortly, and remember, be quiet down the hall. The baby's sleeping."

They tiptoed out of the room.

"They are adorable, Johnny. I hope you know that," Dori said.

"I know. I love them to the moon and back," he said softly and then gathered up the sack of cookies and his empty glass and headed for the sink. "Let me get the boys through in the bathroom, and then it's all yours," he said and left the kitchen.

She killed time cleaning up after their snacks and tried not to think about Granddaddy lying cold and alone in a cherrywood box. Even if his spirit wasn't there anymore, it was all there was left of the man she'd loved. It hurt her heart.

Her steps were slow as she picked up a couple of baby bottles and filled them with milk, then set them in the refrigerator for later. This was the second night in the Pines' home and nothing was routine, nor should it be. She was simply passing through their lives.

She glanced out the window into the dark and then on impulse walked out onto the back porch, curious to see what night was like on this side of town.

Lack of burning streetlights made the stars brighter and the night sky seem closer. She saw lights on in different houses around the neighborhood and one with the garage door open, the house lit up in every room including the garage. She could hear the faint sounds of music coming from there and guessed by the number of cars parked nearby, someone was having a party.

It was a vivid reminder of how the world went on, regardless of death and loss.

She heard an owl and a hissing cat, and then a dog barked sharply, as if announcing both his presence and the parameters of his territory. She saw a shadow move between where she was standing and the house next door. When she couldn't figure out if it was man or beast, she decided she'd been outside long enough.

She went back inside, locking the door behind her, then gave the kitchen one last look and turned out the lights as she headed down the hall. The bathroom door was ajar and the room was dark. After checking on Luther to make sure he was still sleeping, she got her nightgown and headed for the bathroom.

Johnny had laid out a clean towel and washcloth for her and wiped up the floor. The idea of taking a long, hot soaking bath was enticing, but she opted for expediency and chose the shower.

The water was lukewarm, but she didn't care. She showered quickly and dried off fast before putting on her nightgown. After brushing her teeth, she opened the door and turned out the light.

The hall was dark, but the night-light in the bathroom shed just enough light for her to get back to her room, and the dim lamplight was kind to the shabby furnishings. She got into bed, pulled Luther's blanket up over his shoulders, then stretched out beside him and closed her eyes. The knot in her stomach tightened as Granddaddy's face slid through her mind.

"Lord, help me through this," Dori whispered and fell asleep to the sound of Luther Joe sucking his thumb.

—⁓—

Across town, Pansy Jones stood at her living room window, looking across the street at the blackened skeleton of what was left of Meeker Webb's house and reliving what she'd done. No matter how many ways she tried to justify it, she failed in her Christian duty and was blaming it all on Bart. This whole mess was his fault.

And when she heard his footsteps coming up the hall, she rolled her eyes. He was obviously ready for bed, which meant he wanted his sixty seconds of sex so he could sleep. The sound of those plodding steps grated on her last nerve, as did the bellow that followed.

"Pansy! I'm ready for bed."

She turned and yelled back at him. "I'm not in the mood to pretend I enjoy your 'wham, bam, thank you, ma'am' sorry excuse for sex, so you might as well go on to bed without me."

Bart's mouth dropped. "You cursed."

She rolled her eyes. "You'd make a preacher curse. Go away, Bart. I'm not in a very good mood, and you're not making it better."

He walked off, mumbling about wifely duties, which she promptly ignored. She needed to figure out how to put herself back in good standing in the community. She went to the kitchen to make a cup of tea and then sat down at the table while waiting for the microwave timer to go off.

Right now Dori Grant was everybody's tragic heroine, living in the same house with a boy from the other side of the tracks who'd become Blessings's knight in shining armor. And none of this would be happening if she had ignored Bart and done what she thought was right. Trouble was, she couldn't figure out how to fix her reputation unless she destroyed theirs first.

———∿∿———

In Oneida, which was the next town over, word was spreading about the tragedy in Blessings. Lots of people had known Meeker Webb from his days as a roofer and were saddened to learn of his fate.

But there was one man in Oneida who was hearing the news for the first time and wondering about the dead man's granddaughter, the girl he'd fucked outside the high school gym. Frankie Ricks would never have remembered her name except that the next time he saw her she'd been big as a barrel with his kid. Now he was wondering if he might capitalize on it. He kept staring at a spot on the wall of his apartment and thinking that if the girl got anything in her grandfather's will, he might reconsider his options.

———∿∿———

Dori woke up about four in the morning to change Luther and give him a bottle. Her eyes burned from lack of sleep and so much crying, but there was a smile on her face as they played "catch Mama's finger" while he drank. She would wiggle her finger just out of reach of his hand, and he would grab for it over and over until she'd relent and lower it just enough for him to reach. When Luther finally caught it, his eyebrows arched in surprise as Dori chuckled.

"You surprised yourself, didn't you?" she whispered.

By the time she got him back to sleep, it was nearly

five. She went to the bathroom and then crawled back in bed, but she slept lightly, half listening for the family to start moving around.

It was the boys' footsteps running in the hall and Johnny's quick caution to be quiet that alerted her to the fact they were up. Luther was sleeping soundly, so she got out of bed and dressed, then headed for the kitchen, hoping she could help in some way.

Johnny was at the stove, stirring another pot of oatmeal, which made her wonder if they always ate it because it was less expensive than eggs and bacon or because it was the quickest solid meal to fix.

"Good morning," Dori said.

Johnny turned at the sound of her voice and smiled.

"Hey, you," he said softly. "I heard you two up earlier this morning. Did you get any sleep?"

"Yes, I'm fine. Is there anything I can do to help?"

"You can get bowls and spoons for me."

She moved around the room without hesitation and gathered up what he needed and set them within reach.

"You're pretty handy to have around," Johnny said.

She glanced up at him and then quickly looked away, telling herself he meant nothing by it. He was just a really nice guy. She wished she'd gotten to know him better when they'd been in school and then was shocked that had even crossed her mind. She'd already paid a high price for poor judgement.

"I can make the boys' lunches if you haven't already done that," she offered.

"Ham and cheese with mayo for Marshall. Ham and cheese with butter for Beep. Two ham and cheese with mustard for me. Their lunch boxes are on the back counter by the washer and dryer. Marshall's is *Duck Dynasty*. Beep has Iron Man. Mine is red Tupperware."

"Got it," she said and got to work.

The boys came in for breakfast, saw what she was doing, and made a beeline for her.

"I like mayonnaise," Marshall said.

Dori smiled. "I know. Johnny told me."

"I *don't* like maynaze," Beep drawled.

"You want butter, right?"

He grinned. "Yep. I'm a butter man."

She laughed again, which made Johnny stop and look—really look—at her. She was so pretty when she smiled. Then he shook off the thought and started dishing up oatmeal.

"Can I have raisins?" Marshall asked.

"May I, and, yes," Johnny muttered.

"I don't want no raisins," Beep said.

Johnny stopped and turned to the boys.

"Guys! Every morning I make oatmeal. Every morning you both feel the need to remind me how you like to eat it. I have a real good memory. You really don't have to tell me every time."

Marshall shrugged. "Okay. Whatever."

"I sure don't want no raisins," Beep mumbled.

Johnny shook his head. "You like grapes. You should like raisins."

"Why?" Beep asked.

"Raisins are just grapes with most of the juice dried out of them."

"I don't like dried grapes," Beep stated.

"I think you've lost that battle," Dori said.

"That happens a lot around here," Johnny said and put

the bowls on the table. "Eat up, guys. Today's Friday. Let's make it a good one."

He dipped oatmeal for Dori and paused.

"Would you like some raisins in yours?"

She took the bowl out of his hands.

"I don't like no dried grapes either," she said and took her bowl to the table with Johnny's laughter following like a warm breath on the back of her neck.

Chapter 12

DORI WAS DOING LAUNDRY AND LUTHER WAS ON A pallet in the living room, waving fat baby fists at the spinning ceiling fan, when Peanut Butterman called.

She saw the caller ID and walked away from the noise of the washer and dryer to answer.

"Hello."

"Dori, it's me. I got your text about the deposit box key. Where on earth did you find it?"

"Mrs. Harper at the funeral home gave it to me. She said it was in Granddaddy's jeans."

"Your granddaddy, God rest his soul, was really thinking ahead to take that with him when you were running from the fire. Listen, I have some things to bring over when I pick up the key. Is it okay to come by now?"

"Yes, sir," Dori said. "I'll be watching for you."

"Is your little guy awake?" he asked.

Dori walked toward the living room to check and saw Luther waving at the fan and smiled.

"Yes, sir. At the moment he seems to be having a conversation with the ceiling fan."

Peanut laughed. "See you soon."

When he disconnected, Dori went down the hall to the bathroom to brush her hair and freshen up.

A couple of minutes later, she put down the hairbrush and looked at her reflection. Something was the matter with her hair. There were dry patches that frizzed up no matter how long she brushed—probably burned by sparks from the fire. There were dark shadows under her eyes, and she knew she was still too thin, but there was nothing to be done about that, either. After making sure her shirt was still clean, she went back to the living room to check on Luther and was sitting on the floor playing with him when she heard a car. She got up to look and saw two cars instead of one coming up the driveway.

Peanut got out of the first car, with a briefcase and a large sack. The driver in the second car parked, popped the trunk, and got out as Peanut headed to the house.

Dori opened the door as Butterman came up the steps.

"Good morning, Dori! I come bearing gifts. Where's that boy?"

Dori stepped aside as Peanut entered and pointed.

Luther was still in deep conversation with the fan, his gazed fixed, his hands flailing.

Peanut laughed. "Hypnosis! That's a unique way to put them to sleep."

Then the man who'd been driving the other car was now standing on the threshold holding a very large box.

"Where do you want this, Mr. Butterman?"

"Just set it anywhere and then wait for me. I won't be long."

The man grinned at the baby, nodded politely at Dori as he carried the box to an empty space behind the couch, and then made a quick exit.

"What's in that?" Dori asked.

"A collapsible playpen that can double as a baby bed. I had a feeling you might need something like that."

Dori gasped. "Oh, you have no idea! This is wonderful. Thank you so much."

Peanut patted her arm in a fatherly manner.

"You're welcome, dear. If you have a few minutes, we need to talk."

"Yes, sir," she said and sat down on the sofa.

Butterman sat at the other end of the sofa and then seemed to remember he was still holding the sack.

"This is for you. I had my secretary pick it out. It's something for you to wear to the funeral. She checked with Lovey Cooper about the sizes."

Dori opened the bag and pulled out a black-and-white baby-doll dress, black stockings, and black wedge sandals. The outfit was young and stylish but still perfect for a somber event.

Her hands shook as she felt the soft knit fabric. His thoughtfulness was so beyond what she would have expected.

"It's beautiful, and the shoes are perfect. Thank you. Thank you so much, Mr. Butterman."

Peanut smiled. "You're welcome, Dori. I'm pleased that you approve. Now, down to business."

She stood up to get the safety-deposit key from her pocket and handed it to him.

"Thanks," Peanut said. "This will make my job easier. The box has to be opened in front of witnesses and the contents listed and recorded. There's a lot of paperwork attached to the business of dying. Now, let's see…"

Dori watched him shuffling through the papers in his briefcase, and then he paused and handed her a debit card.

"This is from the joint account belonging to you and Meeker. You stated that you had signed the card to write checks on the account, but the debit card for you was never picked up. Even though his estate is in probate, your name on the account does allow you access."

Dori sighed. Now she had access to his money too, when hers ran out.

Peanut handed her an envelope.

"These are some bank checks for you. One is for your personal account. The other is the joint account. You can use those while waiting for your replacement checks to arrive. I gave them this mailing address, although your old address will still be on the checks. You'll have to deal with that later. For now, you should get them within five or six days."

"Thank you. This is so thoughtful," Dori said and laid them in her lap on top of the card.

"And last but not least," he said and handed her a set of car keys, "the car I drove here is a rental. Per your insurance policy, they have to furnish one for you until yours is replaced. That's the beauty of full, comprehensive coverage. I took the liberty of acquiring one for you."

Dori sighed. "This is so thoughtful of you, Mr. Butterman."

Peanut paused in the act of closing up his briefcase to explain.

"My job is rarely pleasant. I'm almost always trying to solve a criminal issue. This is different. This was a tragedy coupled with the legal issues of a good man's passing. I really liked Meeker Webb. I admire your courage, and I'm sincerely honored to get to do this for you."

"Then, thank you," she said, struggling once again not to cry.

He shut his briefcase and stood.

"The gas tank is full. There's a baby seat in the back

for your boy. If you need me, don't hesitate to call. I'll see myself out."

Moments later, he was gone.

Dori got up and locked the door behind him, then laid the checks, the debit card, and the keys on the side table and turned and looked at Luther, who was still mesmerized by the spinning blades.

"You've stared at that thing long enough," she muttered and turned off the fan. She dragged the box with the playpen away from the sofa and tore into it.

Luther squawked, then heard the noise his mother was making and squawked again because he couldn't see her.

"You sure are bad off," she said, laughing as she dragged his pallet out where he could see what she was doing, and then she finished setting up the playpen and put him in it.

The phone had been ringing all day at the Curl Up and Dye. Women who would normally be getting their hair done on other days were all trying to get their appointments changed to today so they'd look good to attend Meeker Webb's funeral tomorrow. It wasn't so much that they'd held Meeker in such high esteem as the fact that they wanted to see if Dori Grant showed up with Johnny Pine.

Ruby was juggling customers without complaint, but there was a bead of sweat on her upper lip and her blond curls were in serious disarray. The twins were working double-time but with less grace. Grumbling was a part of their repertoire, and no one thought too much of it.

Even Mabel Jean was being pushed to take as many manicures as she could squeeze in. The place was full to overflowing, with ladies still sitting up front and waiting to be called back. So when the bell jingled over the front door signaling yet another customer coming in, everyone turned to look.

———⁓———

Dori buckled Luther into the car seat, tucked the blanket around him, and then got into the car. She took a couple of minutes to locate all the controls, then adjusted the seat and the rearview mirror before backing out of the drive.

It felt good to be in control of something, even if it was just a car. She had a baby bottle and extra diapers in the diaper bag and Luther's favorite teething ring, but she was hoping he'd be so interested in his surroundings that he'd be good for the short time she would be at the salon.

As soon as she knew she had wheels, she'd called the Curl Up and Dye to see if Ruby could trim the ends of her hair and get rid of those dry places. She had no idea that her call would put Ruby in a tight spot or that most of the clients in the shop that day were indirectly there because of her.

Upon arrival at the salon, Dori was surprised by the lack of parking and circled the block twice before a spot became empty. She got out with the diaper bag and her purse, unbuckled Luther from the car seat and cradled him in her arms, blanket and all, and walked in.

The women up front stopped talking.

Dori smiled at them as she noticed all the seats were taken.

A couple nodded a hello, others stared, and none of them budged.

Without an empty seat to sit in, Dori shifted the baby to her shoulder and moved back against the wall to wait.

By now, the customers already in the stylist chairs had spotted them and chatter inside the shop dwindled to almost nothing.

It was the sudden lack of noise that made Ruby pause and then turn around to see what was going on. When she saw Dori and the baby standing, and five women seated and looking at her with unconcealed disdain, the hair crawled on the back of her neck.

"Excuse me a minute," she told her client and marched to the front of her store and took Dori by the arm.

"Dori, honey, I'm so sorry there are no more empty seats up here, but there's a spot in the back. You'll be up next."

The other women had been waiting for some time and began to fuss and whisper among themselves when it appeared the girl was going ahead of them.

Ruby turned around and gave them a look that silenced the whispers before she led her toward one of the dryers.

"Sit here, honey. We don't use the dryers on these chairs as much as blow-dryers these days." She saw Luther peeking at her from under his blanket, and she lifted it and grinned. "You are such a cutie pie," she said and poked her finger lightly at his belly.

Luther immediately giggled, and the sound carried through the salon.

Ruby poked his belly again and he giggled even louder.

Now everyone was turning to look. The sound of a baby's laughter was a hard thing to ignore.

"He is so darling," Vera said.

Dori smiled. "He likes that game. Granddaddy used to play that with him."

Ruby sighed. "I'm sorry, honey. I had no idea."

"Oh no, I'm glad he's happy," Dori said.

Ruby patted her knee. "Give me a couple of minutes, and I'll get you in and out before he loses his sense of humor. How's that?"

"Perfect," Dori said and settled back to wait.

A few moments later, the lady in Ruby's chair got up and began gathering her things and walked straight to where Dori was sitting.

"Honey, my name is Rachel Goodhope. I run the bed and breakfast, and I wanted to give you my condolences. I know eventually you'll figure out what you're going to do, but if you find yourself in need of a place to stay for a short while, give me a call. I'm rarely booked solid and the cost would be on me."

"Thank you, Mrs. Goodhope. That is a very generous offer, but I think Luther and I are going to be okay. A friend from high school has kindly taken us into his home. It will take a while for everything to go through court, but eventually I will find Luther and me a new home."

Everyone heard what she said. The fact that she had spoken of moving herself and her baby away from Johnny Pine didn't fit the gossip.

Rachel smiled and then cupped Luther's face.

"He is a beautiful boy. You must be so proud."

"Yes, ma'am, I am, and thank you," Dori said.

Rachel waved as she went up front to pay, and then she was gone.

"You're next, Dori. Into the chair with you," Ruby said.

Mabel Jean came out of the workroom and saw Dori trying to maneuver the baby around the cape Ruby was fastening around her neck and hurried over.

"Hey, honey, why don't you let me hold this little chunk while Ruby gets you fixed up? I don't have any kids, but I sure wish I did."

Mabel Jean scooped Luther up and into her arms. He took a look at her, popped his thumb in his mouth, but kept his eyes on Dori.

"We'll make this quick in case he decides to complain," Ruby said. "Now tell me what we're going to do here."

Dori ran her fingers through her long, dark hair and then grabbed one of the places where it felt dry and frizzled.

"There are these dry places that stick out like fuzz. They weren't there before the fire, and I didn't notice…" Her voice broke, and then she took a deep breath and started over. "It feels burned, so I guess it happened the night of the fire. I don't remember much after Granddaddy died, so I could have been on fire myself and wouldn't have felt it. Luther wouldn't stop screaming, and everyone was gone except the firemen, then Johnny Pine walked up and took him out of my arms. Luther likes men, you know, because Granddaddy took care of him every day I was at work. He took one look at Johnny and laid his head on Johnny's shoulder and closed his eyes. I figured if Luther was okay with him, then I should be too."

There was a lump in Ruby's throat as she ran her fingers through Dori's thick hair.

"I think you made a wise choice," she said. "Now then, do you want length cut off or just trim the burned ends?"

"I think just the trim. I don't have time for a hairstyle these days, and I need it long enough to put in a ponytail."

Ruby led her to the shampoo station and then a few minutes later back to her chair, and she began cutting.

Meanwhile Mabel Jean was taking Luther on a tour of the shop and talking to him in a sweet, singsong voice, and for the first time since his birth, he was being presented up close and personal to some of Blessings's residents. The consensus was final. He was a darling baby, even pretty some said as they touched his soft baby curls and took note of how sweet and clean he smelled. Dori didn't know it, but her little man was about to sway more public opinion her way.

Ruby was finished within fifteen minutes, complete with trim and a blow-dry, leaving Dori's hair in soft, wavy curls.

"Luther has your hair, doesn't he?" Ruby said as she put down the brush and hair dryer and gave the style a quick spritz of spray to hold it in place.

Dori nodded. "My hair and eyes, and my daddy's name," she said softly. "How much do I owe you?"

"Not a thing," Ruby said. "I'm happy to help in any way I can. If you need help with the baby tomorrow during the services, we'll be there. Just send someone to find us, and we'll be happy to hold him."

Dori hugged Ruby's neck.

"Your kindness is more appreciated than you can know," she said, then opened up her arms as Mabel Jean handed the baby back. "Thank you for the help too."

"It was totally my pleasure and ditto to what Ruby said. I'll gladly do it again tomorrow."

Dori nodded. "I appreciate your offer."

She slung her purse and diaper bag on her shoulder, cradled the baby in her arms, and walked out the door.

Ruby stood in the middle of the salon, watching until she saw them drive away, and then put her hands on her hips and gave everyone in the salon a look.

"Amazing young lady, isn't she? Sweet baby, isn't he? Anyone want to talk ugly about them again, you won't be doing it in here. Are we clear on that?"

Silence.

Ruby glanced at the women waiting.

"I've lost track of who's next. If you can make that decision without a fight, come on back," she said and then smiled at the lady who got up and walked toward her. "Morning, Sue."

"Morning, Sister," she said.

Ruby smiled as she whipped out a fresh cape. She liked it when people in town called her by her nickname. It made her feel like she belonged to a real family. Even if they were a little hateful now and then, what family wasn't?

"Take a seat and we'll get you all fluffed up."

Johnny came back from the job site at noon, hauling the dozer. He'd already called his boss to tell him the hydraulic system was leaking.

Mr. Clawson was disgusted by the news, but not at Johnny, as he unloaded the dozer and moved it into the repair bay.

"Did it go out all of a sudden, or could you feel it going loose?" Clawson asked as Johnny killed the engine and jumped down.

"I think it blew a seal somewhere," Johnny said. "It seemed okay one minute and then it wasn't and there was fluid spray all over this side here."

Clawson saw it and shrugged. "I guess I can't complain. It's almost as old as you are. Listen, the other two dozers and drivers are on jobs, and this one's gonna be down. Why don't you call it a day and go on home? We'll finish up work on that job site first thing Monday."

"You sure?" Johnny asked. "I don't mind helping here if you need me."

"I'm sure," he said. "I have mechanics. They can earn their pay today."

"Okay. See you Monday, then," Johnny said and headed for the car.

It wasn't often he got to go home in the middle of the day, and he welcomed the downtime to catch up on some other things. Dori was on his mind as he started home. He thought about calling her to see if she needed anything and then decided he'd find out when he got there and go out again later if need be.

When he turned down Admiral and saw the strange car in his driveway, he frowned, wondering who else was there. He parked on the other side of it and got out, then headed to the house.

～

Dori was in the kitchen when she heard someone at the front door. Then she heard a key in the lock and headed to the living room with the dishrag still in her hand and saw Johnny.

"Hey," she said. "Is everything all right? Are you sick?"

The answer was on the tip of his tongue, and then he saw her—really saw her—standing barefoot with her hair down and framing her face in long, soft curls. She was wearing a pink T-shirt and blue jeans and the rag in her hand was dripping water, and he forgot what he was going to say.

"Johnny?"

He jerked. "Oh. Sorry. I, uh…what did you say?"

"You're home, and I asked if you were sick."

"Oh, right. No, I'm fine. Hydraulics went out on the dozer. Mr. Clawson sent me home for the rest of the day." Then he saw the playpen and Luther in it asleep and sucking his thumb.

"Mr. Butterman brought it," Dori said. "Did you eat yet?"

He shook his head and held up his Tupperware container.

"Then come in the kitchen. I just made myself a sandwich. I'll make you something to drink," she said.

He followed her, still shocked by what he was feeling.

"Whose car is that?" he asked as he opened his lunch box and took out the food.

"It's a rental. Mr. Butterman brought it too. He said it was a benefit from the insurance coverage Granddaddy had. I can use it at their expense until they issue the money for me to replace the one that burned."

"Nice," Johnny said, but his mind was racing.

Did that mean she would be leaving soon? He wasn't going to ask, because it might seem like he wanted to be rid of her when he'd just realized that wasn't entirely true.

"Is iced tea okay?" Dori asked.

"Uh, yes, thank you," he said, sitting down and beginning to unwrap his food.

She set his drink in front of him and then took a seat on the other side of the table.

"Want a chip?" she asked as she pushed a bag of potato chips his way.

He realized she'd bought some groceries on her own, and he helped himself to a handful. This was the first time they'd been together like this without the boys. It was like being on an almost date without his chaperones. He wanted to know her, to know about her, and he took a chance.

"Can I ask you something?" he asked.

She looked up and met his gaze. There was a long moment of silence and then she nodded.

"What do you want out of life?"

She paused, a little surprised by the question. "I want to be happy, and I want Luther to grow up to be a good man. After I took the GED, I began taking college courses online to design websites. I am…was getting pretty good at it."

He was both surprised and pleased by her answer. Like him, she wanted more than to settle for where life had thrust her.

"You can get right back in it as soon as you get a computer, right?"

She nodded.

"That's a very creative outlet and a great avenue for income," he said.

Dori smiled, pleased that he didn't make fun of the idea, and took another bite of her sandwich.

Johnny put his elbows on the table and leaned forward, his food forgotten. "Can I ask you another question?"

She tensed. "You can ask."

Johnny heard the hesitance in her voice and panicked. He didn't want to hurt her feelings. "I don't know what you think I was going to ask, but it had nothing to do with your privacy. I would never presume to—"

"I'm sorry," she said. "Ever since Luther, I have this big thing hanging over my head... It's like being shot at. After it happens once, you find yourself ducking for the rest of your life."

Johnny reached across the table and took her hand. "I'm sorry. I don't know what happened between you and your boyfriend to cause the separation, but I would never—" He stopped, shocked by her reaction to what he'd said.

She had doubled her hand into a fist, and there was a muscle jerking at the side of her mouth. "There was no boyfriend, and that's more than I've ever said to anyone."

When she went to pull her hand away, he grabbed it and held on.

Dori looked up. His face was a blur. She was crying and hadn't even known it. She tried to pull her hand away again, but he wouldn't let go. It was the firm, steady grip that finally broke her—a feeling that no matter what she said, he wouldn't turn away.

"I couldn't tell. Granddaddy would have killed him."

Johnny flinched. The look on her face was one of

such devastation that he knew what had happened without hearing the word.

"Where is he now?" Johnny asked.

"I don't know and I don't care," Dori whispered. "I went to a dance at the school gym. There were a few people there I didn't know—party crashers I guess— and I think someone slipped something in my drink. I got dizzy. Someone took me outside to get some air. I don't remember a lot except his face and me telling him no, telling him to stop." Her shoulders slumped. "But he didn't. And now I have Luther. I don't understand why I had to go through all that to have him, but I know with everything I am that he was supposed to be mine."

Rage swept through him so fast it took his breath away. He kept looking at her, imagining her fear, hearing her cries for help while no one came.

"Do you know his name?"

"Just his first name," she said.

"Does he live here in Blessings?" he asked.

"I don't know where he lives," Dori said. She slipped her hand out from beneath his grasp and covered her face.

Johnny's voice was so soft, she almost didn't hear it.

"The son of a bitch," he whispered. "Why didn't you tell? Why would you let everyone in Blessings believe the worst of you?"

She looked up. "Granddaddy would have gone looking for him with a gun. Someone would have died, and someone else would have gone to jail. Either way, it would have made my life worse and it wouldn't have changed a thing. It's always the girl's fault, Johnny.

Don't you know that? I didn't want my baby to grow up knowing he was born from an act of violence. It's better people think that it was me being foolish. I won't have him thinking he was a mistake."

Johnny got up from the table and dumped his food. He couldn't swallow. When Dori followed him to the cabinet, he took the plate out of her hands and pulled her into his arms.

She stiffened.

"It's a hug, nothing more."

His arms were so strong, and she could feel his heartbeat against her cheek. Before she knew it, she was sobbing; fifteen long months of shock, horror, and misery came bubbling up, and Johnny didn't let go.

Chapter 13

DORI HAD MOVED THE PLAYPEN INTO HER BEDROOM for the night and was giving Luther a bottle. The rocker creaked every now and then, but Luther's eyes were nearly closed. The milk in his mouth was running down the side of his cheek. He was already too far gone to swallow.

She set the bottle aside, put him on her shoulder, and began to pat his little back in a steady, rhythmic thump as she continued to rock. One good burp and she'd put him down.

She glanced at the clock.

Johnny had been gone for hours. He would have picked up his brothers at school a long time ago, and she thought they would have come straight home. But they hadn't.

She was a little worried about what she'd told Johnny. He knew her secret now, and while he seemed very supportive, she was afraid that he'd come to judge her. She wouldn't stay here if that happened. She couldn't. No matter what kind of hardship it caused.

Luther grunted and shifted uncomfortably in her arms. The gas on his belly was hurting, but she just kept patting and rocking.

She was dreading the funeral tomorrow and at the same time was so ready for it to be over. They were serving a meal at the church before the service, and even though they didn't have any family left, her grandfather had made a lot of friends during his lifetime. They would be there and so would she.

Luther finally burped and went limp.

She kissed the side of his cheek, loving the silky-soft feel of baby skin on her lips, and then laid him down in the playpen and covered him up. Bless Peanut Butterman for his thoughtfulness. She paused to make sure Luther was settled and then left him, confident he would be safe in the new bed.

A car passed by out on the street with a radio playing so loud, she could hear the bass thumping from inside the house and hoped it didn't wake Luther.

Tonight they were eating the ribs and baked beans Ruby had brought, and Dori had made potato salad out of the leftover mashed potatoes from last night. When she got to the kitchen, she rinsed out the baby's bottle and set it aside to wash with dishes later, then leaned against the cabinet as she looked around the room. It felt like she'd lived a lifetime in the short two days she'd been here. The house was even becoming familiar.

The blue and white floor tiles were clean. The white walls were a little dingy and could have done with a coat of paint. The pale yellow oilcloth on the old wooden table was a bright note in the room, and the pendulum tail on the red rooster clock was still swinging, ticking off time.

It was almost 5:00 p.m. She couldn't imagine what was keeping Johnny and the boys. Still, they'd have to show up sometime, so she began to set the table.

Johnny was still in shock. He didn't know how to cope with the revelation of Dori's story without wanting to hit something. He understood why she hadn't told Meeker Webb. She was right in believing that Meeker wouldn't have stopped until he'd made the man pay. What Dori didn't know was that Johnny felt the same way, even though she wasn't his to protect.

They had not discussed the funeral tomorrow beyond the fact that she would go. But after what she told him, there wasn't a way in hell he was going to let her face her grandfather's funeral alone. The gossips were already working their jaws about her presence in this house. Accompanying her to the funeral couldn't make anything worse.

This afternoon, he'd spent money he didn't need to spend on three dress shirts for him and the boys. He already had a good pair of dress jeans, and the boys would have to wear school jeans. They wouldn't be dressed fancy, but they wouldn't embarrass her, either. What they all needed were haircuts, but when he'd called the Curl Up and Dye to ask if they had an opening, he'd been told no. He started to hang up when Ruby Dye picked up the phone.

"Johnny Pine?"

"Yes, ma'am?"

"I thought I heard Vera say your name. What do you need, son?"

"My brothers and I are taking Dori to the funeral tomorrow. I've been cutting our hair and it looks like it. I was wondering if you had any time this evening after school to trim us up?"

"What time can you be here?" Ruby asked.

"I pick the boys up at three thirty."

"Come straight here afterward. I'll work you in," Ruby said.

"Yes, ma'am, and thank you," Johnny said.

He didn't know what three haircuts were going to cost him, but it didn't matter. He had a little money socked away for hard times. He'd make it work.

He caught Miss Jane at school so she'd know he was taking the boys, and then he waited near her van for them to come out. When they saw him, they began to run, excited to be going home early with him.

Beep came to a sliding halt at Johnny's feet a few seconds after Marshall's arrival.

"Yay!" Beep said. "We get to go home with you."

"Can we get ice cream?" Marshall asked.

"Let's get in the car first, and I'll explain," he said.

By the time the boys figured out there was no early playtime at home and it was haircuts instead of ice cream, they were verbally expressing their disapproval.

"Look, guys. This isn't punishment. Tomorrow is the funeral for Dori's grandfather, and we're gonna go with her to the church. We want to look our best, understand?"

"Oh," Marshall said and leaned back in the seat. "Will it be like Mama's funeral?"

Johnny sighed. Nothing would be like that funeral. One spray of flowers, no other family, and a few of the people she got high with.

"Bigger," he said shortly.

Beep was confused. Church was just a building to him. "Is Mama gonna be there?" he asked.

Johnny stifled a groan. "No, buddy, Mama's not here anymore. She's in heaven."

Beep's shoulders slumped. "Okay."

Marshall patted his brother's leg. "It's okay, Beep. Mama wasn't around all that much anyway, remember?"

Johnny sighed. Out of the mouths of babes. "We'll get ice cream another day, I promise," he said.

"When we get haircuts, can I get a 'hawk?" Marshall asked.

Johnny frowned. "No, we're not shaving heads in this family. You can comb it like that, but that's enough."

Marshall nodded. He hadn't expected a yes, but he'd had to ask.

Then Beep had a question too. "Hey, Johnny?"

Johnny glanced up in the rearview mirror. "What, buddy? And stop picking your nose."

Beep took his finger out of his nose and wiped it on his jeans. "Are they gonna cut my hair better than you do?"

Johnny grinned. "I sure hope so."

"Okay," Beep said, then leaned back against the seat and closed his eyes.

Johnny could only imagine what he was thinking, then let it slide as he turned down Main Street and parked a half block away from the Curl Up and Dye.

"Let's go, guys. And please behave. We want to leave a good impression on people wherever we are, remember?"

"I 'member," Beep said. "I won't pick my nose."

"Much appreciated," Johnny muttered, and then they got out and headed down the street—one very tall young man and two mini-versions of the same, all with the same stride in their walk and the same expressions on their faces. It was as if they'd been born leading with their chins, expecting the worst out of life.

Ruby Dye was dead on her feet. Vesta was in the back, washing towels, and Vera was in the bathroom. Mabel Jean had gone to the Beauty Supply for extra shop supplies, and Ruby's last appointment had been gone exactly three minutes when the bell jingled over the door.

She turned around and smiled. The Pines had arrived.

"Come on back," she said.

Johnny ushered them through the salon with a hand on each shoulder.

"I really appreciate this," he said.

"It is my pleasure," Ruby said. "And what a coincidence that you came in on Family Special Day. Today, all haircuts are half-price."

Johnny breathed a sigh of relief.

"That's good to hear," he said. "Money's always tight, which is why I'm the barber at home."

Ruby smiled and patted her chair.

"Who wants to be first?"

Beep's hand shot into the air.

"Me! Me! And I won't pick my nose."

Johnny sighed.

"Thank you for that info, Beep." Ruby chuckled as she slid a booster seat into the chair.

Johnny helped him up into the seat, still careful not to squeeze the ribs, and removed the mask for his nose.

Ruby pointed to the empty chairs at Vesta's and Vera's stations.

"You guys can sit there and watch."

Ruby eyed the little spots growing back in on the back of Beep's head, where the hair had been cut away, and was horrified all over again that something that simple had caused such a horrible incident.

"We're just trimming you guys up, right?"

"Right," Johnny said.

She combed through Beep's hair to check length and the way the hair grew, and then she got to work. As soon as she'd finished, she moved him to the shampoo station and washed out the bits of hair, then used the blow-dryer to dry it.

The minute the air blew across Beep's face, he closed his eyes and hunkered down.

"Is that too hot?" Ruby asked.

"I don't like it," Beep said.

Ruby turned it on low.

"Is that better?"

"Yeah," Beep said.

"Yes, ma'am," Johnny corrected.

"Yeah, ma'am," Beep echoed.

Ruby grinned. The kid was adorable.

A few minutes later, she traded Beep for Marshall.

"And you're Marshall, right?"

"Yes, ma'am," he said and flashed a quick grin.

She looked at Johnny and rolled her eyes.

"Lord, Lord, this one's gonna be a heartbreaker."

Johnny grinned as Marshall blushed. Ruby caped him up, then ran the comb through his hair. As she did, Marshall looked in the mirror in front of him and caught her eye.

"Uh, ma'am?"

"What, honey?"

"Don't cut too much off. I like to wear my hair in a 'hawk."

"Will do," she said and patted his shoulder. "Trust

me. I'm a fan of the 'hawk myself, but not the buzzed kind. How about you?"

"Yes, ma'am. Pines don't buzz their hair," he said.

Johnny couldn't look at Marshall without a lump in his throat. He'd never thought about the bond between them so much until Beep got hurt, and now it was all he thought about. The boys were his life, but as Ruby just reminded him, they would grow up and be gone. Then where would he be?

He thought of Dori again and willed himself not to care. He was only helping, not getting attached to someone who would likely never trust another man for as long as she lived.

Ruby went through the same routine with Marshall and then got Johnny in the chair. His hair was just as thick and just as black as the boys', and it had the same little cowlick in the crown.

"Anything special here?" she asked.

Johnny met her gaze in the mirror.

"Just make me presentable. I don't want to embarrass Dori."

"I can do that," Ruby said and got down to business.

When she'd finished, they looked like three versions of the same person—small, middle-sized, and full-grown—and all of them lookers.

"That does it," Ruby said and glanced up at the clock. It was a quarter to five.

"How much do I owe you?" Johnny said as he pulled out his wallet.

"Family special—eighteen dollars for the trio."

Johnny took a twenty-dollar bill out of his wallet and handed it over.

"Thank you for taking us at such short notice," he said.

"Follow me to the front and I'll get you your change."

"No, ma'am, you keep it, and I'm sorry it's not more," he said, and then they were gone.

Vesta and Vera came out of the workroom, grinning from ear to ear. "We heard everything. You weren't running any family specials. You're a pushover, Sister, and we love you for it. As for those guys, they're adorable. And that Johnny…do you think he likes Dori Grant?"

Ruby shrugged.

Vesta stared off into space.

"I think he does. I wish they could get together somehow. It's like they sort of need each other. Know what I mean?"

"You don't hook up with someone because of necessity," Vera stated.

"I don't know why not," Vesta argued. "These days some people do it for no reason at all."

Ruby sighed. She'd had enough of customers and arguing and haircuts.

"We don't have any more appointments, and unless you two want to stay here and close on your own, I'm shutting this place down."

The back door opened and Mabel Jean came in, loaded with sacks.

"Help," she cried.

They ran to relieve her of the supplies and began putting them up.

"That does it," Ruby said and headed to the front of the shop and turned the Open sign to Closed.

She began counting the money in the till to deposit in the bank as Mabel Jean swept up the floor.

Vesta put the last of the clean towels in the cubbies, and Vera quickly cleaned out the shampoo bowls.

As soon as Ruby had the money in the deposit bag, they were gone.

Dori was on the verge of being really concerned when the Pines finally came home, and then she realized she'd become far more invested in their world than she had intended.

Two days and now they mattered? She wasn't going to go there, yet when the trio came barreling through the door with big smiles on their faces, her heart skipped a beat.

Yeah, they mattered. But she wouldn't let it be too much.

"Hey, you guys look happy."

"We got haircuts so we'll look nice for the church," Beep announced and then strode down the hall with his backpack to dump it in his room, with Marshall behind him.

Johnny shut the door and turned to face her.

"We're going with you tomorrow. You don't do this alone."

"Oh my God," Dori muttered as her eyes filled with tears. "I've cried more in the last two days than I've cried in my whole life. I didn't expect you to do this, but I won't lie. I am so grateful."

Johnny relaxed, thankful his instincts had been right. Then he held out the sack with their shirts.

"I got dress shirts for us. Should I wash them first, or just iron them and put them on?"

"Give them to me," Dori said, wiping away tears. "We'll wash them first, or they'll feel scratchy from all that sizing. Let me see the tags…oh, good. Wash and wear!"

"I'll put them in the wash," Johnny said.

"Then I'll heat up supper."

"Deal," he said and then looked around. "Hey, where's little man?"

"Asleep in the bedroom. That playpen is a gem. No more fear of rolling off the bed."

"So, let's get this show on the road," he said and headed to the utility room, taking tags and pins out of the shirts as he went.

Supper was long since over. Everyone was in bed, and Johnny couldn't sleep. The three-quarter moon cast a faint glow through the blinds, leaving wafer-thin slices of light on the hardwood floor. The water stain in the corner of his ceiling looked darker. He needed to get up on the roof and see if that place needed patching again. The whole roof needed replacing, but that wasn't going to happen anytime soon.

He heard a noise and raised up, thinking one of the boys must be out of bed, and then heard it again and realized it was outside. He got up, moved the blinds aside to look out, and saw two kids having a fight out in the street.

He grabbed his jeans and put them on, then headed for the front door and walked out onto the porch.

"Hey! Take that crap somewhere else," he yelled.

Suddenly their fight was no longer front and center as they aligned themselves against him.

"Make us!" they yelled.

Johnny came off the porch on the run, and they scattered like quail, going in two different directions. Johnny Pine didn't take shit from anybody, and everyone knew it. They were running for their lives.

"Stupid kids," he muttered as he pivoted in the damp grass and walked back into the house. Now he was even wider awake.

He went into the kitchen to get a drink of water and opted for a piece of pie to go with it, then stood at the living room window and ate it in the dark, just to make sure the two kids were gone for good.

Even after he'd gone back to bed, he couldn't get the image out of his head of Dori being assaulted, begging for help, and no one coming to her aid.

He tried to remember her in high school and, after a few moments, realized she was one of the smart ones, one of the students who tutored others who were in danger of failing. He remembered seeing her before school in empty classrooms, tutoring first one student and then another in different subjects. She'd helped one of the guys in his class pass science so he could graduate.

So, Dori Grant was smart, really smart, and she wanted to design websites. Given half a chance, he was guessing, not only could she do it, but she would also see much success.

Finally, he fell asleep and dreamed he was on the dozer and moving dirt for a new road that ran from his old house, all the way up the hill, across the railroad tracks, and onto the good side of Blessings, straight to a new house sitting empty on a tree-shaded lot. All he had to do was build the road, and when he got there, it would be his.

—◊◊◊—

Dori had also been awakened by the commotion outside and flew out of bed and ran to the window.

She'd heard Johnny yell at the boys fighting in the street, and when she heard them yell back, challenging him, her breath caught in the back of her throat. Were they going to come up and attack him?

All of a sudden, they turned and ran in two different directions, and before she had time to wonder why, he appeared in her line of vision, running across the yard toward the street, wearing nothing but a pair of jeans. Not only had he heard their challenge, but he'd taken it to them. Now they were gone, and he was standing alone in the yard, his hands doubled into fists, his feet apart in a fighting stance, ready to protect what was his.

Dori took a deep, shaky breath, mesmerized by the glow of moonlight painted on the bare skin of his upper body. She watched until he walked back toward the house, then turned and stared at her doorway, listening as he moved through the rooms. She heard him in the kitchen and thought about joining him, then knew that wasn't a good idea. She crawled back into bed and tried to go back to sleep, but her head was filled with so many what-ifs and maybes that she couldn't relax. She dreaded tomorrow in the worst possible way. It would be the last time she would see Granddaddy this side of heaven, and she needed to be strong.

Luther let out a small squeak, but before she had time to get up, she heard him sucking his thumb and closed her eyes.

When she opened them again, it was hours later and

Luther had rolled over onto his back, kicked off his blanket, and filled his diaper. She could smell it.

"Way to wake up your mama," she mumbled and glanced at the clock. It was just after 4:00 a.m. She threw back the covers and got out of bed to change him, then carried him with her to the kitchen to warm up a bottle while he held on to her hair, trying to get it in his mouth.

"No chewing on hair," she said and flipped it over her other shoulder as she put the baby bottle in the microwave.

She stopped it a second before it dinged, so as not to wake anyone up in the back of the house, then popped it into Luther Joe's little mouth and carried him back to the bedroom, cradled in her arms. She carefully shut the door, eased herself down in the rocker, and pushed off with her toe, rocking gently as the baby sucked down the milk one greedy gulp after the other.

Twenty minutes later, he was back in the playpen and she was in bed. She pulled the sheet and blanket up over her shoulders and closed her eyes. Even though a dog barked somewhere nearby, the house was quiet. It never occurred to her to lock her bedroom door or feel afraid. From the moment Johnny had taken her screaming baby out of her arms and brought her home to the scene she'd witnessed only hours earlier, watching him protect all that was his, she felt safe.

And that was Johnny Pine's gift to her.

He'd given her a soft place to fall.

When morning came, Dori didn't speak about the incident during the night and neither did Johnny, and the morning flew by until it was time to go to the church.

She dressed Luther in a blue one-piece outfit with a little yellow-and-brown giraffe embroidered on the front and blue socks on his feet. The black-and-white baby-doll dress she was wearing was so pretty that when she first put it on, her instinct had been to show Granddaddy, and then she stopped, crushed all over again by her loss.

The empire waist on the smocked bodice of the jersey knit fell in loose gathers beneath her breasts, while the hemline ended just above her knees. The black tights made her long legs longer, and the black wedge heels added two inches to her height. Ruby Dye had solved her hair problem, and because the day was calm, she'd chosen to wear it down.

She had the diaper bag packed with everything she might need for the baby. Now all she needed was the baby himself. She wrapped him in a lightweight blanket, slung the diaper bag and her purse over her arm, and out the door they went.

Johnny and the boys were dressed and waiting for her in the living room. He had to admit the boys looked good in the pale blue dress shirts and jeans. Their cowboy boots were worn but shiny. Struck by the solemnity of the event and remembering their own mother's funeral, they were on their best behavior.

When Johnny heard Dori's footsteps, he stood. Then she came into the living room, and he took a slow, deep breath. The only thing he could think was that she was the prettiest thing he'd ever seen.

Dori saw Johnny get out of the chair and for a few moments forgot what she'd been about to say.

The white dress shirt against his sun-browned skin and black hair was a stunning contrast, and the fabric of his Levi's molded to his body and long legs in a perfect fit, leaving nothing to the imagination. The younger boys were mini-versions of him.

"You all look so handsome," Dori said.

"And you look beautiful," he said softly.

"Thank you," Dori said. "Can we drive my rental? The baby seat is already buckled in."

"Absolutely," Johnny said and picked up the car keys from the side table before ushering everyone out the door.

He took the diaper bag and Dori's purse so she could put the baby in the seat in the middle, then the boys got in, one on either side of Luther. When Johnny gave them a look, they quickly put their hands in their laps.

The silence inside the car was telling as they headed for the church. A muscle was jerking at the side of Dori's eye and her hands were shaking. She dreaded this day even worse than the day she'd had to tell her grandfather she was pregnant. When Johnny put a hand on her arm and gave it a quick squeeze, it pulled her out of the moment.

"Thanks," she said.

"I'm sorry this day is going to suck," he said.

She sighed. "So am I."

A few minutes later, they pulled into the parking lot. It was full.

"Oh Lord. Everyone in town must be here," Dori said.

Johnny glanced in the rearview mirror at the boys.

"Remember what we talked about?" he said.

They nodded as he parked, then he gave them one last order. "Okay, we're getting out now. Walk with us. Stay with us. Do not run around anywhere. This is not a time to play."

"We'll be good," Marshall said. "I promise."

"Want to take the car seat inside?" Johnny asked. "Might make it easier for you to keep up with Luther and discourage a lot of people from wanting to pass him around."

"Good idea," Dori said.

"I'll carry him inside in the carrier," Johnny added.

And so they walked into the church, looking like the little family they weren't and upping the gossip meter even more.

Pansy Jones was in the church dining hall, putting serving spoons in the dishes of food, when she saw them arrive. When she saw Johnny carrying the baby like he owned the right, she smirked and glanced at her women friends, as if to say, *See? I was right.* But then the blanket came off and the baby was revealed, and at that point, one thing became blatantly clear. The three Pine boys looked alike—thick, straight black hair, brown eyes. Luther Joe had blue eyes and soft brown baby curls. He did not look at all like Johnny Pine.

The women looked at Pansy and frowned. It made her anxious. This would poke a huge hole in her attempt to add credence to her story that the baby was his. She sniffed and continued with her duties. So what if he wasn't the baby's father? They were living in sin and that sure wasn't right.

The meal was endless. Dori couldn't swallow more than a few bites. She fed Luther and then held him, because it comforted her to hold him close as people stopped by to pay their respects.

Johnny stayed nearby, trying to anticipate her needs before she asked. People had been gathering inside the church for over forty-five minutes and the sanctuary was nearly full. When Dori was finally alone, he scooted into a seat beside her.

"Do you want to go freshen up or something? It won't be long before the services start. I'll hold Luther if you need a break."

Dori's eyes were swimming with unshed tears.

"Yes and thank you."

He lifted Luther out of her arms.

"Come here, little man. You're gonna sit with me a minute."

Chapter 14

DORI SMOOTHED DOWN THE FRONT OF HER DRESS AND headed for the ladies' bathroom. The cinnamon-scented air freshener hit her in the face like a slap. Wrinkling her nose at the too-strong scent, she slipped into a stall only moments ahead of two women who came in behind her. It was obvious they didn't know she was in there, because the first words out of their mouths had to do with her.

"Dori Grant looks so pretty, and that baby of hers is a real cutie. I love curly-haired babies, don't you?"

"Yes, he's a cute baby, but then aren't they all?"

Dori held her breath, trying to stay quiet. That last voice belonged to Pansy Jones, and she didn't want a confrontation.

"Personally, I think it's terrible that sweet baby is being subjected to such immoral behavior," Pansy added.

Rage went through Dori so fast, she stifled a gasp. Her hands were shaking as she flushed the toilet and jumped to her feet.

The moment the women heard it flush, they hushed.

Dori straightened her clothing and came out of the stall with her chin up and her hands curled into fists.

Pansy Jones looked like she'd seen a ghost. Before she could form a thought, Dori was in her face.

"All these years you were my neighbor, and I thought you were such a nice lady. But I will be the first to admit my mistakes. You are a mean woman, Pansy Jones. I don't know what I ever did to make you hate me this way, but I won't have it. How dare you tell lies? How dare you insinuate something bad about me and Johnny Pine? Just because he helped me when no one else would does not make him *or me* guilty of anything. You should be ashamed of yourself."

Then she pushed past them and out the door, letting it slam behind her as she strode back into the dining hall with her chin up.

Johnny saw the flush on her face and could tell she was angry.

"What happened?"

Dori saw Ruby Dye heading her way and shook her head.

"It's nothing," she said as Ruby arrived.

"Dori, you look beautiful. Your grandfather would be proud," Ruby said.

Johnny couldn't agree more as he watched Dori touch the bodice of her dress and then her hair, as if uncertain of her appearance.

Then Ruby pointed at the pastor who was waving them toward the door.

"I see they're about ready for you to enter the sanctuary. Do you want me to take the baby during the service? I'll gladly stay in here with him," Ruby said.

Dori glanced at Johnny and then nodded.

"That would be great. I've been worried that he would start crying. You're sure you don't mind?"

Ruby hugged her. "Of course I don't mind."

"Here you go, and I think he's getting sleepy," Johnny said as he handed over the baby.

Ruby snuggled him close and kissed his little cheek.

Dori cupped the top of Luther's head, feeling the soft curls against her palm.

"There's his car seat and diaper bag. If he gets fussy, he can have a bottle. Everything else you might need is in the bag."

Ruby had already settled into a chair and had the baby on her shoulder.

"The service won't last long, so don't worry about us. We'll be right here when you get back," she said.

"Thank you so much," Dori said.

Johnny eyed his brothers.

"Boys, tuck in your shirts."

They quietly obeyed.

Everything after that felt like a dream. Dori vaguely remembered the congregation standing as Johnny and the boys walked with her down the aisle, and because they seated them in the front pew, she didn't see a single person—or hear a thing the preacher said afterward. All she could see was the cherrywood casket they would be putting in the ground with her grandfather in it, buried beneath six feet of Georgia dirt where she would never see him again.

She hurt too much to cry.

———

By the time they'd followed the hearse to the cemetery to see Meeker Webb to his final resting place, it was almost three o'clock. Luther was asleep, so Johnny and the boys stayed in the car with the baby as Dori proceeded to the grave site alone.

The preacher said a brief prayer and then Dori sat

through what felt like an endless receiving line of people who came to pay their respects. She didn't know the boys had slipped into chairs on either side of her until Marshall patted her arm and handed her a fresh tissue.

"It's okay to be sad. We were sad when Mama died," he whispered.

She wanted to hug him. Instead, she took the tissue.

"Thank you, Marshall. That was very thoughtful of you."

He nodded.

Beep leaned his head against her shoulder.

"Are you tired, honey?" she asked.

He nodded.

"So am I," she whispered and gave him a quick hug.

She looked up and caught the preacher's eye, and he quickly came to her side.

"Pastor Lawless, the service was beautiful, but I'm not feeling well, and I need to get the baby home. Would it be rude of me to leave before all the others were gone?"

"No, no, absolutely not," he said. "I'll see you to your car."

"Thank you, but the boys are here. They'll walk with me. Please give everyone my thanks." Then she looked down at Beep and Marshall. "Ready, guys?"

They glanced at each other and then nodded in unison.

Beep took one hand and Marshall took her other, and they walked away. About halfway to the car, Beep stumbled, and Dori caught him before he could fall.

"Are you okay, honey? I didn't hurt you, did I?"

"I'm not hurt," he mumbled and ducked his head.

Marshall frowned and then followed his brother's line

of sight, right to the group of boys just up the hill who were picking up trash that had blown across the graves.

"I know what's wrong," Marshall said and pointed. "That's the guys who hurt Beep. They are on kid parole and have to do work every Saturday for a long, long time."

Dori paused, then looked up the hill at the four boys walking up and down the rows, dragging trash bags behind them. Off in the distance, she could see a police officer. It was true; it looked almost like being in jail and was no more than they deserved.

"Don't worry, Beep. They're in trouble and you're not. So let's go. Johnny's waiting," Dori said and gave his hand an extra squeeze.

He didn't say a word, but he held on a little tighter as they walked back to the car.

When Johnny saw Dori holding hands with the boys, he felt like he'd missed out, and then he took a slow breath, taking comfort in the fact that they were coming to him. He got out, held the door open as she slid into the seat, got the boys in the back without waking the baby, and then drove away.

"Hey, Johnny, did you see them guys?" Marshall asked.

"Those guys, and who are you talking about?" Johnny said.

"The ones who hurt Beep. They're back in the cemetery picking up trash. They have to walk on people's graves and everything. I'm sure glad I'm not one of them," Marshall said.

"I'm glad you're not either," Johnny said and then realized that's why Beep had stumbled and why Dori had stopped to talk to him.

He glanced at her, intending to say thanks, but there was something about the way she was sitting, like she was holding herself still so she wouldn't fall into pieces, that told him to let it go.

He kept an eye on her as they drove back through town. She was pale and too silent, and there were dark circles under her eyes. He knew she hadn't eaten enough today but understood why.

It had taken him all day to figure out why he had a knot in his belly that got tighter every time she cast a glance his way—or why the brush of her hand against his arm when she leaned on him for support made him think he could fly. With very little effort, he could fall hard for Dori Grant.

Dori had been silent ever since they'd left the cemetery. She was grateful for the fact that Luther was a good traveler. Between the sound of the car engine and the gentle movement of the seat, he was lulled into a semi-conscious state.

She kept thinking back over the day; the incident in the bathroom with Pansy was far overshadowed by the kindness of everyone else. And then there was Johnny. Watching him moving among the people during the day had been eye-opening in more ways than one. It was obvious he had the regard of many and seemed far older than his years. He'd gained character through responsibilities, sacrificing everything a young man his age might have wanted to do just to keep his family intact.

Now it was time for her to set aside her own feelings too. Luther had to come first. But where would they go?

She needed to finish her college courses, so she could set up her website business and begin generating some income. What Granddaddy had left her was wonderful, but it wouldn't last forever if she wasn't putting anything back.

Still, thinking about where to go was frightening. The way it was now, she would not be able to work and make enough to pay a babysitter and pay her bills. Being with the Pines felt safe. It felt good to think she wasn't entirely alone.

She glanced over her shoulder. Beep's eyes were closed and his head was nodding, and Marshall seemed transfixed by the sight of the sleeping baby. When she looked at Johnny, her heart tightened. He'd become so dear to her in a very short time.

She touched his arm, an innocent gesture that got his attention.

"Are you okay?" he asked.

She nodded. "I just want to thank all three of you for helping me through this awful day. I don't know what I would have done without you."

"We were happy to do it," he said.

"Can me and Beep go to the park when we get home?" Marshall asked.

The park he was referring to was an empty lot a couple of houses down where some of the neighborhood kids played ball.

"Can Beep and I," he corrected, "and we'll see. It looks like it might rain."

"Oh shoot," Marshall muttered.

Dori glanced at Johnny again and then offered up a suggestion. "If it does rain, you could make a cave indoors. That's what I used to do when I was little."

Marshall's eyes widened. "How do you make a cave?"

Dori was surprised. "You mean you guys never made a fort or a cave in the house when the weather was bad?"

"No."

Johnny frowned, surprised by the answer. Surely that wasn't true. Then he thought about the shape his mother had been in after they were born and sighed. The last few years of her life had been spent chasing a drug high, not teaching her children how to play.

Unaware of Johnny's revelation, Dori kept talking. "Then I'll show you, but once the cave is built, you have to figure out who you are and why you're in the cave, and that's how the game starts."

"I don't want to go to the park," Marshall said. "I want Dori to show me how to make the cave."

Johnny grinned at her. "You've done it now," he said.

Dori shrugged. "No, no, I want to. It will be a good way to change the focus of this day. Besides, it used to be my favorite thing to do when I was little."

"Well, we're home, so prepare yourself," Johnny said as he pulled up into the drive and parked by the house. "Beep, wake up, buddy. We're home."

"Dori's gonna show us how to make a cave," Marshall said.

Beep woke abruptly. The thought of playing something new was intriguing. The boys jumped out and raced to the front door, then waited impatiently until Johnny unlocked it.

"Go change out of your good clothes and hang them up," Johnny said.

"Okay," they echoed and ran inside giggling and pushing.

Dori was unbuckling Luther from the car seat when Johnny came back.

"You take the baby. I'll get the rest of the stuff for you," he said.

A rumble of thunder sounded in the distance.

"Sounds like your prediction was right," she said and carried Luther inside and put him to bed. He stretched to full length, as if glad to be out of the seat, and poked his thumb in his mouth.

"Mama's sweet boy," Dori whispered and tucked his blanket around him.

When she turned around, Johnny was coming in the room with the diaper bag and her purse.

"Just put them on the bed," she whispered. "I'm going to change clothes before we begin cave construction. I hope you don't mind that I offered—"

Johnny put a finger to her lips.

"You don't apologize for being kind to my brothers," he said softly and then ran the tip of his finger along her chin and smiled. "You better change fast. They'll be swinging from the ceiling fan if you don't show up soon."

"I'll hurry, but I have one request. I need two of the biggest and oldest blankets or bedspreads you have in the house, something you wouldn't mind getting a little dirty. I'll wash them up for you when they're through."

"I'll get them. Where do you want to erect this magic place?"

"Do you mind if they play in the kitchen?"

"Honey, I don't mind where they play in this house. The fact that you've made them happy is all that matters. So I'll leave them in the kitchen and the rest is on you."

He left Dori by the bed and closed the door on his way out.

She closed her eyes and took a slow breath. He'd called her honey, and the imprint of his finger was still warm on her lips. It made her anxious and achy—and at the same time, a little leery.

"Oh, Granddaddy, I need to talk to you. I wish you were here."

But there would be no more warm chuckles or wise words of advice. Right or wrong, the decisions were on her now. She began taking off the pretty dress, the nice shoes, and the tights. Cinderella had gone to a funeral, not a ball, even though she had come home with the prince. Now the real world beckoned. It was time to get back to work.

A few minutes later, she was in the kitchen with the boys. They pulled the kitchen chairs a few feet away from the table but still surrounding it, the boys bouncing on their toes with every step.

"Beep, you take this quilt and crawl under the table and make a good nest. Marshall and I are going to build the roof and walls with this one."

Beep's smile was from ear to ear as he went down on his hands and knees and crawled under the table, dragging the quilt with him.

"Marshall, you take this side and I'll take the other, and we're going to spread this quilt over the table and then drape it over the backs of the chairs and let the rest fall on the floor, understand?"

"Yeah, yeah, like making a tent only better."

She grinned. "Yes, like a tent but better."

After a few adjustments of the chairs, and centering

the quilt on the table and weighting it down to keep it from slipping, the cave was almost done. All they had to do was leave the short end of the table that was closest to the wall uncovered. It would be the doorway and also make it appear that the opening was concealed.

"So they can't sneak up on you," Dori said as she showed Marshall how far to pull down the quilt and how much to leave open. "There. So, what do you think?"

Marshall dropped to his knees and crawled inside with Beep.

Dori squatted down and peered in.

"It's good and dark in there, don't you think?"

"Yeah, it's great!" Beep said.

She could tell by the look on Marshall's face that he was already moving into imagination mode. As she watched, the first ripple of thunder rolled across the sky.

Rain, just like Johnny predicted.

"I'll get your camping supplies, and then you guys are on your own," Dori said.

She made a quick raid of the refrigerator, then pulled a plastic bowl out of the cabinet and began piling it high. She cut up an apple into several chunks, made celery sticks and carrot sticks, added a handful of crackers, and then slipped the bowl in front of the cave without a word.

She stood there long enough to see one little hand slip out of the opening and pull the bowl inside.

"Mission accomplished," she whispered.

She could already hear the boys planning their strategies and smiled to herself, remembering what all she'd played. When she turned around, Johnny was standing on the other side of the table. He took her hand and led her out of the kitchen and into the living room.

"You rock the world, Dori Grant. In the middle of a very sad day for you, you went out of your way for them."

"Truth? It is as good for me as it is for them. And you were right about the rain."

He wanted to put his arms around her but saw the exhaustion on her face.

"Go to bed, Dori. At least sleep until the baby wakes up. We have leftovers and pie. No cooking. Just a chill-out evening, okay?"

The thought of sleep was enticing.

"You talked me into it," she said. "See you later."

"Yeah, later," he said and watched until she disappeared into her room.

———

Pansy Jones stood at the window, looking out at the burned remnants of what had once been Meeker Webb's home, watching the rain come down and thinking about what had happened at the church. Bottom line, she was in a sticky situation. Dori Grant had given her a verbal slap down in front of one of the biggest gossips in Blessings. What had happened would be all over town by morning, and then she'd have to go to church and face everyone in her Sunday school class without a way to deflate Dori's accusations.

Besides all that, Bart wanted biscuits and gravy for supper, and she wasn't in the mood to cook. If only she could take back what she'd done the night of the fire, then none of this would be happening. She thought about taking her licks and admitting she was wrong, but then worried about how she'd be received afterward. In the end, maintaining her reputation was more important to her than feeling guilty for ruining Dori Grant's.

She turned away from the window, went to the desk, and began digging through five years' worth of phone books before she found the one she was looking for.

She'd gone to school with Ethel Carter; she'd been Ethel Justice then. Ethel was a caseworker for their county's Division of Family and Children Services. DFCS. The same dreaded department that tried to take Johnny Pine's brothers into state custody.

Pansy Jones was about to open up a great big can of worms.

—◦◦◦—

Runoff from the downpour flowed through the streets in dirty rivulets. The rain blew against the windows and hammered the roof in a steady, repetitive drone. It was music to sleep by, and Dori slept, exhausted by the day and the emotional toll.

Johnny lay stretched out on the living room sofa, listening to the excitement in his little brothers' voices as they played in the other room, and he felt like crying. They'd missed so much of what being a child was all about, and he'd been so busy trying to keep a roof over their heads that he hadn't seen it. Dori was good for them—for all of them. He didn't want her to go. He killed time by watching television and catching up on paying bills, then popped some corn and shared it with the little animals beneath the table.

Along about a quarter to six, Johnny went into the kitchen and began digging through the refrigerator to make supper. The boys heard him and emerged from their play long enough to make a request.

"Hey, Johnny, can me and Beep eat supper in our cave?"

Johnny grinned. "Yeah, sure, as long as you don't throw the bones down on the floor."

"We won't! We promise!" Beep yelled and began leaping about the kitchen on his hands and feet.

"What are you doing?" Johnny asked.

"I'm a baby wolf playing in the rain."

Johnny chuckled and started picking out a couple of pieces of leftover fried chicken to heat up for the boys.

"I want mine cold," Marshall said.

"Yeah, I want mine cold too," Beep said and then stopped hopping and looked at Marshall. "Why do we want it cold?"

"Because we're wild animals, remember? They don't eat their food cooked."

Beep frowned. "I don't want no raw chicken."

"You don't want *any* raw chicken," Johnny said.

"I already said that," Beep cried and bounced all the way back into the cave.

While he was digging through the leftovers, the baby woke up, which got Dori out of bed. She changed him and carried him to the kitchen to heat up a bottle.

When Johnny saw her coming, he got one out of the refrigerator and put it in her hand.

"Thanks. You are handy to have around," Dori said as she took the bottle to the microwave.

Johnny smiled, but she didn't see it. She was playing peekaboo with Luther while she waited for the microwave to ding. As soon as it was ready, she cradled

Luther in her arms and poked it in his mouth, then leaned against the counter to let him drink while she watched the boys crawling in and out of the cave in an obviously pretend foray for food.

"They are having so much fun," she said softly.

Johnny stuck a spoon in the leftover baked beans and then got plates from the cabinet.

"You're really good with them," he said.

Dori shrugged. "It's not hard to like good kids."

"Seeing as how we no longer have a dining table tonight, why don't you and Luther go into the living room, and we'll eat in there? I'll bring you a plate if you trust me to fix it."

"Sure, but don't put much food on it. I'm not very hungry."

"Okay," he said and fixed food for the boys and set it down in front of the cave. "Wolf food is ready," he said. "Put your dirty plates in the sink when you're through."

They howled in unison, took their plates, and crawled back in the cave.

He was still chuckling as he took their food into the living room, set her plate on the sofa beside her, and went back to get drinks.

Dori took a bite of the chicken and then licked her fingers as Johnny put a glass of iced tea on the end table.

They ate in silence for a few minutes while Luther finished his bottle. It wasn't until Dori put him on her shoulder to burp him that Johnny put down his plate and leaned forward.

"I've been thinking about this situation," Johnny said.

Dori stifled a groan. He'd probably heard Pansy

Jones's gossip. This was where he told her she needed to find someplace else to be.

"I know I need to start looking for a place for Luther Joe and me. I'll get a newspaper and check out the rental properties," she said quickly.

"No, no, that's not what I meant at all," Johnny said. "I want to run something by you and see what you think. Keep in mind it's totally your call, and I'll be cool with whatever you say, but it would benefit me as much as it might help you."

"I'm listening," Dori said and kept patting Luther's back.

"First off, we like having you here," Johnny said.

Dori smiled. "I like being here too. You were a lifesaver."

"I know the funeral is over, but you said Butterman has yet to file all the probate papers, so you really can't make final decisions on anything until all of that's over, right?"

"As far as I know, that's correct," she said.

"School will be out in a couple of weeks. I always have a really hard time finding people to keep the boys during the summer, because Miss Jane doesn't do all-day day care and she also takes the summer off. I don't believe you will be able to find a job that pays enough for rent, day care, and living expenses. Believe me. I know what they pay people our age."

She sighed. "I've already been worrying about that. What I have to do is finish my college courses so I can set up my design website and start taking clients. Eventually, I would hope to make enough to work from home full-time."

He shifted nervously, trying not to sound too desperate.

"How would you feel about staying here, maybe through the summer or however long it takes you to finish your classes? And in return, you could take the boys to school and pick them up for the two weeks until it is over, and then this summer, you would be here with them while I'm at work. You wouldn't have to be paying rent, and I would save money not paying day care."

Luther burped.

Johnny grinned. "If that was his opinion, I'm not sure if that was a yes or a no."

Dori was still trying to come to terms with what Johnny had just asked while thinking about Pansy's accusation.

"You know what people will say," she said.

He shrugged. "They're already saying it."

She sighed. So he'd heard the gossip too.

"You don't mind?"

Johnny shrugged. "The way I see it, we're both trying to keep our families intact any way we can. I don't see anyone else offering to shoulder our burdens, and I'm willing to chance it if you are."

Dori didn't have to think twice. The moment she'd heard the offer, the relief she'd felt had been visceral.

"I would love to be able to stay here for a while longer."

He didn't know he'd been holding his breath until she spoke. He exhaled slowly and tried not to look too excited.

"I promise you won't need to worry about...uh, that I would assume anything personal would happen between us."

"I trust you," she said softly.

"Good. Then it's settled," he said.
She nodded. "Yes, it's settled."

Chapter 15

DORI WOKE UP SUNDAY MORNING WITH TEARS ON HER face. She didn't remember what she'd been dreaming, but it didn't matter. Her reality was explanation enough.

She rolled over onto her side and got up quietly, so as not to wake up the baby, then darted across the hall to the bathroom and back again before she got caught in the hall in her nightgown. Once inside her room, she began sifting through her new clothes to find something to wear and settled on another clean shirt and jeans. Sometime today, she'd do laundry again.

She could smell coffee brewing as she dressed and knew Johnny was up. She didn't know what the Sunday routine was in this house, but she remembered hers.

Sunday breakfast was usually pancakes, then getting ready for church and listening to Granddaddy singing "The Old Rugged Cross" as he shaved.

And bracing herself to show up in church as the unwed mother she was, putting up with a combination of overdone pity or disdain.

Granddaddy hadn't seen it, but then men rarely hear the sarcasm behind a woman's sharp words and sweet smile.

Ordinarily she dressed without looking at herself, but today was her birthday, and in the eyes of the law, she was no longer a juvenile. She didn't feel different but wondered if she looked different. One glance and it was plain to see she was still the same too-thin girl she'd been yesterday, but whatever decisions she made from this day forward would be hers to make. And her first decision was to ignore the day of her birth. For the first time in her life, there would be no celebration. As Beep would have said, she was too sad for cake.

But as it turned out, sad had no place in her day. Luther woke up smiling, and when she got him out of bed to bathe, his antics made her laugh. Taking care of him took her out of herself, and her dark mood soon lifted.

She had him on her hip and was on her way to the kitchen to make his oatmeal when the boys came out of the kitchen, their feet dragging.

"Hi, guys," Dori said.

"We had to take the cave down," Marshall muttered.

"We can't be wolves no more," Beep added.

"You can build it somewhere else," she said.

Their expressions shifted to one of instant relief.

"Really? It doesn't have to be the table?"

"'Course not," she said. "You saw how we did it yesterday, so take it into your bedroom. You can tie corners to one end of the bed and then find something else to hold up the other end. You'll figure it out."

They bolted back into the kitchen at high speed.

"Johnny! Johnny! Wait, don't wash them quilts!" Beep yelled.

Dori chuckled, and when she did, Luther crowed, trying to mimic her sound. She laughed.

"Monkey see, monkey do," she said and tweaked his nose as the boys came flying back out of the kitchen, dragging the quilts behind them.

Johnny was cleaning up breakfast dishes when she walked in.

"Sorry we were late."

He shook his head. "You're not late. They were up at the crack of dawn wanting to play some more. I ruined their party when I told them they had to give the table back. I don't know what you said, but whatever it was, thanks."

"They're making another cave in their room."

"Ah. Usually they mope around when they can't go out and play. This may be the best rainy day in this house ever. Can I make you breakfast? It won't take long to make a little more oatmeal."

She shook her head. "Thanks, but I'm just not hungry. I'm going to feed Luther his cereal. I might eat some toast later."

He frowned. "Don't skip meals. You can't keep up the strength you need to take care of him if you get run down, okay?"

She looked up. "You sounded like Granddaddy just then."

"Smart man," Johnny muttered and pointed to the cabinet. "I'm going to make a run to the grocery store this morning. If you need stuff, add it to that list. I'm going to go change the sheets on their bed before they get the new hidey-hole all set up."

Dori fixed Luther's cereal and then cradled him in her arms to feed. Tomorrow she was getting a high chair, but right now, adding items to the grocery list came first.

It was also raining in Oneida, the next town over.

Some of the less faithful worshippers in the various churches had opted to stay home, rather than slog through the rain to be chastised for their shortcomings.

Others' plans to go fishing had been shifted to sleeping in or driving into Savannah for a day out at the mall.

For twenty-three-year-old Frankie Ricks, the rain had in no way dampened his curiosity about what was going on with Dori Grant. He was completely worthless and something of a gigolo. He got what he needed from willing, and sometimes unwilling, women, because of a better-than-average resemblance to the actor Johnny Depp. But he wasn't dumb, and he was really good at waiting for handouts. Today was a bust, so he kicked back in the recliner in his apartment and reached for the phone. No way was he going out to eat in this downpour. He was ordering in.

～～～

Pansy wasn't going to church. She'd used the "I have a headache" to get out of sex with Bart last night and was going to lay low in her bedroom today to continue the ruse. Fearing the news of her smackdown from Dori Grant was probably common knowledge by now, she couldn't face her church friends and was fed up with Bart. Since he'd caused all of her troubles, he should be miserable too.

When he came back to their bedroom to get dressed for church, he gave her "that look," the one where she was at a disadvantage and he had an itch needing to be scratched.

"I see that look on your face. Just because I'm in bed doesn't mean you can take advantage of me, Bart Jones. I'm sick, and you will respect the misery of my condition, do you hear me?"

Bart glared. "I didn't say a thing."

"You didn't have to," Pansy said. "Go about your business and give the pastor my regrets."

Bart paraded around in his birthday suit, a less than sexy image considering his paunch and skinny ass, not to mention a poor excuse for an erection. He kept casting hopeful glances in Pansy's direction as he took his Sunday suit from the closet.

Pansy was getting nervous. "For Pete's sake, Bart Jones, put your pants on. I've seen all that before."

He paused. "How about just a little poke, Pansy? I wouldn't take long."

She thumped the bed with her fists. "So what else is new? You take just long enough to make yourself happy, which is my problem with you and your pokes. This is Sunday and you should be ashamed of yourself for wanting to fornicate on the Good Lord's day."

Bart's shoulders sagged along with his ardor. "Sorry," he muttered, then dressed in record time and made himself scarce.

The minute Pansy heard him drive away, she second-guessed her decision to stay home. Maybe she should have gone and pretended nothing was wrong. In a panic, she jumped out of bed and fell to her knees beside the bed and began to pray, begging the Good Lord to not only forgive her, but to also get her out of this mess with her good name intact.

Even after the prayer was over, Pansy was pretty sure she'd overstated her troubles to the Lord. Her life wasn't in danger. Her health was fine. They owned their home and their car, and they had food to eat. She didn't know where gossip fell in the sin category, but then she remembered that verse in the Ten Commandments

about not bearing false witness against her neighbors
and started bawling.

"I'm fucked," she wailed and got off the floor and
headed for the kitchen.

She needed a drink of something stronger than coffee.

—⁓—

Johnny had the grocery list and the extra money Dori
had given him. The worst of the wind had stopped blowing as he headed uptown to the supermarket, turning
the rain into a mere downpour instead of a gale. As he
drove, he remembered he needed to call Miss Jane at the
Before and After about Dori taking over her duties, so
as soon as he parked, he made the call. It rang a couple
of times, and then she answered.

"Hello?"

"Miss Jane, this is Johnny Pine."

"Why, hello, Johnny. I hope nothing is wrong with
the boys."

"No, ma'am, but I need to let you know that Dori's
going to take over getting them to and from school for
the last two weeks."

"That's wonderful," Jane said. "I know this will help
you immensely."

Johnny smiled, thankful she understood.

"Yes, ma'am, and they won't have to get up quite as
early either. It will be a big help all around."

"How is she doing today?" Jane asked. "She looked so
stressed out yesterday. My heart just aches for her loss."

"Yes, ma'am. I guess she's doing okay. She doesn't
complain and has the baby to keep her thoughts on
other things."

"Well, give her my regards, and you all have a good summer."

"You too, Miss Jane, and thank you for being my backup quarterback all year."

He heard her chuckle. "I like being called the backup rather than the babysitter. Maybe I'll change the name of my day care to Backup Quarterback."

She was still laughing when he disconnected. He patted his pocket to make sure he had the list and then looked out at the rain. There was no good way to do this, so he slapped his cap on his head, bailed out of the car, and made a run for the door.

———∿∿∿———

Dori was putting a load of clothes in the washer. Luther was in his playpen, sucking his thumb and fighting sleep. Johnny had been gone almost an hour, and Dori was thinking about what to make for dinner at noon when she heard Beep scream. She dropped the clothes and ran.

The makeshift cave was at the end of the bed, and Marshall was on the floor in front of it. He was on his hands and knees trying to cough, but his face was turning blue. Beep was pulling on Marshall's arm, trying to help him up when Dori ran in.

She grabbed Marshall around the waist and yanked him up. She knew he was choking, but she didn't know on what.

"Beep! Beep! Stop crying and tell me what's in his mouth."

"A marble. I think he swallowed a marble."

When Dori saw a handful on the floor beside him, it was evidence enough. She locked her hands beneath his rib cage and began the Heimlich maneuver, repeating it over and over with a prayer in her heart.

God help me. Help me. Don't let this child die.

Beep's screams masked the sound of running feet as Johnny suddenly appeared in the doorway, his eyes wild with fright. Before he could move, he saw a marble shoot out of Marshall's mouth, landing with a thunk at his feet.

"Thank you, God!" Dori murmured and then held him close as he began gasping and coughing, drawing life-giving breath back into his body.

Beep was still sobbing as Johnny reached the bed.

Dori staggered backward, taking Marshall with her as she flopped backward onto the mattress.

Johnny turned. "Beep, stop screaming, buddy. Marshall is okay. See? See? He's breathing on his own."

Still, he picked Beep up and sat down beside Dori and Marshall, so shaken by what he'd witnessed that for a few moments he couldn't speak. He kept remembering all the times he'd been gone on brief errands and left Marshall in charge. Today, if Dori hadn't been here, Marshall would have died.

Dori's heart was still pounding, but the relief of knowing Marshall was breathing had lessened the panic she'd first felt.

Johnny cupped Marshall's face and pushed the sweaty hair away from his forehead.

"Hey, Marshall…hey, buddy, are you okay? Do you hurt anywhere? Does it hurt to breathe?"

Too weak to speak, Marshall was drinking air like water as he shook his head and went limp against Dori's chest, her hands still locked tight against his belly.

Johnny clutched her arm, his gaze locked on her face. "You saved his life!"

Dori shuddered. "And he nearly scared the life out of me."

"What happened?" Johnny asked.

"I was in the utility room when I heard Beep scream. By the time I got here, Marshall was turning blue. I don't know for sure how it happened, but he swallowed a marble, and that's what came out."

His hand tightened at the back of her neck as he glanced down at Marshall's face again. His color was returning to normal. He felt his pulse. It was rapid but steady.

Beep was still snuffling and shaking. "Marshall had a marble in his mouth," he offered.

Johnny frowned. "What the hell for?"

"It was a red one. We was pretendin' they was starberries."

Johnny sighed. He couldn't believe this had happened, and at their ages. He glanced back at Marshall.

"Pretending is fine. Putting stuff in your mouth that could choke you is not. Are we clear on that?"

Marshall nodded and then crawled out of Dori's lap and into Johnny's arms as Beep gave way to his bigger brother's presence.

Dori got up and took Beep by the hand.

"Let's go get your face washed up and bring a washcloth back for Marshall, okay?"

Beep clung to her hand as they walked out, leaving Johnny and Marshall alone.

As soon as they were gone, Marshall started talking.

"I saw Mama. She was telling me to hang on. I saw Mama, Johnny. I swear on my life."

Johnny wrapped his arms around his little brother as his vision blurred.

"Well, I'm damn glad you hung on, okay? I don't know what I'd do without you."

"I know. I'm sorry, Johnny, I'm sorry."

"It's okay, son, just promise you won't do anything dumb like that again."

Marshall spit on his hand then slapped it against his heart.

"I swear," he whispered.

Beep came back with the washcloth Dori promised and handed it to Johnny, who began wiping Marshall's face and then wiping away everyone's tears.

"Are you crying too, Johnny?" Beep asked.

Johnny sighed. "A little bit, I guess. You guys scared me."

Beep crawled up on Johnny's other knee as Johnny wrapped his arms around them and held them close.

"I love you guys. Don't ever forget that, okay?"

"We love you too, Johnny," they echoed.

It took Johnny a moment to realize Dori had not come back with Beep.

"Where's Dori?" Johnny asked.

"She said the Pine men needed some time alone. Are we men too, Johnny?"

Johnny managed a shaky grin.

"You're working on it," he said. "Now do me a favor. Beep, you pick up those marbles and throw them in the trash. Marshall, I want you to get in the bed and rest for a little while, okay? You can turn on the television, maybe find some cartoons. I'm thinking a little down-time before dinner would be a good idea."

They nodded in agreement as Johnny kissed them both and then got up and left the room, in search of Dori.

Chapter 16

AFTER DORI SENT BEEP BACK WITH THE WET WASH-cloth, she went straight back to the utility room and put the clothes she had dropped into the wash. Her hands were shaking as she stuffed them in the tub and sprinkled in the soap. She was seeing spots before her eyes as she set the water temperature and started the machine, and then on her way back into the kitchen, weakness overwhelmed her.

Oh my God, I am going to faint.

She staggered to the sink and then stood for a few moments with her head down and her eyes closed, trying to catch her breath, unaware what was happening was a result of the adrenaline crash.

All of a sudden, there were hands on her shoulders. It was Johnny. She felt him give them a slight squeeze and then he turned her around.

Their gazes locked.

He lowered his head to brush a kiss across her fore-head, then wrapped his arms around her. When he spoke, his voice was shaking. "I have no words."

"I thought I'd found him too late."

He tightened his grip. "Thank God, you didn't quit."

Dori looked up and saw tears swimming in his eyes. "I'm not the quitting kind," she said.

"I really, really want to kiss you," he whispered.

Awash with sudden longing, Dori wanted that too. "I wouldn't mind," she said softly.

And so he did.

First, it was a mere brush of his mouth across hers, then another pass that lingered. Then he took a breath, centered his mouth upon her lips, and he was lost. He knew she was trembling, but she was also hugging him back. That simple fact gave him hope.

When he stopped and pulled away, the room tilted beneath his feet, as if he'd lost his anchor to earth. He cupped her face, then ran a thumb across her lower lip, still moist from the kiss.

"Please don't regret that happened."

"No regrets, Johnny," she said and managed a shaky smile.

"Promise?"

"Yes, I promise."

"I would never want to scare you. If I just did, I swear that won't ever happen again."

She put a finger to his mouth and shook her head. "I wasn't scared."

He kept looking at her face and shaking his head in disbelief. "I never expected this to happen."

"What? That you would kiss me?" she asked.

"No, that I would find myself falling for you."

Dori shivered. "I, uh—"

"Don't answer," Johnny said. "I don't expect anything from you. I just had to say it. And on another note, I think I need to get the groceries off the porch. I dropped them when I heard Beep screaming, and the rest of the stuff is still in the car."

"I'll get the porch. You get the car," she said, glad to be focused on something safe.

He ran a finger down the side of her cheek. "I believe

I've said this before, but you're real handy to have around," he said.

They walked outside together, and when Dori began gathering up groceries from the porch, Johnny picked up his cap, put it back on his head, and made a run for the car. He grabbed the last two sacks of groceries and dashed back across the yard and up the steps, past Dori, as the rain blew into his face. He hurried inside, dropped off his sacks, and was on his way back to help her get the groceries he'd dropped when she met him at the threshold.

"I've got it. You get the door," she said.

Johnny closed and locked the door behind her and then followed her into the kitchen, dripping water as he went. He dried his face and hands, and then they began sorting the food, putting some in the refrigerator and the rest in the pantry.

Dori turned on the oven and got out the hamburger meat, then went through the groceries until she found everything she needed to make meat loaf.

"Johnny, do you have a loaf pan or some kind of dish or pan that I can use in the oven?"

"Yes," he said and dug through the back of the cabinet next to the stove before he found what he was looking for. "I can't remember the last time we used this. I think I need to wash it first."

He cleaned up the casserole dish and handed it to Dori.

She sprayed it with nonstick spray then mixed up the meat loaf, popped it in the baking dish, and put it in the oven.

"You made that look easy," he said.

She shrugged. "A lot of years of practice."

"I'm going to change clothes and check on the boys," Johnny said.

Dori didn't comment, but when he walked out of the kitchen, she was watching every step he took. Soaked to the bone, his clothes were plastered to his body like a second skin, highlighting his long, steady stride and the play of muscles across his back. When he finally walked out of sight, she shuddered. She was attracted to him in so many ways, and now this only added to her confusion.

"Lord, Lord. This could be a disaster in the making or the best thing that's ever happened to me. Please let it be good."

Unaware of her quandary, Johnny stopped to peek in on the boys. They were side by side in the bed, watching television, and didn't even know he was there. Satisfied that they were okay, he went across the hall to change.

He stripped standing by the closet, leaving the wet clothes in a pile, and then got clean underwear, a pair of sweats, and a T-shirt and put them on over his still-damp body. He left the room barefoot, with his wet clothes, and as he stepped out in the hall, he heard Dori's voice coming from her bedroom. *The baby must be awake.*

They'd only been here four days, and yet the routine they'd fallen into had been easy, as if they'd been doing it for years. He'd never thought about his boys' future beyond bettering their living conditions until Dori Grant and her baby came into their lives, and now in four short days, they had become a huge part of that dream.

The washing machine was still running, so he dumped his wet clothes on the floor. The meat loaf Dori put in the oven was beginning to cook, and the enticing scent was a hint of the good meal to come. He'd already calculated he would save four hundred dollars each month by not paying Before and After or a summer babysitter, and since Dori was insistent on paying for their part of the groceries, for the first time in a long time, Johnny felt good about the future.

—◦◦◦—

Bart Jones came home from church expecting to smell roast and potatoes, or at least a fat hen baking in the oven. Instead, he found an empty whiskey bottle from his secret stash on the kitchen counter, and Pansy passed out on the living room sofa with an empty shot glass stuck between her chin and her chest.

To say he was shocked was putting it mildly. Not only was he was pissed Pansy had emptied his liquor, but he was also stunned that she was still in her nightgown and drunk off her ass.

"Pansy Jones, what the hell do you have to say for yourself?" he yelled and yanked the shot glass from beneath her chin.

She opened one eye, burped, farted, then rolled off the sofa onto her face.

"Oh good grief!" Bart muttered and manhandled her back up onto the sofa into a sitting position and went to get a wet cloth.

When he came back, she'd slumped over and face-planted herself into the cushion. He shoved her back into a sitting position again and slapped the wet cloth on her face and neck in angry, repetitive swipes until he had her attention.

Pansy came to enough to swat at his hands, trying to take the cloth out of his hands. "You shtop. You hear me, Bar' Jones? Shtop dat righ' now."

He paused. "What do you have to say for yourself?"

She burped again and then started to cry. "Goin' to hell."

Bart frowned and swiped the wet cloth across her forehead. "So were you planning on drinking yourself there?"

Pansy swatted at his hand again. "Drinkin' ta forget."

"Forget what, for heaven's sake?"

She pointed a shaky finger in his face. "Issh all your fault. Do not bring a girl and cryin' baby in my house, you shaid. You wouldn't let me do my Chrisshun duty."

His frown deepened. "Are you talking about Dori Grant? What does she have to do with you getting drunk?"

"We shunned her. Ever'buddy hates us."

"Oh, that is so not true. You're full of shit, Pansy."

"Full of Jim Beam whishkey, is what, and issh true. I tried fix it. Made it worse."

Now they were getting to the real truth. His eyes narrowed. "Exactly *how* did you try to fix it?"

Pansy started to cry harder.

"Pansy...what did you do?" Bart asked.

"I might'a lied," she said, bawling louder and then grabbing her head. "Oh dear Jesus, my head is breakin'. I feel a crack."

Bart felt the back of her head and pulled out a hair clip. "Your head's not cracking. It's your hair clip."

Pansy stared at the clip, blinking rapidly as she tried to clear her vision, and then poked it with the tip of her finger, confirming the identity. "It *is* m'clip! I love dat clip, and it broke my head."

Bart rolled his eyes. "Enough about your hair clip. What lie did you tell?"

"Shaid Johnny Pine wuz baby's father and livin' in sin with her and kids."

Bart shrugged. "So what? Maybe it's true, maybe it's not, but they'll never know you said that."

"No. People heard. She heard."

"What? Where the hell did that happen?"

She mashed her face into a throw pillow, but Bart yanked it from her hands and tossed it on the floor.

"Pansy…?"

"The funeral."

"The funeral! What the hell possessed you to do that?" he yelled.

She started to wail all over again.

Bart sighed and then tried to head off a new wave of hysterics. "Well, again it's not the end of the world. Before you know it, someone else will be the subject of fresh gossip and everyone will forget."

Pansy wailed louder.

Tears flowed.

Snot ran.

"Dere's more," she mumbled.

He groaned. "What else did you do?"

"Called DFCS."

Bart gasped. "Why would you do something like that? Why would you want to cause them more trouble?"

"If dey look bad, I look good."

Bart stared at her like he'd never seen her before and then backed away, needing to put some distance between them. "I'm going out to dinner. When I return, I expect the kitchen cleaned up and you with it. Then we're going to forget this conversation ever happened. However, the next time I want a poke, you do not get a fucking headache. Understand?"

Her shoulders slumped as she nodded wearily. "Am I still goin' t'hell?"

"I'm not the one to answer that," he said. "I'm leaving now. Get up and get busy."

The door slammed behind him.

Pansy sighed. "I am. I'm goin' t'hell, but firss I have ta clean up da kishen."

———

It stopped raining halfway between meat loaf and dessert, but no one noticed. The food Dori had put on the table was being devoured in huge gulps. Even Luther, who was sitting in Dori's lap having some pureed plums, was gulping it down, taking his cue from the other males at the table. Dori would have laughed, but he was also spewing as much out onto her as he was swallowing.

"Good grief, Luther Joe! I'm going to have to take a bath when I get through feeding you," Dori muttered.

"You need that high chair in the worst way, don't you?" Johnny said.

"You have no idea," Dori said and then sighed when Luther slapped at her hand and plums went flying. "Or maybe you do."

The boys laughed. Johnny got up and got a couple of paper towels.

"Thanks," she said and wiped Luther down, then dabbed at the spots all over her jeans. "You're going to spend some time on your own now, my little man."

Despite one squawk of disapproval as she put him in the playpen, he poked his thumb in his mouth.

She began cleaning up.

"I'll do that," Johnny said. "You cooked. I clean."

"But I don't—"

"That's the deal," he said. "Take it or leave it."

She grinned. "Take it. I think I'll go outside for a little air."

Johnny eyed his brothers. "Guys, when you're done, take your plates to the sink."

Marshall nodded, still eating mashed potatoes.

Beep scraped his plate with his fork and looked longingly at the leftovers.

"Beep, you can have some more for supper, okay?"

Beep looked longingly at the bowl and slowly pushed his plate away.

"Okay, but it sure is good."

Johnny remembered being hungry and didn't have it in him to tell the guys to stop eating. He got up from the table with the bowl of mashed potatoes and then paused long enough to put one last spoonful on Beep's plate.

"Thanks, Johnny! You're the best," Beep said and dug in.

After checking on Luther to make sure he was okay, Dori went outside and sat down in the porch swing.

The rain was still dripping from the eaves, and the muddy runoff on both sides of the street was capped with froth, like whipped cream on a mug of hot chocolate, as it rushed downhill.

She pushed off in the swing and closed her eyes, and as she did, she flashed back to a memory from her childhood. After she'd gone to live with her grandparents, she used to swing with her eyes closed, and one day her grandmother asked her why. She remembered exactly what she'd said.

If I don't see who's pushing me, then I can pretend it's Mommy.

Now she hardly remembered what her parents looked like, but she remembered longing for them to come back. Here she was, swinging again with her eyes closed and wishing Granddaddy could come back too. The likelihood that would happen was zero, just like before.

Tears welled, but she kept on swinging, wondering why it was that some people lost all of their family and others had so many family members but couldn't get along. She thought of Johnny. Even though his father was still alive, he might as well be dead for all the good he would ever do his sons. She swiped angrily at the tears on her cheeks. No need for crying. It wouldn't change a thing.

She heard the door creak and then the heavy step of boots, and knew it was Johnny. When she heard him stop suddenly, she also knew he'd seen the tears. She sighed. She didn't really want to talk.

"I'm going to make a quick run to Walmart, and I'm taking the boys with me. I have seventy plus dollars left over from the money you gave me last. Want me to look at high chairs for you?"

Grateful for the ordinary question, she nodded.

"Any specific thing I should know?" he asked.

"Make sure the footrest is adjustable to allow for when Luther Joe grows."

"Will do. What's your favorite candy?"

She opened her eyes, startled that he was standing

near the steps and looking out into the streets instead of at her.

"Peanut M&M's."

He nodded.

The boys came out, smiling.

"We're ready, Johnny. We brushed our teeth and peed and everything," Beep said.

"Good job," Johnny said. "Let's load up. The sooner we leave, the sooner we'll get back."

They went loping off the porch like raucous puppies and ran all the way to his car.

Johnny turned and caught her watching him.

"When you cry, it hurts my heart," he said softly and then followed the boys to the car.

The boys waved at her. She waved back, and then they were gone.

———

Ethel Carter had been a county caseworker for DFCS for almost twenty years, and during that time, she'd heard every excuse known to man as to why parents had neglected or abused their children. And she'd seen the same abused children screaming to stay with the parents, all the while knowing what would happen to them if they did. Experts found that the children had learned how to navigate that world of abuse and were afraid of something new. She'd come to understand that for them, it was a case of "better the devil you know than the one you don't," but it had made her hard. She was burned-out and marking time until the end of the year, at which time she would retire.

For the past few days, she'd been at a human

services convention in Savannah and was glad to be home. She'd already gone through her mail and poured herself a glass of iced tea as she sat down to go through her phone messages.

There were messages regarding follow-up visitations and a couple of messages from her superior. There was one from her gynecologist's office, reminding her of her next appointment, and one from her bank telling her that her account was overdrawn. It wasn't the best news she'd ever had, but it was also not the first time it had happened. Ethel had a thing for playing the slots.

When she got to phone call number nine and heard the caller identify herself, she leaned back and smiled. Back in the day, she and Pansy Jones had been good friends. But then she focused on the message and, as she did, began to frown. Pansy didn't want anyone to know she was making this call, but she claimed, as a God-fearing Christian woman, she believed it was her duty.

Ethel was making notes as the message continued and wrote down the name of Dori Grant and baby boy Luther Joe. And then she heard the name Johnny Pine and the hair crawled on the back of her neck. She knew that name. She'd been the caseworker who'd testified in court against him being given custody of his little brothers, and the court had overridden her opinion. According to Pansy, not only was Johnny Pine sleeping around with an unwed mother, but he'd taken her and the baby into his home, exposing all three of the children to illicit carnal behavior.

Ethel made note of the name, date, and time she'd received the call. Regardless of Pansy's wish to remain anonymous, Ethel was by the book and listed the caller's name, as well.

She went to her computer and entered the information in the database and, when she sent it to the office, requested to be assigned to this case, stating prior knowledge of the family situation.

The next morning, when she received a confirmation from her boss, she juggled her visitation schedule to do this interview first and began getting ready for work.

—⁓—

Johnny's sleep was restless all night, and when his alarm finally went off, he was glad to get out of bed. He headed across the hall to the bathroom and showered and shaved before going back to his room to dress. Without having to wake up his brothers, he kept feeling like he was forgetting something. He thought of Dori asleep on the other side of the wall and wondered what it would be like to wake up with her every day for the rest of his life. In theory, it sounded like heaven, but he'd learned not to expect too much from life.

Once he was dressed, he went to the kitchen to make coffee and oatmeal. It would save Dori time later, considering she had to feed Luther and the boys before she could leave.

He was stirring oatmeal when Dori walked in the kitchen. She was already dressed and her hair up in a ponytail, but there were still dark circles under her eyes.

"Hey, you're up early."

She smiled. "I thought I'd make lunches before Luther woke up."

"I was going to do that, but since you're here, have at it," he said. "Remember, Marshall—"

"Likes mayonnaise, Beep likes butter, and you like mustard."

He grinned. "You're hired."

She laughed and the sound made the hair stand up on the back of his neck. Five days in his life and already she was weaving her way into his heart.

He finished the oatmeal as she finished the lunches, and then he dished up two bowls for them.

"Hey, good-lookin'. Can I buy you breakfast?" he asked.

"I don't want no dried-up grapes."

He grinned. "I remembered too."

They ate in comfortable silence for a few moments before Johnny got up to refill his coffee and topped hers off too.

"Thank you. And thank you again for getting the high chair. It's going to make such a huge difference for me," Dori said.

"The boys picked it out," Johnny said, eyeing the blue-and-white stripes on the back and seat. "They said it had racing stripes."

Dori laughed again, and it was all Johnny could do not to get up and kiss her. Instead, he took a drink of coffee and then carried his bowl to the sink and rinsed it.

"You have my number. If you need anything, just call. I don't know where I'll be working today, but it's so wet that if they're not through fixing my dozer, I might wind up working on it down at the garage with the mechanic."

"We'll be fine," she said as she rinsed her bowl and

stacked it in his. "I'll wash these after I come back from taking the boys to school."

He nodded, then stuck his hands in his pockets to keep from putting them on her.

"You can wake them up about 6:30 and drop them off at school anytime after 7:45. School starts at 8:00."

"I remember," she said. "Some things never change."

"So, I guess I'll be leaving now," he said.

"Don't forget your lunch," she said and handed him the red Tupperware container.

"Right. So, I'll see you this evening," he said and headed for the door.

"Johnny?"

He stopped and turned so fast he nearly dropped his lunch. "Yeah?"

"Have a good day."

He smiled. "Yeah, you too."

Chapter 17

DORI WAS HESITANT TO WAKE UP THE BOYS, BUT AS IT turned out, they were on their best behavior. She suspected that when Johnny had put them to bed last night they'd heard a speech about cooperation. They dressed without fanfare, combed their hair before they came to the table, and when she put their oatmeal in front of them and served it correctly without their input, they were elated. Raisins for Marshall. No dried-up grapes for Beep. As they ate, they watched her feeding Luther with great interest.

"Hey, Dori, didja hafta teach ole Joe there how to swallow, or did he come knowing how to do that?" Beep asked.

Dori stifled a laugh. Ole Joe. That was priceless.

"Well, he came knowing how to swallow milk, because he lies down in my arms when I feed him his bottle, but he is learning how to swallow sitting up, which is a whole other thing, see?"

Beep's eyebrows arched. "Oh yeah! I guess Mama had to teach us the same thing."

Dori sensed his need to maintain any kind of connection to the woman who was gone from his life.

"Yes, she sure did. She had to teach Johnny and Marshall *and* you."

He and Marshall looked at each other and burst out laughing. When they did, Luther Joe laughed too, spitting oatmeal everywhere, which caused even more laughter.

"What was so funny?" Dori asked as she began wiping up the oatmeal Luther had spit out.

"That Johnny didn't know how to eat either."

She grinned. She guessed the image of their big, strong, take-charge brother not being able to spit or chew *was* funny.

"Nobody knows how when they're born. That's stuff everybody has to learn. Now hurry up and finish your cereal and go brush your teeth. I don't want you guys late for school."

They quickly did as she asked, leaving their bowls rinsed and in the sink before they left.

Dori made a face at Luther as she spooned up the last of the oatmeal for him to eat.

"Now if I could get you to be as polite as those two, I'd be in business."

He made a face back at her and gobbled down the bite, then she began cleaning him up.

"We're going for a ride, little man, and I need you to be a good boy."

Luther didn't seem ready to object, and when Dori lifted him out of his high chair and plopped him on her hip, he grabbed at her ponytail.

"And no hair in your mouth either," she muttered and flipped her ponytail away from his grasping fingers.

"We're ready!" the boys yelled as they came barreling into the living room.

"Don't forget your lunches," she warned as she picked up Luther's blanket and the diaper bag.

They grabbed their lunch boxes and followed her out the front door. She buckled Luther into his little car seat and made sure the boys had buckled up as well.

It was straight-up 7:45 a.m. when she started the car and backed out of the driveway.

"Do you know the way to school?" Marshall asked.

"I sure do. I went to the same one you're going to. I know the parking rules and the unloading zones and everything. Don't worry about a thing. I've got this," she said.

Marshall nodded, seemingly pleased that his need to be involved in this process was unnecessary.

Dori drove straight to school without incident and wheeled into the unloading zone. The boys unlocked their seat belts.

"Both of you get out on the same side," Dori said. "Marshall, you'll have to scoot around Luther's car seat. Have a great day, okay?"

"Okay," they said, shutting the door and waving before running into the building.

Dori waved back and then put the car in gear and drove away.

"One job down, one to go, Luther Joe. We're going to the grocery store. I'm making a special supper tonight and breakfast tomorrow, and it's not going to be oatmeal."

Peanut Butterman was in the bank waiting with Herman Lewis, the vice president, to go through Meeker Webb's safety-deposit box. They, along with Lewis's secretary, were standing inside the vault, waiting at a table for the clerk to bring them Meeker's box. Since the owner was now deceased, it had to be opened in front of witnesses, and the contents identified and listed.

"Here we go," Lewis said as the clerk brought the box over to the table. "Butterman, you do the honors."

Peanut opened the lid and, at first sight, saw it to be an odd assortment of items.

Peanut eyed the secretary. "Are you ready?"

Her fingers were on the keyboard of her laptop as she nodded, so he picked up the small jewelry box that was on top.

"Okay…we have one diamond ring with rubies."

She began to type.

"A property deed for plat 10, lots 22, 23, 24, and 25 in the town of Blessings, Georgia."

"Got it," she said, continuing to type.

Peanut pulled out a few more items, mostly what he identified as family keepsakes. The last thing in the box was a large manila envelope. He took it out and then pulled out the folder inside and began to read. A few moments later, he paused and let out a slow whistle.

"Hey, Herman, get a load of this," he said and handed it to Lewis.

The vice president glanced at the file and then his eyes widened. "Did you know about this?" he asked.

Peanut shook his head. "No. Is the name of the stockbroker listed anywhere?"

"There's a business card on the inside flap," Lewis said as he handed back the file.

Peanut glanced at the secretary. "The last item to the list is one stock portfolio purchased eighteen years ago and belonging to Adorable Leigh Grant. Contact information: Myles Goodman, stockbroker. This would have been when she was born," Peanut said.

The secretary frowned. "Adorable?"

"That's what it says. I guess Dori is a nickname. As soon as you get that typed, I need a copy that has been witnessed and certified."

"She'll get right on it," Lewis said.

"In the meantime, I'm taking the contents to my office and following up with the stockbroker."

―⁓―

Dori had Luther down for a nap. There was cookie dough chilling in the refrigerator, and she was mopping her way through the house. She'd just finished the living room and was getting fresh water to do the kitchen when she heard a knock at the door. She dried her hands and went to answer.

Dori took one look at the heavyset, middle-aged woman on the threshold and felt uneasy.

"Can I help you?"

"Are you Dori Grant?"

Dori frowned. "Yes, and who are you?"

She whipped out a card and handed it to Dori as if she were flashing a badge.

"Ethel Carter, DFCS. May I come in?"

Dori's heart skipped a beat.

"What for?"

"I'm here to investigate a complaint lodged against you and Johnny Pine."

"A complaint? What kind of complaint?"

"In these instances, I'm the one who asks the questions."

She pushed past Dori and strode into the house without waiting for a proper invitation.

Dori didn't know what was happening, but she wasn't doing this alone. She pulled out her cell phone and sent

Johnny a text while the woman was circling the room like a bloodhound trying to pick up a scent.

> Caseworker from DFCS here. Complaint filed.
> Can you come home?

Then she dropped the phone in her pocket and closed the door.

Ethel Carter turned at the sound, and as she did, Dori's phone signaled an incoming text. She read it, then put the phone back in her pocket.

Ethel's eyes narrowed.

"Where is Johnny Pine?"

"He was at work, but he's on his way home. Why don't you take a seat and we'll both wait for him. In the meantime, could I get you something to drink? I have water, coffee, and Pepsi."

Ethel blinked. The girl was brazen, not the least fazed by her appearance.

"How did he know I was here?"

Dori held up her phone.

"While you were investigating the living room, I sent him a text."

Ethel flinched. That almost bordered on sarcastic, but the girl didn't appear defiant or defensive.

"Nothing to drink for me," Ethel said and then strode across the room and took a seat in the easy chair, leaving the sofa for them.

Dori sat with her hands in her lap and struggled to keep her composure, but her head was spinning. If someone had filed a complaint against them, then she would bet money it was Pansy Jones.

"I don't suppose you'd be willing to tell me who filed the complaint?" Dori asked.

"That's none of your business," Ethel said.

"Well, actually, it is indeed my business, since whatever was said seems vile enough to warrant your presence. But since you feel you can't divulge that, it doesn't matter. The only person in Blessings who has an ax to grind with me is Pansy Jones, so I'll assume it was her until someone tells me different."

Ethel was surprised that the name had come out so easily and wondered if something else was going on that she didn't know about.

Dori's heart sank when she saw the reaction. Damn Pansy, anyway.

"I see I was right."

And then she heard a car speed around the corner and knew it was Johnny. Moments later, the tires squealed as he hit the brakes and then turned up into the drive. Her fear eased.

"It appears our wait is over. I believe Johnny is home."

———

Johnny was underneath the dozer when his phone signaled a text. He pushed himself out, and when he saw it was from Dori, he smiled. But when he read the text, his heart nearly stopped.

"Oh Jesus," he muttered and sent a three-word text back.

On the way.

"What's wrong?" Clawson asked.

"A caseworker from DFCS is at the house. I've got to go."

Clawson frowned. "DFCS? What the hell?"

Johnny was already cleaning his hands. "I don't know, but I'll be back when they're gone."

He took off at a lope and drove home, trying not to panic. But when he saw the strange car parked beside the rental, he got a knot in his gut.

"Please, God, please don't let this be bad," he said and then got out of the car with his shoulders back and his head up. Whatever was happening, he couldn't show fear.

As he walked inside, his gaze went first to Dori and then to the woman sitting in his chair, and for a moment, his heart literally stopped. Taking a slow breath, he laid his cap on the side table as he closed the door behind him.

"Miss Carter, as I live and breathe. What brings you back to my home?"

Dori was shocked. He actually knew this woman? And then it hit her. This must be the woman involved in his custody battle to get his brothers. She looked at the woman again, trying to gauge her reaction.

Ethel was surprised by his attitude. This wasn't the green kid she'd seen in court. She'd lost track of how old he would be now, but he looked and acted like a man.

"I'm here to investigate a complaint," she said.

"Pansy Jones made it," Dori said. "I knew when I caught her telling lies at Granddaddy's funeral that I'd made her mad. I didn't think she would be this low."

Ethel frowned. "I never said who filed the complaint."

Johnny sat down on the sofa with Dori. He saw calmness on her face, but there was a tiny muscle jumping near her left eye. She was as scared as he was.

"Well, we're here, so let's get this over with," Johnny said.

Ethel pulled a file and a recorder from her briefcase.

"I will be recording this interview," she said and then waded in.

"Miss Grant...it is *miss*, right?"

"Yes."

"My information states that you are underage."

"No, ma'am, that's not correct. I'm eighteen."

Ethel frowned. Pansy had that wrong, but it didn't change the basic reason she was there.

"Mr. Pine, state your age."

"Twenty."

She frowned. He'd been eighteen...barely when they'd met in court.

"And how long have you been living together?"

"Five days," Johnny said.

Ethel blinked.

"I'm sorry, would you repeat that please?"

"Ever since last Thursday," Dori added. "That's when my granddaddy's house burned down."

"Why were you living with your grandparents?" Ethel asked.

"Because my parents died when I was nine. My grandmother died a couple of years back. There was just me and Granddaddy left."

"And where is he? Why aren't you still with him?"

Dori took a deep breath. "Because he —" Her voice broke.

Johnny answered for her. "Because he had a heart attack and died the night of the fire."

Ethel frowned. Ordinarily, this is where Ethel would

have gotten up and walked out of the house without a backward look. But this was Johnny Pine and the grudge still rankled, and there were still the children to consider.

Ethel ignored Dori's tears.

"I understand you are an unwed mother."

Dori inhaled sharply, but Johnny was already pissed on her behalf.

"Excuse me, Miss Carter…surely to God that cannot be of concern considering most of the people you do business with are in the same boat and worse."

Ethel glared.

Dori clasped his arm.

"No, no, Johnny, it's a fair question and not like I haven't heard that said before. Yes, Miss Carter, you are correct. I have a child. He's six months old and taking a nap."

"Where's the father?"

"I have no idea nor do I care. He has no part in our lives," Dori said.

"Mr. Pine, I assume your little brothers are in school?"

"Yes."

"How old are they now?"

"Ten and seven."

"According to the complaint, you had an altercation with the law regarding the youngest one a few weeks back. Is that correct?"

Johnny's heart was hammering against his chest so hard he felt sick.

"Inadvertently, that is correct."

"What do you mean 'inadvertently'? Either you were in trouble with the law or you weren't."

"We were not. My youngest brother was the victim

of an assault at his school. The perpetrators have already been found guilty and sentenced. He's healing, thank you for asking."

Ethel frowned. Damn Pansy Jones for twisting facts. Ethel was a stickler for proper procedures.

"Yes, well, I'll be checking into the court records," she said.

"You might save yourself some time and talk to my lawyer, Peanut Butterman," Johnny offered.

Ethel blinked twice. Butterman was well-known within the county, and the man cost money.

"Do you have a job?" she asked.

"Yes. The same one I had last time we met. I drive a dozer for Clawson Construction."

"And you, Miss Grant. Do you work?"

"I did until the fire. Granddaddy kept the baby. Now I don't."

Johnny had heard enough.

"Exactly what was the nature of the complaint?"

"That you are corrupting the children under this roof by the lascivious behavior you display in front of them."

Johnny's face went blank and then he stood up.

"That's a lie, and an ugly one at that. I would like to see proof. I want to know exactly what was offered up to you to speak such slanderous statements."

"An accusation does not demand proof. That is why I'm here. To find the proof for myself."

Dori stood up beside him, her hands clasped in front of her belly. Her voice was shaking and her eyes were, once again, filled with tears.

"Five days ago, I was washing dishes in the restaurant downtown, and then I went home and went to bed and woke up to a house on fire. I watched Granddaddy die in front of me while the firemen were trying to put it out. The crowd of onlookers was large as they watched my world go up in flames, but not a one of them offered me and my baby shelter. Johnny Pine and his little brothers saw the fire, and they saw everybody walk away from us. He offered shelter. I took it. My house burned Thursday. I buried Granddaddy on Saturday. I have cried most of the time I've been here, and now I am to sit here calmly and listen to you accuse me of having wild sex with a man who, up until Thursday, I knew only through school?"

Before Ethel could respond, the baby let out a wail, as if mirroring the shock and sadness in his mother's heart.

"Excuse me. I need to tend to the baby, and I'm not coming back. I've said all I'm going to say to you, lady, and you can tell Pansy Jones when you talk to her again that she is going straight to hell for what she's done."

Dori left the room, and Johnny went to the door and opened it, then stood aside.

"I believe we're through here."

Ethel was angry. She was the one who said when it was over. She was the one who made the recommendations and filed the reports.

"You might be, but I'm not," Ethel said. "I'm the one who's in charge, not you."

She gathered up her things, and the moment she crossed the threshold, Johnny shut her out.

Ethel heard the lock turn behind her, and she headed for her car. Once again, Johnny Pine had been involved in making her feel like a fool.

Johnny bolted down the hall and into Dori and

Luther's room. Dori was sitting on the bed, holding Luther in her arms, and sobbing.

"What's happening?" she wailed. "Why is this happening?"

Johnny sat down beside her and pulled her close.

"I'm sorry, Dori. I'm so sorry. I guess the complaint is what brought her back, but I know she was mad as hell the day the judge ruled in my favor and gave custody of the boys to me. I don't trust her to deal in facts. I don't trust her at all."

Dori buried her face in Luther's neck. "I can't cope with anything else. I just can't do this. They can't take my baby away from me."

Before he could answer, Dori's phone began to ring. She took it out of her pocket and handed it to Johnny.

"I can't talk," she said and began to cry.

Johnny saw it was from Butterman and answered. "Hello, this is Johnny. Dori can't come to the phone right now."

Butterman smiled. "Then I'll wait. I have some very good news for her."

Johnny sighed. "We have a huge problem, Mr. Butterman. Pansy Jones reported us to DFCS, and the caseworker who showed up was Ethel Carter, the caseworker who testified two years ago that I was unfit to care for my brothers. I think she's still holding a grudge. Nothing either one of us said seemed to matter. She even brought up the assault on Beep, inferring it happened because I was unfit."

"Shit," Peanut said.

"Exactly. She is going to try and take the kids away from us. I know it."

"Well, she tried before and didn't," Peanut said.

"I'm not willing to risk losing my brothers again by assuming anything."

"Let me talk to Dori," Peanut said.

"Just a second," Johnny said, then handed Dori the phone. "He wants to talk to you, honey. Give the baby to me."

Dori handed Luther to Johnny and then wiped her face before she answered. "This is Dori."

"Dori, I'm sorry about what's happening."

Dori shuddered past a sob. "Sorry? Sorry won't fix this if they take Luther away from me and the boys away from Johnny."

"I know. Poor choice of words, but I have news, and I might have a suggestion that would fix the problem."

"What news?"

"We opened your grandfather's safety-deposit box. There's a diamond-and-ruby ring and some other family keepsakes."

"The ring belonged to Grandy's mother. I knew it was there."

"Did you know about the stock portfolio in your name?"

"The what?"

"A stock portfolio he bought in your name the month you were born."

"No, I didn't know about that," Dori said.

"Well, it seems he chose stocks wisely, bought and sold some through the years, and a few years back, at his stockbroker's advice, bought some stock in what was a new high-tech company that is now a top-notch business. Bottom line, my girl, you are rich. As in millionaire rich."

Dori gasped and then started to cry all over again.

"None of that will mean a damn thing if I don't have my baby."

"And now we get to my suggestion. Do you like Johnny Pine?"

"Yes, of course. He's been wonderful to us."

"No, I mean, could you like him as relationship material?"

"That possibility exists," she said.

"Good. Now let me talk to Johnny."

She handed the phone back to Johnny.

"Now he wants to talk to you."

She took the baby and Johnny took the phone.

"Yeah?"

"I have a suggestion that could bring an end to your troubles with DFCS."

"Like what?"

"Do you like Dori?"

"Well, sure. She's great."

"Do you like her enough to consider a personal relationship with her?"

Johnny looked at Dori, then cupped her face and ran his thumb down the side of her jaw.

"Yes, I like her enough to consider a personal relationship."

Dori shivered beneath his touch as she realized Butterman was asking Johnny the same question he'd asked her.

"Put the phone on speaker," Butterman said.

"Just a minute," Johnny said and then pressed a button. "Okay, you're on speaker now."

"Here's the deal," Butterman said. "You two are

very young to have such adult responsibilities. You're both trying to take care of your families on your own, and now DFCS has their nose in your business and is threatening you with removing the children from your custody, right?"

"Right," they said.

"So this would end tomorrow if you were married."

Johnny took a quick breath, started to speak, and then found himself staring at Dori instead, waiting for her reaction.

Dori already knew Johnny cared for her because he'd told her. What he didn't know was that she was very attracted to him.

"Well? Did both of you faint or what?" Butterman asked.

"I'm game if she is," Johnny said.

"I'm willing to do whatever it takes to keep our boys," Dori said.

Butterman chuckled. "Congratulations on your upcoming nuptials. If it were me, I wouldn't waste any time. Go get the license and find a preacher, and your trouble with Miss Carter is a thing of the past. I assume I am invited to the wedding."

"We'll be in touch," Johnny said and disconnected. Dori was still staring at him as if she'd seen a ghost. He started talking fast, desperate for her not to back out. "It can be in name only for as long as you need. I understand how you must feel about men and—"

Dori put her fingers across his mouth.

"I do not have a blanket hate on the male species. I was drugged. I barely remember what happened—only the face of the man and feeling like I was standing outside my own body, watching it happen. I do not fear you in any way. I like you, Johnny Pine; even if this sinful relationship is only five days old, I really like you. I think we can do this. We owe it to the boys to give it a try."

Johnny rubbed the back of Luther's little baby neck and then kissed Dori squarely on the mouth.

"I don't have to try. It's a dream come true for me. I think we're both due some happiness, honey, and you and buster here make me very happy."

Dori blinked. Johnny had just called the baby buster, which was Granddaddy's nickname for Luther Joe. It was like she'd just gotten permission from Granddaddy to do it. She shivered, remembering what Butterman had just told her about that stock portfolio—and the life insurance, the money for the house, and the money for a new car. She was sure Johnny was going to pass out when she told him.

"Oh, Johnny, you have no idea how happy you're going to be."

He pulled her and the baby into an embrace and then held them.

"This is certainly going to set the gossip wheel rolling," he muttered.

"Let it roll," Dori said. "Once we're married, there will be all kinds of new gossip for them to chew on."

"Like what?" he asked.

She smiled. "You'll find out soon enough. What I want to know is, what do we do first to get this started?"

"We get a marriage license and find a preacher. No waiting period in Georgia and no blood tests required."

Luther's patience finally wore thin. He threw back his head and let out a howl.

"I need to change him and feed him," Dori said.

"You do the diaper; I'll heat the bottle. We're in this together, honey, all the way."

Chapter 18

JOHNNY HEATED UP THE BOTTLE AND THEN CALLED HIS boss. Clawson answered quickly.

"You guys okay? What's up with DFCS?"

"We *will* be okay. I'll explain it later. Is it cool with you if I take my lunch hour now? I'll work even later tonight to make it up," Johnny said.

"Well, good news is, you can take more than the lunch hour. That part we put on your dozer didn't fix it. It's still leaking transmission fluid somewhere else, and we've had to order another part, which won't be in until sometime tomorrow."

"Okay. I will be there later, and thanks, Boss. This crazy part of my life is about to smooth all the way out. I'll see you after a while."

Dori came in carrying a very dissatisfied baby. Johnny grinned and handed her the bottle. The moment she plugged it in his mouth, the fussing ceased.

"Magic stuff," Johnny said. "Come sit down with me until he's through."

Dori followed him into the living room and sat right beside him.

Johnny touched her arm, then the side of her face. The urgency of this wedding was frightening, but at the same time, he was so worried about how this would make her feel. He'd always heard that the wedding ceremony was a great big deal to girls, and now she was going to be cheated out of all the preparation.

"We don't dare wait to do this, agreed?" he asked.

"Agreed."

"What about tomorrow? We can keep the boys out of school, and they'll be my best men. Is there someone special you would like to be there?"

Tears blurred her vision as her granddaddy's face slid through her mind.

"Not really. My so-called friends at school dropped me when I dropped out. I could ask Lovey and Ruby. They've been so helpful and sweet."

"I told Clawson I was taking my lunch hour now. We can go to the courthouse and get the license. I don't know how much it costs, but I'm sure it's under a hundred dollars. I think I have about thirty dollars on me."

"I have some money too. I cashed a check this morning when I got groceries. I was going to make a special supper tonight and a special breakfast tomorrow."

"You still can," he said. "And if that breakfast is anything but oatmeal, I'm first in line."

She laughed. "There is nothing wrong with oatmeal, but I wanted to do this for you guys. Oh wait! I have to find out if Preacher Lawless can marry us tomorrow."

"I'll call him. You can talk," Johnny said and looked up the number. He made the call on her phone and then took the baby so she could talk.

It rang twice before the call was answered.

"First Baptist Church, Ron Lawless speaking."

"Preacher Lawless, this is Dori Grant."

"Dori! How are you, my dear?"

"Oh, we're okay. Thank you. It seems I am going to need your services once more."

"Certainly. What can I do for you?"

"Can you marry me and Johnny Pine tomorrow?"

She heard a slight gasp, and then Lawless quickly cleared his throat.

"Did you say marry?"

"Yes, sir. Are you free? If not, we can always find a justice of the peace, but I—"

"No, no, of course I can perform the ceremony. I just had no idea you were—"

"It's a long story, sir. We'll tell you tomorrow. Will the church be free in the afternoon?"

"Yes, as a matter of fact, it will. Did you have a time in mind?"

Dori looked at Johnny. "What time?"

He shrugged. "Noon?"

She smiled. "Would twelve o'clock, noon, be okay with you?"

Lawless chuckled. "I think I can delay my lunch for this."

"Thank you so much," Dori said. "See you tomorrow." She laid the phone down and then looked at Johnny.

He started smiling.

She grinned.

Luther took advantage of the silent moment to fill his diaper.

Johnny looked startled.

Dori laughed. "Give him to me. As soon as I clean him up, we can go get the license."

Johnny and Dori went into the courthouse, got the license, and walked out without explanation or conversation.

The clerk who waited on them immediately told her coworkers, who also shared the news when they went to lunch. Before the noon hour was over, half the town of Blessings knew Johnny Pine and Dori Grant had applied for a marriage license. The news was like pouring water on a flame; if they were no longer living in sin, there was nothing to gossip about.

Pansy Jones had decided to make herself scarce for a couple of weeks and left to visit her sister in Savannah early the same morning. There would be no follow-up call to Ethel Carter regarding their change in status because Pansy wouldn't know.

Johnny drove Dori to the Curl Up and Dye to ask Ruby if she'd be a witness in their wedding, then waited in the car with Luther, who'd done them all a favor and gone to sleep.

"I won't be long," Dori said.

"We're fine," Johnny said. "Take your time."

She got out, careful not to wake the baby, then hurried inside the salon while Johnny called Peanut Butterman to tell him about the time of the ceremony and where it would be held.

Every stylist in the shop had someone in their chair, and Mabel Jean was cleaning off her workstation from the last manicure when Dori walked in.

Mabel Jean went to the front to greet her.

"Hi, Dori. Do you want to make an appointment?"

"No, ma'am. I just need to speak to Ruby for a second if that's okay?"

Mabel Jean turned and yelled, "Hey, Ruby! Got a minute?"

Ruby saw Dori and waved.

"Sure, just give me a minute."

She put a bouffant cap over the color job she'd just done on her client and set the timer, then patted her on the shoulder and headed for the front.

"Dori! Great to see you, honey. How are you doing? Did you get any rest last night?"

"Some," Dori said. "I'm sorry to bother you when you're so busy, but I wanted to ask you something. Johnny and I are getting married tomorrow at noon at the Baptist Church and—"

Ruby threw her arms around Dori. "What? Oh wow! I am so happy to hear this! I can't think of any two people more deserving to have some good news in their lives than you guys. Congratulations."

Dori smiled, a little embarrassed.

"I wanted to know if you would be one of the witnesses for me. I'm not doing a big wedding, so technically you wouldn't be a bridesmaid, and if you're busy, I'll totally understand."

Ruby's eyes widened with undisguised delight.

"Oh my sweet Lord! I have never had the pleasure. I would be honored. What time and where did you say this would be?"

"The Baptist Church at noon tomorrow. Just come as you are. We're not doing anything fancy. We just need to get married really fast."

Ruby frowned. "I know it's none of my business why, but are you two in trouble in any way?"

Dori's eyes welled with tears. "Yes, ma'am. Someone called DFCS and implied that we were unfit to care for the children and that they should take them away. Even if I moved out right now, the damage was already done to Johnny's character. They even brought up Beep getting beat up at school as if it was Johnny's negligence that caused it to happen. Our lawyer suggested the marriage as a solution, and we both agreed it was the quickest way to bring the accusations to an end."

Ruby gasped. "Who turned you in?"

"It doesn't matter," Dori said. "It can't be taken back."

Ruby glared. "It was Pansy, wasn't it?"

Dori shrugged. "I have no way to prove who I think did it. But I thank you for agreeing to be at the services. You have been so good to me, helping us after the fire like you did. I was hoping you would say yes, so I'll see you at noon tomorrow?"

"Absolutely," Ruby said and then hugged her again. "Bless you, child. You don't know it yet, but I think you two are going to find that this turns out to be quite a blessing."

"I'm already blessed," Dori said. "I'll see you tomorrow, and thank you very much."

Ruby watched her get back in the car, saw Johnny touch her shoulder in a gesture of comfort, and nodded.

"They're going to be just fine," she muttered. "On the other hand, Pansy Jones is going to be a long time living this stunt down."

She strode back to the work area with a smile on her face and quickly announced, "You will not guess who is getting married tomorrow or why."

—⁓—

Dori called the restaurant to see if Lovey was there, but she was not.

"I'll call her later," Dori said. "Let's go home. You

need to eat some lunch before you go back to work, and I have cookies to bake before I go pick up the boys."

"Sounds good to me," Johnny said. "And you know what else sounds good? The fact that you think of that old house as home."

Dori heard the apology in his use of "old" to refer to his house and didn't want him to feel like it was necessary.

"Don't say that. It's a wonderful house. I found out at an early age that it isn't where you live that matters as much as who you're living with, and I consider myself very blessed that you came to our rescue. You will forever be my white knight."

Johnny blinked away tears, and as soon as he braked for a red light, he reached across the seat and took her hand.

"I'm no hero, honey, but I will make you the same promise I made the boys. We aren't going to live on that side of town forever."

Dori shook her head. "But you are a hero to me. You took on so much when you chose to raise your brothers, and now you have taken on even more by adding Luther and me to the mix."

"We'll make it work," he said. "You'll see."

Dori smiled. She wanted to tell him about her inheritance so badly but decided that would be her gift to him after the ceremony was over.

―⁂―

Dori took the last pan of cookies out of the oven five minutes before she had to leave to pick up the boys from school.

Luther was sitting in the high chair, banging his

teething ring against the tray and talking to the red rooster clock hanging on the wall.

Dori laughed as she dried her hands and went to wash Luther's face and hands before they left.

"I swear, Luther Joe. Ceiling fans and rooster clocks are all the same to you, aren't they?" she said and kept digging the wet cloth beneath his little fat chin, wiping away the drool and cracker crumbs.

Then she made a face at him, and he promptly made one back. She was still laughing when she put him on her hip, slung the diaper bag and her purse on her other arm, and headed out the door to get the boys.

She pulled into the pick-up area at school and parked, then left the car running and the air conditioner on as she settled in to wait. Her head was still spinning from the events of the day, going from abject horror and fear to relief and anticipation. She wasn't sure if she knew what love felt like, but she certainly cared for Johnny Pine in a very special way. Five days and counting. Tomorrow would be the sixth day since the Pines had taken them in, and when she woke up on the seventh day, she would be one of them.

Luther thought about fussing, then poked his thumb in his mouth and was still sucking when Dori heard the last bell ring across the school yard. She sat up to watch for the boys, and when she saw them coming across the grass looking for her car, she got out and waved. As soon as they saw her, they started running.

Dori circled the car and opened the door for them to get in. When Luther heard the sound of kids squealing and talking, his thumb sucking quickly ended, and he began kicking his feet and waving his arms.

Dori laughed. "You're glad to see them too, aren't you, little man?"

Marshall reached the car first.

"Hi, Dori! Hi, baby!" he said and climbed past the car seat and buckled in, then poked Luther in the belly just enough to make him laugh.

Beep was lagging, and Dori frowned when she saw his face.

"What's wrong?" she asked as he dumped his backpack in the seat and crawled in the car.

He shrugged and ducked his head.

Dori got in the car and then looked in the rearview mirror at Marshall.

"What's wrong with Beep?"

"He wanted to buy a book at the book fair after school, but we forgot to ask Johnny for money."

"Is it still open? Can you still buy the books?" she asked.

Beep looked up. Had hope sprung anew?

"Yes, in the library," Marshall said.

"Well, we can fix that," Dori said. "Hang on while I get out of this line and go find a place to park. We'll all go to the book fair and see what's what, okay?"

"Okay!" Beep cried.

Marshall looked relieved that Beep's sadness was gone as Dori headed for the school parking lot. A couple of minutes later, she found a space and killed the engine.

"Here's the deal, guys. We'll go in, and you can pick out one apiece, okay?"

Marshall looked surprised and then happy, but felt obligated to bow out.

"I don't have to have one," he said.

"I know, but I want you to if you want it," Dori said.

"Can ole Joe come inside too?" Beep asked.

Dori chuckled. "Yes, he's coming too."

They got out of the car, and by the time Dori had Luther out of the car seat and her purse and diaper bag on her arm, the boys were doing a two-step, anxious to get back inside before the "good" books were gone.

She had a moment of déjà vu as they walked into the building, remembering only a few short years ago when she'd been in this same elementary school. Now, here she was with a baby on her hip and Johnny's little brothers bouncing along beside her. This morning she thought her world was ending and now she felt like a million bucks—maybe even more.

She laughed to herself as she followed the boys down the hall to the library. As she had expected, it was full of kids shopping and parents standing in line to pay.

"Go pick out the book you want, guys. I'll wait here near the checkout line, okay?"

"Okay!" they cried and headed for the racks where the books were displayed.

Luther was fascinated by the room full of kids and started wiggling in Dori's arms.

"No, you can't get down," she said softly. "They'd squash you in a minute and never know you were there."

She watched the boys, their heads together as they talked, trying to make their choices, and thought how great it must be to grow up with a sibling. She was still watching them when someone tapped her on the shoulder.

She turned and recognized Gigi Potts, a woman who had been one of Grandy's best friends.

"I thought that was you," Gigi said. "I'm here with my youngest grandson, Nate. Remember him? He's the one with the green stripe in his hair. Fetching, isn't it?"

Dori laughed. "Hi, Gigi. Last time I knew anything about him, he was a toddler. Time sure passes quickly."

"Well, your little guy is a charmer. Look at all that curly hair. He has your eyes and smile, doesn't he?" And then her smile slipped. "I was so sorry to hear about the fire and about Meeker. My husband and I were in San Diego. We just got back into town late last night or I would have been at the funeral."

"The last five days have been long and hard," she said.

Gigi gave her a hug. "I can only imagine," she said and then rolled her eyes when she realized she could no longer see her grandson. "I better run that boy down and get him home. I'm still jet-lagged and in no shape to be babysitting. It was good to see you."

After Gigi left, it didn't take long for other people to recognize her and come up to talk. Some came to offer their condolences, while others came to make a fuss over the baby.

She was still talking to a lady she knew from church when the boys came running up.

"We're ready!" Beep cried and then threw his arms around Dori's waist. "Thank you, Dori. Thank you for my book."

"Yeah, Dori, thanks a lot. I have been wanting to read this," Marshall said.

"You're welcome, and we better get in line." She waved good-bye to the lady from church. "It appears we are done here. It was nice to see you."

She ushered the boys toward the checkout line while

Luther tap-danced against her belly, kicking in excitement. They paid and left the library, talking in tandem, and then when they got in the car, they clammed up, both intrigued by their books.

The ride home was quiet. Luther had fallen asleep, and Dori was hoping she could get him in the house and down for a nap without waking him up.

"We're here," she said as she pulled up into the driveway and parked. "Give me a second to get Luther out. If we're quiet, maybe he'll stay asleep."

The boys stayed quiet. They'd heard him cry before and didn't want to precipitate a new crying spell.

Marshall got out so Dori could reach the baby carrier, and Beep crawled out on that side after she'd gotten her stuff and the baby. She locked the car and handed the keys to Marshall.

"Will you unlock the front door for me, please?"

They ran ahead, and by the time she got inside, the boys had moved from the living room to the doorway of the kitchen. She removed the keys and locked the door, then walked up behind them. It was obvious what had their attention.

"Two cookies apiece before supper," she said.

They bolted toward the cookies cooling on the racks as she headed down the hall with the baby, then put him down for his nap. When she came back into the kitchen, the boys were at the table, nibbling on their cookies with their noses in their new books.

"Wanna split a root beer?" she asked.

Their eyes widened. "We get cookies *and* pop?"

"You do today," she said.

"You're the best," Beep said.

Marshall glanced up and then smiled shyly. "Yeah, you're awesome."

Dori smiled, a little surprised her capacity for joy was still intact. "Does anyone have homework?" she asked.

"I have a little," Marshall said and put his new book aside and got it out of his backpack and went to work.

Dori got the roast out of the refrigerator, seasoned it up, and put it in the oven, then began preparing the vegetables she'd cook with it later.

By the time Johnny came home, the scents of his surprise supper drew him all the way into the kitchen, where he found Dori setting the table and Luther banging on the high chair with a teething biscuit.

Johnny paused in the doorway, absorbing the homey atmosphere and the girl who'd soon be his wife.

Dori looked up and smiled. "You're home!"

Johnny swallowed past a lump in his throat. He hadn't had anyone to come home to in so long, he couldn't remember when the last time had been.

He set his lunch box on the counter and then hesitated.

"I would sincerely love to give you a hug, but I'm too dirty."

"There's no such thing as being too dirty for a hug."

He laughed, scooped her up in his arms, and swung her off her feet, then stole a quick kiss before putting her down.

Dori felt like she'd taken flight, and when his laugh sent a chill up her back, she hung on for dear life.

"Where are the boys?" he asked as he put her down.

"In their room, reading their new books. I hope you don't mind but the—"

"Oh man, the book fair!" Johnny said and slapped the side of his head. "I completely forgot. You took them?"

She nodded. "You don't care, do you?"

"No, no, of course not! I'll pay you back as—"

"No more yours and mine, Johnny Pine. After tomorrow, everything we have is ours. Okay?"

He hesitated and then agreed. "Yes, okay. I'm just not used to having anyone to depend on but myself."

"There will be lots of things changing after tomorrow," she said.

He frowned. "Like what?"

She shook her head. "You'll see but not until after the wedding."

He grinned. "You have a secret?"

She nodded. "Yes, but trust me, it's all good."

"Yeah, I trust you," he said softly.

"Go wash up, and while you're back there, tell the boys that supper is ready. We have much to discuss with them. I sure hope they won't care."

"They won't care," he said. "I promise you."

Chapter 19

THEY WERE ALL THE WAY TO DESSERT, WHICH CON-
sisted of more chocolate chip cookies, when Johnny told
the boys they needed to have a talk.

Beep gave Marshall a frantic look. "You said you
wouldn't tell."

Marshall rolled his eyes. "I didn't."

Johnny frowned. "Beep, what did you do?"

"It was an accident," he mumbled.

Johnny kept waiting.

Beep sighed. "I axaldentally broke the night-light."

"Well, accidents happen," Johnny said. "Besides, it
was already half-broken, wasn't it?"

Beep's eyes widened. "Oh wow, Johnny! I thought I
was gonna get the wax for sure."

Dori stifled a laugh. Beep's expressions were
priceless.

"No, buddy. You're good. I'm the one who broke
the first half of it when I was little. You're the one who
finished it off."

Beep sighed. "But now we won't have no light to
sleep by."

"Any light," Johnny said. "I'll leave a light on in the
bathroom tonight and get a new night-light tomorrow."

Dori arched her eyebrows, as if to remind him there
were other things on the agenda for tomorrow too.

"Right," Johnny said. "And we still need to have

a talk. How would you two feel about Dori staying with us?"

"But she's already with us," Marshall said.

"No, I mean for always."

Beep looked at Dori and then at the baby in her lap.

"Would ole Joe stay too?"

Dori nodded. "Yes, where I go, Joe goes."

Marshall gave Johnny a long look and then glanced at Dori the same way.

"Are you guys gonna get married or somethin'?"

"Yes, we're going to get married tomorrow," Johnny said.

Marshall smiled. "I told Beep you guys were in love, but he didn't believe me. I think it's a good idea."

Dori glanced at Johnny, but he was staring intently at the boys.

"Why did you think we were in love?" he asked.

"'Cause you guys watch each other when you think no one's looking. I know how that stuff goes down."

Johnny rolled his eyes. "Let me guess. You were watching romantic movies at Miss Jane's too?"

"No, just the afternoon soaps. There's lots of love stuff going on in those shows."

Dori saw the look on Johnny's face and burst out laughing, which made Luther laugh.

Beep wasn't sure what was funny, but he was still so relieved that he wasn't in trouble for breaking the night-light that he went ahead and laughed too.

"What? What did I say?" Marshall said.

Johnny grinned. "So, Beep, how do you feel about me and Dori getting married?"

"I like it. She likes us, and she makes good stuff to

eat, and she's really, really nice. And when ole Joe gets a little older, me and him can play together."

Marshall frowned. "What about me?"

Beep shrugged. "You're gonna grow up and get a girlfriend just like Johnny did. I'm gonna need someone to play with, aren't I?"

This time it was Johnny who laughed. "So how do you feel about staying home from school tomorrow and being my two best men at the wedding?"

"Yes! We feel like that's a good deal," Marshall said. "Don't we, Beep?"

Beep nodded. Anything that had to do with missing school was fine with him. "Can we go watch TV?" he asked.

"Yeah, sure," Johnny said and then grinned at Dori as they ran out of the kitchen. "I told you they would be fine with this."

Luther squawked because the boys left, then poked his thumb in his mouth and leaned against Dori's chest.

"Even ole Joe doesn't seem to mind," Johnny said.

Dori glanced down at the baby and then back up at Johnny. They'd do whatever they had to do to keep their boys where they belonged.

"Do you have something clean to wear tomorrow?" Dori asked.

"All I have is what I wore to the funeral."

Dori smiled wryly. "I find myself in the same position. I don't think Granddaddy would find that so strange. He and Grandy were big on recycling."

Johnny circled the table, then got down on one knee and put his arms around the both of them.

"I know you don't love me, but maybe one day, if I'm

lucky, you'll look up and realize you can't live without me. In the meantime, I can love you enough for both of us."

The declaration was so moving to Dori that, for a moment, she was speechless. And then she cupped his face with one hand and leaned forward until their lips were only inches apart.

He could feel the warmth of her breath against his face, and when he suddenly saw his reflection in her eyes, it felt like she'd captured his soul.

"I already see you, Johnny Pine, and if it's just the same with you, I'd rather live my life beside you, not without you."

He kissed her because he could no longer talk, and when the baby grabbed his ear and then his hair, he laughed.

"Hey, little guy, we don't intend to leave you out. You're coming too. Okay?"

Dori leaned forward until their foreheads were touching.

"We are going to have a most wonderful life," she said softly.

Johnny put his hand on the back of Luther's head and ruffled the soft baby curls.

"Yes…yes we will."

———

Ethel Carter had put in a request for a copy of the school incident involving Brooks Pine and the police, and had filed her report at the office before leaving on visitations with some of the other cases she was working. When she finished for the day, she went straight home. She had a bone to pick with Pansy Jones and intended to call her up as soon as she got off her feet.

After changing into something comfortable and

slipping into her old house shoes, she poured herself a glass of sweet tea and sat down with her phone and her notebook.

The ice clinked against her mother's crystal as she took a good long swig of the tea and then set the glass aside as she thumbed through the notebook for Pansy's number. The phone rang so long, she thought it was going to voice mail, and then a man suddenly answered.

"Hello?"

Ethel frowned. Drat. Bart Jones. Bart didn't like her, and she didn't like him either. Still, she needed to talk to his wife.

"Hello, Bart, this is Ethel Carter. Is Pansy home? I need to speak with her."

"No, she's not here. She took herself a little vacation and went to Savannah to see her sister. I'll tell her you called."

He hung up in her ear before she could ask for Pansy's cell phone number, but she shrugged it off. Maybe it was for the best. Maybe by the time Pansy returned, Ethel would have this mess all sorted out. She reached for her iced tea and the remote, then turned on the television to catch the evening news.

Lovey Cooper was over the moon about standing up for Dori and Johnny but furious as to why it was happening. Once she learned Ruby Dye would also be a witness, she gave Ruby a call.

Ruby was locking up the salon when the phone began to ring. She almost let the answering machine pick up and then changed her mind.

"Curl Up and Dye, Ruby speaking."

"Ruby, it's me, Lovey. Are you as pissed off about what happened to Dori and Johnny as I am?"

"Yes, but I have a good feeling about those two. I think they'll make this work, even if it was a choice made under duress."

"Maybe," Lovey said. "I called Pansy Jones this afternoon. I was gonna give her what for, but Bart said she had gone to Savannah for a couple of weeks to visit her sister. If you ask me, she hightailed it out of town hoping this would all go away before she returned."

"Stirred up all that trouble and then ran off, did she?"

"She sure did. She's going to come back to a cold reception if I have any say about it. There was no call for all of this ugliness. But enough about her. I wanted to know what you're wearing tomorrow. Dori kept stressing that they had to keep it simple, but I think she at least needs a bridal bouquet, don't you?"

"Yes, and a cake. Every bride and groom should have a cake," Ruby said.

"And pictures, lots of pictures for remembrance," Lovey added. "My nephew, Junior Cooper, is the photographer down at the *Tribune*. I'll get him to come down and snap some shots. It would make a good story, anyway. I can see the headlines: *Married to save a family*...rather than getting married to *have* a family. What do you think?"

"I think it's too long for a headline," Ruby said.

Lovey giggled. "I always take too long to tell a story. They'll figure it out. I'm still going to give Junior a call. As for the cake, the bakery owes me a favor. They screwed up on a great big order I had last month. I think I can wrangle us a wedding cake for tomorrow. We can have the reception at the party room in the restaurant."

Ruby's excitement was growing. She loved making people happy.

"Then I'll get in touch with Franklin's Floral and get them to do her up a little bouquet," Ruby added. "And who's gonna throw the birdseed when they come out of the church?"

"Birdseed?" Lovey cried. "What about rice for good luck?"

"Oh, they quit using rice when someone figured out the birds ate what was on the ground, then it swelled up in their little bellies and killed them. A mass bird killing is not a very auspicious beginning to a marriage."

"Well, I'll swan. I didn't know that," Lovey said. "We could spread the word about the wedding and let whoever wants to come just show up."

"That's an idea," Ruby said. "In fact, I like that. I'll run by the Walmart on the way home, get a sack of birdseed and some net and ribbon, and make up some packets to give out to whoever makes it to the church."

Lovey giggled. "This is fun! We should go into the wedding planner business."

Ruby groaned. "I wouldn't want to change my calling. I like making people look pretty. As for what I'm wearing, I think I'll wear a dress like I'd wear to church."

"Me too," Lovey said. "So, see you tomorrow."

"Straight-up noon," Ruby added.

"Will do. Bye now."

"Good-bye," Ruby said and then locked up the shop and headed to Franklin's Floral before they closed.

—〜〜—

Night came and Johnny was in bed but couldn't sleep. This time tomorrow, he would have a wife but in name only. He didn't know when or if they'd consummate the marriage, but he wanted to; God knows he wanted to.

On the other side of the wall, Dori was sleepless as well, contemplating what it would be like to be married. Would Johnny expect her to sleep with him right away? She remembered how her grandparents had been with each other. Even at their ages, the love they had for each other was obvious. She wanted that; she wanted a partner in life, but she thought she was ready for a lover too. Then she rolled over and willed herself to sleep, convinced that she would know when it was right.

—〜〜—

Granddaddy was smiling at Dori and blowing her a kiss when he suddenly disappeared. She woke up with a gasp and remembered he was gone and that today she was getting married. She abruptly burst into tears, sick at heart that he would not be here to give her away. Still crying, she went across the hall to the bathroom, did her business, and washed the tears away. Today was not a day for crying. Today was the beginning of the rest of her life.

She hurried back in the room to get dressed so she could make breakfast. This was not an oatmeal morning either. She'd shopped purposefully for this and hurried up the hall to get busy before everyone woke up. As soon as she started the coffee, she dug through the refrigerator and then got to work.

Johnny opened his eyes to the smell of bacon frying and immediately two things went through his mind: they were not having oatmeal, and today Dori would be his wife. He rolled out of bed and hurried across the hall to the bathroom, resisting the urge to dance. He shaved with care, thinking about the wedding taking place at noon, and as soon as he was dressed, woke up the boys.

"Hey, guys…time to get up," he said.

Marshall groaned without opening his eyes.

"I thought we got to skip school today," he mumbled.

"You do," Johnny said.

Beep whimpered then shifted into a whine.

"Then why do we have to get up?"

Johnny grinned. "Take a deep breath and tell me what you smell."

They sniffed and then as if on cue, sat up.

Marshall grinned. "Bacon! Dori is making bacon!"

"What else is she makin'?" Beep asked.

"Get yourselves dressed and come see," Johnny said.

They passed him on his way out the door and were laughing and giggling as they ran into the bathroom.

Johnny paused in the kitchen doorway, looking for stress on her face, saw nothing but joy, and let the truth of their future settle in his heart. It was the best day of his life.

He walked in with a smile on his face.

"Something smells wonderful."

"Special supper last night. Special breakfast this morning," Dori said.

"That roast and vegetables last night was super. I can't wait to dig in to this. What can I do to help?"

"You can set the table, and we'll need butter and jelly there as well. And you can taste test this bite of bacon, just to make sure it's edible."

He grinned and opened his mouth as she popped in the piece.

"Yum," he said and headed for the cabinet, chewing as he went.

The boys were fast on Johnny's heels and in the kitchen before he'd finished setting the table.

"We smelled bacon!" Marshall cried.

"There's eggs! We got us some eggs!" Beep added and threw his arms around Dori's waist. "We sure do love you."

Dori's heart stopped. She shoved the eggs off the fire and put her arms around Beep's neck.

"Thank you, honey. I love you guys too."

Johnny smiled. She had enchanted all the Pines.

"Guys, come sit and let Dori finish, okay?"

They pushed and shoved on their way to the table to get the same seats they always sat in, which made Johnny roll his eyes. Why they thought they had to fuss to sit in the same chairs cracked him up.

Dori dished up the eggs and added hash browns and bacon on each plate.

"Oh man, this looks good," Johnny said and carried plates to the table while Dori got the plate of toast.

She sat down, watching as the Pines dug in, and knew she was right where God meant her to be. Regardless of what had precipitated this relationship, it had become a blessing. Aware that Luther could wake up at any moment, she picked up her fork and began to eat with them.

And so the morning went. The closer it got to noon,

the more frantic the activity became. Dori knew they would likely miss dinner, so she made some small sandwiches and let them graze from the platter as they passed through. Just as everyone needed in the bathroom at once, Luther took the opportunity to spit up on his clean outfit, and Dori had to stop and change him. By the time they left for the church, they were frazzled.

"Getting married makes me tired," Beep moaned as Johnny drove over the old railroad crossing.

"I'm hot, and the baby looks mad," Marshall stated.

Johnny turned up the fan on the air conditioner, and Dori reached over the seat and rubbed Luther Joe's curls. He squawked his disapproval, then popped his thumb in his mouth and the moment passed.

Johnny glanced at Dori to see if she was upset by all the whining, but she looked absolutely Zen. He didn't know how she did it. He didn't know that she was storing all of the moments up for the years to come and the "remember whens."

When they arrived at the church, there was a rather large assortment of cars, and that was when the boys realized they were at the same place where the funeral had been held. They looked at each other and panicked.

"Did someone else die?" Marshall asked.

Johnny frowned. "No. What makes you say that?"

"We're back at the dead house," Beep said.

Johnny was stunned. Yet another sign of how he had neglected their upbringing. He looked at Dori.

"Sorry."

She shook her head.

"You have nothing to be sorry for, and, no, this isn't a dead house. It's a church. People come here every

Sunday to sing songs and learn about the stories in the Bible. People also get married in churches."

"We don't go to church," Marshall said.

"Well, we will today," Johnny said.

Beep frowned. "I don't wanna go where no dead people are."

"Me either," Dori said. "Let's go inside and get ourselves married. Okay?"

"Yay!" Beep cried and then poked Luther's belly just to hear him laugh.

"I'll get the baby and the carrier," Johnny said. "You get the outlaws."

Dori smiled at the boys as she grabbed her purse and the diaper bag.

"Let's go hold the door open for Johnny and ole Joe, and remember, quiet voices and best behavior in church."

"Yes, ma'am," Marshall said. "I've got Beep covered."

They were almost at the door when it suddenly opened and Ruby and Lovey came out, all smiles and waving.

"Come in, come in," Ruby said. "Dori! I love how you did your hair, up on top of your head with those pretty curls down around your face."

"You all look amazing," Lovey said. "Guys, come with me. Dori, give me the diaper bag. Mabel Jean is going to take care of the baby during the ceremony."

"Oh thanks," she said and watched her man and men-in-training all disappear around the corner of the hallway.

"You're with me," Ruby said and took her by the hand as they went in the other direction.

"What are all the cars doing here?" Dori asked. "Is there another event?"

"They belong to your friends, honey, and Johnny's

friends. They heard about what happened to you two, and they wanted to show their support by coming. I hope you don't mind?"

"Mind? It's wonderful," Dori said.

Ruby frowned. "Don't cry! You'll mess up your face."

Dori dutifully blinked away tears as they entered one of the classrooms.

"You got me flowers!" Dori cried as she picked up the bridal bouquet and held it beneath her nose. "I didn't think we'd have any—"

Ruby was grinning from ear to ear.

"Oh, that's not all! Junior Cooper from the *Tribune* is going to take pictures, and Lovey has a wedding cake and a reception set up at the party room at the restaurant for afterward."

Dori's eyes widened and then she took a deep breath to keep from crying all over again.

"So everyone pretty much knows about why this is happening?"

"Yes, and they're livid. Pansy Jones's name is mud in this town right now, and it's going to be a cold day in hell before all is forgiven."

"I never said her name. I can't prove she did it," Dori said.

"Well, the fact that she hightailed it out of town says a lot," Ruby muttered. "But enough about her. I hear the music beginning. We've got to get you into the chapel. As soon as the wedding march begins, Lovey and I will head down the aisle. Marshall and Beep are walking out with Johnny to the altar. We didn't think Beep could handle too much ritual."

"Wise decision," Dori said, and then she shivered

as Ruby led her back into the hall. "I can't believe this is happening."

Ruby paused. "Are you okay with it?"

"I am very okay."

"Good. That's what we want to hear."

—⁓—

Lovey shuffled Johnny and the boys into a classroom where Mabel Jean was waiting. Mabel Jean took the baby in his carrier and the diaper bag and was sweet-talking to the little guy all the way to the sofa on the other side of the room.

Johnny looked a little anxious and then decided to give in and let the rest of this happen without his control.

"Uh, hey, Lovey, what's with all the cars outside?" Johnny asked.

"Oh, they're friends. When they found out why this was happening so fast, they wanted to do their part to make this special for you."

He couldn't believe it. After all the years he'd spent trying to live under Blessings's radar, people were suddenly showing support. Lovey was fussing with the boys' collars and their hair when Peanut Butterman walked in.

"There you are!" he crowed, slapping Johnny on the back and winking at the boys. "Johnny, I have something for you." He opened his hand and dropped the diamond-and-ruby ring into Johnny's hand.

"This was in Meeker Webb's safety-deposit box. Dori said it belonged to her great-grandmother. I think today is a great day to give it to her, don't you?"

Johnny stared at the huge square-cut diamond and the smaller rubies set on either side and gulped.

"Is this thing real?"

"Yes, it is," Peanut said. "Have you and Dori talked about uh…finances yet?"

Johnny nodded. "Yes, we know it will be tight, but she's going to get another computer and finish her online classes, and I'll be saving money by not having to pay a babysitter. We'll make it work."

Peanut grinned. "Boy, you are in for one really great surprise, but I need to get back into the sanctuary. I don't want to miss a moment of this. The whole wedding is going to be the lead story in tomorrow's paper. You know that, right?"

Johnny stared. "What? Why?"

"You two have become something called 'big news.' This wedding isn't to start a family. You're both getting married to save yours. It's what's called a feel-good story, and I can promise it's going to hit the Associated Press before it's done."

Now his head was spinning. He didn't know if this was bad or good.

"Uh, does Dori know this?"

"She didn't, but if I know Ruby Dye, she does now. How do you feel about that?"

Johnny shook his head. "I don't care. We both agreed we'd do anything to save our boys."

"But how do you feel about her?" Peanut asked.

And just like that, all the anxiety he was feeling went away; his voice lowered as the tone softened. "She and that little baby have become the light in our lives."

Then they heard the organist tuning up.

"Here we go," Lovey said. "Johnny will lead the way, then Marshall and then Beep, in that order. Boys, you will stand beside Johnny and you will not talk, fidget, or move out of position, is that clear?"

The three looked at each other, then at Lovey, and spoke in unison.

"Yes, ma'am."

She giggled. "This is going to be so much fun. I have to go and catch up with Ruby. See you soon."

Chapter 20

JOHNNY AND HIS BROTHERS WALKED OUT INTO THE sanctuary, and the moment he saw the pews filled to capacity, he nearly stumbled. The boys were right behind him, moving like little soldiers with their faces set and their arms swinging at their sides. He saw face after familiar face, and the ones that weren't smiling were dabbing tears. When they stopped at the pulpit, he turned to face the congregation and the boys turned too. He took the ring out of his pocket and bent down and whispered into Marshall's ear.

"Hold this for me, buddy. And whatever you do, don't put this in your mouth. It's worth more than my weight in gold."

Marshall eyed the big diamond and then curled his fingers around it so tight his knuckles turned white.

The music changed, and moments later, Lovey and Ruby walked together down the aisle. The organist shifted chords once more, and then everyone in the congregation stood up and turned toward the doorway and saw the pretty, long-legged girl in the black-and-white dress, with the curls piled on top of her head standing there alone.

It was not lost upon one woman there that the bride had worn that dress only three days earlier to her grandfather's funeral, and now she was wearing it to her wedding. They knew because of the fire it was probably all she had, but in a way, it became symbolic of bringing her missing grandfather with her.

When the organist struck the notes signaling the bride to start down the aisle, Dori felt a slight breeze against her neck and, for a second, wondered if it was her granddaddy's spirit standing with her after all.

She looked around and then whispered, "If it's you, Granddaddy, I hope you brought Grandy with you. I'd hate to think either of you missed this day."

Then she took a breath, exhaled slowly, and started walking toward the pulpit to the three dark-haired males who waited for her there.

Breath caught in the back of Johnny's throat as he saw her walking toward him, and then his vision blurred. He didn't see her clearly again until she was standing at his side. When she looked up at him and smiled, calm washed through him.

Preacher Lawless went through the preliminary ceremony with heartfelt eloquence, but all Johnny was waiting for were the questions that would bind them together for life. And then, all of a sudden, it was happening. They were standing face-to-face, their hands clasped, waiting for Lawless to begin.

Lawless cleared his throat and began to speak, the holy words tolling through Johnny's head. When the pastor called her Adorable, Johnny blinked and then looked at Dori. She smiled. He hadn't even known her real name. Then he repeated the pastor's words.

"I, John, take thee, Adorable, to be my wife, to have and to hold, from this day forward, for better or for worse, for richer, for poorer, in sickness and in health, to love and to cherish, from this day forward, until death do us part."

Lawless cleared his throat again and turned to Dori, giving her the same vow that she repeated.

"I, Adorable, take you, John, to be my husband, to have and to hold from this day forward, for better or for worse, for richer," at this point she paused to wink, then continued without missing a beat, "for poorer, in sickness and in health, to love and to cherish, from this day forward, until death do us part."

Johnny had missed the wink and was beginning to shake. It was happening. It was really happening.

"May I have the ring?" Preacher Lawless said.

Johnny turned to Marshall and held out his hand.

Marshall opened his hand over Johnny's palm, but the ring didn't fall. There was a moment of panic when Johnny let out an audible groan. He grabbed Marshall's hand and turned it over, then breathed a sigh of relief. Marshall had been holding the ring so tightly, it had stuck into the flesh of his palm. The congregation giggled at the momentary hitch in the ceremony, which lightened the mood.

The preacher blessed the ring and then gave it to Johnny.

When Dori saw what he was holding, she started to cry.

Johnny held his breath as he aimed the ring at her finger, praying it would fit enough to finish the ceremony. To their surprise, they found it was a perfect fit for her ring finger as it slid all the way down. Then he looked up at Dori, his voice shaking.

"With this ring, I thee wed. Wear it as a symbol of our love and commitment."

"Let us pray," Lawless said, and he did. And when he finished, he looked up. "Those whom God has joined together, let no man put asunder. John Andrew Pine, you may kiss your bride."

Johnny bent down and cupped Dori's cheeks.

Their kiss was slow and sweet, and when they stopped, there was an audible sigh from the congregation.

"Ladies and gentlemen, may I present Mr. and Mrs. Pine."

Dori turned and whispered to the preacher, then glanced down at the boys.

"Come here," she said, and moments later, Marshall was standing on her right and Beep was standing between her and Johnny as they all held hands.

Mabel Jean had been watching from the back of the church, and the moment she saw what was happening, she jumped up with the baby in her arms and headed for the pulpit.

"Wait a minute! Wait a minute!" she cried and handed Luther off to Johnny, which elicited another round of giggles from the congregation.

Lawless cleared his throat again. "Ladies and gentleman, may I present Mr. and Mrs. Pine and family. There will be a reception held at Granny's, and you're all invited."

The congregation began to clap, and down in the middle of the aisle, Junior Cooper was taking pictures.

Johnny caught Dori watching him, leaned over Beep's head, and whispered in her ear, "I love and adore you, Dori Pine."

"I adore you too, Johnny Pine, and as soon as we get in the car, I have something to tell you," she whispered back.

Johnny arched an eyebrow questioningly, but she didn't elaborate. Instead, they were herded back down the aisle toward the exit. Dori walked hand in hand with the boys, and Johnny and Luther brought up the rear.

Lovey corralled them outside the sanctuary and steered them into the classroom to get their things and put the baby in the baby carrier.

"You better put this blanket over Luther's head," she said and draped it so the birdseed she knew was coming wouldn't hit him in the face.

The church was empty as they headed for the front door. Then they saw the people standing on either side of the walk and all of a sudden Dori knew why Lovey had covered the baby's face.

"Brace yourself, boys, and run for the car," Dori said.

The moment they exited the church, the birdseed started flying.

"Holy crap! Run for your life," Beep yelled and bolted for the car with Marshall right behind him.

The crowd roared with laughter and then headed for the parking lot. The wedding had been a blast. They didn't want to miss a bit of the reception.

As soon as everyone was buckled in, Johnny started the car. "So, we're off to the reception?"

Dori nodded. "Drive slow. I have something to tell you, and I want you to know I wasn't purposefully keeping secrets. I only found out part of it the day after the fire, and Butterman told me not to tell until probate was over because I was underage. But then my birthday was on Sunday and—"

Johnny looked stricken. "You didn't tell me."

"Johnny. Think about it. The last thing I wanted was a celebration."

"Oh, right."

Dori continued. "So, I only found out the rest of the secret yesterday. Remember Butterman called right after that woman from DFCS left, and honestly I was too upset to care."

"Found out what?" Johnny asked.

"We're rich."

Johnny laughed, and when Dori didn't, he hit the brakes. "That's a joke, right?"

Dori threaded her fingers through his.

"You took me and the baby knowing it would be more of a burden, and still you did it without hesitation. You are my hero. Remember when you said one day we'd move to the other side of the tracks?"

He nodded.

"Consider yourself moved. Granddaddy has over fifty-five thousand dollars in his checking account. He had full coverage on his car and money to replace it is coming in. The house was insured for two hundred thousand dollars. I own the deed to the four lots it was on and we can rebuild, and the boys will have room to play forever."

Johnny gasped. "Holy shit!"

"Johnny cussed!" Beep cried.

"I'm not through," Dori said. "He had a five-hundred-thousand-dollar life insurance policy. I am the sole recipient."

Johnny's face paled. "That's half a million dollars."

"I know. And yesterday, when Butterman called, he said there was a stock portfolio in my name in the safety-deposit box that Granddaddy started the month I was born. There is an account in my name in a bank in Savannah with over a million dollars of earnings over the past eighteen years."

Johnny gasped. "You are not fucking serious?"

Marshall gasped. "Johnny! You can't say that word, ever! Remember?"

Dori started to cry. "As serious as Granddaddy's heart attack, and I'd like to think he's over-the-moon happy for us right now."

Johnny unbuckled her seat belt and dragged her across the seat and into his arms. He couldn't talk, and Dori didn't want to. He smelled too good and looked too fine.

Marshall rolled his eyes at the lovey-dovey stuff and poked Luther's little belly.

Luther squawked and cackled.

Beep poked him too, and Luther farted.

The boys fell into hysterics.

Johnny looked at Dori. "You know what people are going to say. That I did all this for your money."

"No, because I'm going to ask Mr. Butterman to release it through the story they are supposed to do about our wedding. It will state the reasons and the details of the secrecy and why you weren't told until after the ceremony. You're going to be in the clear on this, Johnny. I promise."

"I can't believe this. I just can't believe this."

"You're not mad, are you?" she asked.

"Mad that we will be able to buy extra milk without waiting until payday? Hell no. I'm just in shock."

"Good. So let's get to the reception before everyone eats our cake."

Johnny glanced up in the rearview mirror. The boys were still laughing about the baby's farts, oblivious to how their fortune had changed. He felt like he was floating, like he'd won the lottery *and* married the princess. He put the car in gear and drove away.

By the time they reached Granny's, the place was packed. Lovey was standing out front holding a parking place just for them, and when she saw them coming, she waved them in.

"That's service!" Dori said as she got out.

"Special service for special people," Lovey said. "Come on in. You've got cake to cut."

As they walked into the café, the customers began to clap, calling out words of congratulations as the little family followed Lovey to the big room reserved for parties. It was packed to capacity.

Peanut Butterman was standing near the door and caught Dori's arm.

"Does he know?" he asked.

Dori nodded and stopped long enough to whisper, "Would you please release the info to the *Tribune* to go along with the story? Make sure the explanation is clear that Johnny didn't know until after the ceremony."

"Ah, yes, good call," he said and gave Johnny a thumbs-up. "Next time you need me, it's gonna cost you."

Johnny grinned.

Ruby pushed her way through the crowd to claim the baby.

"It's my turn to play with the little one. You two get that cake cut."

Once again, Dori handed her baby off and let herself be led away. She and Johnny cut the cake together, and Dori fed a bite to Johnny, then one to Marshall, and then one to Beep.

"Hey, don't I get my own piece?" Beep cried, eyeing the very large, four-tiered cake with an overabundance of thick white icing.

The crowd laughed again. Brooks Pine was becoming a favorite.

"Open wide," Johnny said and fed Dori her bite, then kissed the icing off the corner of her mouth. "So sweet," he whispered.

Lovey and two of her waitresses began cutting and serving cake, making sure both boys got their pieces first. Ruby took charge of finding them a place to sit, and Johnny had to trust the boys would hold it together.

Johnny stayed at Dori's side for over an hour before people began dragging him aside to talk of work-related subjects. As time passed, Dori began to realize she couldn't see him anywhere and was struck by a sinking sensation of déjà vu. For a few frightening moments, she was back at the school dance, looking across the dance floor, trying to find her friend. She had wanted to tell her friend that she didn't feel well and was going home, but she hadn't seen her anywhere. She hadn't known her cup of punch had been doped or that she was being stalked by a party crasher. All she had known was she wanted to go home.

Then someone called out her name and lifted their glass of punch in a toast, and the memory passed. But it also reminded her that the man was still out there, and she wondered what might happen if he found out about her money. She had never filed charges. She'd never even reported the rape to the police, so he was not in any danger of being arrested. But if he found out she was wealthy and that they shared a baby?

She shuddered. She needed to talk to Johnny. As she looked around for him, she noticed the boys were sitting in a corner, half-asleep. Then she heard the baby fussing and guessed he was sick and tired of the noise and strangers too. She went after the baby and, in the process, spotted Johnny. She quickly gathered up the boys and began moving them toward the back of the room. When she reached the men gathered around him, Dori slipped a hand on his arm.

He turned and smiled. "Hey, honey! Are we done?"

"Yes. I think we need to get the kids home," Dori said.

One of the men laughed and thumped Johnny on the back. "Not exactly what you normally hear a bride say to her new husband on the day they're wed."

Johnny shook his head. "It's what we signed up for, right, honey?"

Dori nodded.

Johnny took each boy by the hand and led them out, making a path for Dori and the baby as they went. Cheers and best wishes followed them. It was the end to an absolutely crazy week and Dori was mentally exhausted. She'd gone from a state of shock and depression, to utter joy and hope. It was time for the universe to scale back on any more surprises.

—◊◊◊—

Home was blissfully silent as the new family walked in.

"Change out of your good clothes," Johnny told the boys as they dragged themselves down the hall to their room.

"I'm going to put the baby down for a nap," Dori said.

"Do you want me to bring you a bottle?" Johnny asked.

"Yes, please," she said and went to her room to change the baby.

He came in just as she had finished changing his

diaper, and he leaned over and kissed the side of her cheek as he handed her the bottle.

"The boys have already piled down on the bed and are watching television. As soon as you get the baby down, lie down and take a nap too, if you want."

She looked up. "I want to spend a little time with you, if that's okay. There's something I need to ask you."

His eyes darkened. "That's very okay," he said and left, closing the door behind him.

Luther Joe had partied hard. He drank less than half a bottle, and when she lifted him up, he burped in his sleep, saving her the task.

"Poor, tired little man," Dori whispered.

She kissed his cheek, then laid him down in the playpen and covered him up.

The house's old air-conditioning system was humming as she changed out of her dress, into work clothes, then tiptoed out of the room.

She still couldn't get past the thought of Luther's father crawling out of the woodwork, and she had a feeling she should be prepared.

Johnny heard her coming down the hall and jumped up, opened the front door wide, and then went to meet her. Before she could speak, he swept her up into his arms, carried her outside and then carried her back across the threshold, put her down, and then kissed her senseless.

"Welcome home, Mrs. Pine," he said as he closed the door.

"I am happy to be here, Mr. Pine," she said softly. "Come sit by me. Something occurred to me during the reception, and I'm not sure what to do."

He sat down and then waited for her to settle, but when he saw her shoulders sag, he knew it wasn't good.

Dori hated to bring it up. Even mentioning it would take away from the joy of this day, but it was not wise to ignore its existence.

"It occurred to me that once the news gets out about my inheritance, people might try to take advantage."

"Yes, that is entirely possible, but it's nothing to worry about. All we have to do is send them packing."

She ducked her head.

He tilted it back up until she was looking into his eyes. "What?"

She sighed. "What if the person who showed up was Luther's father? In retrospect, I realize I have left a great big door open for that possibility."

Johnny reached for her hand and felt her shaking.

"What do you mean?"

She leaned against him and dropped her head, ashamed by what she was about to admit.

"I never reported the rape. There was no rape kit done. There was no police report filed. In the eyes of the law, he *could* try to cash in on the money by making some claim on the baby. I mean, it's my word against his that anything bad ever happened. He could claim otherwise."

"Shit," Johnny muttered. "All I ever thought about was breaking his neck. This would never have occurred to me."

She shrugged. "Me either, until money dropped in my lap, and money makes bad people worse."

"So, what if you file a police report now?" he suggested.

She leaned back. "I don't know. Isn't it too late?"

"I suspect there's a statute of limitations, but I doubt that it's less than two years, and Luther is what?"

"Just barely six months."

"So that's fifteen months ago. I would think that shouldn't be an issue, but we can sure find out. If you can, then I say do it. At least you will have something on file if he shows up, and then his focus might shift from trying to scam money to not going to jail." When she didn't comment, he added, "If you could, would you want to file charges against him?"

She looked up, her eyes swimming with tears. "If it didn't mean a big ugly trial, yes."

"So what if it did? So what?" Johnny asked.

Her voice was barely above a whisper. "Then everyone will know Luther's father was a bad man."

Johnny shook his head. "Honey, look at my life. Look at my brothers. Both of our parents were losers. It's not a baby's fault or responsibility how they get here, and if it will make you feel any better, we'll get Butterman on the job and file papers for me to adopt Luther right away. I planned to anyway, and this is a good reason not to delay."

Dori crawled into Johnny's lap and put her arms around his neck. "Thank you. Thank you for being understanding. Thank you for not being mad at me."

"The only person I'll ever be mad at is him. He made your first experience with a man frightening, painful, and humiliating. I would give anything if it had been me making sweet love to you. Then you wouldn't be afraid."

Dori laid a hand on his chest, then on his cheek. "I'm not afraid of you, Johnny. I swear. I am not afraid of you. Do you have any condoms? Are the boys asleep?"

His heart fluttered to a stop. Two questions that absolutely made his day, and she was so calm, she might as well have been asking if there was any milk. It was all he could do to spit out an answer. "Yes, and I can check. Why?"

"I want to be with you, Johnny. I don't want this marriage to be in name only. I want to grow old with you. I want your face to be the last face I see before I die. I want to do this right."

"God in heaven, Dori. Don't talk about dying before I've held you naked in my arms. I'm going to check on the boys."

"I'll be in your room, just in case."

Johnny bolted down the hall with his heart in his mouth. "Please, please, please be asleep," he muttered. And they were.

He made a U-turn and saw Dori slipping into his room. He followed her inside and turned the lock, then stood there shaking. He wanted this so bad, he could hardly think. Their first time had to be perfect.

Dori was nervous, but this felt right. He was her husband and this was the way they should begin their life: with love. When she started to undress, Johnny stopped her with a touch.

"Let me," he whispered, and then he cupped her cheeks and brushed his mouth across her lips—not really a kiss, but a promise of what was to come.

He could see the rapid thud of her heartbeat in the pulse at the base of her throat.

"No fear, baby. No fear. Not with me, not ever."

"I'm not afraid," Dori said. "Today I became a bride, and now I want to be your wife."

Johnny slid his hands beneath her shirt, then around her waist, and then carefully lifted the shirt up and over her head.

She looked fragile, but he knew how tough she was. He slid his fingers beneath the waistband of her jeans and popped the snap, and the zipper followed. When he started to push them down her hips, they fell too easily, a reminder of what life had put her through. Now she was standing in her underwear, her jeans down around her ankles. He picked her up and laid her down on his bed and then stripped without ceremony until he was standing before her, naked as the day he'd been born and seriously erect. He looked quickly at her face. If this didn't scare her, he was good to go.

Dori sat up on the bed and undid her bra, then tossed it aside. Johnny groaned as he crawled onto the bed and pulled off her panties.

"Are you okay?" he asked. "You're not afraid?"

"Only that I'll disappoint you," she said.

"Not in this lifetime, you won't."

He put on a condom then stretched out beside her. The first place he kissed her was at the back of her ear. From there, he moved to the curve of her cheek, down to her lips and points south, all the while making sure he wasn't going too fast.

Dori had been anxious, even embarrassed when he began, but had long since lost her inhibitions in the feel of his mouth on her body, then rolling her nipples with his tongue and trailing kisses from her breasts to her belly. When his fingers slid even farther, she opened her legs and closed her eyes.

Johnny wanted to be inside her so bad, he thought

he would die, but she needed to know what this was about before he went there. And when he slid his fingers between her legs and began to massage the little nub, he heard her sigh and kept on rubbing. When he saw her shudder and then heard her groan, he knew it was good, so he didn't stop. When she arched her back and then bit her lip to keep from crying out, he knew she was close. He increased the pressure, moving his fingers a little faster, and when he did, she grabbed the bed and held on, as if she were about to take flight.

"Look at me, Dori. Look at me. You need to see the face of the man who loves you when you come."

She opened her eyes as the climax hit and then abruptly lost her mind. The blood was still surging through her body when he slid inside her. She wanted to watch him, to see the passion in his eyes, see the lust wash over his face, but the rhythmic motion of him deep within her was a feeling too intense. She couldn't focus, couldn't form a conscious thought. And when the second rush began, she wrapped her arms around his neck and closed her eyes, waiting to take flight in his arms—and she did.

Johnny couldn't think. The blood was hammering so hard inside his head that he thought it would explode, and then the climax washed over him and he fell apart. Moments passed as he lay weak and spent upon her body, and yet he knew he had to move or he would crush her. He rose up on his elbows just enough to roll over and took her with him.

"I love you, I love you, I love you," he whispered and buried his nose beneath the curve of her chin.

Dori rose on one elbow to look down into his face.

The word *husband* was still spinning in her head as she accepted the truth of what she felt.

"I love you more."

Johnny groaned as he kissed her nose, then her lips, and then wrapped his arms around her neck.

"Oh, baby, thank you. I wasn't sure I'd ever hear you say that. This is true wealth, and I will never take it for granted."

Chapter 21

ONCE THE KIDS WOKE UP, THE NEWLYWEDS SPENT THE afterglow of making love putting her clothes into Johnny's room and turning the other room into a nursery for Luther. Dori was a little anxious about leaving the baby in a room on his own, but Johnny solved the problem by making a run to Walmart and getting baby monitors, so she could hear even the tiniest of peeps. Once Dori realized how well they picked up noise, she was relieved.

Neither of the boys thought a thing of her moving in with Johnny. Their biggest concern was what to call her now that they all were married, and the issue arose as they sat down to supper.

Luther was in his high chair, talking to the rooster clock and gnawing on a teething biscuit. Dori had already fed him, so he was happy just being where the action was.

She had kept supper simple by making baked beans and wieners, then frying up some potatoes and heating a can of corn. The boys were in their chairs, waiting for the food to get to the table when Beep introduced his problem.

"Hey, Johnny."

Johnny was putting ice in glasses and answered absently. "Yeah?"

"So now that we got married to Dori and ole Joe, how does that work?"

Johnny paused and turned around.

"How does what work?"

"Well, you're my brother and Marshall is my brother. So what is Dori and ole Joe?"

Dori winked at Beep as she set the casserole of baked beans and wieners on the table.

"You can call me Dori," she said.

"But what are you? Are you my mother now?"

The intent expression on his face nearly broke her heart.

"No, sugar, I'm not your mother. I would never pretend to take her place."

"I don't mind. She wasn't a very good one," Marshall said too fast.

Johnny was stunned. He hadn't seen this coming.

"Look, guys, technically Dori is now your sister-in-law and the baby, well, the baby is going to be your brother because we're going to adopt him. He will have our last name."

Beep frowned. "Dori is my sister now?"

Dori could tell he was still confused.

"What do you guys want me to be?" she asked.

Beep dug a booger out of his nose and blithely wiped it on his jeans.

"Me and Marshall talked, and I was thinkin' I might call you Mama," he mumbled.

Breath caught in the back of Dori's throat as she looked at Marshall.

"What do you think, Marshall? What do you want to call me?"

He glanced at Johnny, trying to gauge his mood, and then shrugged.

"I guess me and Beep already got ourselves a brother. What we need is a mama."

Johnny shook his head. "I did not see this coming," he said softly, but Dori was already in fix-it mode.

"Seeing as how I already know how to be one, and seeing as how ole Joe is going to be your brother too, and when he learns to talk, he will call me Mama, I think it's a good idea that you guys call me Mama too."

Beep sighed loudly. "Boy, that's a relief! I'll sleep good tonight."

It was all Dori could do to keep a straight face.

"So will I, guys, and thank you very much. Me and ole Joe were sure needing a family. We really appreciate that you came to our rescue and married us."

"No problem," Marshall said.

Johnny grinned. "Yeah, no problem. We were happy to do it."

Dori gave him a look, which made him laugh, which made Luther Joe laugh too. He was accommodating like that.

Supper came and went, and they moved into the business of getting back into the normal bedtime routine. Tomorrow was a school day and Johnny would go back to work.

By the time they got all three kids in bed and sound asleep, they were exhausted.

"You shower first," Johnny said. "I need to call my boss and see what's up for tomorrow. Unfortunately for us, the honeymoon is over."

"I hear honeymoons are highly overrated," Dori said.

"You are my favorite wife. One day, I will take you on a honeymoon of exaggerated proportions."

"Along with three boys? Then start thinking about Disneyland," Dori said.

Johnny swept her up into his arms and kissed her soundly, then set her back down on her feet.

"Go take your bath. We still have tonight."

And they did.

When the alarm went off the next morning, it was a quick hug and kiss good morning before Dori flew across the hall to the bathroom and then went to tend to Luther as Johnny slipped into the bathroom behind her.

By the time he left for work, the boys were eating breakfast and Dori was making lunches.

Johnny didn't take a daily paper, and so Dori didn't think about their wedding becoming the headlines in the *Blessings Tribune*, or the fact that the story, as Peanut had predicted, was making national news. She dropped the boys off at school and decided to stop at the supermarket. It wasn't until she saw the headlines on the different papers on the newsstand that she realized shit was about to hit the fan. Their picture, the one of all five of them taken right after the ceremony, was splashed all over the papers, each with their take on the headlines:

Married to Save Their Families
DFCS Called on the Carpet
Hero Marries Secret Heiress—Surprise of His Life
Blessings Come from Blessings

"Dear Lord," she mumbled as she fastened Luther's car seat into the shopping cart and took off down the aisles. She needed to get out and get home and then call the police station. The sooner she filed that rape report, the better she would feel.

Ethel Carter was wishing Pansy Jones to hell and back
for setting her on that witch hunt while refusing to admit
it was her prejudice against the family that had put Ethel
on the hot seat. She'd already endured a stringent slap
down by her boss and knew he was writing her up and
putting it in her file. Because of this, she would never
see another step raise on her paycheck. It was a good
thing she was retiring in the fall.

———◆———

Johnny's morning wasn't any better. He'd reported in
at the garage long enough to get his work orders and
then headed out for the job site where he'd spent the
morning shoring up a pond dam that had been destroyed
by muskrats. The owner had drained the pond to kill
the last of them and needed it repaired before it was
viable again. He got in the truck cab to call Dori when
he stopped for lunch, but the call went to voice mail.
Because she was always busy with the baby, he didn't
think much of it, ate his lunch, and went back to work.

Back at home, Dori and Officer Pittman were at
the kitchen table as she retold the incident of her rape.
She'd heard the phone ring but let it go to voice mail and
kept answering Lon's questions. She had already gone
through the part where she began feeling dizzy and dis-
oriented, and how she'd been looking for her friend, and
was at the point in the story when she said someone took
her by the arm and told her she needed to get some air.

"I remember walking from the light into the dark, and
I wanted to sit down on the bench outside the gym, but
he kept pulling me farther into the shadows."

"Did anyone see you?" Pittman asked.

Dori shoved her hands through her hair in frustration. "I don't know. I could barely focus."

"And you stated you didn't know him."

"I'd never seen him before. He didn't fit. He didn't belong."

"What do you mean?" Lon asked.

"He was too old, way too old to still be in school. I told him I needed to go home. I was sick. I couldn't think."

"Sounds like someone slipped something in your drink," Lon said.

She shrugged. "I didn't see it happen, but I think so."

"What else do you remember?" Lon asked.

Dori ducked her head. "I felt him pulling at my clothes. Then I passed out. I came to and saw his face above me and knew what he was doing, but I couldn't move. I passed out again, and when I came to, he was gone."

"Did you ever see him again?" Lon asked.

"Yes. I was about seven months pregnant and was walking out of the pharmacy when I saw him coming out of Granny's restaurant across the street. I didn't know the people he was with, but they were getting into more than one car. I heard one of them call him Frankie."

"What did you do?"

"I got in the car and drove home as fast as I could go."

"Why didn't you tell someone?" Lon asked.

Dori shuddered. "Granddaddy would have killed him. I didn't want him in jail, and I guess I was afraid the law would find the guy and I wouldn't be able to prove anything. It was my word against his, and I felt like a fool, like it was somehow my fault."

"I'm sorry that happened to you. I'm sorry you were afraid to tell, but I understand."

"So what now?" Dori asked.

"I have your statement on video, and I have the written statement you gave me, as well. I understand why you felt the need for this to be on record, but without a last name, I doubt this investigation can go much farther."

"I don't want to find him. I'm doing this in case he comes looking for me," Dori said.

"I understand," Pittman said. "I can do some preliminary investigating and then bury the file. It will be there if the need arises."

Dori sighed. "I'm not even going to ask if this is proper police procedure. I'm just grateful."

Pittman stood up to leave and then stopped. "I've felt guilty ever since I was called away from the fire and found out no one helped you. I assumed the paramedics would see to you and the baby's welfare."

"They had already assessed us before Granddaddy died. We hadn't suffered smoke inhalation and weren't burned. They wouldn't let me ride in the ambulance. No one could have predicted what happened that night, but I am forever grateful Johnny and his boys came to my rescue. Look how it all turned out."

Pittman smiled. "I'd say Johnny's pretty happy about it too."

Dori nodded. "You should have seen the look on his face when he found out about the money."

"It's not a bad thing to hear," Pittman said. "However, I'm very sorry you had to lose your grandfather to get it. You take care, and I'll see myself out."

Dori heard the front door open and close, and then he was gone. For better or worse, she'd done it. If the story came out later, then so what if it did? She refused to worry about it any longer. She went to get her phone to see who'd called, and when she saw it was Johnny, she sent him a text.

> I talked to the police. The report has been filed. Making beef potpie for supper. I love you. Be safe.

She glanced at the clock. She'd missed lunch and started to ignore her hunger pangs, then changed her mind. Johnny had told her to quit skipping meals, and he was right. She had punished herself long enough for becoming a victim. She made a peanut butter and jelly sandwich and poured a big glass of milk. Instead of eating it standing up, she sat down in Johnny's recliner and turned on the television while she ate.

It was later that afternoon when Johnny saw the text. Satisfied all was well, he read it twice just to reread "I love you," then loaded up the dozer and headed back to town.

Frankie Ricks was drinking beer in a bar in Savannah and waiting for a friend to show up. The television was on over the bar, and every now and then, he'd glance up, waiting for the weather report to see if it was a good day to go fishing. He had just signaled the bartender for a refill when a picture of a man and woman and three kids flashed on the screen. Beer slopped out of his glass as he recognized the girl, and when the story popped up on the crawl beneath the picture, he nearly fell off the stool.

Married to save their families from DFCS, groom discovers after the ceremony that he married an heiress.

Frankie slapped money on the bar and ran out the front door like the cops were coming in the back. All the way back to Oneida, his head was spinning, thinking up one scenario after another and trying to figure out how he could make this work to his advantage.

That little piece from Blessings wasn't the first girl he'd doped up and fucked. The good part about Rohypnol was the amnesia that came with it. None of them ever remembered what had happened, let alone who'd done it, so he wasn't worried about being accused of rape. He just needed a story that would tie him to her, so he could lay claim to the kid. He could claim a prior relationship with her and say they broke up without him knowing she was pregnant. He could claim seeing her picture in the paper was the first he knew she'd had a child—maybe point out the fact that, since she was a virgin when they'd had sex, by the baby's age alone, he suspected the child was his. The DNA test would surely prove it. By the time he reached Oneida, he had the story well rehearsed.

He knew she'd claim she didn't know him, but that was easy to explain. They had been sneaking around behind her grandfather's back because of the age difference, and she just didn't want to admit what she had done. It was a risky move, but Frankie Ricks was used to taking risks. What he needed now was a lawyer.

—◦◦◦—

Pansy Jones saw the headlines and the wedding picture in her sister's morning paper and her heart stopped. They had gotten married! She had not seen that coming, and the longer she looked at the picture, the more certain she was that she would never go home again. What she had to decide was if she was going to divorce Bart and stay here with her sister or call him and give him a chance to leave with her. Finally, it was the faint memory of her own wedding vows that decided for her.

She reached for her cell phone and called home, then waited for Bart to answer. When her call went to voice mail, she started talking.

"I saw the papers. I can never come back to Blessings again. I am staying in Savannah, with or without your. If you want a divorce, all I want are my things: clothes, my car, and Mama's crystal, china, and silver. You can have all the rest."

Then she hung up. She'd know by the end of the day whether she was going to be starting over alone or with the yoke back around her neck.

Two days later, Peanut Butterman hung up the phone and then sat for a moment, trying to think what to do first. He'd known from the moment that stock portfolio was discovered that something like this would happen, but he wasn't sure how Dori was going to respond. The fact that a man was coming forth claiming a relationship with Dori that resulted in a child was somewhat daunting. She had a baby and had never named the father. The man already had a lawyer, and there was a hearing scheduled in Blessings day after tomorrow at ten a.m. to present the evidence. The so-called father was asking for joint custody and a suitable monetary sum to go with it. Dori was going to be upset. Johnny Pine would be out for blood.

Still, there was no way to ignore it.

—·····—

Unaware of her lawyer's phone call, Dori was in the middle of cleaning kitchen cabinets when there was a knock at the door. She wiped her hands on her jeans and went to answer.

The man standing on the porch had a disarming smile.

"Adorable Grant Pine?" he asked.

"Yes?"

He thrust a piece of paper forward and slapped it in her hand.

"You have just been served."

He walked away as abruptly as he came, leaving her standing on the threshold in a state of shock.

She stepped back into the house to shut the door and then opened up the summons, quickly scanned the words, and then reread them again before it hit her.

She let out a scream of rage and headed for the phone. It rang before she could pick it up, and when she saw it was Butterman, she answered, screaming in his ear.

"The son of a bitch filed for joint custody of my baby. He wants child support and my baby for raping me? I will kill him first! I swear to God, I will kill him."

Peanut blinked. He didn't know she had this in her.

"Dori! Dori! Stop screaming and listen to me. There is a hearing day after tomorrow at ten a.m. I need you to come in sometime today so we can go over—"

"I filed a rape report with the police department two days ago. I don't know if this is the same man, but I will recognize him if it is."

Peanut was impressed. "You filed a rape report?"

"Yes. I know it was late, but Johnny said the statute

of limitations was not up, and now that Granddaddy was no longer around to get in trouble, I did it to protect us from this very thing. Oh my God, I cannot believe he had the gall to pull this."

Peanut's thoughts were turning. "I am guessing he does not know about the report, which is good. You did the right thing. I am also guessing he's going to claim a prior relationship and that he had no knowledge that you'd become pregnant during that time."

"He was a stranger. He drugged my drink at a school dance, dragged me out of the gym into the dark, and raped me. I barely remember any of it except for seeing his face above me and knowing what he was doing, but I couldn't move. It all felt like a bad dream until I found out I was pregnant. I filed a report. If it's him, they have to arrest him, right?"

"Right now, without evidence to prove otherwise, it will be your word against his. If he is the father, Luther's DNA will prove it."

Dori screamed again.

Peanut flinched and held the phone away from his ear until she was through.

"I will get a copy of the police report and be in touch. Stay calm. We'll figure this out."

She was still shouting and stomping when he hung up the phone.

She tried to call Johnny, but he didn't answer, then she remembered he was working on a job site not far from Savannah. He was too far away to come home and hold her hand. She was a big girl. She could handle this herself. In the meantime, telling him had to wait until he got home.

When the baby started crying, she groaned. All her screaming had been a mistake. She'd just gotten him down to sleep and now he was awake. She was just full of bad decisions.

~~~

Frankie got a call from his lawyer that everyone had been notified and served, then suggested Frankie get a motel in Blessings and set up his story. He needed to appear distraught about missing out on the first six months of his son's life and seem anxious to form a relationship with him. He said it would be vital to swaying public opinion in his favor should this come to trial.

Frankie was somewhat nervous to show up there, but he'd cooked up the scheme and now had to follow through. So he packed up a suitcase and headed for Blessings. He got a room in a local motel and then headed straight for Granny's Country Kitchen to get some food. It was just after one o'clock. The lunch crowd should just about be gone.

~~~

Dori was sick to her stomach. Yesterday's elation was gone, and the reality of her life was back on the ugly side. As soon as she fed Luther his dinner and got him cleaned up, she headed uptown. She needed to get tampons at the pharmacy and pick up the birth control prescription her doctor had called in. She loved Luther Joe to the moon and back, but she didn't want another one anytime soon. She and Johnny had all they could handle right now, and he didn't even know it.

She buckled the baby in the car seat, poked his belly just to hear him giggle, and wished to God her grand-daddy was still around to hear it too. Then she shrugged off the pity party and got into the car. She needed to get her errands done before it was time to pick up the boys.

Her first stop was Phillips' Pharmacy. She walked in with Luther on her hip and headed toward the back to pick up her prescription. Four customers stopped her on the way—one to congratulate her on her wedding, one to fuss over the baby, and two wanting to borrow money. She gave the last two a long, silent stare. They got the message and left.

Mr. Phillips was on the phone when she walked up to the counter. He put the caller on hold.

"Afternoon, Dori. I have your prescription right here."

"Thank you, Mr. Phillips. Have a nice day."

"You too, honey," he said as he waved and smiled.

He got back on the phone as she turned left at the next aisle to get tampons. LilyAnn was stocking shelves when Dori walked up.

"Hi, honey. Anything I can help you with?" LilyAnn asked.

"I need a large box of those," she said, pointing to her brand.

LilyAnn grabbed it from the shelf.

"Are you ready to check out?" she asked.

"Yes, please," Dori said.

"Follow me."

Dori handed her the prescription and headed toward the front. Still holding Luther by one arm, she sat him down on the counter to dig through her purse for her wallet.

She paid for her stuff while Luther was trying to put her hair in his mouth and LilyAnn was rattling on about her baby on the way. Dori had no idea what LilyAnn was saying and hoped that she'd smiled in all the right places.

When LilyAnn began sacking up her purchases, Dori absently glanced out the window and across the street toward Granny's Kitchen and, as she did, had a horrifying moment of déjà vu.

The man who'd raped her was walking out of the café.

"No," she muttered. Then her voice got louder. "Hell no," she said and set the baby in LilyAnn's arms. "Hold him for me, please." She ran for the exit.

She grabbed a walking cane from a display near the front door and out the door she went. Moments later, she jumped the curb and bolted across the street without looking for traffic.

One driver slammed on the brakes to keep from hitting her, then honked his disapproval, but she kept on walking, the cane clutched firmly in her fist. The sun was hot on her face, but it was nothing to the heat inside her belly. She was out for revenge and nothing was going to stop her.

A second car coming from the other direction also honked, hit the brakes, and turned sharply into a curb to keep from hitting her, but she never missed a step.

―⁓―

Frankie heard the first car honk and turned around to see what was going on. At the same time he saw the car, he saw the girl coming toward him, hair flying out around her face like some warrior woman from one of his video games. Before he could react, the second car honked and hit the curb, and she kept coming. After that, everything seemed to happen in slow motion.

He thought she was screaming, because her mouth was open and the rage on her face was impossible to miss, but sound was roaring in his head. He couldn't come to himself fast enough to move. He watched her raise her arms like she was swinging a bat and then he went down like a poleaxed steer.

"Sorry son of a bitch!" Dori screamed, unaware of the gathering crowd, and swung the cane again.

People came pouring out of Granny's, as well as stores up and down the street. By then, Frankie was rolled up in a ball, trying to protect his head and face. He was screaming for help when she swung at him again.

"Cowardly bastard! You doped my drink."

Whack!

"You dragged me out of the gym into the dark and you raped me."

Whack!

"You raped me and left me bleeding and never looked back."

Whack! Whack!

"Help! Somebody help me!" Frankie shrieked.

Dori swung at him again, cracking the bridge of his nose, and when he rolled away, she swung again, right behind his knee. He shrieked when it popped.

Whack! Whack! Whack!

"Now you have the guts to think you can come in here and think you're going to take custody of my baby just so you can get some money?"

She swung again, and just before it came down across the back of his head, someone grabbed her from behind and lifted her off her feet.

"Let me go! Let me go!" she screamed. "That's him! That's the man who raped me."

The gathered crowd gasped in unison, and then the hum of their angry voices sent a cold chill up Frankie Ricks's spine.

"Dori! Stop it!" Pittman yelled and yanked the cane from her hand before he put her back down. "I've got this. Do you hear me? I've got this."

Dori was so angry she was shaking.

"I got a summons to go to court this morning," Dori said. "He wants joint custody of my baby and child support to take care of him. I want him arrested for rape."

Frankie moaned. He had not seen this coming. He scooted backward and tried to stand up, but someone in the crowd pushed him back down with their boot. He crawled toward the cop and then pulled himself up. He was bleeding from the nose. He had a cut over his eye and a bloody lip. His shirt was torn, and there was gum on the knees of his pants, not to mention a plethora of bruises he could not see.

"I did not rape this girl!" he shouted. "We had a relationship that went sour, and I'm taking her to court to—"

Officer Pittman frowned, yanked him around, and cuffed him.

"And I have a rape report that fits your description and your first name. If the DNA test I take on you matches Dori Pine's baby, you are going to be arrested and charged with the crime of forcible rape. That's what you'll take to court first."

Frankie gawked. He couldn't believe this was happening.

"I didn't rape you," he said and gave Dori an imploring look as Pittman dragged him off to his cruiser, taking Frankie and Dori's weapon to jail.

Dori was still standing in the middle of the street. Her hands were curled into fists and her body was shaking. She stood until the police cruiser disappeared, and then she turned around and walked back toward the pharmacy in a daze, oblivious to the silence of the crowd around her.

LilyAnn and Mr. Phillips were standing on the sidewalk with the baby, Dori's purchases, and her purse. All Dori could see was her baby.

She stumbled as she reached the back end of her car and then caught herself, took a deep breath, and walked straight up to LilyAnn.

"Thank you for your help," she said, taking the baby out of LilyAnn's arms and buckling him into the backseat of her car. She put her purse in beside Luther, got in, and drove away.

Chapter 22

THE PEOPLE DISPERSED IN A DOZEN DIFFERENT DIREC-
tions, each person carrying a cell phone. Once again, Dori's life had become everyone's business. Half of them were spreading the word; the other half had had the foresight to film the event and were uploading it to social media. It was inevitable what would happen to it next.

Dori spent the rest of the day in a daze. She did a load of laundry and cleaned out the boys' clothes' closet, then drove to school to pick them up. Luther was fussy and wanted out of the car seat, so she got out of the car with him to walk around.

Miss Jane was in her van, waiting for her kids, and when she saw Dori, she jumped out and waved.

"Come stand in my shade," she cried.

Dori walked over, grateful for the offer. Luther was still fussing and rubbing his nose against Dori's shoulder. She knew he was sleepy, but until she got the boys home, there was nothing she could do to make him better.

"What's wrong with the boss here?" Jane asked as she patted Luther's curly head.

"He's sleepy and cranky," Dori said.

"May I hold him?" Jane asked. "I haven't held a baby in years."

The statement struck Dori as sweet, and in that

moment, some of the ugliness of seeing Frankie Ricks slipped away.

"Be my guest," she said and handed him over.

Luther was immediately intrigued by a new face, although there was a moment or two when it seemed he was debating as to whether he would object to the trade. And then Jane tapped her finger against his nose and smiled, and he smiled back.

"There's my smile," Jane crowed and kissèd his cheek. "Oh my, he is such a sweetheart. He must make your days a delight."

Dori sighed. Her priorities were slipping back into place. She ran her fingers through his curls and then rubbed the back of his head.

"You're right. He does make my days a delight."

"Congratulations on the wedding. I doubt you saw me, but I was there. I have to say the boys certainly added color to the event."

Dori grinned. "Yes, they did, and they add color to my life. They are so sweet. Just last night, they decided they wanted to call me Mama, which I love."

"That's wonderful," Jane said. "They certainly needed one. Oh, that's not to say Johnny wasn't doing a good job, because he was. But they're so young, and every kid needs a good mother."

Dori nodded, remembering how scared she'd been when her mother never came home. ▾

And then the bell rang, and moments later, kids began pouring out of every exit.

"Well, here come the hooligans," Jane said, kissing Luther's cheek and handing him back. "Have a nice day, honey."

Dori smiled as Luther buried his nose against her neck. "You too, Miss Jane. You too."

She saw the boys coming and paused to wave. Then she heard them yell, "There's Mama," and the last of her panic slid away. It would all work out. Life wouldn't take another thing away from her now. It wouldn't be fair.

—〰—

Frankie's lawyer, a man named Guidry, showed up three hours after Frankie had been booked and tossed in jail. He got Frankie out on bond and read him the riot act as they exited the jail.

"But you told me to come here," Frankie whined. "You told me to gain public sympathy for my case."

Guidry threw up his hands in disgust. "And instead, you wind up getting your ass whipped by the woman you will face in court, and the whole pitiful event is on YouTube. At last count, it already has over a half a million hits and the blood has yet to dry up on your face."

"I need to go to ER," Frankie moaned.

"Where's your car?" Guidry asked.

"Still in front of the café."

"I'll drop you off on my way out of town. Get in. I need to be back in Oneida before seven. We have guests coming for dinner."

Frankie frowned. "I am your client. Am I not more important than dinner guests?"

"No," Guidry said. "Get in."

They drove back downtown. Guidry paused to let Frankie out and gave him one last piece of advice. "Stay out of trouble until the hearing or forget it. I won't be coming back to bail you out again."

He drove away, leaving Frankie to stumble to his car alone. He started to unlock it, then remembered he'd done that just before he got hit. He opened the door and slid inside, his body one massive ache.

He had a vague idea of where the hospital was, so he started the car and began to back up, but realized something was wrong. He put the car in park and got out to look. All the tires were flat.

"Son of a holy bitch!" he moaned, then got back in the car and drove off.

By the time he got to the hospital, he was driving on the rims. He called for roadside assistance to come change the flats, and then he went into the ER. When he came out later, he found the car up on blocks, all four tires missing.

At that point, he got the message. He was in enemy territory, and he needed to lay low. He got his stuff from the car and called a cab to take him to get a rental. He paid the cabbie and made his way into the rental office. The woman behind the counter looked up, saw his wounds and his limp, and then took a slight step backward. It was the only hint she ever gave that she knew who the fucker was.

"How can I help you?" she asked.

"I need to rent a car."

"We're really short right now."

"Please, lady, I just need something that runs and has wheels. Anything but a motorcycle and I'll take it."

"Well, we do have one car. It's small but gets good gas mileage."

"I'll take it," he said, grateful that something was finally working out.

He filled out the papers, presented his identification, and paid extra for insurance—the way his luck was going, he would likely need it.

He followed the lady outside and across the parking lot, past two very large vans, a Cadillac, two pickup trucks, a Town Car, and two midsized sedans. Then she stopped and pointed.

"Here we are. Let me check it out for scratches and such before you get in. Wouldn't want you having to pay for someone else's fender bender."

Frankie was in shock. It looked like a clown car from the circus.

"What the fuck is that?"

"It's a hybrid. I told you it was small. Don't you want it?"

"No, no, it's fine. It just looks like a clown car. And it's yellow."

She laughed. "That's what everyone calls it. They'll see you coming in this one, right?"

He rolled his eyes. Just what he needed. A sign on his butt saying, *Here I am. Kick my ass again.*

After a few more signatures and a copy of the rental, he got in. It took a moment to acquaint himself with the controls, and then he drove away, cursing his luck and wishing he'd never left Savannah. He drove straight to the motel, and as soon as he got in his room, he took two of the pain pills the doctor had given him and collapsed.

—⁓—

Johnny drove into Blessings a little after five and parked his rig inside the fenced lot, then headed for the office.

His boss grinned when he walked in. "The excitement at your house never ends, does it?" he said.

Johnny blinked. "What do you mean?"

"You mean you don't know?"

"Know what?"

"About your little wife taking a cane to that man. Boy, did she ever put a whuppin' on him. I haven't seen that much fury since Sherman marched through Georgia."

All of a sudden, he remembered that missed call from Dori and headed out the door.

"If you want to see it, there are a dozen different versions of it already uploaded to YouTube. She's really something, that girl. You got yourself a winner!" Clawson yelled.

Johnny kept on moving, trying not to panic. The minute he got in his car, he called home, but his call went straight to voice mail. He didn't bother leaving a message and kept on going.

He pulled up in the driveway, relieved to see she was there, and smelled something good as he rushed up the steps. He walked into what appeared to be normalcy. The boys were side by side, fixated on the television. They didn't even look up. Luther was in his playpen close by, talking to the ceiling fan. Dori walked out of the kitchen with a dish towel in her hand.

"Hi, Johnny. I'm glad you're home."

"I missed your call. I forgot to call back. What the hell happened?" he asked.

"Look, Johnny!" Marshall said. "It's the bad man who hurt Dori. She caught him for the cops."

He turned around just as Marshall upped the volume on the evening news and saw a blow-by-blow video of what she had done.

When it was over, he turned around, looked at her

like he'd never seen her before, and then took her in his arms and held her.

"I'm sorry I wasn't here. I'm sorry I wasn't the one who laid into him. I'm so sorry."

"Don't be," she said, her voice so calm and matter-of-fact after witnessing that rage gave him a chill. "I needed to do that. I had no idea I'd been harboring so much pent-up rage until I got that summons. After that, I sort of lost it."

"You got a summons?"

Her shoulders slumped. "It's why he's in town. I have to be in court, day after tomorrow, for a hearing. He's suing me for joint custody of Luther and money for maintenance, so to speak."

"Thank God you filed that report," he said.

Marshall got up on his knees and looked over the sofa at Dori.

"Mama caught a bad man. I won't ever be afraid again. If Johnny's not around, we got ourselves a mama who knows how to whip ass."

Dori tried to look serious.

"It's not a good idea to be violent. We don't like what happened to Beep, right? What I did to that man happened for a very special reason, and I can promise it won't happen again."

"If he needs whipping again, I'll be the one doing it," Johnny said and pulled her close again.

Dori sighed. If felt good to be loved and even better to know she didn't have to fight another battle alone for the rest of her life.

"Supper is ready. Everyone go wash," she said.

"I already washed," Beep said, holding up his fingers. "I licked them with my tongue."

"Do it again, and this time use soap," Johnny ordered and off they went.

Dori picked Luther up and set him in his high chair. He greeted the rooster clock with a squeal and supper was served.

—~~~—

When Frankie woke up, it was dark. His belly was growling from hunger, but his jaw was too sore to chew.

He opened the door to look out and saw a fast-food restaurant nearby. Ignoring his clown car, he walked across the parking lot and then across the street to get a milkshake. No chewing involved. He had to wait in line for almost fifteen minutes, but the cold, sweet ice cream was worth it.

When he got back to his room, he saw the door was ajar and groaned, certain he'd been robbed. He pushed it open, expecting to see the room trashed, but to his relief, nothing seemed to be missing. When he went inside and tried to shut it, he discovered it didn't catch properly and decided that was what had happened. He leaned against it to make sure the dead bolt caught and then sat down on the bed to watch TV while he drank his shake.

An hour later, he peeled off his clothes and took a shower, hoping the hot water would ease his misery. Then he took two more pain pills, crawled between the sheets, and turned out the lights.

Within minutes, his head began to itch. He scratched and rolled over, punched the pillow into a new lump, and once again closed his eyes. Then the back of his ear began to itch, then his shoulder, then the hair around his dick. He threw back the covers and turned on the light, thinking he must be breaking out in some kind of rash. To his horror, there *were* spots on his body. But when he looked closer, they weren't red like a rash, but they were moving.

Fleas! He'd heard of fleabag motels but thought it was just a phrase for "cheap." Obviously he was mistaken.

He ran into the bathroom, cursing and moaning, and scrubbed until his skin was raw. Then he put on clean clothes, threw his suitcase in the car, and headed for the front desk.

The clerk, a fifty-something woman with a cigarette stuck to her lower lip, looked up as he entered.

"Can I help you?" she asked.

"My room has fleas," he cried.

She took a puff on her cigarette and squinted as the smoke she exhaled lifted upward past her nose.

"Really? What room were you in?"

He slammed the key down on the counter.

"Room 122."

"Ah. The haunted one," she said.

"Haunted! What the hell does that have to do with fleas?" he asked, then scratched his head and checked under his fingernails to see if he'd missed one, but there was nothing.

"It's haunted by the motel cat that got run over in the parking lot last year," the clerk said, and this time when she took a draw on the cigarette, she blew smoke back in his face.

"Like hell," Frankie said. "I want another room."

"We're all full up," she said.

"There aren't but six cars in this whole parking lot," he argued.

"They walked in," she said, leaning forward and shaking ash on the back of his hand. "Just like you better be walking your ass out of this office. We don't take to people who rape young girls around here."

The skin crawled on the back of his neck as he backed up. He turned and ran to his clown car, crawled in, and drove away, thinking he'd seen a bed and breakfast coming into town. It might cost him a little more, but by God, he was going to sleep in a decent bed or know the reason why.

Rachel Goodhope checked Frankie Ricks into the B and B without prejudice for what he was driving, even politely ignoring his wounds. She gave him the key to the first room up on the right and offered to bring breakfast to his room in the morning around nine, since he seemed to be ailing.

Frankie accepted the offer, settled into his room, and fell asleep.

By the time morning came, Rachel had figured out she was harboring the bastard under her very roof and set about preparing him a meal he would not forget.

She carried the tray of food up to his room and knocked promptly at nine, then waited for him to let her in.

"That sure looks good," Frankie said as he tried flashing her one of his best Johnny Depp smiles, but his lip was too swollen and his nose was leaning just the teeniest bit off to the right.

"I hope you enjoy it," Rachel said. "I didn't ask you last night, but will you be staying long?"

"No, ma'am. Just one more night, and then I'll be leaving."

"I don't serve meals at noon, but if I have guests at night, I will make dinner unless they have other plans."

"No plans, and dinner will be fine," Frankie said.

Rachel smiled sweetly and closed the door behind her as she left.

Frankie dug into the fluffy scrambled eggs, popped a sausage link into his mouth along with it, and then buttered one of what appeared to be a blueberry and chocolate chip muffin. He wouldn't know until later that the chocolate chips were Ex-Lax, and by then it would be too late.

He ate until everything was gone and then set the tray out into the hall, crawled back into bed, and turned on the television. To his horror, he caught just enough of the morning news to realize he and Dori Pine were trending on social media. There was a moment when he thought about quitting and leaving, and then he realized things had gone beyond that. Besides the upcoming court date he'd scheduled, he had another hearing to face: the one where a judge decided if they had enough evidence to bind him over for trial. If he left town now, he'd be jumping bond. It was the first time he realized a good dose of Rohypnol did not automatically guarantee amnesia. He wished he'd known that sooner.

He fell asleep during a game show and woke up about an hour later with a bellyache of massive proportions. He wasn't sure if he was going to throw up or blow up. He barely made it to the bathroom and fell onto the commode with a groan.

First he got his butt whipped, then flat tires, then fleas, and now diarrhea. No way did he think this was an accident, but he was in desperate shape and couldn't get far enough away from the bathroom to run away. It was late afternoon before the trots finally dried up. His butthole was sore and his innards were clean as a whistle. He was pretty sure that if he took a drink of water, it would run right through without stopping and wet his pants.

Rachel wasn't around when Frankie paid up and made his getaway. He drove until he found a bar on the outskirts of town and slunk inside, grateful for cool air and low lights. He sat down at the back of the room and ordered a beer. The weary barmaid who waited on him barely gave him a glance. He felt safe, his identity was unknown. But he was wrong. Word had spread. The bastard trying to get Dori's baby and scam her out of her money was driving the clown car.

A short while later, two brothers named Bo and Billy Weaver came into the bar. They glanced his way and then sat down at the bar and ordered beers. When the bartender passed them over, they took them to a nearby pool table and began to play.

Frankie watched them for a while until he'd finished his beer, and when the barmaid came back around, he ordered another and asked for peanuts too. He was working on his second beer and wishing he had an ice pack for his nose when he began feeling a bit dizzy. He popped another handful of peanuts in his mouth and then went about the business of trying to chew them enough to swallow. In the back of his mind, he began thinking that drinking beer on a completely empty stomach might not have been such a good idea. He chased the peanuts with another swig of beer and then decided he needed air. He left money on the table and staggered out to his car, rolled all the windows down, and then took off from the graveled parking lot as fast as the little car would take him.

Bo and Billy left their pool cues on the table, threw down a twenty for their beers and the game, and left the bar right behind Frankie. He was headed out of town, which they considered perfect. They stayed just far enough behind him so that he wouldn't be alerted to their presence. And when his car began to weave back and forth, they knew he was just about gone.

"Think we oughta try and run him off the road before he hurts someone?" Bo asked.

"Maybe," Billy said.

But before they had the chance, Frankie ran himself off the road, right into a ditch, where he stopped the car, managed to get it into park, and then passed out behind the wheel with the car still running.

Bo pulled off to the side of the highway, beside Frankie's car, and then stopped.

"We couldn't have done a better job," he said.

They got out, waded into the brushy ditch, dragged Frankie Ricks out of the car, and killed the engine before dragging him up onto the road.

"How much of that drug do you suppose May put in his beer?" Billy asked.

Bo shrugged. "She didn't say when she called. She just said he'd pass out soon."

"What do you want to do with him?" Billy asked.

Bo looked around and then looked farther down the ditch and pointed. "I see a patch of poison ivy."

Billy grinned. "Why, I do believe you're right, Brother."

They grabbed Frankie by both arms and set to

dragging him down the blacktop toward it. When they reached the edge, they started to toss him in, but Bo piped up with a new idea.

"We could pants him first," he suggested.

Billy grinned. "Why don't we just pull them down around his ankles? When he wakes up, he'll think he did it to himself, and we're both in the clear."

Bo grabbed Frankie's belt, and Billy undid the zipper. They yanked his pants and underwear down past his knees and then rolled him off the shoulder of the road, down into the ditch again, where he landed facedown in the patch of poison ivy.

"I believe we're through here," Bo said.

"I think you're right, Brother," Billy added.

They walked back to their truck, made a U-turn on the blacktop, and headed back into town, leaving the yellow clown car in the ditch with the door open and the key in the ignition.

———————

Frankie woke up hours later and rolled over onto his back, but when he went to open his eyes, they felt weird. He looked up, saw the sun was heading toward the western horizon, and then realized he was half-naked and lying in a ditch.

"Oh man. First time I ever got drunk on two beers. I shouldn't have had them on an empty stomach," he muttered, scratching at his privates…then his leg. Then he remembered the fleas and crawled out of the ditch on his hands and knees before he realized that, this time, he did not have fleas. He had a rash. A bad rash. He looked back down at the ditch and the poison ivy and yanked up his pants, but it was too late. He was already poisoned.

"Oh son of a holy bitch," he moaned and staggered back down the road to his car. He crawled back down the ditch to get in and then had to back the clown car nearly a quarter of a mile in the ditch before he found a place shallow enough to drive the tiny car out. Once he was back on the blacktop, he turned around and drove back into town. The only place he could think to go was back to the hospital before it was too late. His eyes were swelling shut.

Chapter 23

BUTTERMAN HAD BEEN ON THE PHONE FOR ALMOST thirty minutes with Dori, trying to reassure her. He felt certain Frankie Ricks was not only going to get his case thrown out of court, but that he was going to jail for rape. But until it happened, Dori was scared, and he understood that.

"Listen, honey, just meet me at the courthouse. Stuff has been developing since that video was uploaded to YouTube. It's going to be okay. You have to trust me on this. This is what I do best, understand?"

Dori sighed. "Yes. I'll see you there. Room 202."

"Right, and don't be late. Judge Beecham doesn't tolerate tardiness."

"I won't be late," Dori said.

She hung up the phone and put her head in her hands. Luther was asleep and the house was so quiet, she could hear a faucet dripping in the bathroom down the hall.

Johnny had stayed home from work to go to court with her, so he took the boys to school, but she'd expected him home an hour ago. When her phone rang, she assumed it would be him. It was Lovey.

"Hi, honey. It's me. I know your hearing is this morning. Do you need a babysitter? I can come to your house and stay with Luther until you guys get back. It would make everything easier on the baby and on you."

"Oh, Lovey, how am I ever going to pay you back

for what you've done? Yes, it would be helpful, and I accept. We have to be there by ten, so if you could get here no later than nine thirty, that would be great."

"I'll see you soon," Lovey said.

Dori hung up and then looked at the clock. It was a quarter to nine. Where on earth was Johnny?

When he finally walked in the front door, he had an armful of bags. She'd just given him several hundred dollars to pad the family budget and couldn't believe he'd been shopping. He gave one bag to her and kept the other one for himself.

She stood up. "What's this?"

"It's something for you to wear to court. You have one dress. You've worn it to a funeral and to a wedding. I didn't think it was proper to wear it to a hanging."

Dori burst out laughing and threw her arms around his neck.

"Just when I think the world is crashing down on me, you always manage to rescue me in the nick of time. I love you, Johnny Pine."

"I loved you first," he said and then glanced at the clock.

"So, let's try this stuff on and see what, if anything, needs fixing."

They went back to their bedroom and dumped the contents of the sacks out on the bed.

Johnny had a dark blue Western-style shirt with white pearl snaps all the way down the front to wear with a pair of jeans. It wasn't fancy, but it was nice, and he wanted her to be proud of the way he looked. He began taking off tags and pulling out pins.

Dori picked up the dress that had been in her sack and held it up to her body.

"Oh, Johnny," Dori said. "This dress is gorgeous."

He grinned. "The Uniqué Boutique lady said it would look good on you."

"Honey, this dress would look good on anyone."

She took off her jeans and shirt, and stepped into it, then pulled it up over her shoulders. Johnny stood behind her to zip it up and then turned her around to the full-length mirror.

"What do you think?" he asked.

The dress was a floral print in pastel pink, green, and yellow. It had a scoop neck and cap sleeves, a built-in bra, a fitted bodice, and a handkerchief hem, which gave the dress a dash of flash and a hint of sexy.

"I think it's beautiful. I think you are the most thoughtful husband in the world to even consider this."

Johnny leaned down to give her a quick kiss, but then she wrapped her arms around his neck and kissed him until his ears were ringing. It took a few seconds more for him to realize it was his phone.

"Hang on," he said and answered quickly. "Hello? Who?" Almost instantly, the smile disappeared. "Are you kidding me?"

Dori could tell by the look on his face, he was shocked.

"Yes, I guess I'll accept," he said and then turned around. He was looking straight at Dori when he answered. "Yeah, it's me, Dad. What's going on?"

Dori's eyes widened with surprise. She started to walk out of the room to give him privacy when he caught her wrist and pulled her close. She wrapped her arms around his waist and listened to the hurt in his voice and wished she could make it go away.

"Oh, right, you saw the story in the paper. Yes, she's

beautiful, and, yes, I love her very much. Yeah, the boys have grown."

Then he was listening and when the tears started rolling down his cheeks, she held him tighter.

"Yes, I'm glad you called, and thanks. I'll tell her. Yes, good-bye."

He hung up, tossed the phone on the bed, and wrapped both arms around her. He didn't move. He didn't speak, but she could feel his heartbeat and knew the call had moved him.

Finally, he began to talk. "He said to tell you that you sure are pretty and that he hopes we have a very happy life."

"Are you okay?"

He sighed. "I'm fine. It just took me by surprise. He said he was proud of the man I had become."

"Oh, Johnny, that's wonderful, right?"

He shrugged, but she could tell he was proud.

"When was the last time you talked to him?"

"About six years ago. Beep was a baby, Marshall was four, and I was fourteen. It doesn't matter. He's never getting out, and I'm not letting my brothers grow up thinking its normal to visit family in prison. Now, let's get the tags off of this pretty dress and get cracking. We've got to be at the courthouse soon."

"It starts at ten. Butterman said don't be late, and Lovey is coming here at nine thirty to stay with the baby."

"That's great. Someday, we're going to have to have a great big party and invite all of the people who have helped us through this mess." Then he glanced at the clock. "We have just under fifteen minutes. You can have the bathroom first. I'm going to toss this shirt into the dryer a few minutes to take out the wrinkles."

And just like that, the shock of the phone call had passed.

Lovey arrived promptly at nine thirty. She got a quick run-through of where bottles were kept and was told everything else she would need was in his room.

"Please help yourself to anything you would like to drink," Dori said. "We have iced tea, Pepsi, and you can always make coffee, if you'd prefer. The coffee is in the apple canister on the cabinet."

"I'll be fine," Lovey said. "And may I say, you look beautiful."

Dori smiled. "Johnny picked this out for me."

"Did I hear my name mentioned?" Johnny said as he strode into the room.

"If I could whistle, I would," Lovey added. "You look downright handsome, young man."

"Can't embarrass this pretty woman," he said. "Honey, we need to leave. Are you ready?"

Dori picked up her purse.

"Let's get this over with. I want our life back," she said.

—◦◦◦—

Frankie spent the night in the hospital. He had finally found a place to sleep that couldn't turn him away. They'd pumped him full of IV meds trying to dry up the rash and managed to get medicine on his eyes before they swelled all the way shut. He'd called Guidry and asked him to pick him up at the hospital entrance and said he'd explain when he arrived.

When Guidry pulled up to the entrance, he was not expecting the man who came out. In fact, he wouldn't have recognized Ricks at all except for that long, stringy-haired, Johnny Depp hairstyle he favored. Ricks was walking spraddle-legged, like he'd gotten off of a horse without knowing how to straighten out his legs. His face was so swollen it didn't look human. The rash on his face had turned into large, seeping red patches from all the scratching he'd done. His eyes were mere slits, and his hands were in bandages, partly because they were swollen and cracking, and partly to keep him from clawing himself to the bone.

Guidry got out and opened the back door.

"What the hell happened to you?" he asked.

"Poison ivy. It's a long, ugly story. Just get me to the courthouse. You've got to make the judge believe that me and the bitch had a relationship going, or I'm going to jail for rape."

"For starters, it would help if you did not refer to her as 'the bitch.' It would also be beneficial had you not assumed she would never recognize you. Now get in. We don't have much time."

"Why am I getting in the back?" Frankie asked.

"Can you get in the front?"

Frankie glanced at the small seat, thought about trying to curl himself up to fit, and groaned. "Probably not. Fine. Just give me a second."

Frankie swung one leg into the car and then scooted sideways, groaning and moaning with every move until he was inside.

Guidry slammed the door, got back in the driver's

seat, and headed for the courthouse. It was nine thirty—thirty minutes before the hearing began.

———ᴡᴡ———

Room 202 was packed. The only empty seats were down front, where the lawyers and their clients were to be seated. Ruby Dye had gotten there early, looking sharp as a tack in a light blue pantsuit with her soft blond curls styled in a simplified version of the Shirley Temple look, and she'd brought herself a pretty little folding fan to use if the air-conditioning could not keep up with cooling off the mass of humanity inside the room.

She was sitting right behind the table where Peanut and Dori would sit, and she had saved Johnny a seat beside her so he'd be as close to Dori as he could get.

When the doors opened, everyone turned. When they saw Peanut Butterman leading the way and Dori and Johnny right behind him, there was an audible sigh, then soft whispers.

Dori didn't know how to feel but embarrassed was a good part of it. How totally white trash that she was in court with her husband, fighting a man she didn't know for custody of their child. Miss Jane's soap operas had nothing on her life.

"Johnny! Here!" Ruby hissed and scooted over so that he could squeeze in.

"Thanks, Ruby," Johnny said as he squeezed into the seat. He nodded to the man beside him and then watched Dori take a seat beside their lawyer. When she glanced back, he winked, and she almost smiled. He knew she was scared. He wasn't about to let on how scared he was for her. He glanced around the courtroom and saw nothing but friendly faces. It wouldn't help the judge's decisions, but it made him feel better.

Peanut saw the panic in Dori's eyes. He patted her hand and leaned closer, using his church-whisper voice for the conversation. "You look beautiful, my dear. Meeker would be very proud, but I want to get down to business. You may not be called upon to speak. All of this is to determine if there is anything to merit a trial, which means the opposing council has to have enough proof to make their case."

"I understand that," she whispered. "But we're no better off than they are. You said that yourself."

Peanut winked. "That was before you took a cane to the man and called him out in front of God and everybody. To date, five other girls have come forth claiming he doped and raped them too. Two have even admitted to having abortions afterward. I have copies of their depositions. Not only is this going to kill his claim that he did not rape you, but it is going to send him up the river for a very long time."

Dori jumped like someone had poked her with a prod. "Sweet Lord, are you serious?"

"Yes, ma'am, I sure am."

She turned around, intent on telling Johnny what he'd said, and then the door opened again. This time, opposing council and his client walked in, although it could have been better stated that opposing council was the only one walking. His client was waddling like a baby with a loaded diaper, and he looked like pure hell.

"What on earth?" Peanut mumbled.

Johnny's eyes widened in shock, and then he saw Bo and Billy Weaver grinning and giving him a thumbs-up.

He didn't know what they'd done, but he owed them, big-time.

Guidry nodded at Butterman and then pointed to the chair where Frankie would sit.

The room was awash in whispers and supposition, but the conversations didn't last long. All of a sudden, they were ordered to rise, and as they did, they witnessed Judge Beecham's entrance.

Frankie itched so bad, it hurt. He'd just gotten comfortable, and now he had to move again. By the time he stood up, the judge was seated and glaring at him. The proceedings started with Beecham chastising Guidry for his client's faux pas.

"I'm sorry, Your Honor, but as you can see, my client is seriously indisposed."

Beecham waved a hand and the hearing began.

Guidry explained his client's reasons for being there and went into great detail about how devastated Mr. Ricks had been to learn that the girl he'd had a relationship with some months earlier had gotten pregnant and given birth to their child without informing him of the fact. He stated that Mr. Ricks was asking for joint custody of the infant named Luther Joe Grant and sufficient monetary recompense to care for him.

Dori was angry all over again just listening to the lies. Then it was Peanut's turn to speak, and he went straight for the heart with his first shot.

"Your Honor, we reject every word of that claim and are instead claiming that the fact of my client's prior pregnancy was nothing but the result of a brutal act of rape after slipping a drug into her drink at a school function. Furthermore, we have affidavits from five other young women, from as far away as Savannah, who have recently come forward with similar claims against this same man, Frankie Ricks. Two of the five women also testified in their affidavits that they, too, became preg-. nant after the rape and terminated the pregnancies."

Guidry's face turned red as he stood up.

Beecham pointed at him. "Sit down. You presented your evidence. He is presenting his."

Guidry looked at Frankie in disbelief and then leaned over and whispered in his ear. "I asked you if there was anything else I needed to know. I asked you if—"

Frankie put his head down on the table and moaned as Butterman was giving an officer of the court copies of the affidavits for the judge.

Frankie moaned again and then straightened up in his chair and started to cry.

Judge Beecham glared at Guidry's table as he took the copies.

"Counsel, please tell your client I will have none of that in my courtroom and to pull himself together."

Guidry hissed a warning in Frankie's ear.

Frankie groaned but did as he'd been told.

Beecham asked if a DNA test had been done on the infant in question.

Guidry quickly stated that was on the agenda.

Beecham rolled his eyes and chided Guidry for being unprepared, then he looked at Dori. Her hands were balled up into fists and she was shaking so hard, he thought she was going to faint.

"Butterman, is your client ill?" he asked.

"No, sir," Peanut said.

Beecham frowned. "She appears most distraught."

"Oh no, sir. She's not ill. She's mad. She's about as angry as I've ever seen a woman get."

Beecham blinked. Like everyone else, he'd seen the YouTube video, but seeing this much rage up close made the accusation of rape almost palpable.

"Dori Pine."

Dori took a deep breath and looked him straight in the face.

"Yes, Your Honor?"

"Are you indeed angry and not ill in any way?"

"I am not ill. I am not fragile. I am not having a nervous breakdown. I do, however, wish that man a one-way ticket to hell...Your Honor."

The people broke out in laughter.

Judge Beecham pounded his hammer on the bench.

"Quiet! Order in the court! One more outburst, and I'll clear the courtroom!" he shouted.

A hush descended. No one wanted to miss what happened next.

Frankie was shaking just as hard as Dori, but for an entirely different reason. His skin was crawling, burning, itching. He was going out of his mind in the tight, binding clothes, and the misery he was in. He just wanted all of this over. It was the fleas. It was the poison ivy. It was Dori Pine.

He jumped to his feet.

"I can't take it any longer! Damn it to hell, I don't care! I gotta scratch. I gotta scratch. Put me in jail. I don't care."

Beecham was pounding the gavel again.

"Guidry, get your client under control now or this hearing is over."

Guidry grabbed at Frankie's arm, but he tore it away, screaming.

"I quit! I quit! I'm dropping the lawsuit. I don't want anything but out of here."

Beecham pounded the gavel once more.

"This hearing is dismissed," he said, then looked toward the back of the room and nodded at the two police officers standing at the door before he got up and left the bench without waiting for the formalities.

Frankie was stumbling up the aisle toward the door, yanking at his tie and unbuttoning his shirt when two police officers arrested him for rape and yanked his hands behind his back. Before he knew it, he was cuffed. He couldn't move. He couldn't loosen his clothing. He couldn't even scratch. It was his worst nightmare come to life.

Lon Pittman caught Dori's eye and almost winked as he began dragging his prisoner out the door while the other officer read him his rights.

"Frankie Ricks, you are under arrest. You have the right to—"

Peanut Butterman was already on his feet when Dori jumped out of her chair and hugged him. She leaned over the railing and hugged Johnny, then turned around hugged Butterman all over again.

"You did it! You saved us," she cried.

Peanut shook his head. "You saved yourself, Dori, and you should be very, very proud. If you hadn't stood up for yourself the way you did, I doubt if any of the other victims would have come forward."

"Is it over?" she asked. "Is everything over? Will I have to testify at his rape trial?"

"Maybe, but I would seriously doubt if it goes to trial.

I'm betting he'll plead out and take his chances with a judge—one other than Beecham, of course."

Johnny leaned across the railing and shook Peanut's hand.

"We are so grateful."

Peanut grinned. "It was my pleasure. I'll send you a bill."

"It will be the best money we ever spent," Dori said. "So, can we go now?"

"Yep, you're free to go. Go have a great life while you're at it, okay?"

"Okay!" Dori said and then looked around for Johnny again, but he was already coming around the railing to get her.

He picked her up in his arms and swung her off her feet. She was laughing with joy when their friends surrounded them.

—◆◆◆—

It was just after sundown on a hot Sunday evening when the Pine family loaded up the car to go get ice cream. All of the boys were in the backseat, and Johnny and Dori were buckled in the front. When they drove across the railroad tracks and started uptown, instead of turning right, Johnny turned to the left.

"Hey! This ain't the way to ice cream!" Beep yelled.

"This isn't the way," Johnny said.

"I already said that," Beep muttered.

Dori was puzzled too, but in the two short months she'd been his wife, she'd learned that Johnny never did anything by accident, so she stayed quiet, waiting.

He took the back streets of neighborhoods she hadn't

been through in years, and then he turned back north. When she realized where she was, her heart started pounding. She sat straighter, unaware she was also leaning forward. Two blocks more and he tapped the brakes and pulled over.

They were at the scene of the fire—only all evidence of the fire was gone, the debris on the lot long since hauled away.

The house across the street, where the Joneses used to live, sat empty, with a For Sale sign in the front yard. While she was staring, remembering, he reached across the seat and took her hand.

"We start building a pad for the house tomorrow, and I'm doing it. I just wanted you to see, to know that everything bad is gone and tomorrow is for good times."

The boys were silent in the backseat, aware of the momentous occasion. Dori knew she was looking at their future, but she was also remembering the past. He'd come out of the night in her darkest hour to give them shelter, then ultimately his love. She squeezed his hand as she turned to face him.

"People have mentioned often in the past few months how crazy brave it was of us to get married after only one week together. I've always smiled or laughed it off, because that was our business, not theirs. But the truth is that when you've survived the worst, it doesn't take nearly as long to recognize the best."

The lump in Johnny's throat was so big, he could barely breathe. He'd never considered their life blessed in any way before Dori and the baby walked into their house, and then it had become instantly clear that they were what had been missing.

Then a little voice from the backseat whispered, "How about that ice cream?"

Dori laughed.

Johnny grinned at Beep. "Yeah, how about that ice cream. I'm getting chocolate."

"I want starberry," Beep said.

"I want vanilla," Marshall added.

"What about you, Mama? What do you want?" Beep asked.

Dori looked over her shoulder at the trio in the back and then back at Johnny.

"I think I want vanilla too, but I don't want no dried-up grapes on it."

———

The next morning, Ruby Dye walked in the back door of the Curl Up and Dye to begin her day. She dumped her stuff in the workroom and then went through the salon, turning on lights, turning the Closed sign to Open, and unlocking the front door. As she did, she saw the Greyhound bus pulling to a stop a few blocks up. They always saw the bus go through town, but she couldn't remember the last time it had stopped. Curious, she stood, watching to see who was getting off.

The driver got out and went right to the luggage compartment beneath the bus, and still Ruby waited, wanting to see what passenger claimed the large duffel bag the driver laid out on the sidewalk.

Finally, she saw a leg, then the side of someone's shoulder. Well, it was a man, but that's all she could see. The driver got back on board, and moments later, the bus pulled away, leaving a puff of black cloud from the exhaust behind.

When she saw the uniform, she realized it was a soldier, but he was too far away for her to recognize his face. She watched him pick up the duffel bag and walk away, limping.

"A wounded warrior. Blessings on you," she said softly and then went about her business.

Throughout the morning, she kept wondering who he was and where he'd gone, but it was something to find out for another day.

IN CASE YOU MISSED IT, READ ON FOR AN EXCERPT
FROM *THE CURL UP AND DYE* BY SHARON SALA

LILYANN BRONTE ALREADY KNEW HOW FAST LIFE
could change. Her past was a road map to prove it. But
on this particular Friday in the first week of November,
she experienced one of those déjà vu moments as the
Good Lord hit Rewind on the story that was her life.

She was sweeping the front sidewalk of Phillips'
Pharmacy, where she worked, when she heard the low,
sexy rumble of a hot-rod engine. The skin crawled on
the back of her neck as a shiny black pickup truck went
rumbling down Main Street.

Before she could see the driver, sunlight hit the windshield, reflecting directly into her eyes. At the same time
she went blind, she heard him rack the pipes on the muf-
fler, just like Randy Joe used to do when he picked her
up for their Saturday night date. But that was a long time
ago, before he went away to war in Afghanistan and got
himself killed.

She had no idea who was driving this truck, and when
she looked again, it was turning the corner at the far end
of the street and then it was out of sight.

For LilyAnn, seeing that truck and hearing the pipes
rattle felt like a sign. Was it the universe telling her she
was living in the past? Because if it was, she already
knew that.

LilyAnn had been a constant source of pride for her
parents through all her growing-up years. She was an

honor student and a cheerleader, and was voted prettiest and friendliest every year by her class. When she was chosen head cheerleader her senior year, Randy Joe Bentonfield, the star quarterback, also chose her for his steady girl.

But it wasn't until she won the title of the Peachy-Keen Queen that her parents broke out in full braggadocio. Lily felt as if her life could not get any better. But as the old saying goes, once you've reached the top, the only place to go is downhill.

On the morning of September 11, 2001, two planes flew into the World Trade Center in New York City and another one into the Pentagon. When the fourth one was taken down by the plane's passengers, crashing into a cornfield and killing all on board, the world suddenly stopped turning.

National outrage followed the shock as young men and women from all over the country began enlisting in the army, including a lot of the young men in Blessings.

Randy Joe was one of the first to sign up. She cried herself silly, after which they made love. Randy Joe was so full of himself about being a man going away to war that he gave her a promise ring before he went away to boot camp. He came back long enough to have his picture taken in his uniform and then he shipped out, returning a month later in a flag-draped casket.

People said it had been a good thing he'd had that picture taken beforehand because he'd come back to Blessings in pieces, no longer fit for viewing.

His death devastated Lily. She dropped out of college that year and wore black, which went really well with her long blond hair. She visited his grave site every day for a year, and people said what a faithful young woman she was, grieving for her lost love in such a fashion.

One year turned into two and then three, and everything became a blur. Her daddy had a heart attack and died, which turned her mama into a widow, and Lily barely remembered her dreams for the future and had forgotten how to get there.

The worst were the times when she could no longer bring Randy Joe's face to mind. At that point, the guilt would set her to eating a whole pint of chocolate-chip ice cream, just because it was his favorite treat. It didn't revive her memory, but it did pack on the pounds.

The years came and went without notice until Lily was eleven years lost. Now she only visited his grave when she thought about it and had unwittingly masked her emotions with a bulwark of extra weight.

LilyAnn was stuck in a rut: too afraid to step out for fear of getting too close to someone and getting left behind all over again.

At least, that's how Lily *had* felt, until today when she'd heard the rattle of those pipes. She felt off-center, like she was trying to balance on one leg, and became convinced that truck was an omen of great change.

At noon, Lily clocked out and headed for her weekly appointment at the Curl Up and Dye. When she reached the salon, she was relieved. This was a safe place, where people came to get pretty. If only there was a place where people could go to get their lives back, she'd be the first in line.

The bell over the door jingled as she walked inside. The owner, Ruby Dye, who everyone called Sister, was already smiling, which prompted Lily to smile back.

"Hey, LilyAnn. How's it going, honey? Boy, that wind is sharp today, isn't it?"

Lily nodded as she hung up her jacket. "Yes, it's getting cold. I sure hate to see winter coming."

"I kind of like it," Ruby said. "The short days and long nights give me time to den up with a good book and some popcorn, or watch old movies."

The last thing Lily needed was more time to eat through the loneliness.

"I guess," she said as she sat down at the shampoo station.

As soon as Ruby put the cape around her neck, Lily leaned her head back in the sink and closed her eyes. Getting her long blond hair washed by someone else was pure luxury. When Ruby began scrubbing and massaging Lily's scalp, the tension in her shoulders began to ease. By the time they were through and she was back in the stylist chair, Lily was two shades shy of having been put into a trance.

Ruby eyed the young woman, watching the way Lily looked everywhere but in the mirror at herself. If only there was a way to get her out of the rut she was in.

"I don't suppose you're interested in a new hairstyle?" Ruby asked.

Lily frowned. "I wouldn't know what to do with it."

"No matter. One of these days we'll figure something out," Ruby said.

Her thumb was on the Power button when they all heard the sound of a hot rod passing by. Whatever the driver had done to that engine, it rumbled like a stereo with the bass set on high.

Lily's eyes widened. It had to be the driver with the truck like Randy Joe's. She swiveled her chair around so fast to get a look that Ruby got the round brush tangled up in her hair.

"I'm sorry. Did that pull?" Ruby asked as she began trying to unwind it.

Lily was oblivious. "No, no, it didn't hurt," she muttered, still craning her neck to see the driver.

And then to everyone's surprise, the truck pulled up to the curb in front of the salon and parked, the driver racking the pipes one last time before killing the engine.

Vesta and Vera Conklin, the twin fortysomething hairstylists, had been eating their lunch in the break room and came out to see what the noise was all about.

The rest of the women in the shop turned to look as the driver walked in.

He was a thirtysomething hunk in a tight, long-sleeved T-shirt tucked into a pair of fitted Wrangler jeans. He had wide shoulders, long legs, slim hips, and a face bordering on cute rather than handsome, but he was working with what he had just fine.

He immediately swept the dove-gray Stetson from his head, revealing dark wavy hair, and smiled at the room like a star granting an audience to his fans.

Even though Vesta had yet to meet a man worth her time, she wasn't dead and buried. She handed Vera her bowl of salad and scooted toward the counter.

"Welcome to the Curl Up and Dye. Can I help you?" she asked.

"I sure hope so, darlin'. My name is T. J. Lachlan and I'm new in town. I went to get a haircut and learned the local barber is in the hospital. When I saw your Walk-Ins Welcome sign, I wondered if I might trouble one of you fine ladies for a trim."

"Sure, I have time," Vesta said.

Vera glared at her sister, then smirked. "No you don't, Vesta. Sue Beamon is due any minute." She set the bowls with their food back in the break room and sauntered to the front of the store and introduced herself.

"Welcome to Blessings, Mr. Lachlan. My name is Vera, and I'd be happy to cut your hair."

"Y'all can call me T. J., and isn't this something. Excuse me for saying this, but twins are truly a man's finest fancy," he said and then flashed them both a wide grin.

Ruby arched an eyebrow at the twins as a reminder that this was a place of business, then turned Lily's chair around and the blow-dryer back on.

It wasn't until she was about through that she realized Lily was staring at the stranger as if she'd seen a ghost.

Ruby paused. "Hey. Are you okay?" she whispered.

Lily blinked, and when she met Ruby's gaze in the mirror, her eyes were filled with tears.

"I'm fine, Sister. He just reminded me of someone." Then she shook her head and looked away.

Ruby's eyes narrowed. This was the first time she could remember the woman even showing an interest in another man. Even if it was a negative interest, it was better than nothing.

"How about we do something a little different with

your hair? Maybe pull the sides away from your face and fasten them up here at the crown…or maybe at the nape of your neck? Hmm? What do you think?"

She pulled the sides back and held them up at the crown to show Lily what she was talking about.

Lily frowned. Pulling her hair away from her face like that only emphasized her double chin.

"I don't know. I guess," she muttered.

"Good," Ruby said. "A little change never hurt anyone."

When Ruby finished, Lily frowned again. She felt naked—like she'd revealed too much of herself. She didn't much like it, but it was too late to change it.

"Same time next week," she said as she handed Ruby her money and bolted out the door like the place had just caught on fire.

But what had caught fire was LilyAnn's lust. She hadn't felt stirrings in her belly like that since the last time she saw Randy Joe naked. Only then she'd been just as naked and proud of her body, not like now.

Not once in the last eleven years had she given her changing shape much thought. It had never been an issue to her existence until today. The stranger was hot like Randy Joe and drove a fine fancy truck, just like Randy Joe. And once upon a time he would have looked at LilyAnn and wanted her…just like Randy Joe. But that man sitting in Vera's styling chair would never give her a second look.

So the question was…what, if anything, was she going to do about this?

About the Author

New York Times and *USA Today* bestselling author Sharon Sala is a member of RWA as well as OKRWA. She has ninety-five-plus books in print, published in five different genres: romance, young adult, Western, fiction, and women's fiction. First published in 1991, she is an eight-time RITA finalist, winner of the Janet Dailey Award, a four-time Career Achievement winner from *RT Book Reviews*, a five-time winner of the National Reader's Choice Award, a five-time winner of the Colorado Romance Writers Award of Excellence, and winner of the Heart of Excellence as well as the Booksellers' Best Award. Writing changed her life, her world, and her fate. She lives in Oklahoma, the state where she was born.